"A sprawling, epic novel of classic dimensions that vividly recreates the psychedelic sixties—the hopes, the fears, the naïveté, the knowing that was at the heart of those turbulent times."

>—Joel Selvin, culture and music columnist, *San Francisco Chronicle*, and author of *The Haight: Love, Rock, and Revolution*

"In her exciting novel, Pamela Johnson has crafted a work of literature that conveys big-picture ideas through the most intimate of characters. A Nation of Mystics sings with the sense of wonder and awe that inspired a generation to change the world—one atom and synapse at a time."

>—Nicholas Schou, author, *Orange Sunshine: The Brotherhood of Eternal Love and Its Quest to Spread Peace, Love, and Acid to the World*

"The deeply insightful and knowledgeable presentations of spiritual practices in both Eastern and Western traditions and the grueling rigors of cleansing and renewal to attain the blessings of sacred plants, are dramatically documented. These quests are captivating. I would rank Pamela Johnson among the best of modern storytellers. She has the rare ability to combine valuable history lessons with highly entertaining portraits."

>—Jim Ketchum, MD, author of *Chemical Warfare Secretes Almost Forgotten: A Personal Story of Medical Testing of Army Volunteers*

"I was particularly moved by the story because Pamela captured the feel of the Brotherhood of Eternal Love. The book explores many of the facets of the scene, including LSD manufacturing and hash smuggling, from 1965–1970, both the sweet and the bitter, in a way that is very hard to accomplish in nonfiction."

>—Tim Scully, underground chemist, Orange Sunshine

Also by Pamela Johnson

Heart of a Pirate / A Novel of Anne Bonny

A Nation of Mystics series

Book I: *Intentions*

Book II: *The Tribe*

Book III: *Journeys*

Soon to be released:

In Violation of Human Rights

A NATION OF MYSTICS

BOOK THREE: JOURNEYS

PAMELA JOHNSON

STONE HARBOUR
PRESS

Published by Stone Harbour Press
PO Box 206
Oregon House, CA
http://www.stoneharbourpress.com

Distributed by River Grove Books

For ordering information or special discounts for bulk purchases, please contact Stone Harbor Press at PO Box 206, Oregon House, CA 95962

Design and composition by Greenleaf Book Group
Cover design by Greenleaf Book Group
Cover images: ©iStockphoto.com/shylendrahoode; ©iStockphoto.com/selimaksan ;
©shutterstock.com/juliagubankova; ©gettyimages.com/©ZenShui/Laurence;
©colourbox.com/LaurenceMouton/AltoPress/Maxppp
Original photo of Benares, India by Pamela Johnson

Publisher's Cataloging-in-Publication
Johnson, Pamela, 1947–
A Nation of Mystics, Book III: Journeys / Pamela Johnson. – 1st ed.
p. cm.

1. Counterculture–United States–History–1961–1969
–Fiction. 2. Hippies–California–Fiction. 3. Social
justice–United States–History–1961–1969–Fiction.
4. Nineteen sixties–Fiction. 5. Bildungsromans.
I. Title.

PS310.O369N38   2010813'.6
QBI10-600059

PS310.O369N38   2010813'.6
QBI10-600059

Print ISBN: 978-0-9981171-9

eBook ISBN: 978-0-9981171-5-7

First Edition

To Timothy—friend and alchemist—because 1969 was your year

"The thing the sixties did was to show us the possibilities
and the responsibility that we all had. It wasn't the answer.
It just gave us a glimpse of the possibility."

—John Lennon,
KFRC RKO Radio interview, December 8, 1980

A list of characters and a glossary can be found in the appendices at the back of the book.

PREFACE

This tale was a long time in the making. Shortly after I graduated from the University of California, Berkeley, in 1980, I began to reflect on stories and incidents from the sixties that eventually became this series. Many of those remembrances concerned the motivations of the youth movement. As I looked around, I saw that those fragile and hard-fought ideas of the counterculture were beginning to bear fruit— environmental organizations, the peace movement, women's rights in the workplace, the ongoing public awareness of racism, emerging gay pride, populist political groups, and the proliferation of health food stores, organic food, and yoga classes.

I also knew that the catalyst for those ideas had been a mass leap in consciousness brought about by the use of psychoactive substances, by the ripping apart of "the filmiest of screens" as William James, the great American philosopher, declared after his initial experiments with nitrous oxide in 1882. At the apex of the sixties, over half a million people gathered at Woodstock in 1969, a single moment in time when those present became one person in mind, in large part because of a shared psychedelic experience. From Woodstock, the tribes moved across the nation and the world, bringing with them a shift in personal values, from competition for money and transitory objects to a world- view that regarded humans as a single community and the planet a living organism shared by all life.

What I also saw in the eighties was a declared war on drugs, a lumping of all drugs into one notorious category, and a deliberate stigmatization of those who altered their consciousness. Tens of thousands of families were affected by the incarceration of a loved one for nonviolent offenses against laws that were becoming more draconian and that often denied the spiritual conscience of an individual.

In between raising three boys, volunteering in schools, and working in the community, I researched and wrote at a time before computers, searching through the stacks of UC Berkeley's libraries, the Berkeley Public Library, and reading through numerous volumes on the sixties found in bookstores. Not having a computer myself, I wrote by hand. About 1988, almost eight years after my first line, I purchased my first computer and typed the work, saving it on large floppy disks. By the end of that year, I had a printed work of enormous size.

In 1989, I decided to return to school for a teaching credential. Having spent so much time volunteering in schools, I thought it might be a good idea to get paid for my work. Little did I realize that a teacher's life was a twelve-hour-a-day job, weekends included. The floppy disks and the ungainly manuscript sat on a shelf forgotten for almost twenty years.

Then, in 2007, on a whim, I took down the box with the old manuscript, dusted it off, and decided to read the first chapter, then the next, and found that I could not put the story down, having forgotten what I had written years ago. The pages were yellowed, the text was definitely a first draft—many revisions were necessary—but what I had was the kernel of a good novel, a remembrance for the children of the sixties who were now older. For many months, I searched for ways to convert the old floppy disks to a contemporary Word document, praying I would not have to retype the entire manuscript. Some of the disks were converted and some of the work was retyped, but much of what was recovered was feisty on the page, refusing to be altered by margins and having a mind of its own. Through a great deal of finessing, I eventually came up with a document with which I could work and began the editing process.

Book 3: Journeys is the conclusion of the *A Nation of Mystics* trilogy. In *Book 1*, readers are introduced to the characters, their motivations, and events that help develop the ideas of the youth movement. *Book 2* follows the strengthening relationships of the Tribe as they search for enlightenment through mind-expanding hallucinogens and work for political change, all intersecting in the historical events of People's Park in Berkeley, California.

In this last book of the series, the intentions of the flower children and the threads that hold together the tribe culminate in both a conclusion and a new beginning. Standing on the brink of a new decade—the seventies—the family members resolve old conflicts and look back over the last years to understand that their ideals have become the groundwork for a new culture.

No one person shapes the characters of these pages. They are an amalgam of the stories told to me in hours of interviews, scholarly and scientific texts, spiritual works, autobiographical and biographical readings, writings on the history of music, and days in libraries searching through old newspaper records for day-to-day events.

This story is for all of you who have dared to dream and imagine and who have worked for a better world.

ACKNOWLEDGMENTS

Words cannot begin to express my deepest and sincerest thanks to many people who made this work possible: Michael John Murphy, whose handwritten notes became the catalyst for the story; Dolores Muldoon and Kathleen Caswell, who spent many hours helping to type the original handwritten manuscript; my forever readers and friends for their encouragement and advice—Katherine Czesak, Anne Einhorn, John Hornung, Cynthia Josayma, Clifton Buck-Kauffman, Wendy Lee, Kelsey Magness, Leonard Post, Annie Reid, Patrice Sanders, Tim Scully, Carol Whitnah, and all you others who have taken time to read parts of the story; Julia Cooper Smith for helping me to understand how to cut a story to make it more powerful; Donald Ellis for his friendship, eternal support, and amazing knowledge of the publishing industry; Greenleaf Book Group, especially Hobbs Allison, for the time, concern, and orchestration of the editorial comments that led to the trilogy, Pam Nordberg for the hours of proofreading, and Neil Gonzalez, for his artistry and patience in working with me on the cover designs. I must especially thank Nathan True, copyeditor, who has worked with me daily over the last year with humor, good advice, vision, and most importantly, friendship. My forever gratitude to Susan Hauptman for sharing both her time and extraordinary artistic eye in helping to choose the cover art. To the dozens of you kind enough to take the time to give interviews, again, my sincerest thanks.

To Peter McGuire, Jim Ketchum, Jean Millay, Nicholas Schou, Tim Scully, and Joel Selvin—busy people all—for your generous endorsements. As always, thanks to my family, to Erin, Owen, and Adam, who grew up watching Mom write whenever there was a spare minute; to the women who love them, that they may know the waters from which these men spring—Sophie, Danielle, and Clarice; to Nicolas, Liam, Emery, Cayden, Nora, Dyllan, and Marley, for inspiring the fortitude to leave you a greater awareness of the world.

And finally, to Erik—always my inspiration.

1

KATHLEEN MURRAY AND CHRISTIAN BROOKS
WOODSTOCK, NEW YORK
AUGUST 1969

The journey had begun before dawn on an airplane leaving San Francisco. Now, eight hours later, the hired bus carrying them to the Woodstock Music Festival passed scores of small towns on its way into the mountains. Just off the Saugerties turnoff, traffic slowed. As far as the eye could see, a long chain of bumper-to-bumper cars jammed the two-lane highway—an unexpected, unbelievable sight. Local residents stood along white picket fences or sat in old rockers on porches to watch as mile after mile of cars and trucks, vans, old bread wagons, hearses, and paisley-painted vehicles slowly wound their way along the road in stop-and-go traffic.

Kathleen Murray stood in the bus, looking from the windows, both astonished and gleeful, an arm around Christian's shoulders.

"Danny!" she cried, and turned to peer at him over her shoulder. "What a party for your eighteenth birthday!"

Then, shaking a finger at Richard, she scolded teasingly, "And you didn't want to come! Thought you'd miss something by leaving the Bay! Well, think about missing *this*!"

"Yeah, well," Richard mumbled, "I just wish Alex and Honey had come with us."

The discomfort in leaving Alex behind in Marin County showed clearly on Richard's face. Alex was his business partner, his friend since third grade, but Alex had decided he couldn't make this journey with the rest of the family. Kathy knew his absence bothered Richard, not simply because Alex resisted being a part of the whole, but—truth be told—because Richard was concerned about just what Alex might be doing in his absence.

Marcie leaned against Richard, holding baby John on her hip, and laughed at the delight in Kathy's voice. "Well, *we're* here. We'll just rub it in when we get back. Richard, there are so many of us!"

Two years ago, in the fall of 1967, Richard had given up the lease on the Ashbury Street flat in the Haight-Ashbury district of San Francisco. All throughout the Summer of Love, the home had offered shelter to travelers and a safe space to make the psychedelic journey. Although the Victorian home with its brightly painted walls of flowers and rainbows was now a piece of history, the people who had joined hands in friendship and spiritual experience were still close—a family, a tribe—bound by their original intent to create revolution through psychedelic discovery.

Since moving from the Haight, there had been marriages, children born, and more children on the way. Greta and Merlin, original members of the Haight commune, had just had their second daughter, a tiny infant, three weeks old—Eden Azura, named for the paradise of their mountain home in Humboldt and for the color of the azure blue sky on the day she was born. Other friends were now experimenting with environmental organizations, wellness through yoga and meditation, neighborhood food communes, organic farming, new clothing designs, left-wing newspapers and small publishing companies for poetry and experimental fiction, innovations in music and art. The Youth Movement was growing, beginning to mature into something permanent. Yet, no one truly had any idea how large or diverse the culture had grown, not until today, when they stood staring from the bus windows at miles and miles of a snaking line of vehicles filled with the young.

"This is about as far as I can go," called the frustrated bus driver, gratefully nodding to the festival gates ahead. The drive had taken a good many more hours than planned. "I have room here to turn around."

"This is okay." Richard told him. "Thanks."

Near the entrance to the festival, the communal family unloaded the bus, picked up their bags and camping equipment, and looked for a gate. Richard held the tickets ready. But instead of a manned ticket kiosk, the only entrance was a gaping hole in the wire fence originally meant to establish a queue. Now, a continuous stream of people ducked through the clipped metal.

Shrugging, Richard pointed to the hole, and on they hiked until they found flat ground for a campsite. Racing the setting sun, they put up two-man pup tents, Marcie, Richard, and John in one; Kathy and Christian in another; Danny—alone for the moment—in the third. The air of the forest was filled with the scent of pine pitch as they collected firewood and gathered stones to create a circle for the campfire. Venus appeared near the horizon—brilliant and solitary. Distant stars emerged, one by one, filling a sky shifting from pale pink through vibrant orange to a deep violet.

As day faded into night, each family member took a place around the campfire, and passing the peace pipe, speculated on what the next day would bring, until, exhausted, they crawled into sleeping bags to await tomorrow's music.

Christian Brooks woke as the sun rose. He crawled quietly from the tent and regarded a sky that was a dawning purple. The smell of hay and pine mingled in the morning air. The night chill was slowly dissolving, white wisps of cloud floating up from the valley. Nearby meadows merged with timbered forests that ran in fingers up the slopes of hills. Behind them, in the far distance, the Catskills rose tall and blue. He settled into lotus position, filled his pipe, toked, and began the meditation that Lama Loden, his spiritual teacher, had taught him.

"Clear the mind," Christian heard the Lama's words as he sat facing the sun. "Remember that, ultimately, information gained through the senses is false. Meditate so that you can directly perceive truth. Know the emptiness of inherent existence. Know the nature of ignorance, the belief that things are self-propelled, that they exist of and by themselves, that subject and object are different entities. Know that the separation between things is false and that ignorance based on this notion of separation is the fuel for desire and hatred."

Christian began to breathe slowly, offering a special prayer for being allowed the beauty of the morning, for having the time to sit in meditation to consider the *dharma*. For his human body. Lama was back with him. Once again, they sat at the pipal tree in Bodh Gaya, in India, candles by the thousands flaming around them.

"You have been given a valuable gift," Loden Rinpoche said. "The jewel of leisure."

"A jewel?" Christian had asked.

"Leisure, Christian. You have been granted leisure time to meditate, to study. Can you comprehend how valuable this is? Life is short. This human life so precious. If we are given both leisure and fortune, what a great waste if we do not practice the Path."

Then Christian felt arms around his neck, warm breath near his ear. "My love," Kathy whispered, kneeling next to him.

All that day, he could not take his eyes from her face, her body. She was exquisite, everything to him, beautiful and relaxed, light and unburdened, soft and compassionate, the woman he had known on Maui—the way she always was when she got away from the business. The nagging thoughts about her continued desire for "independence," her sales and smuggles, the fact that she would not put her trip aside to help him with the work his acid lab demanded, all disappeared under the bright skies of upper New York State. He saw her as an exotic princess, her long, dark hair tied back with a narrow, beaded headband. As they walked, he reached over to slip a hand underneath her vest, savoring the touch of her breast, her beads and feathers and long, beaded earrings swaying as she leaned into him. He strode the new paths of the festival with his arm around her, bare-chested, in cutoffs, with beads, necklaces, and roach clips around his neck. She'd laughed and pulled away the band that tied back his hair so that it floated freely around his shoulders and down his back. Together, they were the *tao—yin* and *yang*—woman and man, her radiant darkness contrasted with his vibrant blondness and clear blue eyes.

Sometimes, when he drifted in the privacy of his own thoughts, he would remember another woman who had been a part of his life, Lisa. In those quiet, stoned moments of perception, he would wonder about her life in the New Delhi ashram. Would wish her well. But Lisa was far away. She had chosen her guru and studies instead of a life with him. It was Kathy who lay in his bed in the evenings. When he uncomfortably compared the two women, he knew them both to be strong, unique, conscious, but also . . . very different. Occasionally, on some mind trip, he would try to put his finger on just what the difference was, but found that knowledge elusive.

On this first morning of the music festival, he made his way toward the stage, his arm around Kathy's shoulders, drawing her to him, the feel of her soft against his body. Thousands and thousands of people were already sitting before the enormous stage, territory staked out with blankets and tapestries. The crowd was an outrageous lot of campers in shorts and jeans and T-shirts, but there was also a good bit of deerskin with long fringe and cowboy hats with bands of feathers, Mexican dresses and San Blas *mola* blouses, embroidered cotton dresses from India and tapestry skirts, antique clothing and sorcerer's robes, necklaces of beads and bells. American flags and peace symbols were sewn onto pants and shirts and jackets. And when the crowd saw each other that first morning wearing all their colors, an astonished murmuring began.

Christian laughed aloud when he saw Danny chose a place next to two young girls in halter tops. Then, he waited while Kathy and Marcie pulled at the corners of the blankets they'd brought—an old custom now, the women adept at getting the family settled for a concert. Packs held down the corners, snacks and food and drinks inside. Just as Danny had struck up a conversation with the girls, Christian heard the first words from the stage float out over the enormous speakers.

"Ladies and gentlemen," the voice called, "since this morning, this has become a free concert . . . !"

A cheer of approval spread over the arena. People began to feel their joined power. They were listening to one another, playing off an enormous flux of energy, learning to work with it.

". . . And since this morning, this has become the third largest city in New York State!"

Again, a great roaring vibration erupted from the crowd, now mighty thunder, powerful.

"Now, we didn't expect you. Like, we expected maybe fifty thousand people a day. What we got is about three hundred thousand of us! Unprepared as we are, we're gonna make it. We're gonna do that by helping each other make it. We're gonna keep our cool. The world is watching! They want to know if we mean what we preach. Let's show them that this many freaks can live together and still be hip. So, are we together, man?"

A roaring "Yeah!" exploded from the multitude. "Yeah!" the energy flashed from person to person.

The announcer spoke from a concert stage larger than anyone had ever seen. Across the top, toward the rear, a wooden ramp had been built to hold equipment—speakers, lights, and the cables that supported the stage tarp used for shade. Around the perimeter of the set were more speakers and microphones. In the very center stood a huge circular platform, a mini-stage on the larger stage. And in front, a narrow aisle bordered by a tall fence held the press box, where photographers prepared 35-millimeter cameras, and network-broadcasting systems readied reel-to-reel cameras and tape recorders. Most striking were the three tall towers on each side of the stage, where lights were still being lifted by crane to the top platform.

Then, like a ray of light, Swami Satchidananda appeared on the stage, garbed in a pale pink tunic, and flanked on either side by devotees dressed in white. In a laughing voice he began to teach of peace through service to others, and to lead those seated in the arena in yoga. He spoke of the power of music, of sound. In that morning's meditation, he lifted the crowd's intentions, imparting a sense of good-will that carried the multitude for the rest of the day.

Soon enough, it became clear that no one knew how to feed the masses who had gathered, many expecting to purchase meals from vendors. Christian and Kathy found the Hog Farm camp, with its psychedelic bus, rows of rough tables, and tented cooking area, and volunteered for the morning to help prepare the meals that would be given away. As donations of food were delivered to the kitchen, Christian assured Kathy that this was the twentieth-century version of the parable of the loaves and fishes.

Nearby, the festival organizers had set up a huge hospital tent. In the days to come, its staff would care for the sick, assist in the births of babies, tend to the drug overdoses, and talk people down from difficult trips before sending them back to the crowds. Next to it, a red and white trailer dispensed legal aid and drug information. A long row of portable toilets had been set up to service the crowds, and eventually, planks would form a bridge across the mud, allowing access. Paths were already cut through the forest, and in the center, between routes already named High Way and Gentle Path and Groovy Way, a medieval pavilion sold pipes, roach clips, and papers. Hawkers stood on the trails just as on Haight Street or Telegraph Avenue or MacDougal Street, calling out their wares.

Waiting for the music to begin, the family members explored the festival grounds, shared good weed and Afghani hash and conversations with the people around them, altered consciousness, listened to the stories and ambitions, hopes and plans of new friends. The sun was warm, the air humid. Time slowed.

The music began. Richie Havens opened the concert late Friday afternoon, his impassioned voice and acoustic guitar flowing across the crowd with his cry of "freedom." The power of the sound reverberated through their bodies. Bert Sommer followed him, singing of bombers turning into butterflies. Evening approached. Colors and lights floated over the stage. The family lay on blankets watching the stars that peeked between clouds. Light raindrops sprinkled the air while

Ravi Shankar's fingers rushed over his sitar. The evening raga brought Christian immediately back to India and he drifted with the notes, memories assailing him.

Tim Hardin took the stage with "Simple Song of Freedom," the lyrics speaking to the possibilities of peace amid the realities of war. When Melanie Safka began to sing in the drizzle, Richard pulled a camping candle from his pack and joined others in holding up a light to dispel darkness. Arlo Guthrie was next up, late into the night, with a smooth rendition of "Amazing Grace." Finally, there was beautiful Joan Baez, six months pregnant, carrying David Harris's baby as he did prison time for resisting the draft. At the first notes of "We shall overcome," everyone stood with arms around each other to sing with her of the struggle of the common man for justice and freedom from bias.

In the smoke that was shared, in expanded consciousness, in the lyrics that offered a glimpse of a world that all here could create, with the forests and meadows and lakes holding them in an embrace, stars above, each person at Woodstock became bound to hundreds of thousands of others, knowing that every man and woman here could make a difference.

On Saturday, Danny celebrated his eighteenth birthday, and Christian watched as Kathy wept in relief. Now, no matter what, no one could return him to Arizona as a juvenile runaway. He'd been sixteen when she'd picked him up hitchhiking by the roadside just south of Tucson. He had come to live with her, becoming her brother and partner, helping her to put together a strong weed business, one that matched anything the long-time dealers from Haight Street had going.

Quill began the music that Saturday. Country Joe was there from Berkeley, Joe in his green army jacket singing about Vietnam. Santana's conga drums got everybody to their feet. John Sebastian played acoustic guitar, completely awestruck and singing for the children. Britain's Keef Hartley Band, performing for the first time in the States, gave the crowd psychedelic rock and roll. The Incredible String Band sang of change. Canned Heat and "Going Up the Country." Mountain with its blues-rock music. The Grateful Dead, so familiar to the family from the Haight.

On through the night the music continued. Creedence Clearwater Revival belting out "Proud Mary." Janis Joplin knocking everyone over with "Piece of my Heart." The heavy beat of Sly and the Family Stone. The Who playing Tommy, the rock opera—Roger Daltrey an avenging angel, the arms of his fringed shirt outstretched like wings ready to fly. Jefferson Airplane, with Grace Slick singing the haunting "White Rabbit."

In the early afternoon on Sunday, near 2:00, the family had just returned to the bowl to sit in a circle, once again awaiting the music. Saturday night had been a very late night, because they'd stayed on until the wee hours of the morning to catch The Who and Jefferson Airplane. As the day gradually warmed with the new sun, Christian looked out over the crowd with its color and banners and peace symbols and announced, "This festival is the New Age Sermon on the Mount. Only this time, the message is electric. This time, the teachings are passed in the music."

The son of a missionary father in India, he knew his Bible and recited the Beatitudes from memory, quietly speaking the words spoken a long time ago by a revolutionary Jew fighting the system with love, one who emphasized the inner spirit of each man, the humility that should guide our actions, the necessity of social justice, and the quality of mercy. "Blessed are the peacemakers," Christian recited, "for they will be called children of God."

"A good start to the day," Kathy murmured, smiling and passing him a plastic bag.

"Our last day," he nodded. Then, he opened the bag and began to pass out acid tabs.

Kathy leaned back on the blanket that defined their space in the concert bowl, watching the sky overhead, coming on slowly, drifting with
the music. Joe Cocker, waving his arms, his rasping voice filled with
emotion, was singing about getting high with a little help from his
friends. As she began to melt into the blanket, she watched Christian,
wondering whether he would once again look far away to see a riot in
Amritsar in northern India, relive the death of Lama Loden on that terrible night, and question the disappearance of Nareesh, his childhood
friend and spiritual brother. Five years had passed, and still Christian
grieved. On a night in Merlin's cabin last December, she had finally
heard the story of melee and conflagration, how Christian had almost
been killed, and how the lama had protected him with his body and
taught his overwhelming lesson of compassion.

That trip by the fireplace had given Christian license to speak of his
past, and afterward, Kathy had at last understood his occasional, but
fierce, nightmares. Now he often spoke of Nareesh, their friendship,
growing up in a village in India, the all-boys boarding school they had
attended together in Jalandhar, the decisions each had made at the end
of secondary school.

Nareesh had planned to attend divinity school in Ohio, with plans
to go on to medical school. Christian had been expected to accompany
Nareesh, but had chosen instead to study in a monastery in Nepal with
Lama Loden. His father had not been happy.

Then, the night of riot.

Lama had died. Christian had been immediately sent out of harm's
way to Ohio. Nareesh had disappeared, never to appear at school.

Kathy knew Christian well enough to sense that a huge part of
his suffering was his guilt, his mortifying belief that his actions had
caused the death of a loved one. He believed the fault was his, and
making a mistake did not come easy for Christian. Everything he
touched was done with consideration. Usually he was smart, strong,
and overly confident. But when he considered the evening of the
riot and its dire consequences, there was no focal point for him, no
steady floor on which he could plant his feet and fight his thoughts.

His mind was a broken record, trapped in a groove, always asking if there was something—anything—he could have done to prevent all that had happened that night.

As Christian lay on the ground next to Kathy, his mind was not on Amritsar or his Lama, but gently floating with warmth and color and the physical love of this family surrounding him. Joe Cocker had just stepped away from the microphone. His eyes gazed into an acid sky that had become a screen above them. He was still coming on, colors intensifying, boundaries falling away, his mind moving up the ladder of consciousness, already merging with the minds of those around him, when slowly, from one corner of his vision, black clouds pushed into view. He watched those clouds, trying to understand their meaning, what significance they held in his life.

The wind picked up, strong enough to be noticed. Christian felt a ripple, an electric spark passing from one person to the next, spreading out, a premonition like the flutter of startled birds before flight. Above him, the clouds continued to move, fanning across the bowl. Then, a gust of wind, harder than anything before. The new energy was something apprehensive, an intangible perception moving into realization. Something profound was happening, but Christian had yet to understand exactly what this energy was, to give it a name. The knowledge of it pierced his mind slowly. The awareness tried to find form in ordinary reality. All he could sense was that the sky was growing darker.

Moments later, lightning flashed and clouds roiled, heavy with water. Around him, a low murmur began. Anxious people stood and looked up, speaking with their friends, putting things away, folding blankets, collecting belongings, ready to move. But . . . move where? Where could half a million people go for shelter when there was none to be had?

Kathy felt Christian's hand move against her arm, an electrical tingling. Completely at ease, desiring nothing else in this world than to be here with Christian, watching paisleys colorfully bloom and imprint on all the tangible surfaces around her, she knew it would not matter if this moment ever passed. She laid her head against his chest and held absolutely still, listening to the music of his heartbeat. She lifted her face to look into his, wearing the silly acid grin, reveling in the loving emanations from his eyes. His face was pulsating, and she laughed, drawing him further into her mind with her gaze, love shining in her eyes.

"My love," she said softly, grinning with him.

Then she watched his eyes travel to the sky. A few more heartbeats passed. He pointed, then he slowly stood and looked around, trying to put it all together. Kathy stood with him, following his gaze.

A new energy surrounded her from this height, and she tried to steady her trembling legs, heavy with released energy. But she could only laugh, unable to deny her own happiness, unable to understand wind and clouds and moving people.

"Alright, everyone," the voice on the loudspeaker called, "it looks like we may have a little rain. Now we're just going to have to sit back and ride it out . . . "

Wind whipped through the air in small whirlwinds, scattering debris and dust and leaves. The growing crowd murmur rose, ascending in the same circulating wisps. Frantic activity appeared on the stage.

". . . I know we can hang in there," the voice continued, controlled but high-pitched, "just like we've hung in there for three days now. It's just one more test of our courage. We're going to have to cut power in a few minutes. Everyone needs to move away from those towers!"

For the first time since dropping, Kathy looked past Christian, regarded the towers, wondered why they might be important, looked toward the crowds who were standing, packing, to Marcie pulling a large plastic cover from her pack, to Jeff, the kid sitting to one side of them who had just dropped for the first time. At Jeff's face, her gaze stopped. His face was red, angry, scared.

Kneeling beside him, acid-flushed, her eyes hugely dilated, she grinned broadly. "How's it goin'?" she asked.

"Not so good," he was quick to answer, his voice close to tears, his face a mixture of pout and fear.

"Can you feel the power, Jeff?" she asked him, still grinning. "The power of the elements? Water. Electricity. Wind. The elements have come together to make their own music. For you. They'll flow through your body, and you can be the conductor." She lifted her arms and looked toward the sky. "Trust yourself! It'll be alright!"

A deafening clap of thunder and a fearful tremor rolled through the air. The first large drops of rain began to fall. Kathy took one corner of the plastic tarp and helped Marcie cover John. Then, they sat beside him, tarp overhead, and emulated John as he watched, wondering and quietly knowing.

The voice over the microphone yelled, "We'll be back as soon as we can. Get away from those towers! Alright! Cut the power!"

For the first time since it had been born, the crowd was alone, cut from its electric umbilical cord. No longer could the music and sound of the speakers focus them, hold them as one person. Kathy sensed the water touch her skin—soft, fluid—moved as Christian pulled her to her feet and wrapped his arms around her. There they stood as they had in the past, once again subjected to the mercy of things beyond their control—a night in Haleakala crater on Maui with the elements of wind and plummeting temperatures; tear gas and pepper spray in the Berkeley battle for People's Park; the impotent, devastating loss of a brother, Kevin, killed by a narc.

The drenching rain shocked them, much as the first jump into a cold lake might do, falling heavily, beating upon them, but also upon hundreds of thousands of others who huddled desperately under blankets that were soon soaked, the water quickly turning the gigantic bowl into a huge sea of mud.

Then, from somewhere, Kathy heard a chant began. And she immediately understood. The crowd was pulling together, discovering itself, testing its power. "Rain, rain, go away . . . rain, rain go away", the chant repeated over and over, the sound growing louder as more and more people joined the ancient ritual for control of the weather.

Spontaneously, Kathy pulled away the wet blanket covering Christian. She took his hand and reached out to Marcie. A larger handholding circle formed with Richard, and Danny and his new lady, Camille. Throwing back their heads, they laughed and jumped like mad people, John still watching, grinning from beneath his tiny tent. When Kathy glanced over at Jeff, his red face was still huddled underneath his soaked blanket, mean and miserable. She held out her hand to him. "Wanna be crazy too?"

For several moments, Jeff sat staring at the outstretched hand. Then he was on his feet holding onto her, laughing and jumping like the rest.

The circle grew larger, and a new chant arose, accompanied by the striking together of cans or hands or anything that would clack. "Mari-marijuana . . . ," sung with a 4/4 beat, ". . . mari-marijuana . . . mari-marijuana . . . "

The crowd began to dance, to form circles. Long lines of men and women held hands and moved through rain and mud. The chanting spread. A cue formed for a mudslide that began at the top of the bowl and ended near the stage. A thought flashed from person to person, from smile to smile.

No mere rainstorm will put out the fire in this gathering. Nothing will turn us from each other.

The heavy rain began to slacken, and soon after, the stage mike was on again. Sound from the festival organizers once more floated through the air.

Then suddenly, in the middle of that child's dream, that gigantic mud puddle, helicopters appeared. A flash of paranoia spread through the crowd, so thick and strong it was tangible. Kathy gripped Christian's arm. They were back in Berkeley watching the National Guard helicopters spraying the crowds with pepper gas at People's Park. What would the spray be this time? Something lethal? If the authorities wanted to try to stop a movement, this would be the place to start. If they could remove all these people who held to beliefs that would change government and society—this group of the young who had challenged the might and money of the military-industrial complex— the old order could continue unchallenged.

Slowly, the helicopters circled the field, getting closer to the ground, and then . . . they began dropping flowers.

"Oh, my God," Kathy whispered quietly, blown away, "flowers." The symbol of spiritual and political evolution.

"Richard," Marcie cried, holding him and looking intently into this face. "I have an idea! What if they dropped flowers on Vietnam? I mean, instead of bombs. What if they took all that money and helped villages rebuild with seeds and tools and food and medical supplies? What if we could learn about each other? About how we're both different and the same? What if our government offered a hand to nations who were trying to help their people, rather than dictators only interested in wealth and power?"

"Because, my dear," Richard answered, holding Marcie tight against his chest and speaking to her ear, "Dow Chemical and Monsanto wouldn't make its millions manufacturing napalm. And all the little soldiers with stars on their shirts wouldn't have a game to play. And the men sitting in the White House wouldn't feel very important if they were dealers in flowers rather than human lives."

"But, Richard," Marcie insisted, looking up at him again, "doesn't it make perfect sense? Doesn't it?"

Kathy looked over the bowl where an hour ago people had sat comfortably on tapestries with food and backpacks and smoke. Now it was a sodden heap of mud-soaked blankets interspersed with pools of standing water. Crowds were still sliding down the mud hills. Laughter and song surrounded her. Christian's face was aglow, his eyes radiant with light. In her hand, she held a wilted, muddy daisy, a treasure. Country Joe and the Fish had just started to play.

The sun had slipped low on the horizon. In that narrow space between the mountains and the gray clouds still hovering overhead, a layer of gold and reds filled her vision. Still very stoned, she began to walk slowly with Christian back to their tent site for dry clothing. The music followed them as they walked, this time the heavy electric guitar of Ten Years After. On the way, they stopped to stand next to a bonfire. Steam floated from their clothing in the fire's heat. Strangers gathered beside them to share in the warmth, their eyes as dilated and wonder-filled. A man passed a pipe, sharing a smoke with those in the circle. Someone spoke of the storm. Another of the music. Christian of the promise of a new age of mankind.

The sacramental journey, Kathy realized. *Here we are again. Sharing. Humbled by the knowledge of the ancient age of this body, of the reverence for life, of the absolute miracle of existence. This knowledge of deep holiness.*

At their tent, Christian once again held her close. She knew the joy, the sheer pleasure and comfort of his body against hers, the protection of his long arms. She was tired now, getting into the spacy part of the trip. Now she wanted to sit to meditate, to do yoga, to simply be with Christian.

He whispered into her ear, "We gave out a lot of good acid over the last few days. Look around. Acid put this festival together." Completely open and unguarded, he asked, "Kathy, will you reconsider working with me? I need someone I trust to move crystal grams from L.A. to the Bay. Richard says he'll take all we have. And I've got a pound of ergotamine to drive across the Canadian border. Will you think again about giving up your weed business and helping me full time? I'm asking you to become a complete partner."

"I hear you," she whispered, but for the moment, she could not give him an answer. "In the morning. We'll talk about it then."

That evening, there were bonfires everywhere—huge, roaring fires. Smoke rose in the gathering twilight. At the stage, the music continued, but at the campsites, as the mountains darkened, a hush settled over the area, the gathering night pierced by the colors of the psychedelic vision. In the family's circle, they once again passed the peace pipe around the fire, secure in a calm abiding in each other and in the clarity of the visions that had been given to them.

Sometime in the middle of the night, they fell asleep, but shortly after the sun rose they were awakened by music carried across the fields and forests and into the campsites. Jimi Hendrix stood on stage playing the "Star-Spangled Banner," his guitar crying for freedom, justice, and peace.

The family crawled from their tents, wrapped their arms around each other in the morning air, and stood silently, listening.

2

LISA

ANANDA SHIVA ASHRAM, NEW DELHI, INDIA

SEPTEMBER 1969

Lisa awoke in the bedroom she shared with two sisters of the ashram and thought of the letter she had written to Christian not two months ago. Not only was the letter filled with her apologies for not writing sooner, but she had wanted him to know something of the ashram—its ancient buildings, her room with its high ceiling, the gardens—most importantly, her love of the Master. She'd described the work she was doing on the new medical clinic with the Master's Disciple, Padmananda. And she had given him an invitation to visit. In fact, when she thought about it, she'd asked herself if she'd sounded too desperate. "Won't you come?" she had written. "Won't you know the happiness the Master has to offer? Won't you reconsider joining the ashram?"

As she dressed on this warm morning, she wondered if he had received the letter and whether he would respond.

The last days at Ananda Shiva in Santa Monica before departing for India in late December of 1967 had been a whirlwind of emotion. Not only was there both the excitement and the trepidation of leaving for a new country, but thrown into the maelstrom was all the remorse and longing that only meetings with Christian could bring. Her emotions were a pendulum, a constant pull from one extreme to another, leaving her sick and exhausted.

At times, she was angry. Christian had a way of tempting her, of playing on her weaknesses. "Leave the ashram," he'd said. "Be my lady."

Then she would remember that he wouldn't give her the courtesy of a single question about the Master. Nor did he have the grace to call her by her new name—Kali. When Christian showed up, it was always on his schedule, confusing her plans. His world was dangerous, and she knew that he'd be dealing, whether she was with him or not.

In the next instant, she would admonish herself, reminded of his selflessness. He had given her the money to live in India when he owed her nothing, money that came from the very work she insisted he renounce. How could she speak to him of love and right action only to turn and take from him? Over and over, she envisioned him handing her the small paper bag containing the three thousand dollars she would need for airfare and lodging in New Delhi, his eyes large and dilated from the acid trip that had delayed him earlier in the day, his gaze filled with longing and love. Where would she find someone who loved her with such passion again?

Perhaps a letter will come today, she told herself as she finished dressing. *Surely, he will understand just how important the Master and Padmananda are to me.*

Lisa was not the only one who had been unsettled on the evening Christian had come to say his good-byes in Santa Monica. Padmananda, the young disciple visiting from India, had also been in a state of turmoil. In the dim porch light of the ashram, he'd had to look hard to make sure the man at the door was Christian. But even with long hair and a beard, there could be no mistake. What before Padmananda had suspected, he now knew with certainty. The shock was staggering, creating a painful problem of conscience.

The man at the door was his childhood friend, his brother, the one person with whom he had shared everything from the time he was seven years old. Five years ago all had been in balance, his name Nareesh, both their futures clear. He and Christian were to have attended theological college together, return to India, and take up their missions.

But in that fateful spring Christian had made other choices. Instead of following in his father's footsteps, he had decided to take refuge in Lama Loden and live in a new monastery in Nepal.

On the night in Santa Monica when he had watched from the shadows, Christian had held a brief conversation with Kali. He had not heard the words, but had seen the way Christian touched her face, knew the gift of money he had brought so that she might travel to India and the Master. He had watched Kali's stricken face as Christian turned from the door and walked away. Only then did the first twinge of jealousy begin.

Christian and Kali.

Padmananda knew Christian's weaknesses, especially with women. Hadn't Christian shared them often enough?

A few nights after Christian had left Ananda Shiva for the last time, Kali had collapsed at *satsang.* Padmananda had pushed through those who had crowded around to help. Lifting her, he had carried her to her room, oblivious to the concerned questions surrounding him. Her fever had been high, her body shivering and sweating, her hair wet. One of the women had brought a cool bowl of water and a washcloth, and he had held it to her forehead.

"I'm s-sorry to put everyone through s-so much t-trouble," she had whispered through chattering teeth.

"Don't worry," he'd answered gently, so softly that the women at the door could not hear the words. "Kali, are you afraid of what you'll find in India? Or of what you're leaving behind?"

"You . . . you know of my struggle?" Grasping the meaning of his words immediately, she answered her own question. "Of course you do."

"Ask yourself," he had counseled. "What do you want more than anything?"

The answer was simple, her voice low, throaty, her eyes burning with delirium. "I want to be able to give with the kind of love the Master has."

"Then put all else aside and follow your own path. Everything that should be yours will walk with you."

"But . . . the money . . . the way I took it. I hurt someone to make this trip."

Leaning close to her ear, he had whispered the advice he would have given to any of the initiates in the same circumstance. "The money is yours, given to you by God. The man was only the messenger."

On the twenty-hour flight just before New Year's, 1967, from Los Angeles to Hong Kong, then from Hong Kong to New Delhi, Lisa had daydreamed of what she would find in India. She believed the Santa Monica ashram a tiny microcosm of the country, a place where religion guided the lives of the people. But when the plane landed in the early morning hours, when immigration and customs were behind her, when at last she stepped out into the main terminal, she caught her breath in an audible gasp.

Between the chairs and along the walls of the airport lobby were row upon row of sleeping bodies, the heads and faces of many of the men covered by turbans and dirty brown shawls as they huddled close together for warmth in the cold Delhi night. Carefully, Lisa picked her way between them, looking for the exit, unsure. Ahead she saw a door and beyond that, darkness.

Once outside, Padmananda led the group to a waiting bus. Lisa noted the ramshackle huts lining the airport fence, and shuddering against the cold, zipped her jacket closer to her throat. She glanced at her watch. Almost 5:00 a.m. The sky was turning a thin gray. Near the makeshift hovels, people were beginning to stir. Small fires appeared, and figures squatted near the flames. One coughed and spat on the ground. A man pissed on the fence. A subdued quiet enveloped everything, as dead as the haze that hung limply above the ground.

Confused, Lisa huddled down into her parka and closed her eyes. This wasn't the India everyone around her had spoken of for so many years. Bob had talked of buying hash and of the *sadhus* who smoked along the sacred rivers, of shopping and the bargains of the bazaars. But he'd never mentioned the cold or the homeless or the grim poverty that stared at her from the street. Is this why Christian had always only smiled when she'd talked of visiting a country where spirituality was the guiding principle?

Am I ready for this? she wondered, tired and very discouraged. *Did I come all this way to see human misery? Did I leave Christian, hurt him, only to see the pain of others?*

The sun was newly born as the bus pulled onto the ashram grounds. The buildings were old, gray, and stained from years of weathering. A tall, rendered wall surrounded the compound. In a large, central courtyard stood an ancient pipal tree, its enormous trunk stretching up from the ground and branching into giant arms. Along the inside walls, were the same shacks she had seen at the airport, the same fires lit by people huddled in shawls against the cold morning. Even though she was made welcome, given a comfortable room, and encouraged to rest, Lisa could not sleep, torn between the discrepancy of her expectations and the reality she faced.

Then had come evening, and Padmananda had led the new arrivals to their first meeting with the Master. In the room where she waited for his blessing, Lisa had stood transfixed. Daya Nanda was seated on a cushion on a small raised dais, dressed in a white robe, garlands of marigolds and brown *mala* beads around his neck. A radiance emanated from eyes that spoke of love, joy, serenity, and deep wisdom. Padmananda crossed the floor, knelt, and touched his forehead to Daya Nanda's feet, and in the next moment, they were in each other's arms, speaking softly, the love between them—father to son—so strong that witnessing it was a gift.

When it was Lisa's turn to lay her gift of flowers at the Master's feet and touch her forehead to the ground, she moved as in a dream. Then Daya Nanda's hand touched the crown of her head, and the current passing from him electrified her body.

Never again would she be the same. Never simply Lisa, but Kali and the Master.

Kali's days at the ashram began at 5:00 a.m., when darkness gave way to a faint red glow and silent black buildings turned to silver gray. The earth outside her window was all softness in the haze created by thousands of morning fires. In that quiet, she performed her meditation. Sometimes she heard the sound of movement in the courtyard or the far-off blare of a car horn, yet nothing disturbed her sense of timelessness, her absolute presence in the moment.

After breakfast, she would find a seat close to the Master for *satsang*. Each day, Daya Nanda managed to teach the scores of initiates in a singular way. Questions would rise to the surface of the group's mind, and feeling the need or the tone of the many merged minds, the Master would speak, fishing questions from the pool of faces and returning answers like a scattering of food to the hungry. Kali began to detect meaning in even the smallest of gestures—a raised eyebrow, the movement of his little finger, a certain smile—and knew this man had perfect clarity of vision, a consciousness that encompassed not only the moment but other levels of existence as well. Even his laughter, she realized, was not wasted. Here was a man—flesh and blood, bone and tissue, like any other. And his presence proved Christian wrong. How many times had Christian expressed the belief that religion was man-made and self-serving, creating many of the world's problems? The Master was a living testament of man's ability to achieve God-consciousness through religion.

While her spiritual practice grew, remarkably, so did her understanding of ordinary matters. Until she began working as Padmananda's secretary, she hadn't realized the extent of the ashram's businesses. Not only was there the commune and restaurant in Santa Monica, but there were ashrams in Portland, Boulder, New Haven, Tampa, and Kahului on Maui. Portland maintained a restaurant and a metaphysical bookstore. Tampa held the India import trade and incense business. Nor was property limited to the United States. New ashrams had begun to thrive in London, Stockholm, Amsterdam, Hamburg, and Paris.

Kali was equally impressed with two enormous projects: The first, a medical clinic that would serve the poor in New Delhi; the second, the final act of sale on three hundred and fifty acres of land in Connecticut that would operate as a retreat center. The Connecticut property had once housed a Catholic seminary, complete with a main house, bakery, kitchen, outbuildings, and chapel. The proposed plans included a bakery service and an ayurvedic health center.

The months Padmananda had spent in California, Kali realized, were a vacation of sorts. Looking afresh at the people he had chosen to accompany him to New Delhi, she saw that he had indeed chosen the best from the ashram—not only in terms of spiritual inclination, although certainly this played a part, but in terms of their talents for corporate management or in skilled labor. Krishna, for example, had been the able manager of the Santa Monica ashram. He was perhaps overly watchful at times—sometimes willfully denying Christian access to her—but he was certainly a capable administrator. Chandan, another example, was a journeyman carpenter who had taken the Hindu name of pungent sandalwood, "Chandan," as a sign of his art and craft.

Ultimately, she had come full circle to ask a question that had not been fully formed until many months after arriving. *Why me?*

Not until late August did she begin to suspect an answer.

No earth-shattering incident caused the suspicion, just a single touch one evening after *satsang*. She had stopped at Padmananda's office with a copy of the blueprints for the new clinic, thinking he might be interested in an alteration considered earlier that afternoon. On the desk, a small lamp and a scented candle had lent an easy light to the room. Padmananda had stood behind her chair as she pointed to the drawing. In midsentence, she'd paused. His hand had lightly touched her head. Immediately, she recognized the difference between the touch of the Master and the touch of his disciple. Startled, she'd looked up and had caught the unguarded look in his eyes for the brief second before he had looked down at the page and had quickly dropped his hand to his side.

"Uh . . . yes . . . ," she'd said, glancing back down at the drawing, pointing. "Um, here, I thought perhaps because of Param's inquiries, we could move the courtyard here. That way more people could wait in shade."

"You're right, Kali," Padmananda had answered absently. "Go ahead and make the change."

"I'll speak with the architect first thing in the morning."

He'd stood so close she could smell the incense on his clothes, feel the warmth of his body. Caught up unwillingly in what his touch had aroused in her, she'd looked toward his arms. Then, abashed and embarrassed, she'd rolled the plans and stood, looking toward the floor.

"Goodnight," she'd said softly.

Is it my imagination?

She pictured his soft, dark eyes, smiled to think of the humor and wit in them. Thought of his mouth. The strong line of his chin. His shoulder-length dark hair. His youth and humor. With him, she knew safety and security, approval and encouragement—no conflict, no ego battles, just easy conversation and laughter.

For a single tortuous week, she had asked whether she could be falling in love. What was love, really? Was it the huge roar of emotions she felt every time she thought of Christian? The feeling she fought to control whenever she was with him? Wanting to touch him, to be as close as two people could physically become? Or was it something else? Perhaps something to do with true friendship and a part of life separate from the passions of desire.

Over the next few days, she had watched Padmananda more closely, and she noticed that he had watched her in return. On several occasions, their eyes had met, and there was a message for her in his. Confused, she had made some attempt to avoid him, an attempt that had became difficult, considering their work together.

Now, dinner had just ended, and he walked deliberately toward her.

"Kali, will you walk with me?" Without waiting for an answer, he stepped back and held out a hand to the door leading to the garden.

She found that she trembled slightly, her stomach a thick ball of anticipation, one mixed with fear, knowing that everything was changing.

A waxing moon lit the path where they walked. Others were in the garden. The sound of laughter from a group of friends floated toward them. The music of a guitar. From the huts spread against the ashram walls, gentle voices coaxed children to sleep. Cicadas sang their love songs. The bell necklaces of cows deeply resonated as the animals moved rhythmically in the evening shadows. A quiet tension stood between the couple. An expectation.

Suddenly Padmananda looked up to the sky and surprised her by saying, "In a week the moon will be full. I have always loved the beauty of the iridescent light of a full moon." He took the shawl from his shoulders. "Are you chilled? Here . . . " He stopped in lamplight and wrapped the cloth around her, his eyes holding hers, his hands lingering on the cloth.

"Somewhere in my knowing you," he whispered softly, "my thoughts changed. I don't know how it happened, but my feelings have gone beyond those of a teacher. I think you know it as well. The other night, when we were together in my office, I looked at you and saw your hair glowing in the lamplight. I needed to touch it, to touch you at that moment." Then, words rushed from him. "You have the most beautiful heart I've ever known. I've fallen in love with your soul, with the love and kindness in everything you do . . . "

"Padmananda," the word was anxious, and she held up a hand to stop him, "before you go on, there's something I need to know."

She saw him nod.

"Why is it you brought me here to India? Was it because you thought I deserved to come? Or was it for yourself?"

With an intensity that startled her, he said fiercely, "You were chosen long before I began to suspect my feelings. Ask yourself. You've

worked an eight-hour day as my secretary while also studying and performing your religious duties! Don't you see your own ability?"

Kali took a small, shuddering breath. "Then I need to ask something else. When you told me to come . . . the night I was sick with the
fever . . . you knew there was someone else in my life. Was your counsel
to take me away from him?"

"That night I was the disciple," he answered simply. "I swear it on
the love I hold for the Master."

Kali lowered her eyes and looked down at the ground. A startling
warmth spread through her body. Something new. A freedom to feel
emotions she had put aside. A rising, irresistible joy rose to her throat.
This man loved her. Because she was worthy. Yet within the warmth
was a confusion. The so many questions about how to move forward.
How could she explain the complexities of her emotions?

"Then I will answer you honestly. At first, I had for you the love
of a student for a beloved teacher. Then the friendship we knew as we
worked together. But now . . . something more."

Padmananda leaned toward her, and in the dim light, she could
read eagerness in his face. But she shook her head and stepped back.
She had to be sure. All had to be spoken.

"But if what I feel is true," she whispered, "then I must be honest
with you. Some part of my life is still tied to Christian. Several weeks
ago, I wrote telling him about the ashram and the Master. About my
happiness. I suggested he come to see for himself what I have found. I
mentioned that there might even be hope for us if he were to join the
ashram. I feel . . . as if I owe him something."

"Is it because of the money?"

"No." She shook her head. "It's because he's always been kind to
me. He loved me enough to let me go. He gave me the freedom to
decide for myself what I wanted to become."

For several long moments a heavy silence loomed between them,
then he smiled. "You're right. We should continue to know each other
as friends. Would you spend some time with me? Not as student to
teacher, but as friend to friend. Next week the moon will be full. Would

you like to travel with me and a few others to see the Taj Mahal? In the light of the full moon, the Taj glows like a pearl, speaking all the thoughts of those who built her. The night is filled with such splendid light, that the moon pales in comparison. "

"Oh, Padmananda!" she cried without hesitation. "Yes! The Taj Mahal! I've so wanted to visit the India outside the ashram walls. And," she gently took his hand, "there's so much I've wanted to know about you."

His voice suddenly turned serious again. "At Agra, Kali. At Agra, I'll tell you everything."

The journey to Agra was a blur of images, so strong that for weeks afterward, Kali could close her eyes and see and feel everything just as she had on those days.

As they gathered at the bus just before sunrise, there was the first surprising moment. Padmananda was dressed in blue jeans and a white shirt, a lightweight windbreaker over his arm, sporting a gleam in his eye and the air of a young man on holiday. There was also the uncomfortable instant when she saw that Krishna, friend from California, understood things had changed between her and Padmananda, that they were no longer simply initiate and disciple.

As the ashram gates opened, the sun was just rising. Kali leaned toward the window, anxious for her first view of the outer city in the early morning light. She had been within the ashram compound for almost ten months, working and studying. The bus traveled slowly down a narrow lane and then onto larger side streets. Small groups of goats and dogs wandered in front of the bus. They narrowly missed a bullock cart carrying straw. A donkey loaded with firewood veered to the side of the road. The bus came to a complete stop as a huge Brahma bull slowly meandered across the road.

By the time the bus entered a large boulevard, the streets were brightening by the moment, and the city was waking. Even at this early hour the roadway was crowded with people and vehicles of all descriptions. Every few seconds the driver honked his horn, and a chorus of blaring horns responded. The driver wove his way around three-wheeled pedal rickshaws and motorized rickshaws, cars, and scores of small, dark taxis. At a red light, Kali gaped at the elephant standing in the next lane waiting for the light to change.

The journey became a constant contrast of ancient and modern, poor and rich. Leaning against the outer walls of a large brick apartment building were tiny hovels of cardboard and thatch. Neatly dressed young children rode to school in peddled rickshaws, while half-clad waifs shaped the cow dung they had collected into round fuel pies and slapped them against a wall to dry. Well-groomed men in three-piece suits carried briefcases, as beggars in rags sat on sidewalks and held open their hands for *baksheesh*. The streets were filled with men, only an occasional woman appearing in a colorful sari and embroidered shawl. Corporate managers with briefcases walked past the modest sidewalk stands of fruit sellers and moneychangers.

As they left New Delhi, the September day was filled with sunlight. The vast expanse of urban city changed to spreading agricultural fields. Kali smiled to see the image of a lone woman moving gracefully in a flowing sari, her steps along a raised path between rice fields. This was the India she had come to see—this woman strolling on her way to collect water, the brass jar atop her head flashing in the sun.

Within hours, they were on the outskirts of Agra, and once again, the streets became crowded. From the slow-moving bus, she watched men and women dig into the earth with shovels at a construction site and haul dirt away in baskets carried atop their heads. A potter sat at his wheel turning red clay under his hands. In the shade of a tree, a tailor worked, his feet pushing a treadle sewing machine. Children ran after an old tire, spinning it with sticks. Food vendors sold fruit and pakoras and tea.

When the bus finally stopped near the Taj Mahal, Kali picked up her bag, hoisted it over her shoulder, and stepped uncertainly to the street. The sounds of fierce bargaining in the marketplace carried to where she stood.

Immediately, she was surrounded by three men and four little boys, their voices pleading, anxious, ceaseless, hoping she would purchase cheap postcards or beads of lapis lazuli or sandalwood incense.

"I'm sorry," she tried explaining, "I'm an initiate in an ashram. I have no money."

She took a step forward, and the crowd parted, making a path, but still close, still holding up wares. A boy about eight years old tugged at her sleeve, and, looking into his face, she saw with horror that his teeth were rotting. Ten feet away, a man turned to urinate against a tree. Another lifted one finger against his left nostril and blew his nose, allowing mucous to drip to the ground. Kali looked away, only to notice scores of wads of coughed-up phlegm intermingled with piles of decaying vegetables, garbage, and animal dung. With some relief, she saw that she was approaching a huge red sandstone gate. The last of the heavy haggling from the sellers swarming her began with renewed and frantic appeal.

A few more yards, Kali thought desperately, *and I'll be through the gate.*

Just as she thought she would make it, she froze and began to step back, one foot at a time. A wall of the truly needy rushed her. A leper with a deformed hand reached out. A tiny woman whose age Kali could not guess, her hair matted, wearing brown rags, her eyes filmy with an oily slickness, whined in a language she did not understand. A blind man held up a begging bowl, his eyes white orbs. A tiny child of two was being taught to open her palms, learning her trade early.

They closed in, those desperate beggars, hands outstretched. Kali could not in her heart say no to these desperate people, but there were so many of them, all searching for a face in the crowd that might mean the difference between life and death. Despairing, she wanted to offer each a life of fulfillment, human endeavor, and growth. What good would a coin do, even if she had one to throw? Why was her life so blessed?

Suddenly, attributing it all to karma just didn't cut it.

This is about politics, she thought instinctively, *about those with more who cannot share with those who have less. About the distribution of food, goods, and wealth. Education. Overpopulation. Religion.*

Her involvement at Berkeley came rushing back, and with it, Christian's voice asking how she could hide in an ashram while political change was imperative.

Then, as suddenly as everything had begun, she heard a quiet, familiar voice. The beggars began to slip away, one by one. Padmananda walked among them, offering coins of *paise.*

"The gate is near," he said close to her ear. "No one will bother you once we're inside." He offered her his hand, and shaking uncontrollably, she gratefully took it.

"I'm . . . not sure I can go on." Her voice rose, louder and echoing off the walls as they passed underneath the red sandstone gate. "I don't know what's real anymore. My world? The one for these people? Karma?"

Padmananda put an arm around her. "Both worlds are real. And yes, this is a result of karma. Kali, look. There is another reality as well. Turn your face and look."

Poised like a love poem beyond a stretching green lawn and a shimmering pool of water, was the Taj Mahal, alive and breathing, its four minarets and smooth, round domes cast into a pale blue sky.

"Come," he said gently, dropping his arm from around her shoulders, "the rest of our group is waiting."

The night was like no other Kali had ever known. The Taj Mahal was alive with the reflection of the moon on its marble, aglow with an internal light. Visitors walked quietly through the gardens or strolled the mausoleum's terraces, gazing at the glittering streak of moonlight that fell across the Yamuna River. Below, in the burial chamber, Shah Jahan and his wife Mumtaz rested as they had for three hundred years.

"Legend has it that there was to be a black marble mausoleum built on the opposite shore for Shah Jahan," Padmananda told her, resting against the terrace's railing and looking across the water. "A black marble bridge would join a white marble bridge from this shore in the middle of the river. Unfortunately for Shah Jahan, his son had him imprisoned, so we'll never know whether he could have carried out this plan—or even if it's true." He turned toward her and smiled. "We do know that the love story between Shah Jahan and his wife was remarkable enough to produce this magnificent mausoleum."

"Why, you're a secret romantic!" she teased. "You were right, you know. The Taj does rival the moon."

Then, looking around at the splendor of the architecture and the glow of the marble in the moonlight, she became serious. "It's hard to imagine this kind of beauty after all the things I saw on the street today. You realize nothing much has changed since the time of Shah Jahan. Those with wealth are allowed to experience this beauty. We were fortunate to be able to pay the entrance fee so we can enjoy this evening. An amount that would feed a poor family for many days."

"I think you might have a better understanding now about the need for the medical clinic we're building."

She nodded. "It's more than blueprints on paper." Then leaning back on the marble railing, she asked, "How is it you came to the Master?"

"I have known Daya Nanda all my life. He and my father were the best of friends, both teachers. They planned the ashram together. Daya Nanda has been a part of my life from the time I was a small boy. When I was called Nareesh."

"It must be wonderful to have always known the Master and your path," she said wistfully.

Padmananda laughed. "Actually, my journey was . . . not a straight one. You see, although my family is of the Brahmin class, as a child, I was very poor. My mother died when I was quite young, and my father . . . well, my father put aside this world. Early on, he took a *brahmacharya* vow of celibacy. All his time was spent reading, studying, and teaching. A comfortable life based on the accumulation of wealth neither interested nor concerned him."

"That must have been very hard for you. Growing up alone, without a mother's care. I'm very close to my own mother."

"As a small child, I always had the sense of something missing." He paused, pondering, then took a deep breath. "But when I was seven years old, a friend came into my life. After that, I never felt alone."

At the tremor in his voice, she whispered. "Go on."

No longer looking at her, staring across the river, he continued. "In the days that followed, karma brought me to the father of my new friend. A Christian missionary living in my village for many years. I was blessed. This generous man offered the means of paying for my education at an English boarding school."

Grasping the implication immediately, Kali said, "And you and your friend were in school together?"

"Oh, yes. For many years. Through graduation. In fact, we did everything together." Suddenly, the humor she always known in him returned, and she listened as he laughed again. "We often took the same classes. And we loved the same sports. I was better at cricket. A bowler. He always insisted he was a better footballer. We traveled quite a bit. Occasionally, we got into trouble together."

Kali smiled tentatively at this new Padmananda. "What kind of trouble?"

"More worldly concerns than sense."

Sidestepping exactly which worldly concerns, she asked, "And after graduation? You planned to study with the Master?"

"No. I was prepared to attend a Christian theological college in the United States."

Completely surprised, Kali inhaled sharply.

Once knowing the Master, how can anyone desire anything else, she wondered.

Padmananda took her hand. "You see," he explained gently, "when

I first left my village and arrived at the English boarding school, I had to struggle with new habits and customs. A year later, an Indian toilet seemed just as bad to me as it did to you today. As I grew older, I thought I could clean up the nation, rid it of disease, poverty. To my youthful eyes, the solution was simple."

"What solution was that?"

"Christianity. And Western medicine. I believed Christianity a religion of progress. In fact, I was rather snobbish about my beliefs."

"And your father? The Master? What did they say?"

"The choice was mine to make. Outside of the occasional uncertainty of identity, I was content. Oh, there was some indecision in high school. I experimented with alcohol, thought of those pleasures of a more worldly life. But by senior year, I knew I wanted to become a Christian minister."

"Did your decision have anything to do with a sense of obligation to the missionary who paid for your education?" The wind blowing off the water picked up, cooler. Emotion filled the space around them, something shackled, unspoken, waiting to be released. She shivered. Wrapping the shawl over her head, she said simply, "Tell me everything. I want to know."

With a voice that rose and fell in its emotion, he described the last months of high school, decisions and travels to Bodh Gaya, a visit to the holy city of Amritsar, of a man at the door announcing a riot between Hindu and Sikh, of fire and raging mobs. Of witnessing the death of his father, Ram Seva.

He told the story of a man betrayed by a brother.

"My father stood upon a cart trying to speak to the crowds." His voice was low, impassioned, the harshness of it alarming. "Daya Nanda had been swept away by the mob. I needed to find him. I asked my brother to protect my father. Surely, it was not too much to ask? A mob poured past the cart, the force of hundreds of bodies crushing the wood. My father fell beneath it—trapped and trampled. When I finally returned with Daya Nanda, my brother was . . . nowhere." Covering his eyes with his hands, he moaned, "If he had just stayed with the cart as I'd asked, he could have pulled my father from the onslaught. By the time I returned, all I held was a lifeless body . . . "

She heard pain, saw tears, but something more. Bitterness. His fists were clenched. His tone still incredulous at the extent of the duplicity.

"The next day, I learned that my brother had left the country. He'd run to save himself. He didn't even have the courage to face me. Can you understand? I thought I knew him. He and I . . . inseparable in heart and mind. And he couldn't come to me in my hour of greatest need? Attend the cremation?"

Fearful at the scope of his rising anguish, his vehemence, Kali placed a hand over his. Yet his voice continued to rise.

"The poor, the sick, the hungry . . . these weren't his problems. He had money. Resources. He could leave any time he wanted for the clean streets of America. He was not Indian. He was not . . . my friend."

"The Master," Kali whispered. "What has he said?"

In the moonlight, Padmananda looked at her closely, making sure she understood. "When I knelt over my father's body, my world crashed. Ram Seva had died as he lived, trying to protect his people. Only when Daya Nanda touched my shoulder did I see my decision to leave India akin to running away. My people needed someone who would care for them as my father had. If my brother represented Christianity and what I would find at divinity school, I needed to take a new direction."

Gently she pulled him to her, put her arms around his neck, and whispered in his ear, "Everything has a reason. Together, you and I, we've already begun to make a difference."

Ignoring the disapproving looks of visitors who turned away, he responded. At first, only holding to her tightly, then he was moving his lips over her face, her eyes, her ears, her cheeks, then to her mouth, tasting her lips and tongue, seeking oblivion, enveloped by a kind of madness, one of wild anger and sorrow and guilt and the hunger of deep sexual excitement.

At last, she pulled away, remembering where they were, struggling to gain control of her breathing and the emotions of desire that had been reawakened.

"I've taken a vow," she whispered. Hadn't she wanted to bring her mind and spirit to a higher plane? One that was not centered on the earth?

Savoring the nearness of her body, he spoke to her ear, "Your vow was for a short while. It was always meant to be set aside when you were ready. Will you consider marriage?"

Kali closed her eyes and swayed slightly with both ardor and the desire to heal him. An intuitive understanding of their easy comfort, of friendship and wit and common goals, left her abashed and searching for words. When at last she was able to control the waves of pleasure and promise washing over her, she answered in a hushed voice, "Yes . . . yes."

"I will no longer be your teacher," he said softly. "We will teach each other. Work together. And if you are willing, if God is willing, we will share children."

A subtle shifting in their roles began, with Kali leading. "Come," she said, taking his hand. "I think we should walk for a while. We must first bring this news to Daya Nanda for his blessing."

Filled with a mutual desire of the body, each silently wondering how long they would have to wait for consummation, they followed the course of the river, speaking softly, asking questions, discovering, and making plans.

3

BOB AND JULIE
MAUI, HAWAIIAN ISLANDS
SEPTEMBER 1969

"I'm telling you that after months of effort, they were gone. Just like that!" Keith snapped his fingers toward Dharma and Bob. "After all those prayers. The backbreaking climbs with composted soil for the plants. Fighting jungle roots using that rich earth. Battling rats chewing on the stems. Months of labor . . ." The frustration rose in his voice. "Along someone comes and rips off every plant!"

"Sorry, man," Bob said, shaking his head and wondering whether this was going to be a problem with his own grow plans.

"What we need," Keith exclaimed decisively, "is a place where people won't bother to go. A place that takes so much effort to reach that the crop is safe."

"Where's that?" Bob asked.

"In the interior," Keith told him. "Someplace warm and wet. Up a trail that's rarely traveled."

"Just where did you have in mind?"

Keith took out a map. "There's a long ridge not far from here. See? It's listed as unexplored. Now look. This," he pointed, "is national park land. And here are the park trails. This one," he touched the paper, "ends here. I've been up that trail a dozen times, thinking about just this sort of thing. Where the trail ends, there's a faint, ungroomed path. I know if we keep going, that path will take us to the back side of the ridge. Here," he traced the area, "in the valleys on either side of the ridge. I think we'll find what we're looking for right here."

"But how far does the trail go?" Dharma squinted at the map, trying to envision a path. "Once over that ridge, I mean, we're talking about a climb. The map says 'unexplored wilderness'."

"Yeah, but if we found the perfect spot, we could have a crop every four months," Keith argued. "Four months in summer, six or seven in winter, depending on weather. We wouldn't have to keep making the Afghan run. Not unless we feel the need for really good hash. It's getting harder for me to travel with the family."

"Alright," Bob said thoughtfully. "Let's do it. Let's hike up there and take a look."

"When do you leave for Asia?" Keith asked.

"When Christian picks up the truck."

"Is he going with you?"

Bob shrugged. "He hasn't decided yet." The subject was a source of annoyance. He wanted to know whether he could count on Christian's energy on the journey.

"How does Julie feel about this trip? With the new baby coming and all?"

"Yeah, I hear you," Bob answered. "But I swear this is going to be a quick one. I'm going to be back for this baby." He looked down at the map again. "We've got a couple of weeks until we hear from Christian. Let's plan to hike the day after tomorrow. Where will we come out of the jungle?"

"Here," Keith touched the map. "By this beach. We can have Annie meet us with the Land Rover. It should take about four days for the whole trip. We'll travel light. Bring enough food for two days. Fast for two. Make it a spiritual trip."

The plan to grow on Maui had been a dream of some of the members of the Brotherhood of Love ever since Laguna Beach had gotten too hot. If they had stayed in Laguna, the odds were that they would meet with disaster—arrest and long jail sentences. Keith and Annie had welcomed Bob and Julie and baby Shakti, as well as Dharma and his new old lady, Bliss, to the land on the river. In that fertile red dirt, the men had begun to experiment with growing herb on the island. The results were promising. But to set up the project, to make land payments while they experimented, Bob and Dharma, with a huge investment from Christian, had to make the trip to Afghanistan once more.

This time, they would not be flying in with four surfboards to fill with hash. This time, they planned to ship a special vehicle to Greece, then drive to Afghanistan. Once they arrived in Kandahar, they'd load up the vehicle, drive to a port city in India, and ship the vehicle back to Greece. There, they would change freight lines, shipping the truck back to the States on the original line. On all the visible paperwork, the entire trip would appear to be a European vacation. Much of their investment capital was going into a large truck, a sturdy vehicle that could manage the trek through desert and mountain, and one that could carry at least a hundred pounds of hash. Once sold, the beautiful black-green slabs of Afghanistan would earn them over a hundred thousand dollars, enough to carry everyone until they could grow a good Hawaiian crop.

Bob rolled away from Julie and Shakti and pulled back the tent flap. The sky was still dark, but in the east, a glow appeared, a faint purple, brightening by the moment. He crossed his legs into lotus position, straightened his back, clasped his fingers in a *mudra*, and began the rhythmical breathing. A half hour later, he opened his eyes to emerging color and stretched his head to his knees, breathing out, slowly inching down, following the same steady, rhythmical breathing as he went through a series of *asanas*.

The canvas tent they shared was a single room with its outer tan walls painted in colorful images of the sea—mermaids, shells, fish, waves of blue, clouds, and a sun over the water. Julie had placed two Indian rugs with mandala centers at either side of the foam pad that was their bed. A paisley bedspread and a colorful, geometric patterned tent frieze from Afghanistan considerably brightened the interior. The fabric smelled of months of burning incense. A small trunk held everything they needed. A vase of flowers sat on a small table. In one corner, stored in a basket, were three or four toys and clothes for Shakti. Near the front flap, another basket held papayas, some bananas, green coconuts, and a pineapple.

Bob took a papaya from the basket, sliced it open with a knife, and walked away to spill the seeds under a tree. As he ate, he watched Julie and Shakti curled next to each other on the bed, knowing there was nothing more he could ever want in life than what he had now. A cozy, vibrant home. The feeling of early morning air filled with the fragrance of earth and jungle. Julie, soft and warm and growing round with their second child, a woman who gave him the freedom to be himself. Food grew on the trees for the taking. He could walk without his clothes, one with nature. Here, he could live spiritually, explore his consciousness, and raise his children in peace and love.

If he could help Keith meet the land payments.

Where has all the money gone? he wondered. *All those years of scams—where were all the bucks?*

The thought brought him back to the morning. Leaning toward Julie, he kissed her ear.

"Hi," she mumbled sleepily, putting her arms around his neck.

"I'm leaving now, okay? See you in four days."

"Okay," she mumbled again, closing her eyes.

But this morning, he didn't want to let her go and pulled her once more toward him. "Good-bye, my love," he whispered, his mouth close to hers. "Four days."

"Mmm . . . until then . . . "

When Bob arrived at Keith's cabin, Dharma and Keith were already waiting. A morning toke together, and the three men began the drive to the national park in the Land Rover. Annie would get a ride up later and take the car home.

Parking, they pulled their packs from the car, adjusted the fit on their backs, and walked down the asphalt road toward the earthen trail. As Keith had suggested, they were traveling light—wearing shorts, T-shirts, and rubber flip-flops, carrying nuts and dried fruit for a couple of days, canteens of water, a plastic tarpaulin for ground cover, a machete, a compass, some paper and a pen to map the area, a bag of rolled doobies, and tabs of Orange Sunshine acid, in case they found the perfect spot.

The going was easy as they strode through the park. The trail was laced on either side with bright flowers, vines, ferns, and the sounds of birds. They walked the entire day, finding only at day's end that the path began to steepen, the climbing to become harder. But the air was clean and fresh, and they filled their lungs, breathing deeply. At nightfall, they camped by a stream. Above, they could hear the dull roar of a waterfall. The air was turning cool, and Bob wondered briefly whether they should have brought the sleeping bags. But he'd found a soft bed of moss, and taking out the tarp, he resolved to find comfort in the natural world. The river provided plenty of drinking water, and the men, famished after the long climb, ate more than they had expected. As the hours passed, the night grew colder, and the ground cloth did little to keep them dry and warm. As soon as first light appeared, each of them was glad to be on his feet and traveling again. In a short while, they were warmed as they climbed, and the island was once again beautiful and congenial.

The day was filled with gossip about their women and other ladies who had come to settle on Maui, the men laughing and speculating on the wide variety of sexual possibilities. They discussed what the impact of growing herb on the island's economy would be. Furthered plans for the forthcoming Asia journey.

By the middle of the second day, they reached the trail's end and began the more arduous climb along the makeshift footpath. None of them knew how long this curving venture would continue, why it was there, or who had used it. But that was the point of the expedition—to find out. By the time they stopped at nightfall, the food was gone, a mist had begun to rise, and a pressing cold began to push through to their bones. The trail had become less and less visible, and the easy walking in flip-flops that had been stable for two days had rapidly become more difficult.

"It looks like jungle from here," Bob said into the dusk. "What do you think?"

"I think it's going to be damned cold tonight," Dharma answered, putting his T-shirt back on. "Especially with this mist settling in."

"Food's gone, too," Bob noted.

"I thought we were going to fast," Keith said, looking at them.

"But after today's climb, maybe it wasn't such a good idea. We need the energy."

"Well, we're about halfway," Keith figured. "By tomorrow morning, we should cross the ridge and be in that tangle of valleys. That's what we came for. Or we can go back. It's two days of hiking either way."

"Then let's go on," Dharma said slowly, deciding, staring into the darkness settling into the trees. "I'd like to see those valleys. And you're right—it wouldn't hurt to fast. It just means changing our headspace. Saying we're not hungry."

The night was cold and damp, and more than once, Bob's chattering teeth woke him. With the sparsest of dawn illumination, the men were up and climbing, thankful for the growing light and the movement that brought warmth. By midmorning, the mist lifted, and although the trail became even sparser, they were able to catch glimpses of the line of ridge toward which they were climbing. By the time they reached the top, it was almost noon. The long ridge ran before them, its green slopes stretching into a series of valleys, all tumbling toward a distant, jewel-sparkled sea.

Bob had his first doubts when he saw the length of the ridge and the unknown paths they would have to forge. They had neither food nor proper equipment. Suddenly, the adventure looked a bit foolhardy. Today was the third day of the journey, and they had calculated meeting the women no later than tomorrow afternoon. *Four days*, Bob had murmured to Julie when he'd left. Now the trail spread away into a far distance.

"What do you think?" he asked as they stared to the east.

"It's beautiful," Keith told them. "Rugged. Untouched."

"Yeah," Dharma answered, "and you're right. Somewhere in those valleys, there's a spot that'll grow the perfect plant in safety."

"We're already half a day behind schedule," Bob said uneasily. "Are you sure we're doing the right thing? Can we make it in a day? Or even two?"

"We've come so far already," Keith answered. "And if you have to leave for the mainland soon . . . "

"Then let's get going and not waste time." Dharma started over the ridge, still following the footpath.

By late afternoon, the trail had completely disappeared, and they followed the course of least resistance, pushing forward through the least overgrowth. Where it was necessary, Keith took the lead, hacking away at vines and ferns with his machete. Conversation stopped, and the laughing speculations of love affairs and who grew the best smoke faded into thoughts of simply getting back into the arms of old ladies who loved them. The mist that had disappeared in the morning returned, bringing a chill and an eerie sense of grayness.

By nightfall of the third day, they stopped to drink from the little water they carried and drew lots to see who would sleep in the middle, blanketed by the warmth of bodies on either side. They pulled the thin plastic tarp over themselves, and they lay together, exhausted, cold, and famished, only to be confronted by still another problem—mosquitoes. The small, quick-flying insects hummed and buzzed about them as if the warmth of their blood was a rare feast. Not until morning, when they woke to the same gray cloud cover, did they see they had camped near the beginning of a large bog . . . and there was no way to go forward but through it.

Standing, stretching, and shaking his head, Bob took off his flip-flops and, without preamble, waded in barefoot. The murky water touched the top of his knees. He moved slowly, looking for a way to dry ground. The water deepened to his waist.

"The compass," Dharma asked, swatting a mosquito. "Did we remember to bring the compass?"

"I've got it right here," Keith answered.

"At least we had sense enough to bring that," Bob mumbled, irritably. "We'd be in a critical situation without it."

"Look," Keith called to him, "it's more than we'd planned for, but now, what choice do we have except to keep moving? The one thing we can be certain about is that the coast is out there somewhere. By the end of the day, we should be there."

"Yeah," Dharma added, "and the women will be waiting at the beach with food and doobies."

The strength of Bob's certainty that Julie would be there, along with Annie and Bliss and the children, hit him hard. With that sureness, he knew his commitment to Julie was a partnership. Suddenly, all those other women in their scanty bikinis were just bodies. Julie was eyes and heart and soul.

The swamp seemed to carry on forever. Keith kept a constant check on the compass to make sure they continued in the right direction. It was not until early afternoon that they reached firm land. Grateful at first, the men soon found this new land blocked by a forest of twelve-foot ferns and vines. Not far above their heads, gray clouds still hid the sun.

By nightfall, Keith's wishful thinking that the perfect valley would appear or that the ocean would welcome them, failed to materialize. Instead, there was only the ceaseless, monotonous gray mist and almost impenetrable green foliage. Bob took his turn sleeping in the middle, but this night, none of them slept. The cold seeped right through their plastic covering, making it useless. Their shared body heat was not enough to overcome the terrible pervading damp chill. All they could do was pray that the journey would soon end. And for the first time, try to push away the fearsome idea forming that they might not survive its ending.

When the morning of the fifth day arrived, they awoke with dismay and growing alarm to find the same gray cloud cover and a second swamp. Looking to his friends with a questioning glance, Bob read despair in their eyes. They were frozen, their physical pain bound to hunger and exhaustion. Keith was getting spacey, slurring his words.

"We'd better ration what water we have left until we know how much farther we have to go," Bob counseled.

Dharma nodded, his teeth chattering.

Once again, Bob walked barefoot into the swamp, frightened now. At first, he had thought to ditch his pack. The food was gone, and all he needed was the compass and the canteen. But he would need that pack when he left for Asia. So he held onto it, carrying it on his back like some treasure to be safeguarded.

"Keith," Dharma called, "come on, man, don't lag behind. The last thing we need is to lose one another."

Bob turned to see Keith wavering on unsteady legs at the edge of the bog. With a long sigh, Keith finally stepped into the waist-deep water.

This time, crossing the swamp took only an hour, and the land on the other side began to climb. Up now, through the mist they traveled. The higher they climbed, the denser the cloud cover became. Everything dripped with the wet. Their flip-flops had long ago become useless, twisting and slipping off their feet. They hiked barefoot into growth so dense that Bob could no longer hack a path with the machete. It was too time consuming, and they were running out of time. Instead, they struggled to reach the top of the ridge, crawling over almost impenetrable walls of ferns. Where the stems broke, wooden prongs, like sharpened knives, cut and tore at their feet, arms, and legs. The ferns continued in a seemingly impossible, unending forest, and when they came through it at last, they left behind a trail of blood and much of their hope.

Just before the sun waned, at the crest of the hill, for a brief moment, a breeze cleared the air. There, stretching out toward what the compass told them was east, was a long ridge, almost like a bridge.

On either side of it, valleys fell at straight angles downward toward marshland. The layer of sky beneath the cloud layer turned bright pink, and far into the distance, they saw low hills, and at the very end—a distant blue hint of the ocean.

Left with their own thoughts, they sat together, unable to sleep, tense and tight, shaking from cold and shock and pain, waiting for any light that would send them a measure of warmth and allow them to move forward.

"T-tomorrow," Keith told them, sometime toward dawn. "T-tomorrow w-we'll be there."

Awakening from fitful snatches of sleep laced with vivid dreams, Bob wished he could return to slumber. The visions of his unconscious took him to the beach where the children played in sand and water. On a blanket laid under a tree, was food and drink and nearby, a fire to greet the evening. A twig of driftwood lit the pipe, and in the smoke were visions of eye and mind, an understanding of the wholeness, of the relationship with the tides and moon and the pull of the surf, of the waves rolling into shore, of his balance as he traveled over water on his surfboard.

But when he opened his eyes, the light of a new day had begun to separate dark, homogenous shapes into isolated objects, his body was cold, his thirst terrible, his hunger absorbing.

Remarkably, the mist that enveloped the ridge where they sat was shifting. The heated air from the morning sun gave rise to a breeze that blew away the cloud for several glorious, long minutes of sun. Then the mist was back again, moving, its arms enveloping the men, touching them with damp fingers, the chill hovering around their bodies. In another moment, as if dancing with the sun, the cloud departed, slowly shifting over the hills, dissipating, only to be joined by more rising mist from the valley below.

When the men finally stood and faced the ridge to see what awaited them, they were actually relieved. The fern forests were below in the valleys, and the ridge traveled east, the way they needed to go. Only when they started to move across the length of it, did they discover that the path was treacherous. On either side were sheer drops of pumice rock, covered in vines, and slippery with water.

Bob hung onto his pack and compass with what remained of his will. They represented his way out of the wilderness, his connection with home, with Julie and Shakti and the new baby growing in Julie's womb. His wife and children were all he could see, images that appeared before him. With each labored step, he tried to reach them. The thought that he might never see them again brought tears to his eyes. He blinked, forcing them away. He couldn't break down. He held the compass, and Dharma and Keith followed him.

"Hold up," he called to the men behind.

"What is it?" Dharma asked wearily.

"Look," Bob pointed.

Ahead, the ridge top narrowed to a scant twelve-inch width for perhaps thirty feet or so.

"I'll go first," Bob told them. "Wait here."

Using what control he could still muster over his exhausted body, he crossed foot over foot until he passed over the narrow bridge. Just as he told himself the worst was over, he heard a gut-wrenching scream and turned in time to see Keith sliding feet first on his belly along the long, slippery, vine-covered slope, picking up speed. In wide-eyed horror, he watched helplessly as Keith fell toward the fog and jungle below, almost out of sight.

As he slid, Keith grabbed desperately at the vines clutching the cliff side. They tore away from his hands, but it slowed him. A root caught his foot. He grabbed for it, missed, grabbed for another, slid away once again, and passed below the fog line, finally to crash hard against a tree.

"Keith!" Bob screamed, panicked and hoarse. "Keith!" His voice echoed in the valley until it drifted dead into the cloudy mist below.

"Here," Keith yelled shakily. "Here. Hanging onto a tree."

Bob dropped to his knees and tried to pull himself together. He looked toward Dharma, who stood white-faced and unmoving in the middle of the narrow bridge.

"Keith!" Bob called again. "Are you alright?"

"I'm . . . I'm not sure," he called back. "I'm shaking like a son-of-a-bitch."

"Just . . . just take it easy."

The fog was still moving, as if alive. Now it floated upward, thinning as it did so, the sun burning, swirling the white cloud. Retreating, still dancing to the whims of sun and breeze, the haze thinned to reveal the valley below. Bob could finally see. Thirty feet below, Keith clung to a tree with nothing beneath him. To his right, other trees grew along the hillside. If Keith could make it to the nearest tree, he could slide from tree to tree until he touched bottom, perhaps another fifty feet, where the ground was remarkably flat and firm. The only other alternative was for Dharma to continue on and come back with help. Realistically, that might take days—if Dharma made it—and how long could Keith remain perched on a limb, especially when the night winds blew along the canyons? Bob motioned to Dharma to traverse the narrow part of the ridge.

"Carefully," he called quietly.

Taking no chances, Dharma crossed on his hands and knees until he came to rest beside Bob.

"What do we do now?" he asked helplessly. "There's no way he can get back up. Man, we are talking slick. And there's nothing underneath him."

"He's going to have to go down," Bob answered. "And quickly, while the sun is with us. He's going to have to reach the trees on this side of him." He took a deep breath. "I'm going down. If I can get across from him, maybe I can reach out and pull him over."

"The hill's too steep!" Dharma cried. "What if you can't get to him? Move too fast? What if you get stymied midway there and can't go down?"

"Then we'll call up to you, and you'll go for help. Just leave your pack here to mark the spot."

"That may take days!"

"Then hurry," Bob mumbled.

He slipped off his pack, laid it on the ridge top, and before he could think about what might go wrong, he slid over the side, clutching tightly to vines, praying his slide could be controlled. At ten feet, he held to the first small tree, but as Dharma had feared, he fell away, his wet hands losing their grip. With a curse, he grabbed wildly for a root, caught hold of it, eased toward a second tree, caught it, and held on.

"What the fuck are you doin'?" Keith called up to him.

"Hang on, ol' buddy," Bob called back, the quiver in his voice matching Keith's. He was committed to the descent now. He let go, carefully sliding toward the next tree below him, then the next, and the next, until he was opposite Keith.

"So," Bob grimaced, trying for a smile, "how's it goin'?"

"Are you crazy?" Keith cried.

"If you can make it over here, we can descend using the trees underneath me as a break. We've got to try it. There's nothing underneath you."

"You're tellin' me."

Bob extended his arm full-length. "Stretch," he called.

Keith held out his arm as far as it would go.

They didn't meet.

Getting a toehold, careful, because the vines were unreliable, Bob stretched further. They were still shy the length of a man's arm.

Above, Dharma watched as they struggled. "Well, fuck it," he said aloud.

Throwing off his pack, he wrapped the canteen around his neck, attached the machete to his belt, laid belly down, and slid down as Bob had, braced against the side of the hill, using the vines for ropes until they clutched the same tree.

"Brother," Bob said to Keith, wiping his hand on his pants, "stretch out your hand."

With a final look into Dharma's eyes that said everything, Bob secured a toehold into the hill, held tightly to Dharma's right forearm, and inched across the chasm that separated him from Keith. "Try not to depend on the vines. Use my arm."

Mist began to press upon them, this time floating from above where the ridge peak captured the cloud. His feeling of desperation grew. A descent had to be done quickly, before the fog closed in again, but nothing couldn't be rushed.

"Easy," Dharma groaned, watching Bob push himself against the hillside. "Use your feet . . . steady . . . make sure you have some kind of foothold . . . "

Bob held his breath. He and Keith touched, grabbed each other's forearm, and began to maneuver back toward Dharma. Bob had almost covered the return distance when his foot gave way, the force of it tearing Keith away from the hillside and the vines he held to.

"Jesus!" Dharma cried. "Do something! I'm losing you!"

"There's a tree just below," Keith shouted to Bob in a shaking voice. "Let go."

Bob had no choice. The tree was the only chance for all of them.

Keith hit the tree hard, but it stopped his descent. Above him, Bob still dangled precariously. He searched with his foot for any kind of foothold.

"Come on," Keith called. "Drop."

Almost paralyzed with fear, crucial seconds passed until Bob rasped to Dharma, "You've got to let me go."

"I . . . can't . . . " Dharma groaned, ". . . the distance . . .what if . . ."

Instead, Bob released Dharma's hand and slid. Grasping instinctively at vines, he slowed.

"Here," Keith screamed up at him.

In the next moments, Bob came up against the same tree as Keith, and felt Keith's arms around him, steadying. He cried aloud with relief.

Slowly, one tree at a time, the three men slid themselves down the mountain. The sun was up, warm, and they looked up into blue skies framed on one side by a cloud-shrouded ridge. When at last they were near the bottom of the ravine, they still had a ten-foot drop to the moss- and vine-covered ground. Keith was the last to touch down. As he landed, they heard a snap.

"My . . . my goddamned ankle . . . ," he screamed, rolling on the ground. One of the bones protruded awkwardly.

"And I was just going to ask if you wanted to do that again," Dharma said, lifting Keith's head into his lap. "That was kinda fun, eh? Sliding."

"Real fun," Keith answered angrily, crying in pain and despair.

Abruptly, Bob stood up from where he'd knelt to examine Keith's ankle, and listened. "A waterfall," he mumbled. "Dharma, fill the canteen."

Dharma came back with a full canteen and a smile as bright as the ripening bunch of bananas he carried over his shoulder.

"Let's get you into the sun," he said to Keith, who was shaking from shock and pain. "You'll feel better with some warmth and food."

With the machete, they made a brace for his leg and ankle, then cut two small trees, wrapping the poles in strong vine to form a litter. By the time they'd finished, it was late afternoon. At the waterfall, they once again stopped to refill the canteen in the pool that formed at its base. The pool was surrounded by a grove of wild banana trees, many with a green bunch hanging between long leaves. They loaded the ripening bananas onto the stretcher along with Keith and followed the river as it wound its way across the valley floor.

"Look up there," Dharma nodded to Bob.

"Yeah, I know . . . mist," Bob answered absently.

"That's the way we were traveling. Along that ridge. If we were up there, we'd still be walking in the cloud. But here, in this valley, there's sunshine. Look at the way the mist hugs the ridge top."

Bob looked around. For the first time, he forgot the agony of each brutal step. The moss-like jungle floor was enclosed in a valley dominated by a small, almost hidden waterfall at one end and by a river running east, all the way to the ocean. They still had to occasionally hack at foliage to pass, but bright sunlight shone freely through the trees.

They passed wild banana, guava, and mango trees, following what had to be an old boar trail.

"You know, there's plenty of water and sunlight here," Dharma hissed between heavy breathing. "Just the right combination of heat and cool evenings. Pot plants will love it."

Wasn't that what had brought them on this excursion? The search for the perfect valley? Even the air smelled sweeter.

As night descended, they slept for the first time in many days, bellies full of fruit, the air warmer, lulled to sleep by the gurgling stream and a soft breeze in the trees. Bob's dreams were of Julie's worried eyes, telling him to hurry home. He could almost hear her anguished crying, and he awoke with a start to hear Keith sobbing. Touching Dharma, he motioned toward Keith, and together they lay next to him, holding him in the dark night.

Before dawn, they were already pushing through the jungle, carrying Keith, Dharma and Bob groaning aloud with each painful step. It was the beginning of the seventh day of this journey, and although they traveled the easier, low-lying path, progress was still slow. By late afternoon, the men again knew only despair.

"Where does it end?" mumbled Bob, ready to sit and cry. "How much more?"

Surely, the whole island could be crossed in seven days, not just the tiny part they had tried to explore. Impenetrable, the maps had called it. Now they understood why. With tremendous effort Bob forced back his tears . . . but failed. His legs buckled under him, and he knelt on the ground, sobbing.

"How much more?" he cried out, his feet so torn he wondered whether he could take another step.

Dharma touched his shoulder, tried to reassure him, then, to give him a moment, stumbled to the top of the low ridge hovering over them. Suddenly, Dharma was shouting, "The ocean! It's there in the distance. I can see sunlight on the water. If we move, we'll make it today!"

Bob turned and knelt at Keith's side, both men crying now in relief. "Did you hear?"

Dharma came to kneel beside them. "You see the tower there . . . to the left . . . the tall pinnacle." He pointed. "Mark it. And the flow of the river. With those two points, we should be able to get back here, only starting with a day's march ocean side."

"Do you really think we'll make it home today?" Keith asked pitifully.

"We can damn well try," Bob answered, wiping his face, his confidence returning.

Keith reached into the leather bag tied at his waist to retrieve the ten tabs of Orange Sunshine wrapped in plastic. Another time and they would come back to run naked along the wild boar trails, eat from the trees, swim in the pool of the waterfall, and make love to their women on the soft moss. Today, they would bury the tabs as a promise to return.

True to Dharma's expectations, they reached a widened trail that would surely take them to a road. They were so close they could hear gulls, and occasionally a breath of wind would bring the sound of waves pounding the shore and the tangy smell of salt. Just as they had begun to wonder whether they would have to spend another night in the forest, they heard voices.

"You wouldn't be the three men who tried to hike through from the park, would you?" the leader of a group of horsemen asked. "We have some awfully worried ladies waiting at home." The man sprang from his saddle and looked at Keith's ankle. "Broken," he stated flatly. "Looks like you got held up a bit."

A great amount of weeping and laughing surrounded them once they returned home, the men suddenly smug. The pain had been worth it, they assured everyone. They had found a safe place to grow.

Sometime during Bob's second week home, his feet almost completely healed by comfrey poultices, Julie picked up a message. Christian had telephoned nearby friends to say the truck they would use for the Afghanistan smuggle was ready. As she walked back to their campsite, she watched Bob sitting near the tent, working carefully on a leather headband. In the morning light, he was beautiful. His hair had finally grown past his shoulders. Now he would be cutting it once more to make this new journey. How long would he be gone this time?

During the week he'd been lost, she had been forced to consider the possibility that he might not return. Now he was going far away again, to a wild and distant land. What if something happened to him there? She felt a rising sense of panic, caused not only by her fear of losing him, but by the fact that, for the first time, she wanted some control over his decisions. Life wasn't really about letting everybody do his or her own thing anymore. Life was about providing for the children, being assured of a tomorrow. Bob's decisions affected the whole family. She remembered giving birth to Shakti without him. Bob had taken six months to get back from that trip, and even though he had brought back the beautiful hash, rugs, and dresses of Afghanistan, she had been desperately lonely. A sister of her heart had been at the birth, not her old man. Kathy—not Bob—had stood by her, while, wracked by pain, she had brought his daughter into the world.

"Bob," she said softly.

"Yeah? What's up?"

"There's a message from Christian. The truck's ready."

"Great." Bob smiled. "Just in time."

Julie shook her head. "I'm not so sure."

He looked at her, his brow furrowed. "What's in your head?"

"I'm afraid," she told him.

"Afraid? Of what?"

"I'm not really sure. Of losing you, I think. I've just gotten used to having you around. Sharing mornings with you. Lying with you at night. Planning things around you being here. And now you're leaving us again."

"Come on, Julie. You're not going to lose me. While I was lost in the jungle, you were my strength. I felt you call to me, tell me to hurry. I dreamed of your arms," he touched her mouth, "your lips. You kept me going. How will you lose me?"

She didn't want to have to say this. She had never wanted to make a demand on him. "I don't want to give birth without you. Not this time."

"Listen," he said gently. "It's going to be a quick in and out. Maybe Christian will come. You know how businesslike he is."

"He said he wasn't going. If he gets close, I believe he thinks he'll have to confront his father."

"I'm still hoping he'll come. I'll be back in time for the birth. I promise, lady."

"Bob, I really need you. And I need you now. Not only at the birth. I feel so . . . so vulnerable. You could have died in the jungle. Your presence here gives me a sense of security."

"If I don't make the trip, none of the time and investment I've put into it so far will be worth anything. I want the money to buy the land next to Keith. You know it's not just for me."

"I know," she answered, guilt weighing heavily on her. "What I feel is selfish."

"It's not selfish; you're thinking of our family, but so am I. In a few days, we'll all be off to Honolulu for the Jefferson Airplane concert. Then I'll be gone with Dharma for six weeks. Max. I promise."

"Six weeks to go around the world? Last time, it was six months."

"Trust me, okay? I'll be back. I promise." He stood. "Now go get Shakti. It's almost time for lunch. I told Keith we'd come up to the house."

As she started toward the tent for Shakti, she looked back at him. A look of concentration on his face told her he was already absorbed in planning what needed to be done for the journey to Asia. His demeanor made her realize something she had tried to avoid. The men in her world would always love their women and children, live off the energy of their combined love, wither without it, but they would never be staked to it. They would demand the freedom to come and go at will, the thrill of the elusive deal chased into the wee morning hours or halfway around the world, the smell of money and danger great. They would wield the tyranny of that freedom in the name of common sense, of business, of the financial burden that held together the family. And if they were lonely, there would be some woman to soothe away the night, while she and Bliss and Annie, and ladies like them, waited.

Only occasionally, another woman would enter the business world, sending the energy askew, and also calling the men brothers. Women like Kathy. Suddenly, Julie was as jealous of Kathy's freedom as she was of Bob's. No man, not even Christian, dictated to her, not even through the clever, soft words of "because I love you," "because this is for the family." There were no small children to bind her. And she had money . . . money, the key to her freedom.

But Bob would not want to be with her if she were like Kathy. He wanted her soft and malleable, and if she hardened or insisted on her own needs, she might lose him. The thought frightened her. To be alone with two small children. Fear tempered her anger and her jealousy.

Fretfully, she tried to rein in her fear and the strange bitterness about his leaving. She needed time to gather her wits and her emotions, not just for the little girl who played idly in the red dirt, but for the child within her, who must surely feel her emotions. Sitting on the stump of an old tree, she repeated the mantra she recited each morning and evening. An old idea stirred within—ultimately, you are always alone. No one else can make your life for you. You have to make it for yourself.

Feeling calmer and forcing herself to believe that six weeks would pass quickly, Julie picked up Shakti and took Bob's hand as they walked down the trail to the house.

CHRISTIAN AND KATHY
BERKELEY, CALIFORNIA
SEPTEMBER 1969

Christian walked into his house in the Berkeley Hills holding a copy of *Life* magazine's special edition on the Woodstock Music Festival. For the past two hours, he'd been at Richard's house. Baby John had fallen asleep on his chest, and he had leaned back, content at the baby's warm presence, talking quietly with Richard and Marcie about the meaning of the festival. Woodstock, he believed, represented the hope of the psychedelic prayer. For three days, a half million people had lived as one, each part caring for the whole.

Now, magazine in hand and squinting against the reflection of the sun on the living room window, he looked around for his lady. "Kathy," he called.

"In the bedroom!"

At the door, he stopped, his fingers marking the pages with the pictures he wanted to share with her. Her bag was open on the bed, and she was folding clothes and stuffing them inside.

"You're packing," he said, stating the obvious.

"Hi." She smiled. "Where've you been all morning?"

"Talking to Richard."

"Did you offer him a partnership in the lab?"

"Yeah, but he said he couldn't leave his partner. I really felt for him. I could see he really wanted to do it."

"I'll never know what he sees in Alex," she answered, shaking her head. "Did you tell him about the new equipment?"

"He thought the vacuum sealer was a great idea. With it, we can keep crystal stored indefinitely."

"When are you going to let me see the lab?" she baited him.

"We've been discussing this. When you give up your business and work with me full time."

She grinned, throwing a sweater into the bag. "Christian, I'd never work with you. Only for you."

"Besides," he returned, "I don't want to endanger you."

"But you'll endanger Richard?"

He pretended not to hear and sat down next to her. "The energy of the lab's so intense, I can't figure out how the Man doesn't tune into it. It emits these powerful waves."

Now she laughed. "Christian, if they had the sensitivity to tune into it, they wouldn't be looking for it. They'd understand and be on our side."

"So . . . what's going on with the bag?"

"I've got to go to Arizona for a few days. I'll be back before classes begin next week."

"You're going to Arizona?" Christian asked, discomfort evident in his voice.

"I got a call this morning. A hot tip." Kathy threw him an impish look. "The people I'm doing business with want to talk to me this time, not Danny."

"Larry?"

Kathy's good humor vanished. "Who told you that?"

"Richard. He said you were once pretty tight with Larry."

"An old friend. He was my first acid trip."

The immediate stab of jealousy surprised him. He felt his body go rigid. "I see."

She stopped the packing. "I . . . shouldn't have said it like that, Christian."

"A first trip's important. Life changing."

"They're good people," she said quietly. "Larry and Jose. Carolyn. Miguel and Rosie. Larry and Jose have been partners for some time. They've been brothers since meeting at a pacifist training workshop in Big Sur years ago."

"Richard said that, too."

He turned away, thinking, and put the magazine down on the dresser's flat surface. "Kathy, I'm really serious. I asked you at Woodstock if you'd sell your business and join my team. I mean full time. I need someone who won't fuck up. That load of base needs to be brought down from Vancouver in a couple of weeks. You know how important this is."

Base, ergotamine tartrate, was the alkaloid derived from ergot. With ergotamine a chemist could make lysergic acid. Lysergic acid would then be used to produce LSD, lysergic acid diethylamide. His lab was set up in an industrial area in Southern California, and although Kathy had never seen it, he knew the power of it intrigued her.

"Why can't I help you and keep my business at the same time?" he heard her say.

"Too many variables."

"Like what? My independence?" And she sighed. "Christian, we've been over this before. Since Hawaii. The same reasons still exist. The acid business is your scene. It always will be. If I give up my business, I'll lose control of my life. I need to have my own trip going. How can I make you understand?"

"Couldn't it be something other than dealing? Choose a career and I'll help you out financially."

"If that's what I wanted, I could pay my own way. But I made a commitment to raising consciousness. Just like you."

"Why does trusting me scare you?"

"I do trust you, and nothing's scaring me. It's not about trust."

"As soon as we start getting comfortable with one another, you're off. Hanging out with Danny at your old College Avenue apartment. Sleeping there if you get too stoned to drive back up here." Casting a hand toward the bag with more than a hint of frustration, he added. "Packing."

"Now . . . wait a minute . . ."

She was regarding him closely, and he tried to center himself. This huge flux of frustrated emotion wasn't new, but it was the first time he felt he was losing a grip. Words burned at his lips. Things he'd wanted to say for months. Maybe it was because of Woodstock and the closeness they'd had. He'd actually thought she was going to become his full partner.

"Hey, I only crashed there one night," he heard her say. "And quite frankly, Christian, when I'm hanging out with Danny, I'm usually involved in a deal. Yeah, sometimes I'm visiting. Smoking. But I'll hang out with Danny anytime I want. I'm not living there anymore. I moved all my stuff up here months ago. I'm living here with you."

She glanced at her watch and closed the pack. He moved to stand over her.

"I told you when we first got together that I wanted something more from you." His voice was tight with quiet anger. Another first. He could not remember a time when he'd ever been truly angry with her. "I said we could see how it worked. But what I want doesn't seem to be important to you. I want a life partner. Someone who will always be here. Not someone who comes and goes on a whim. You do whatever you want, anytime you want. It's never what *we* decide to do."

The voice that answered him was soft, unsure. "Maybe . . . maybe I should just leave and we can discuss this when I get back. There's laundry that needs to be done. These sheets need changing. See if you can get Linda to lend you a hand."

His voice rose, anger flashing in his eyes. "I don't want to ask Allen and Linda to do our housework. Ever since this relationship began you've pushed to have things your way. Where does it end? Where's the compromise?" He reached up and unbuttoned the top button of her blouse and watched as her body stiffened. "That's exactly what I mean," he told her, jabbing a finger against her bare chest. "It's always on your time."

"No, it isn't," her tone began to match his own. "I just don't like your first response to any problem you have."

"Which is?"

"To take my body as if you owned it."

The words stung him. He blinked and stepped back. That was part of having an old lady, part of love. You had a place to come and lay down your problems.

"You know I'm in a hurry and don't have time for this. I'll be lucky to make that plane." She pulled on one of the straps to tighten it and mumbled, "You'd just love it if I gave up everything. Then you could go brag to Bob that I was finally under control."

"What were you going to do if I hadn't shown up? Leave me a bloody note? I don't want a bloody note on the dresser."

"We're . . . we're having an argument." Her voice trembled, and her hands were shaking as she tried to buckle the other strap. "I don't want to argue."

"Kathy, I want us to talk to each other. Decide things together."

"Let's get to the root of this. You're pissed off because I've got my own business responsibilities. Something you can't control."

"No. We're having an argument because I want to know exactly, once and for all, where I stand with you."

She looked at him curiously. "You know you mean more to me than anyone else in this world."

"Except yourself," he said, his tone now more sorrow than anger.

"Oh, for God's sake, Christian, this is not about how I feel about you. Or the sacrifices we've made for each other. This is about my financial independence." She picked up the bag. "I have a plane to catch. If I don't go now, I won't make it. Let's talk about this when I get back. I think we both need to chill anyway."

Jesus, he thought, *she's just going to walk out the fuckin' door, leaving this kind of energy in her wake.*

"Look," he said, stopping her with the word. "We've done pretty well up to now. We've both changed a lot to be with each other."

"I know . . . but . . . but right now I have to go." Her hand touched the doorknob.

Just as she turned the knob, he asked the real question, the source of all his ire. "Will you make love to him?" The words were spoken quietly. He waited.

She had never been able to hide anything from him. Didn't want to now. But she was clearly embarrassed that he read the truth in her eyes.

"I see you've thought about it. When you get back, I think you should move your things back to College Avenue."

"Don't do this to me," she pleaded. "Why are you doing this?"

"Because I can't live this way anymore. I love you, but . . . I just can't. I need someone I can count on to share a life with me. I'm twenty-three years old. Everyone we know is having kids." He thought of John lying on his chest, the warmth of it, the unbroken bond with a child.

"Well, go on then," she screamed at him, suddenly just as jealous and angry. "You can have your pick any night of the week at Carousel Ballroom. Get some brainless chickie to screw and then change the sheets when you're through!"

"That's not what I had in mind."

Surprised, she faltered. "You . . . you have someone in mind?"

"As a matter of fact, I do."

"Why is it alright for you to have some fantasy waiting in the wings?"

"I could forget what's waiting if you were my lady. Can you be? Can you let Larry and your business with him go? Can you work with me like I've been asking? Tell him plainly you have an old man who needs you?"

Kathy looked toward the floor, unable to answer.

"I thought not," he answered for her.

"Christian," she whispered, "I love you."

Half smiling, he took three large strides and had her in his arms, lifting her against him, fitting her against his contours so that she folded into him. His kiss took the breath from her mouth with the same easy fit, as if to tell her how well matched they were. "And I love you," he whispered in return, looking deeply in her eyes so that she would know the truth of it. "Remember that, will you? If you leave, remember what it is you're giving up."

He let her go.

"Christian . . ." Her eyes were bright with tears. He watched as she blinked and wiped her cheeks. "I will not be forced to choose between you and my business." She struggled to make her words forceful. "He sounded excited over the phone. A new deal—different weed and a good price. He's waiting. You'll just have to trust me."

She reached out to pull open the door, then turned one last time. "And let's get one more thing straight. We call it 'business' because we have no other word for it. But it's not *business*. You and I both know the money is secondary, only energy used to keep things going. If it was money we wanted, we could get it in any number of ways, without the risks. It's the head trip that's important, but we have to make it available. I need to go to Arizona. I'll be back when the *business* is over."

He stared at her without a word. There was nothing left to say.

"You're important to me," she told him softly, "to other people. You do things no one else can. I believe in you."

A last look and she was out the front door, hurrying toward the airport.

5

KATHY
TUCSON, ARIZONA
SEPTEMBER 1969

Almost a year had passed since Kathy had seen Larry, and at first, she didn't recognize him.

"You . . . you cut your hair!" she exclaimed.

"Oh . . . yeah," he said, taking off his cowboy hat and running his hands through his dark locks, "months ago. I needed a different look for crossing the border. And getting a bank loan. Do I look okay?"

"You look . . . beautiful. I'm just . . . well . . . shocked, I guess. How are you, anyway?"

"Never better." He grinned and leaned over to kiss her gently. "Come on. I'll tell you what's going on."

Kathy took a long, hard look at him as he made small talk about the ranch on the way to the truck. The cowboy boots were scuffed and dusty. His bell-bottomed jeans had been replaced by straight-legged Levi's. His hands were hard, brown, and calloused, his body tight from heavy labor. But he still wore an incongruous Grateful Dead T-shirt and a colorful beaded band around the rim of his black cowboy hat. He was indeed beautiful—rugged, maturing, confident.

"We've got two dozen horses," she heard him say. "Fine ones. We're starting our own breeding program. The bank loan allowed us to add to the original property when the parcel next door came up for sale. It's really a fine piece of land—lots of water and winterfeed. We hope to finish getting it fenced so that we can start running horses on it this spring."

From the corner of her eye she watched him move, only half listening to all the news he told her, aware that everything he said told only of the what and where and how of running the ranch. He threw her pack onto the truck bed, then leaned back against the door, regarding her. "Your hair's longer. I like it." His voice was hard and rough, the same as his body. Kathy didn't know how to take him. For the first time, she felt uneasy with him, kept her eyes turned away. The slight nausea she had felt this morning returned.

"Hey, what's going on?" he asked. "Are you stoned or somethin'?" He took her chin in his hand and turned her face to look at him. "Or have I been running off at the mouth?"

"I . . . I'm glad to be here," she told him. "It's just . . . it's been a long time."

Larry wrapped his arms around her, pulled her close, and looked into her eyes. "I've missed you."

"Ah," she breathed softly, "there you are. For a moment, I thought I'd lost you."

"Let's go," he said, giving her a kiss. "I've got a lot to tell you." He opened the truck door, and she slid onto the seat.

"I think I've finally done it." Larry had both hands on the wheel and a self-satisfied smile on his face. "It took a long time, but I think this is it. I've finally found the right connection. The samples look good. Wait until you see them. We're not talking bricks anymore, but loose buds. Moist and sweet. Just like you said you wanted. They smell like bananas or papayas. Straight from the tropics."

"So you're moving into loose grass. I'm telling you, it's a pain to deal with, but so tasty!" She laughed. "What's my price going to be?"

"Probably about fifty dollars a pound."

"Fifty a pound! Larry! That's a fuckin' good price!"

"Yeah, well, I owe you. Wait'll you see it. Even Jose thought you'd go for it." He gave her a sly, sideways glance. "And you know he's always on your side."

Near the road leading to the ranch, Larry made an unexpected turn and headed down a dirt road Kathy had not been on before.

"Where are we going?" she asked.

"I want to show you the new parcel we bought."

The truck bounced and jolted its way along a deeply rutted track, over two small hills, and then into a valley. At a long curve in the road, a small stream joined them alongside, growing wider as they drove. Large, flat rocks laced the banks in places. The valley became a canyon with steep sides, the land wild, primitive, all sand and cactus. Larry finally stopped the truck and waited for the dust to settle. When it did, Kathy looked out toward a rise in the land. A waterfall of some thirty feet cascaded freely through the air, falling into a deep green pool.

"This place is paradise," he said to the smile on her face. "No one around for miles. Just you and the river."

"Water pretty cold?"

"Freezing. But in summer, it warms toward afternoon. Come on. You have to see this."

He started up the hill, climbing almost straight up. Kathy felt the backs of her legs burning, but doggedly followed his easy gait until he stopped in front of a narrow crevice that faced the waterfall.

"Let me check first for critters," he said, surprising her by slipping through the opening. In a few moments, he was back and pulling up a handful of dry grass. "Come inside."

The cave was not as small as the entrance led one to believe. The space was cool, with a sandy floor that spread back and toward the right into a tiny alcove. Sleeping bags were stored there. Light filtered in from an open hole above a fire pit circled in stones. The cave's ceiling was blackened by smoke. Next to the fire pit, firewood had been neatly stacked. A basket nearby held dry, pale-green sage, an eagle feather, and an abalone shell.

"Like it?" he asked. "My special place."

He knelt down to begin a fire, the dried grass and smaller bits of kindling nurtured by his breath. Gradually, he added larger pieces until he had a warm, dependable flame going.

"Just what did you have in mind?" she asked.

"I thought maybe we'd just get warm."

"Take off your hat and let me look at this haircut."

Larry unrolled one of the sleeping bags, sat, and leaned back on his elbows. "How about my boots? Can you help me with these?"

"Larry . . . "

"Yes?"

Kathy knelt down beside him, staring out toward the waterfall through the slit in the crevice. "It's so beautiful."

"I'd like to conceive a child here," he told her, "and when he's born, bring him to the river to baptize him, giving him to the earth. He'll grow strong—swimming, riding, climbing. A man of the earth—Adam, I may call him."

"What if it's a girl?" she asked.

"Then she'll be a beautiful earth goddess. Mother Spirit. I'll teach her the Oneness. Aren't you getting warm? Why don't you take off your windbreaker?"

Sitting cross-legged on the sleeping bag, Larry reached into the basket and lifted the abalone shell and a small branch of sage. Then, holding the branch to the fire, he lit the sage and fanned it with the eagle feather until a sweet smell filled the cave. Once the flame was out, the branch smoldered, gray smoke drifting. He lay the smoking sage into the abalone shell and knelt to cleanse himself, pulling the sacred smoke over his hands and arms, over the top of his head to his back. From a pocket of his jacket, he removed a bag of buds and a pipe, swirling them through the smoke, purifying them. Then he stood and took a pinch from one of the buds.

"Grandfather of the east," he cried, holding the herb to the east, the source of enlightenment and first morning light. "I make this offering that enlightenment may be furthered. I give thanks for the thoughts you have given me."

Putting the herb into the pipe, Larry took a second pinch of buds from the bag and held his arm to the north, the place of mind and of clarity. "I give my thanks to the north for the clarity of my visions.

"I give my thanks to the south," he continued, "for teaching me the power of love. To the west, the direction of water, I am thankful for my life's nourishment."

A new pinch of herb ascended toward the sky, then went into the pipe. "Father Sun . . . " He touched the ground. "Mother Earth . . . "

From the fire pit, he took a stick and lit the pipe, inhaled three times, and passed it to Kathy. "This should get you high. Enlightenment, clarity, heart, and soul. Blow the smoke to the four directions, to the sky and the earth. It creates a sacred space."

He watched as she followed his instructions. "Jose's been teaching us ritual. We've got to get away from the idea of getting stoned. Grass will never be accepted if we don't legitimize what we feel and experience. If it becomes a sacred thing, perhaps one day it'll be accepted for what it is. If we smoke together in ceremony, the sacrament will become powerful. People need to remember why they share it."

"Is this the smoke you're selling?"

"Yeah. What do you think?"

"Wait a few minutes, and I'll tell you."

"You like the view from here?"

The stone relaxed Kathy, laid her back. Without even thinking, she turned to him and said the first thing that came to mind. "I love what I see."

"Why don't you take off your shoes?"

"Larry . . . "

"That's the second time you've said that. You wouldn't say 'no' to me, would you?"

Kathy stared at the waterfall for a long while before answering. As she sat, she reviewed her earlier conversation with Christian. The light from his blue eyes plagued her. She fought hard to put aside the rising guilt.

He knew, she thought. *How did he know before I did? If it had been anyone but Larry, I'd be saying no. But sharing my first trip with him created a bond, an allegiance that Christian understood better than I did.*

She turned to Larry, could see him wondering, waiting. His dark eyes held fire and laughter. He leaned forward, ready to scoop her up.

Slowly, she began to unbutton her blouse. The flame in his eyes burned hotter. Carefully, she set her shoes aside, slipped off her blouse, letting the silkiness of her hair fall below her breasts and across her bare skin. Her nipples were hard and dark and peeked out from the strands of her tousled hair.

Kneeling close to him, she whispered, "I could never say 'no' to you."

Then he was around her with a strength she had not known from him before, every part of him solid. He played with her in a hard, hot flow that matched the power of his body, and when he finally entered her—his own confidence apparent in his thrust—Kathy sank into feeling that held no room for another thought.

The sun was a red ember on the horizon when they finally approached the quiet, cozy ranch house nestled off the road. Out in the pasture, Kathy could see some of the horses Larry had mentioned. Running among the others was the Appaloosa that was his favorite. Blue Corn, he called her.

"Things are kind of crazy around here," Larry said, taking her pack out of the truck bed. He made quickly for the door, as if the time he'd lost over the afternoon could somehow be made up in the last minutes of the day. "Steve's here."

"Who's Steve?"

"A friend I've been buying from."

Steve? she thought, trying to place the name. *Someone Carolyn's mentioned?*

"Larry, I don't like meeting people. You need to tell me more about this deal."

"Come on in, and we'll sit down with Jose."

The house was just as Kathy remembered. Newspapers lay on the fireplace hearth with wood and kindling, a striking reminder of the times she'd dropped and sat next to that fire. The *kachinas* were in their places on the mantel. The old Navajo rugs on the walls. A huge bowel of harvested Indian corn in a multitude of colors lay in a large basket as a table centerpiece.

"Have you seen the new Chief's Blanket?" a voice asked.

"Jose!" She turned to see him standing at the door, body as work-toughened as Larry's, his face still carrying the self-knowing grin she remembered so well.

"Take care of the lady for a minute," Larry told him. "I want to see where everyone is."

Jose took her in his arms and genuinely hugged her, grinning playfully. "Plane late?"

Kathy dodged the question. "I see you've still got your hair."

"Cutting hair is for white men."

"God, but you're handsome!"

"And you . . . you're still the same," he smiled. "What keeps you away? The man with the sky blue eyes? The one I met at the People's Park march?"

"Did you talk to Larry about Christian?" she asked.

"No." He shook his head. "That's your job."

"What about you?" she teased. "I hear you have girls lined up. When are you going to choose?"

"I'm too young." He laughed.

"Larry's showed me some of the ritual you've been teaching him."

Jose raised an eyebrow. "Has he?" The grin again.

"We stopped to see a waterfall," Kathy mumbled, "and . . . " She paused.

"The cave? Then you're fortunate. The cave is very old. My father first showed it to me when I was a boy. Larry and I are the only people I know who have been there recently. It's a holy place. We go there to make the vision quest."

"Carolyn hasn't seen it?"

"She's not interested in receiving visions."

Kathy paused to consider Carolyn. During the Summer of Love, in 1967, Kathy had hitched back to Tucson with Larry, a man she'd casually met on the street who needed a hitching partner. Carolyn had reappeared at the ranch on the day they'd arrived together, asking to continue a relationship she'd walked out on months earlier. At that point, Larry wasn't ready to let either Kathy or Carolyn go, and so they had worked on the relationship as a threesome. Although it was true that Carolyn was petulant and self-serving, always putting Larry through a slew of games, Kathy also knew that Carolyn had invested a lot of time in the day-to-day of ranch work.

Suddenly, Kathy flashed on where she'd heard the name Steve. When she'd arrived at the ranch that first night—Carolyn had just returned from Laguna Beach—she'd gone there to be with a man named Steve.

And, she thought, still piecing it together, *hadn't Carolyn spent New Year's Eve in 1967 in L.A. with a man named Steve? Hadn't Carolyn become pregnant after that week with him?*

Months later, Carolyn had slipped away to L.A. for a secret abortion that Kathy was sure had almost killed her. Bound by a promise to help and the obligations of their intimate relationship, Kathy had quietly left the ranch, traveling to an address in Topanga Canyon to help Carolyn through the nightmare. When she'd returned, it was to find that Larry had cut her out of a deal, selling a large load to her connection in the Bay, causing a rift that had almost ended their friendship.

But the real problem with Carolyn's petulance was that she was central to a family that had psychedelics at its core, and she had never tripped. Apparently, Kathy's year away had made no difference.

"Then the cave is a special gift," she softly told Jose. "Even more than I imagined."

"Kathy . . . Jose," Larry called from the stairwell. "Come downstairs."

In the basement, Larry carefully moved the wood covering from behind the wet bar and lifted out a large green plastic bag.

"Come over here by the light," he said to Kathy. "Take a look at this sample."

"How much of this do you have?" Kathy asked, taking it to the light, looking at its color and crystals, the tightness of the bud, holding it to her nose for its smell, squeezing to see if it was too dry, whether the resin was sticky when she touched it.

"Plenty. Tons."

"Really? What are you paying for it?" she asked boldly. "Well, I can guess. Two thousand pounds of tops delivered over the border—fifty to me—you must be getting them for thirty. I wouldn't put out that much cash unless I was going to make at least twenty dollars a pound. What is that anyway?" she calculated quickly. "Sixty thousand dollars for the ton, right? That's a lot of cash to have to put out. But a nice profit of forty grand. How often do you plan to do this?"

Larry studied her as she touched and smelled and made calculations. "How much do you think you can do?" he asked.

"If I buy them?" Kathy looked at the buds again. Larry was right. They were nice—not too dry, sweet smelling. The smoke smooth and stony. The loose, seedless buds would sell. Certainly worth the trip down. "Five hundred pounds every two weeks. Delivery shared," she told them.

"You've got yourself a deal," Larry said, holding out his hand. "Before long, we'll be able to get that second section up from the waterfall."

"You want to bring some back this trip?" Jose asked her.

"If I rent a U-Haul, I can take the first five. I have the cash with me. But Cal starts next week. I've got to get it back before classes begin."

"Great," Larry told her. "By this evening, we'll have everything you need."

"You still need to purchase the load?"

He nodded. "Steve set it up. He's made what he wants; now he's retiring. We're buying his connection."

"Have you met the people yet?"

"Yeah," Larry told her, putting the bags away. "It'll probably be alright."

Kathy stared from Jose to Larry. "What do you mean 'probably'?"

Larry threw a quick glance at Jose. Anyone might have called it a slip of the tongue, but none of them believed in accidents. What had that word meant?

"You're going out there with sixty grand, and it'll 'probably' be alright," Kathy said quietly.

"I didn't mean it that way," he told her gruffly. "We've never done face-to-face business with these people before, and we don't know what the energy of the actual exchange will be, that's all. We've met the man and his brother a couple of times."

"What do you think about this?" Kathy looked directly at Jose. "You think it's risky?"

"It's always risky. You know that. Every time you make a buy or a sale, it's risky. But Steve's been doing business with these people for a few years."

"Let me put that bag away," Larry told Jose, his entire manner chagrined.

"So it's cool?" she insisted.

"Yeah," Larry told her. "It's cool."

Although his tone told her the matter was settled, she watched as the storm continued to gather in his eyes. *Damn,* she thought, *that part hasn't changed. He still wants to be one step ahead of me.*

"Let's go upstairs," Jose said to her. "Carolyn's anxious to see you."

"Sure," she answered, looking back at Larry. "Sure."

Halfway up the stairs, Jose stopped and turned back to her. In the dim light, she could not read his face. He looked around with a furtive air before he spoke. "That day we went riding—you remember. The first day. We took the road east and south."

"Yes."

A hushed quiet filled the stairwell, except for the distant sound of the bass from the stereo upstairs. "Remember the place I called Four Corners? Where the southernmost road leads directly to the border?"

Kathy nodded.

"About three miles down that road, toward Mexico, there's the shell of what used to be a homesteader's hut. To the right is a narrow road. Just past the first curve . . . we'll make the exchange there."

"Why are you telling me this?"

"Because of the questions you asked downstairs. And who am I to say where questions come from." He turned, looked back down the stairs, and seeing no one, said, "There's something else I want you to know. If the energy's crazy in this house, it's because Carolyn's having an affair with Steve."

Kathy thought of the hard, demanding way Larry had needed her.

Just then, Larry appeared at the bottom of the stairs, gave a surprised glance upward, and started up.

Jose gave Kathy a warning look. "Dinner's waiting. Wait until you see Rosie's belly. We're taking bets on how much the baby will weigh when it's born."

6

Dinner had ended, the table was cleared, and the dishes were washed. Carolyn stood alone outside, a coat thrown over her shoulders, staring out across the desert toward the hills. A thin slice of new moon was already sinking beneath the horizon line, the glimmer of light from its thin slice departing, only the stars left to dominate the sky.

A good night for the exchange, she thought. *Darkness to cover movement.*

Instead of returning inside, she took off, walking down the road. The air was getting colder, but she was too angry to care. Steve had come in for dinner an hour ago and had immediately become interested in Kathy, telling her stories, finding ways to touch her. And Kathy . . . she'd decided to play, laughing at his anecdotes and teasing him in return. Larry hadn't looked up from his meal. Jose had leaned back, grinning, watching. Rosie had tried small talk about the baby room decorations. Miguel had stood as soon as he'd eaten to begin cleaning the kitchen.

Carolyn pulled the coat tightly around her shoulders.

Kathy. From the first, I've been torn between loving and hating that woman. On the first night, when she and Larry had hitched home from the Haight, she was dirty, bedraggled, tired . . . and sure of herself.

Would Larry still have asked me to stay if he'd seen Kathy as she was the next day? After rest and a bath?

What happens when she gets tired of traveling? Will she just give the word and claim Larry as her own, take the ranch and all the efforts I've put into making it grow?

And yet, in my moment of greatest need, she came without thinking twice, never betraying my secrets. Even when it cost her.

Carolyn continued to walk farther from the ranch house without caring about the time, still angry, some of that anger now turned on herself. Steve had come two weeks ago, and armed with the barbs of an old game, had calmly told Larry that while Steve was at the house, she'd be spending time with him.

"Sure," he told her, "if that's what makes you happy." But it hadn't. Not if Larry didn't care.

Okay, Carolyn admitted. *I'm jealous. Jealous of Kathy. Of Rosie and the baby growing in her womb. Of something everyone here seems to understand, while I can only try to see.*

She shivered against her thoughts and the cold. Over the quiet desert, the wind brought the sound of the motor from the huge truck.

They're going.

The first coyote of the evening howled from the hills. She turned back toward the house, walking slowly because she felt she hadn't the energy to go on—not another day, another minute. Something had to be resolved. Kathy had asked her earlier in the evening to join with them. *Why not trip?* Well, she would. She'd go for broke. Nothing could be worse than her present space. If she dropped now, even if she lost control, she might be on her way down before Larry and Steve returned.

That was the fear—losing control in front of other people, her beauty compromised. Kathy had once teased that she looked like a Beach Boys poster—long blonde hair, blue eyes, white teeth, a perfect body.

But Kathy was here, the one person who had nursed her through a difficult and dangerous abortion. Kathy had already seen her at her worse.

Taking a deep breath, Carolyn made her way back to the house and straight for the tabs Larry kept in his dresser drawer.

7

In the living room, Kathy sat alone, reading an *Arizona Highways* magazine when she heard a quiet step behind her.

"Kathy," Carolyn said timidly as she approached.

"There you are. Where have you been? The guys left almost a half an hour ago. Larry was looking for you."

"Walking. Kathy . . . ," she said, a tremor in her voice. "I dropped. Just now."

"You dropped? You mean . . . acid?"

Carolyn nodded. "I took a tab from Larry's dresser."

Inwardly, Kathy was annoyed. How like Carolyn to do the unexpected! Of course, she wanted her to trip—would help guide her—but tonight, there was a lot of work to do, and she was trying to focus her energy on the movements of a ton of weed. Now that energy would have to be redirected toward caring for a first trip. And to drop this way—without Larry!

"Let's put some music on," she said. "We'll wait for Larry to come home." For a moment, she considered dropping too, so she could be sure of staying awake.

"K-K-Kathy . . . my body's sh-sh-shaking . . . "

"Which of the tabs did you eat—what color?"

"An . . . orange one."

"Orange Sunshine. That's about 200 mics. A good dose of some really good acid. Yes. You're going on a journey."

From the stack of records next to the stereo, Kathy chose Paul Horn's *Inside*. Notes from a flute played inside the Taj Mahal filled the room. She smiled, knew an opening of her spirit, a transcendence of body.

"K-K-Kathy!"

The dose was coming on fast and heavy. Certainly Carolyn smoked pot. Knew how one's body and mind changed. But acid was different. Not only was Carolyn suspicious of a lot of the hype surrounding its negative effects, but she had watched others laugh and roll on the floor and smile broadly and sit in lotus and take flight. A first trip was a brave new world into the mind and the body; more importantly, it was a loss of ego. Looking at Carolyn's frightened face, Kathy decided against dropping with her, thought it best to be the steady guide.

"Come and sit here by the fire," she said gently. She moved pillows around the floor, making a comfortable place. She lit the candles and incense in the room, creating a sacred, peaceful space.

Throwing herself down hard, Carolyn looked dazed and shaky as each cell in her body released energy. She was definitely on her way.

"Let's take your shoes off," Kathy said. "I'll get you a comfortable shift to wear."

"D-d-don't leave!"

"I'll be back in one minute. Believe me. You'll appreciate loose clothing."

Hurrying down the hallway, Kathy searched through Carolyn's closet and pulled out a white cotton Mexican wedding dress with flowers embroidered along the yoke. It was a perfect dress for tripping—feminine, colorful, natural fibers, comfortable.

"Kathy!" Carolyn screamed loudly and hysterically from the front room.

On the landing of the living room stairs, Kathy met Miguel rushing downstairs, naked, his hair disheveled, his face distressed at the sound of Carolyn's scream.

"She dropped," Kathy explained. "Two hundred mics of Orange Sunshine."

"Oh." Miguel grinned, nodded, and understood. "Call me if you need me."

"Here you go," Kathy held up the shift to Carolyn. "Pretty."

"My vision is blurred . . . my mouth . . . it's fuzzy. I . . . I may throw up. I can't keep my eyes open. I'm shaking . . . "

Kathy spoke slowly, softly. "Your body's going to go through some changes. It's part of the trip. You're going to clean out. The L will squeeze out your organs and cells. That's part of the reason people take acid. It's a deep cleansing. You're going to feel a change in your energy balance. Stretch with it. Let it teach you yoga. Breathe. Feel the *prana* in the air. Breathe."

"I'm . . . scared . . . things are . . . so different . . . "

"There's no reason to be scared. You simply have to let go. Let everything you know slip away."

"Everything I know?"

"Just flow. Let the acid take you. Become a leaf on the stream. Trust it. It'll teach you."

For the next three hours, Kathy played the mellowest records she could find in the box next to the stereo and smoked a little to try to keep up with Carolyn's headspace. But now all of Carolyn was an outpouring, and the range of emotions was as wild as Jose's new stallion. Everything she felt produced great fits of crying and shaking and enormous heat release, then great hilarity or, alternately, more crying. The energy filling the room was sexual, and Kathy knew having Miguel's presence would have balanced the male and female, but she didn't want to wake him, not just yet, not if she really didn't have to.

"Shouldn't I have waited for Larry?" Carolyn cried aloud. "Soon I'll be pushed over the edge, maybe even get lost out here somewhere. I don't want to be lost without Larry. I . . . I . . . don't understand . . . ," she moaned, her eyes closed.

Trying to stand, to focus in a material world without distinction, only paisleys and patterns and bright diamonds of shifting color,

Carolyn stumbled and tried to still her grinning mouth and the queasy feeling in her stomach. As she moved, she toppled things from tables, unaware of Kathy's discreet removal of Larry's precious pieces of Anasazi pottery to a safe cupboard.

Then, a new thought stopped Carolyn where she stood. She covered her head with her arms, trying to hide her shame and murmured loud enough for Kathy to hear, "Larry has stood by me, day by day, let me change. Even when I played all those stupid games with Steve!"

Then, with wild eyes, she cried, "What if the baby was Larry's? I couldn't really be sure. It might have been Steve's. What would Larry say if he knew? Does anyone know?" she whimpered. "Oh, Kathy, does anyone know? It's here somewhere." She waved her arms and grabbed at the air, both her visions and her ideas tangible. "Everything's here. Laid out for anyone to see. I'm naked. Naked to my soul." She fell to the floor, curled in fetal position, crying and moaning her guilt, while Kathy sat with her, knowing this was her time to examine the pain, to come to terms with her desperate decision.

"Larry," she mumbled aloud, "all the things I've done to you. Where was the love?"

The passage was hard, but Kathy saw that she was at a new beginning, an understanding that what was important was the human soul, the karmic acts of each day, Larry's feelings, the substance beyond the image. Not the mask of beauty she had worked so hard to perfect.

Carolyn held her hands out to the fire as the music changed—an Indian raga. She took a deep breath, then lifted the Mexican dress over her head. She breathed in deeply once again, and as she breathed, Kathy could see the weight she held inside was lightened. Kathy knew from her own experience that where the mind held a question, an uncertainty, the muscles were tight and taut, but the answers that were found within would cause the knots to dissolve, the yogic stretch to loosen the body. Carolyn breathed again and stretched over her legs, grabbing her feet, holding the pose. When she rose to sit cross-legged in lotus posture, she turned large, dilated eyes to Kathy. "I'm going to be there for him," she said simply. "The child he's wanted—I'm going to give Larry his child."

A huge step, Kathy knew. The beginning of a family and a lifelong commitment.

Suddenly, Kathy needed space, just a moment or two to think through this idea that Carolyn had placed into the world.

"Let me put water on for tea," Kathy said. "I'll be right back."

In the dimly lit kitchen, Kathy welcomed being alone. She leaned over the counter and put her head down on her arms while waiting for the water to boil, stung by what Carolyn had taught her.

"Christian," she murmured, "I miss you terribly."

And at that moment, she knew, like Carolyn, she didn't want to play games anymore. "The man with the sky blue eyes," Jose had said. All she wanted was to see the fire in them for the rest of her life. If there had been a safe phone she could use, one that did not connect the ranch to Christian through phone records, she would have called him, but the nearest pay phone was a long drive away.

Christian's really pissed at me. Christian, who's never raised his voice in all the time I've known him. And maybe he has every right to be angry and disappointed after this afternoon.

But was it really so bad to love Larry?

The answer was clear in the instant. Christian had made a commitment, honored it. She owed him the respect of returning his trust, rather than taking pleasure for a single afternoon in another man. Larry had moved away into his own world and had his own commitments.

Dear God, what have I done? He'll know. One look into my face, and he'll know. How could he feel anything but betrayed?

When the water boiled, she filled the teapot and brought it to the front room. Carolyn still sat in lotus in front of the fire. As Kathy set the tray down, Carolyn opened her eyes.

"Who am I?"

"You are Carolyn," Kathy told her softly, aware of the full weight of the question and the answer. All experience, memory, past lives; all the feeling of sensory awareness; all the choices of the future put into one moment in time—one human—Carolyn.

The room fell quiet as Carolyn closed her eyes again and traveled inward, learning, putting things in place. The stillness was good after hours of movement and music. Kathy was exhausted, drained. She was crashing hard from smoking all evening and looked to the tea and the sugar in the fruit on the tray to give her mind some life. She heard Carolyn begin to speak, to share, and Kathy listened quietly while she peeled an orange, the drone of Carolyn's voice almost putting her to sleep. A sound on the stair bobbed her head up. Miguel stood on the landing, looking down into the living room.

"Things have certainly mellowed out down here," he said.

Kathy waved for him to come down. Now, she needed him. "We're having a good time. Come and have some tea."

When Miguel took a seat next to her on the pillows, Carolyn was crying quiet tears. "Ah, yes." He brushed at one of the tears on her cheek. "It's time for me to take the journey. A special place, isn't it? A place halfway between laughter and tears."

Kathy passed him a cup of peppermint tea.

"Where's Larry?" he asked.

She looked at her watch. A little after two. "He's not back yet."

"Really?" Miguel looked surprised. "They should have been back by now."

8

The deal was a simple one, prearranged in the last weeks—cash for grass. Steve had set up an initial meeting between the two parties, samples of the pot had been passed to Larry and Jose, and a price had been reached: Thirty dollars a pound for loose buds. Steve was to have seen and counted the money. Sixty thousand dollars in hundreds, six neat stacks of ten thousand dollars each—a bundle small enough to place in a man's shoebox. The meeting with Mario and his younger brother Eduardo had cost Larry and Jose ten grand for the introduction. Larry had found the brothers amiable enough. Perhaps they were not in the same headspace he and Jose embraced, but they were professional, and the money motivated a tight operation.

At eight thirty, the two-ton truck that Jose and Larry had bought months ago for hauling loads turned down the road next to the homesteader's hut. The road was dark, their faces lit eerily by a green glow from the lights on the dash.

"You're awfully quiet tonight," Larry said to Jose.

"It's a quiet night. There was a breeze a while ago, but it started dying down just as we took off. Now it's just cold, dark, and still."

Larry laughed but cast a quick, furtive glance at him.

"Let's get everything moved quickly," Jose said. "Open a sack at random. If it looks good, take the load."

"You jittery?"

"Yeah. This first-time stuff."

"Kathy set you off?"

"No," Jose lied.

"Hey, these guys are cool," Steve assured them. "I've worked with them for years."

"There's the truck up ahead."

Larry surveyed the scene in one sweeping gaze. Jose was right. The night was so dark that the contours of the land could only be vaguely seen. Ahead, the road turned left again around the edge of a hill. Mario's dark truck was parked precariously along the rim of an even darker gully that ran along the right side of the road. This spot had been picked precisely because it was enclosed within the road curves with space to park two large vehicles.

Larry passed the parked truck, pulled into the turnout, and watched in his rearview mirror as Mario jumped down from the cab, his frame illuminated by the cab's overhead light. A second later, the younger brother, Eduardo, followed from the same door. Shaking out his sweating hands, Larry realized he'd been gripping the steering wheel tightly. He was dimly aware that his throat was dry.

"Okay," he said tersely to Jose. "Let's do it. You got the money?"

"Once we're out of the truck, we're committed," Jose replied.

Larry turned to him. "What's goin' on, man? Where's your head at?"

"Relax," Steve told them again, all the talk making him edgy. "I'm telling you these guys are cool. We just make a simple transfer. Half an hour. You've done this a hundred times. I'm going to talk to Mario."

Jose and Larry watched as he walked over and settled into conversation. "So what is it?" Larry asked.

"I don't know. I've felt uncomfortable all day."

Larry watched Steve through the mirror. "If we don't get out of the truck soon, things are going to get weird."

Jose took a deep breath. "Okay. Let's do it."

Larry crossed in front of the truck to join Jose on the roadside. Together, they began walking up to the other men. "Give me the box," Larry told him.

Jose passed the money over and knew instantly the truth of his foreboding, could feel the quickened interest in the shadowed faces. They were waiting to make sure of the cash.

Larry felt the pain before the noise even registered with him. There was not even time for a regret or an obscene epitaph. The brilliant red flame entered his back, missed his backbone, and pierced his lung. All that was left was a sense of Jose rolling away from him and the sudden surprised look on Steve's face. In slow motion, he saw Steve turn back to Mario, and then from Mario's hand, a double flash of light pierced the darkness. Steve's body jerked, then arched forward, his hands clutched to his stomach. In the next eternity, Steve's knees buckled, and he was sinking to the ground . . .

Larry never saw him land. A second searing pain exploded into his back, and he, too, spent a long time falling, the box of money dropping away from his hands to lie abandoned in the sand.

So it's over, he thought simply. *Dying isn't so difficult. No panic. Just the same yogic balance I know I could have lived every moment of my life.*

But his body tried to hold onto life. Blood painfully filled his lungs, and it became hard to breathe. Coughing and gagging, he struggled for air. Then a third shot mercifully pierced the back of his head and he stopped feeling anything.

Jose was on guard long before he stepped from the truck. With his father's hand on his shoulder, he walked anxiously, stealthily, as if he were stalking game. Every lesson he had ever been taught was honed at that instant by his anxiety. He was on his toes, ready to move when he saw the flickering motion of Mario's hand. Instinctively, he leapt to one side, hitting the sand and rolling. The bullet intended for his back only grazed his arm. A sudden sharp pain forced an involuntary cry from his throat, but there was no time to give it his attention. The loud rifle firing continued, and he kept rolling through the dust that flew around him as the bullets missed their target in the dark.

Three men from behind, he noted. *From around the hill curve.*

His body hit emptiness. Then he was flying, tumbling down into the darkness of the gully, landing on his face with a thud. Long moments passed before his mind caught up. He waited. Waited for some darkness, or death, or pain. Waited to see if he was still alive or for the pain that would tell him he was dying.

Then there was a hush. The shooting stopped. The crashing noises of his roll into the gully evaporated into the distance. Only his heavy breathing and the ringing in his ears filled the distorted space around him. The rip in his arm caught fire. He wanted to scream against it, but the silence warned him. Again, his father's hand lay on him. In the wind that had begun to blow, he could hear a whisper. "Do not move. Make no sound. Still your breathing."

A man's voice floated down to him. "¿Dónde está el dinero?" *Where's the money?*

"Aquí. Todo está aquí." *Here. It's all here.*

"¿Qué hay de uno que se cayó del borde? Traiga una luz. Rapido." *What about the one that fell over the edge? Bring a light. Quickly.*

Again Jose heard the whisper. "Do not move. Make no sound."

Rifle fire cracked the stillness. The ground erupted around him. Icy fear kept him paralyzed, waiting for the bullet that would finish him.

Again the quiet.

A light flashed over him, spotlighted his body on the rocks, picked up his blood-soaked clothing. A climb down into the gully would mean maneuvering the steep vertical walls, and the men on the road had already spent too much time in this place.

"Vámonos de aquí." *Let's get out of here.*

A motor started, doors slammed. The sound of the engine grew dim as it moved away. Then silence—a silence so deep and painful that it hurt almost as much as the pounding filling his head and the tear in his arm. Pushing himself to his knees, Jose slowly tried to stand.

Where am I hurt?

Then he remembered.

With a growing sense of panic, he struggled against the awful knowledge.

"Larry!" his hoarse voice screamed, breaking the silence. Across the sand, he heard a desert creature scurrying through the brush, the agony of his cry disturbing what life was left to listen.

"Larry!" The scream echoed, penetrating into dark places. "Larry! God, man! Speak to me! Are you alright?"

Only the silence answered.

And then the cold. The temperature began to drop. The shock to his body left him shaking violently as he stood on swaying legs. He took a deep breath and tried to feel his way over the ground. The inky darkness made the rocky terrain almost impossible to see. His sense of touch guided him to the wall he would have to climb. The pain in his right arm was agonizing. Slowly, feeling with his feet and one hand, he'd gained about fifteen feet when the rock beneath his right boot suddenly gave way. He went skidding and crashing the full distance he had so laboriously traveled. The earth spun, stars flashed, circling his eyes. Helplessly, he slipped into unconsciousness.

9

KATHY
TUCSON, ARIZONA
SEPTEMBER 1969

Carolyn's going to be alright, Kathy thought, sipping tea and watching her talk with Miguel. *She's put a lot of things into place. Tomorrow, though, I'll have to have a few words with her about her dropping alone and unguided, about the responsibility it laid on everyone else tonight. At least she picked me. She had a lot to go through that only the two of us knew about.*

The living room was a mess—books and magazines scattered about, furniture moved, art placed out of obvious reach. Kathy thought to leave the cleaning for the morning. The day would be busy—not only cleaning, but weighing out the weed and renting a U-Haul.

So, where's the nearest U-Haul? she wondered and looked toward Miguel to ask, only to notice his anxious glance at the clock.

He's nervous. Could the truck have broken down?

"Miguel, I think I'm going to go for a drive. Would you mind staying with Carolyn for a while?"

"You . . . you know where to drive?" he asked, grasping her meaning at once, relief in his voice. "I would have gone sooner if I'd known."

Kathy's body began to tingle with the extent of his concern. "I'll be back soon."

"The keys to the pickup are in the ignition."

Kathy could not remember a night this dark on the desert before, and Lord, it was cold and getting colder. Tired and bleary-eyed, she bounced along the rutted road, more than a little aggravated with the way things were going. An emotionally exhausting evening had not been in the plan. Nor had this drive and the apprehension that she was walking into something she knew nothing about. These deals sometimes took forever. People were often late. Maybe they'd decided to weigh everything out.

What's Larry going to say when I turn up?

She could already hear that New York heaviness in his voice. Miguel had better back her up if Larry got really pissed!

Ahead, she could see the place Jose called Four Corners. The southern road ran all the way to the border. She followed it slowly, searching for the ruin of a hut.

There it was. To the right. And behind the hut—the other road, just as Jose had mentioned. The pickup bounced and swayed, unable to avoid the potholes.

The meeting place can't be far, she thought. *Here's the left curve.*

The headlights immediately picked up the two-ton truck—parked alone. She stopped, her foot on the brake, wary and a little scared now. If there'd been a bust, would the Man have left the truck? She didn't think so. Then what had happened?

Slowly, she drove ahead. The pickup's lights focused on something in the middle of the road. In the next second, she stopped, her foot hard on the brake.

A man's body.

And beyond it, another sprawled figure.

"No," she whispered aloud. "No. Oh, God, no, no, no . . . please don't let it be . . . "

Shaking, she jumped from the cab, took a few steps forward,

then . . . stopped, immobile, numb with the horror of trying to grasp what was before her.

If I move, it'll become real. Don't move, don't move . . .

But hope pulled her forward to see whether they were alive, and suddenly, she was rushing, throwing herself next to the nearest body. Steve lay in fetal position, his hands still pressed to his stomach. Kathy pushed him gently to his back, then timidly felt his cold face. There was nothing peaceful about the look on it. For what seemed a long while, she just stared, still trying to understand, shocked into stupidity. His eyes were wide and staring, picking up the light of the truck's beam. She willed him to do something—anything. But there was nothing there. Nothing left of him.

Desperately, she turned, wild with grief. The other sprawled body—Larry's jacket.

She knew . . . and still, she pushed the truth away with all the strength of her will.

There was enough light from the pickup's headlights to see the dark holes in his back and the blood on the ground around his head. The gentleness, the tenderness she had shown with Steve was lost as she turned Larry's body over, pulled him into her lap, and shook him hard, as if to wake him back to this world. "Oh, dear God . . . no . . . ," she moaned.

His face was covered with dirt and the blood he had coughed up. She pressed him to her breast, held him, rocked him, wept for him, cried his name over and over, believing her strength, her will, her demands could call him back, set his life flowing again.

Shocked, stimulated, pushed to some far chemical edge, she found herself capable of picking up minute sound and detail, every nerve ending acute. A unique kind of power filled her. If time would not turn back on its own, then she would use her own power to raise the dead.

"I know your spirit is near," she cried. "I can feel it. Come back. Please. I need you. Come back to your body. If you love me enough, you'll come back. You gave me my true self. I can't go on without you . . . "

Like a mantra, she repeated her demand, her challenge, over and over. Larry was out there somewhere. Hadn't she touched that spot on all those trips? If she could only reach him, she could pull him back.

But he didn't move, only grew heavier in her lap. In a long, lucid moment, she understood that his body was damaged beyond repair, beyond use, and even though his spirit was indeed still close, he could no longer use this body.

Slowly, Kathy aged, and a part of her died forever. The nursery rhymes and the happily-ever-after stories were over. Wonderland was a myth. This was reality. No amount of independence or happiness or good times or getting high could give her control over time or death. Life was a long march from birth to the grave. And each time a person died, there was someone who would know the pain she was feeling now. How much pain since the beginning of creation had been released with the death of each person who had been born?

With the weight of the answer, her face grew gray, lined, her eyes sunken into sockets as dark and lifeless as Larry's own eyes. No longer was she powerful, but a small, cringing figure kneeling and crying in sand and dust and blood, tempered with old, unwanted, and unasked-for knowledge, holding to a dead man who could no longer return her embrace.

A sound unexpectedly brought Kathy to her feet, still holding to Larry's hand.

What was that sound?

In her shock, Kathy had forgotten everything else. How could she take her mind from Larry? She held his spirit by a kite string, but once the string was broken, once her attention was distracted, he would float away, be gone from her forever.

Pieces of the evening came back to her. Jose had been with them. She could not see him in the light of the truck.

The sound came again, and this time she knew what it was. A long, shuddering groan.

"Jose!" Kathy screamed into the black void, turning in all directions, her body heaving in long, rasping sobs, shaking uncontrollably. "Jose!" she screamed again, high-pitched, desperate.

The deep-throated moan was coming from somewhere nearby. Kneeling, Kathy kissed Larry's hand and placed it gently on his chest. It took everything she had to let go of it, for in releasing it, she knew she was also releasing her hopes for his life. But Jose needed her. He was alive. Somewhere in the darkness and hurt. She would find him and make sure that he lived.

In the glove box of the pickup, she found a flashlight, and turning off the motor so she could better listen, she ran to the edge of the gully. "Jose!"

"Kathy . . . " The word was thick, husky.

She brought up the light and caught him in the beam as he tried to move. Then she was tearing down the hillside, stumbling and falling even as she focused the light, careless of danger, desperate to reach him. When she did, she helped him to sit, sobbing, holding him, crying over and over, "You're alive. Thank God, you're alive . . . "

Wrapping his good hand around hers, he focused the light on her face so he could see her eyes. "Where's Larry?"

Shaking her head back and forth, she both revealed and denied at the same time.

"And Steve?"

Again, she shook her head and cringed at the tears that filled his eyes. His arm reached out to pull her close, his hoarse sob muffled in her neck, and clinging to her, they cried for what had been precious and would never be again.

Later, the one thing Kathy could remember well of that night was how difficult moving bodies could be. After the arduous climb, pushing and carrying Jose up the steep hillside, she used the torn sleeve of her shirt to tie the feet of the dead together so Jose could help her lift them into the pickup bed with his one good arm.

They took the southern road at Four Corners, making for Mexico, and crossed the porous border at a road Jose had used before. The darkness was a blessing. They were silent, said nothing. The only noise was an occasional grunt from Jose as Kathy hit a pothole too difficult to see in the night. Up into the hills they traveled, anxious, but the job had to be done, and their return over the border could not be detected.

Once they placed the bodies on the ground, there was nothing else they could do but take the money from their wallets as if they had been robbed, and leave them there. In a few days, they would report Steve and Larry overdue from a camping trip.

"We can't just walk away without doing something," Kathy whispered, unable to keep her eyes from Larry.

"No . . . no we can't."

And gathering a branch of sage from the desert, Jose lit the leaves, blew out the flame, and smudged the smoke over his body, over Kathy, finally to purify the bodies on the ground.

"We release these souls," he said softly. "All over the universe, there will be happiness and rejoicing, because we send these spirits back to the center. We offer these bodies to heaven . . . and to the earth . . . to the east, to the north, to the south . . . to the west, where the sun goes down. We release them to the next journey."

"One day," Kathy added, her voice barely above a whisper, "karma will bring us together again."

A long moment passed, and then, with unexpected steel in his voice, Jose looked down at Larry and added, "Mario and his brother will know my reach. I will not fail you, brother."

Kathy could not move, could not stop crying large, silent tears. "I'm not doing this very well."

"Don't," he told her, shaking his head. "Don't interrupt their journey. Don't call them to this place. It wouldn't be wise to give in to emotion." With the words, he fell to one knee.

Suddenly, she remembered how badly injured he was, and kneeling beside him, helped him from the ground. "Don't die," she pleaded. "Please."

"Time to leave," he said, and bending at the waist, holding the branch of sage to the ground, he walked backward, stepping away from the bodies, swooshing away their footprints. "We want to free them. We don't want their spirits to follow." Then he added grimly, "Nor do we want the police to see our tracks."

The sun was up, the desert turning from red to white heat, when the two trucks pulled through the ranch gate. Kathy drove the two-ton truck, desperately worried that Jose would not be able to handle the pickup. Ahead, Miguel was waiting on the front steps, relief clear on his face as he saw them. But when she jumped from the truck, his smile froze as he picked up on her torn, bloodied clothes.

Jose stumbled out of the cab and leaned heavily against the door. Miguel regarded his mangled arm and looked for Larry and Steve.

"They're gone," was all Jose could whisper.

Once everyone had assembled, once explanations had been made, and tears shed, the family went to work—bloodied clothes were disposed of, the trucks cleaned, the living room put back together, the stash moved, especially the heavy stuff underneath the downstairs bar. The two-ton truck would be parked in an industrial area of Tucson. No evidence of what had happened could be left. They couldn't let the authorities know Larry and Steve had died in a pot deal.

"They'll confiscate the ranch," Jose told them wearily. "This land is sacred, bought in blood. The ranch is something Larry loved, the place he wanted to raise his family. We can't let them have it." He turned to Miguel. "Take the car. You and Rosie drive to Mexico until I call you back."

"You're staying?" Miguel asked.

"Someone has to answer questions. Carolyn, you too. You need to leave. Can you go stay with Julie in Hawaii for a while? And Kathy," he looked at her, "you . . . you just need to go home."

Kathy shook her head. "I'm not leaving. Not until you're well."

"Yes, you are. Today. There's going to be a lot of heat. You want your name in a police record connected with a murder?"

"I'm *not* going!"

"Alright," he sighed hoarsely, sickness, loneliness, and gratitude mingled in his answer. "Rosie, stop and see Tara, the medicine woman. Send her here. Tell her it's a deep wound. She'll know what to bring and won't ask questions."

By late afternoon that same day, Jose had fallen into an exhausted sleep on the couch from the herbs Tara had given him to drink. She and Kathy had undressed him, washed his body, and salved his cuts and gashes. The one serious wound was the deep injury through the muscle in his right arm. But the bullet had missed the bone, the tissue was clean, and barring infection, it simply needed time to heal. Tara smoked his body with sweet grass, prayed over him, touched him with quartz crystals, and gave him an injection of penicillin. "He must rest," she told Kathy. "Keep him in bed."

Kathy watched over Jose as he slept on the couch. Everyone was gone, the work done. For the first time since rounding the curve and seeing the truck, she gave in to an exhaustion she had never before known, one filled with pain and guilt and longing. If she slept, time would pass, and Larry would be further away. Now, he was still with her. If she slept, Jose might need her. As it was, she barely took her eyes from his face to make sure he breathed. She stirred the fire and put on two pieces of wood. She would just lie down quietly on the floor and watch him. She wouldn't sleep. She would just watch.

10

KATHY
TUCSON, ARIZONA
SEPTEMBER 1969

When Kathy woke, it was cold. Looking up, she could see that the sliding door was open and that Jose was no longer on the couch. Her heart began to pound, and jumping up, she raced to the door. He was standing naked on the porch, staring at the fading sky, a blanket draped across his shoulders. Once again, the evening was a soft, dull rose. Shivering slightly, she wondered how the Earth dared continue to move.

"You know you should be lying down," she told him, gently touching his shoulder. "Didn't Tara tell you to stay off your feet for a few days?"

Jose turned to look at her . . . and the pain in his eyes caused her to wince.

"It's my fault," he said. "All of it."

She shook her head, desperate for him. "No . . . no . . . "

He leaned forward, stopping her abruptly. "Larry and I got out of the truck. We started walking toward Mario and his brother, Eduardo. Steve was already talking to them." He paused, and when he spoke again, his voice was hard. "I knew. Something didn't feel right. I saw a flicker of Mario's wrist. The first bullet was for Larry, because he held the bucks. They were going to make sure he didn't run. That first shot . . . it was just seconds, but it saved my life.

"I rolled, and I could make them out . . . behind . . . three dark shapes and the flash of rifles in the darkness. They could have just ripped us off, but they didn't want to deal with what we'd do. Or the stories we might tell. So they murdered Larry and Steve and tried hard to get me. And now . . . now I wish they had."

Kathy was crying softly. "Don't say that. Please. Come. Come and lie down."

"Do you know the only thing that sustains me? I'm thinking of how I'm going to kill Mario and Eduardo Garza. The others. I'll find out who they are. And when I do, I'll kill every one of them." His chin dropped to his chest and his voice was a whisper. "Damn, Kathy, but it didn't feel right. You knew it that afternoon. It didn't feel right. And I did it anyway . . . I . . . I did it anyway."

Then, the hardness was back. "God, I'm going to kill those bastards. Slowly, I'm going to track down each and every one of them and let them know why they die." Turning, he walked back into the house.

Kathy followed, closing the sliding door behind her, still crying softly, trying to catch her breath as she shivered. The fire needed building. She tore at paper, stacked kindling, and set logs against each other.

"You can't do that, you know," she forced the words from her lips as she lit the paper underneath the firewood. "Think about the way you and Larry met."

The smell of smoke drifted briefly by her, then the draft brightened the flame, and smoke flumed up the chimney, the kindling crackling, logs beginning to burn. The heat was a welcomed sensation into all the coldness in the room.

"You think I haven't considered that? I've vowed to devote my life to peace. But I also made a vow to Larry. You heard me swear it over his body."

"You swore not to fail him. You know the law of karma. Those men will feel the results of their actions quickly enough."

"*I* will bring them justice. They will know my hunting knife."

Kathy shuddered against the image. "Do you think Larry would want you to kill for him? Just to extinguish your guilt?"

He sent her a quick, angry glance.

"You can best serve your brother by being true to his dreams."

"And Mario is to go free to kill others?"

Kathy stumbled. Where did responsibility lie? If Mario were left unchecked, would he live to kill someone else?

"And once he finds that I'm alive," Jose said, walking closer, "won't he come for me? Send his men to make sure I cause him no trouble? I don't want to spend the rest of my life wondering if they're waiting around the next corner."

Kathy's face paled at this new thought. "Do . . . do you think they will . . . come for you?" She glanced nervously at the door. At any moment, they could come bursting into the house, guns drawn. She and Jose would be powerless. Trapped. Dead. She felt herself freeze in terror, her tears put aside in an uncontrollable feeling of panic. Perhaps they were close by, just beyond the door, ready to surprise her, in a panicky and unprepared-for death.

"Be still. There's no danger for the time being. Mario doesn't know I'm alive and won't for several days. I told you to go this morning."

"I . . . I couldn't," she answered, her voice small now and shaking. "Leave you here. Hurt and helpless. I couldn't . . . I can't let anything happen to you. Don't you see? The world's shifted to some dizzying degree. Someone has to explain to me how evil can exist if the center of all creation is love. If we can feel love running through everything that exists, what is the source of evil? If you're alive, there's a reason to go on living. A reason to try to find the answer . . . "

"Answer? I had to put my brother on the bare ground and walk away from him. You want me to let them live? While Larry and Steve will never have a life?"

Kathy began to cry again. "Don't you see, we've simply given their bodies back to the earth. You need to promise me that whatever the cost, you'll let Mario's fate rest with his own actions. If we can't hold to what we believe, what's the point of living? Promise me. Promise me you won't throw your life away."

Jose picked up the closest thing to his hand, an earthenware jar, and threw it hard across the room. Kathy ducked reflexively and heard it splinter against the wall. The violence started his wound bleeding again, the bandage turning bright red. As if his legs could no longer support him, he fell to his knees before the fire, finally putting aside the hard voice that deflected the pain, crying into his hands.

"It's not your fault . . . ," she whispered, pulling him to her, taking his head to her shoulder.

"I want him back," a child's cry, a moan into her throat, wetness and warm breath mingled against her skin, "and nothing I can do . . . "

"Sh-h-h," she whispered, rocking him, kissing him softly.

His hand twisted in the back of her hair, and he brought his mouth to hers, reaching to touch Larry through this woman he had loved. His hard, angry kiss reminded her of Christian's fervor on the night they'd dropped in Merlin's cabin. She wondered fleetingly of her own karma, that she was chosen to be mother to the distraught. Her chest heaved, ready to accept his needs, searching for a place beyond the pain.

The blanket fell from his shoulders. With his good hand, he pulled the Mexican shift over her head so that they were both naked, his face close, the pain in his eyes so absolute in its mingled despair and longing that she was swallowed by it. "My fault . . ." He drew her against him, desperate.

His body was hard and solid . . . like Larry's. Misery and memory drowned her.

"I have always loved you," she spoke softly to his ear. "Brother of my soul, you have done nothing, and nothing . . . nothing . . . will ever destroy my love for you."

He turned bright eyes to hers, a fever in them, and whispered, "You would still love me? Knowing what I've done?"

"The only thing you have done is to love deeply—Larry, the family that cares for this land, the horses. And you have always worked for a better world." She looked into his eyes and blinked away tears, her voice ragged but firm. "It's not your fault. One day your children will visit the cave and swim in the pool beneath the waterfall. One day. If you don't blow it."

The violence of his body seemed suddenly exhausted.

"You're right," he murmured. Then, sitting back on his heels and clutching the wound on his upper arm, he whispered, "I promise not to track down Mario or the others. That's the oath Larry would have wanted, too."

Staggering to the couch, he lay down, closed his eyes, and slept.

The day after the shootings, it rained hard, and they breathed easier knowing that the desert was washed clean. Kathy stayed with Jose, caring for his carefully concealed wound, deriving some strength from Tara's encouraging visits, keeping house, and answering the door and phone calls that had become ominous. Ten days after Larry and Steve were left over the border, Jose reported them missing. The wound was healing nicely and was invisible when he wore his shirt.

It took only a half day to get a call from the coroner's office.

"Now it begins," he said.

Even though the trauma of the questions and answers with the homicide department filled Jose with the fear of discovery, he was relieved to be able to publicly show his sorrow. The genuineness of it was apparent, and both he and Kathy thought it helped to allay suspicion as to his role in the undertakings. Kathy was interviewed only once at the house and gave a fictitious name. Unimportant, a guest newly arrived. But two days later, the detectives were back, a search warrant in hand, and the house was torn apart. They found nothing— no blood, not even a seed or a tab. Although they were suspicious, the detectives closed the case, and Jose knew he would have to tread lightly in the future.

Gradually, friends began to overcome their fears and to visit the ranch, filling up the empty spaces. The real story of that evening began to circulate through the scene. An old friend from Jose's childhood came to stay, bringing with him a small arsenal of hunting guns and his own physical power.

After the police raid, when things seemed somewhat settled and Kathy felt secure enough to go to the phone at the local market, she'd made several attempts to call Christian, but there had been no answer. She would have had a better chance of finding him home at night but was still too frightened to leave the house in the evening, let alone to stand in the open to make a phone call. As the days passed, she wondered how she could put all the days and nights of terror she had lived into a phone conversation and finally decided to wait until she could sit with him and cry out the whole story. Besides, there would be a lot of explaining to do.

Reaching Danny, she only told him that the deal hadn't gone as planned and that she'd be staying a while longer.

"But your classes have started," he reminded her.

"School will have to wait. Can you pick up the withdrawal forms for me?"

Miguel and Rosie returned, finally able to grieve with those they loved. Rosie had planned to give birth at the ranch, and the baby was due soon. Kathy knew what it would mean to the energy in the house. The baby would bring renewed life, further normalization. Kathy let go of her responsibility to Jose and the ranch a little more.

Around the third week of Kathy's stay, Carolyn called from Hawaii to say she couldn't return. Somewhere between Arizona and Honolulu, she had come down off the high of the acid trip to realize what had happened. At the airport, she had collapsed into Julie's arms. Bob had just left for Asia, and Julie had welcomed her, grateful for the company. Together, they had visited the Hare Krishna Temple on Maui, and she had been able to find some solace in chanting and prayer.

At last, the day came when Kathy knew that life had resumed a normal rhythm—Jose's wound was an angry scab, the animals were being fed regularly, people slept through the night, even the two-ton truck was brought home.

In the early morning, a little over a month from the day she had arrived, she stood outside, watching the sun come up in the east. She'd made it a habit lately, watching the sky turn colors in the morning, as if her soul needed more nourishment than her body. She had not eaten well over the last weeks; indeed, she was regularly nauseous, had grown thin, and slept little. Standing on the porch, she felt someone behind her.

Jose took one look at her face and spoke the words, "You're going."

She continued to stare out over the desert and slowly nodded. "I think it's time. You'll just have to ride this one out carefully."

"You'll come back?"

She turned fierce eyes toward him. "Always."

"We're still going to get that parcel above the waterfall."

"I know."

"There's . . . there's nothing to take back with you."

Kathy shook her head. "I couldn't handle it just now anyway."

"Pedro's going to stay and help run the ranch. I'm hiring two other men besides. We're really going to make a go of this horse business."

"Rosie told me you offered Miguel a partnership in the ranch. And in business."

Jose nodded. "He wants the section that borders north of here. I'll be glad to see him get it. We're going to be cool for a while. And when we start up again, I'll carry a gun."

She gave him a knowing glance. "Try dropping with them first. Before you do any deals."

For a long moment, all was silent. "When do you plan to leave?" he asked.

"This afternoon, I think."

The sun was higher on the horizon now. As she turned for the door, he called to her. In the next breath of time, he had her in his arms, looking closely into her eyes to make sure she understood. "Do you know how much I love you? What you mean to me?"

"Yes," she whispered.

Then, gathering her up, he kissed her with the same hard passion as once before, giving a part of his spirit to her.

Parting with Jose and leaving the ranch was one of the hardest things Kathy had ever done. Not until she was on the plane did she realize how terribly alone she was. The weight of the last weeks sat on her like a vulture picking at dead bones. In the washroom, she really looked at her face—pale and emaciated. The rest of her was equally thin.

Now only Christian occupied her mind. Was it too late to take the job he'd offered? Right now, she never again wanted to be responsible for someone's life in a deal. Christian could make the decisions for both of them. The thought of seeing him, of being with him, took some of the anxiety from her stomach. If she could just tell him the tale, it would melt away. This nightmare, this violent death of a loved one, was one he'd lived through, something he understood. What he'd learned in the years of contemplating his own anguish—the riot and the death of his beloved lama—he would share with her. Now she understood that the faraway look that took over his face in quiet moments was the torment of memories, of trying to touch someone who was gone.

By the time the plane landed in Oakland, she was convinced of her course. Only after she'd paid the driver and watched the taxi pull away did she realize the ludicrousness of her position—showing up at Christian's door without any word after over a month. But there was nothing to do but walk the half block, hoping he would be home and praying that an unknown woman would not be with him. Hadn't he said he had someone in mind?

"Kathy!" Allen exclaimed, opening the door, surprised. "Where have you been? Are you just getting back from Tucson?"

"It turned into a long trip. Is Christian here?"

"You haven't heard?"

Kathy felt her legs crumple beneath her. Leaning for support against the doorframe, she asked in a voice that sounded hollow to her ears, "Is he alright?"

Allen could not mistake the terror in her voice. "He's fine." He took her arm and led her to the couch. "He went to India with Bob and Dharma. I . . . I thought he would have told you. I thought you knew. Here," he sat her down and watched as she put her head to her knees. "I'm going to call Marcie."

He's not hurt or dead, she assured herself, her heart racing. *He's just gone to India.*

Then the full meaning struck her—*India! And with Bob! God only knows how long he'll be gone!*

When Marcie arrived, Richard was with her. Allen had said something was wrong, and Marcie fearfully speculated that Kathy's long overdue return entailed more than a prolonged visit. Something really important must have happened to make her miss the beginning of classes.

In a voice flat and deep and empty, Kathy told the story in tearless pain—of the cave near the waterfall and Larry's belief that weed needed to be blessed to make it sacramental, of fearfully driving out when the man were overdue, of finding the bodies, the trip into Mexico in the dark night, Jose's wounds and the terror of being ambushed at the ranch, anxious conversations with the police, and the care of the home.

Richard shook his head, his face gaunt. "It's just not possible. Kevin. And now Larry. Kevin murdered by a narc. Larry shot in the back by someone who was supposed to be one of our own."

"The next plane," said Kathy's ghost voice. "I want the next plane to New Delhi."

11

CHRISTIAN, BOB, AND DHARMA
NEW DELHI, INDIA
OCTOBER 1969

When Christian thought of India, he pictured the holy river Ganges, its waters flowing from the snow-covered peaks of the Himalayas, crossing the broad, northern Indian plain, reaching Varanasi and Benares, soft, smooth, and steady. But he also knew that when stirred enough by winter rains and snowmelt, an angry Ganges might rise a hundred feet, washing away everything in its path—temples that had stood for a thousand years, towns, businesses, even people. The same passionate and untamed qualities, he believed, could lie just beneath the surface of India's people.

As the wheels of the plane touched down in New Delhi, he closed his eyes. His body trembled. Coming back to India meant remembering. He wondered—not for the first time—what he was doing here, and whether India would change the direction of his life as it had once before.

Bob and Dharma gave each other a knowing smile as Christian quickly moved them through immigration and customs, then out onto the street, raising his voice louder in perfect Hindi, startling the coolies and taxi drivers into action.

"Man," Bob told him as they settled into a taxi, "why didn't you tell me you were so useful? I mean, when you said you spoke Hindi, I had no idea you really spoke it."

Christian stared from the taxi window. As if he'd never left, everything was exactly the same. "Nareesh . . . my best friend as I was growing up . . . was the son of a revered Brahman in my village. A Teacher. Ram Seva insisted that we speak Hindi, Punjabi, and English. And I have a smattering of Tibetan. There's a Tibetan monastery near my boarding school."

"Where's your village?" Dharma asked.

"In the north. Just south of Jalandhar. About two hours from the holy city of Amritsar."

"Why haven't you told us any of this before?" Bob asked, abashed and wondering how much more of his personal life Christian had kept secret. "You know Julie's really involved with the Hare Krishna Temple."

"So what's with you and religion?" Dharma asked, thinking how many times Christian had refused to visit the temple on Maui.

Christian gave him a look that suggested the answer should be obvious. "Think about it. My life has been filled with teachings. Hindu. Sikh. Buddhist. Christian. I've had my fill of religion."

"Yeah, but it's made you different," Bob told him. "I would never have brought you home that first night from the Sunrise Restaurant if there wasn't something special about your energy."

"You were too loose, man. Taking someone in off the street." Bob took a hell of a lot of chances. That whole scene on Maui, for example. Sure, they'd found the valley, but it had almost cost them their lives.

"Not really," Bob argued. "I'd already dropped with you. Let's not forget I gave you your first dose of acid. Besides, even then you had one foot on the earth and the other stepping up on some cloud. The way you're always leaning back and closing your eyes as if, at any moment, you're going to leave us."

"For what it's worth, I'm not feeling very centered," Christian muttered, still staring from the window. "Years ago, before I arrived in California . . . there was an incident."

"You know," Bob said quietly, "if you started talking about it with the people who love you, maybe you'd ease up on it a bit."

Christian sighed heavily. "Then there's my father and mother. They're still here. I haven't spoken with them in years."

"And Lisa, huh? Hard to know exactly what she wants, right?"

Lisa was one of the reasons he'd ostensibly taken this journey. To see if she still cared enough for him to leave the ashram and come back to the States. An act, he was not yet willing to admit, that would cover the pain of Kathy's leaving after an argument and disappearing for weeks without a word.

"What *does* Lisa want anyway?" Christian suddenly cried, frustration seeping into his voice. "Her eyes tell you one thing, her words another."

Bob merely stared at him, a concerned look on his face. "I've never heard you raise your voice."

"And when I get back," Christian added, making an effort to change his tone, "I'm going to have to face Kathy."

Suddenly shifting gears, Bob answered gruffly, "You don't need to worry about Kathy,"

"I should have told her I was leaving."

Now Bob was surprised. "You didn't tell her?"

"She was in Tucson. Business."

"Why didn't you just call her?"

Christian gave him a sardonic grin. "Kathy doesn't give me the phone numbers of her connections."

"I could have . . . uh . . . helped you out. You could have asked me. Julie has the number. She's friends with Carolyn, Larry's old lady."

"She's so fucking independent," Christain told him angrily, in spite of his attempt to be cool. "Never talks anything over."

Again, Bob stared, regarding Christian closely. "What's going on?"

"She was going to be gone only a few days. When we left, she'd already been there over two weeks. No phone call. Nothing."

So I just decided to do the same, he added silently. *Leave.*

"Maybe you're a little jealous about Larry?" Dharma asked, laughing.

"Shit, man, I'd be." Bob shook his head.

"And what's she going to say when she sees I've cut my hair and beard to do this scam? Jesus, she's just going to freak."

"It's not all that short, Christian." Dharma was still laughing. "You should've cut it shorter."

"I don't know about Kathy," Bob mumbled. "No matter how you try to come on to her, she always manages to push you away."

Christian eyed him. Jealous. Deploring the feeling. His rational mind told him that flirting stimulated Kundalini energy at the base of the spine. Flirting wasn't what was important; rather, how that primal energy was used. He took a deep breath knowing he had to come to terms with the destructive nature of afflictive emotions.

If she's not giving in to Bob, he told himself, maybe she really was just doing business in Tucson. Shit! I shouldn't have had Allen move her things back to her old apartment. Not in anger.

"Listen," he heard Bob say, "I've been through this travel routine lots of times. Just start collectin' presents. She'll be happy to see you. And with Kathy," Bob shrugged, "just give her your share of the load to sell. That should chill things out."

Bob leaned back in his seat, and from the way he averted his glance, Christian knew he was still mulling things over about Kathy, still trying to figure her out. Just before leaving Maui, Bob had told him that Kathy was really something else. She could dance with him as if he were the only man in the world, flow with every movement, dark hair swaying, her smile all warm and soft and gentle, all round breasts and hips. An hour later, she could suddenly be into hardcore sales and prices and the management of product.

"Christ!" Bob had grumbled. "How can she be so strictly business? It's like working with another dude."

"We're here." Dharma's voice returned Christian to the moment. "There's the road to the hotel entrance. I just hope the car arrives on time."

Before leaving Berkeley, Christian had arranged to ship the car east—Michigan to New York to Athens. Afterwards, he had traveled west, through Hawaii to meet with Bob and Dharma. From Honolulu there had been a short stop in Tokyo, then on to New Delhi. They would wait a few days for the car to arrive in Greece, and once the shipping company informed them that the car was available, they would fly to Greece to pick it up. From there, they would drive to Afghanistan. After loading up, they would return to India and ship the car from Bombay back to Greece. In Piraeus, they would transport the vehicle to Los Angeles on the original shipping line. All papers would indicate a Greek vacation.

"A few days in New Delhi catching up on jet lag won't hurt," Christian answered. "Man, we need to score something to smoke."

Bob grinned and playfully pushed against Christian's leg. "Hey, you'd better try and keep it together this time. You don't want Lisa looking into your wild, stoned eyes and tossing you out of the ashram again."

The Hotel Imperial was situated behind gracious gardens, tall hedges, and fences that faced Janpath Road. The gardens kept much of the noise of the city at bay—a difficult thing to do since the Imperial was three short blocks from the central hub of New Delhi, Connaught Place. The lobby was small, the couches an uncomfortable vinyl, the wooden chairs old and scratched, the red-patterned rugs worn. The room they were given had a high ceiling, an old couch, two rather dilapidated chairs, two standard beds, and a table with a black rotary-dial phone. The good-sized bathroom was clean and spartan. Although it was aging, the Imperial gave them what they needed: privacy to rest and recover from a grueling flight, and a place to center themselves for the tasks ahead.

Without waiting to rest, Dharma left the hotel to visit with a travel agent he knew well. Rahool would be able to telephone the shipping company in Piraeus to see whether the car had arrived. And he'd also have a select stash of *charas*. Rahool had made arrangements for Dharma before, in fact, he had made travel arrangements for many a Westerner into the high mountainous regions of India, Nepal, and

Afghanistan, searching for the pressed resin that would bring adventure, visions, and money.

Two hours later, Dharma was back, quietly closing the hotel room door behind him. "We're all set," he informed Bob and Christian. "Believe it or not, the truck's waiting. The ship got into port early."

"Did you get anything to smoke?" Bob asked, toweling his hair dry.

"Right here." Dharma took a lump of *charas* and a *chillum* out of his pocket. He filled the pipe and passed it to Bob.

Christian was pacing, uncomfortable. He watched as Bob lit the pipe, then he continued to walk the length of the room, turn, and walk back.

"I've never seen you so uptight." Bob's look was one of disgust. "You're acting like a caged lion. Sit down and have a toke."

Christian forced himself to the sofa and took the pipe.

"What do you think Lisa's up to? Right now?" Bob teased him, a gleam in his eye.

"She's working with one of the Master's disciples. A clinic of some sort."

"You know," Bob continued lazily, "she tried so hard to be honest. About everything. She never let herself off the hook. Always constantly examining her motivation. Let me tell you, by the time we got into bed, she was ready—hungry just to lose herself in every fuckin' minute. Just so she could feel and not think anymore."

Christian sprawled back on the couch, breathing deeply, the smoke forcing him to honesty. "I'm already jealous enough. You know, you haven't been away from your old lady for a full week and you're already talking about other women. How're you going to make it six weeks without getting laid?"

"Or you?" Bob asked.

"I don't have an old lady," Christian told him dryly.

What he really wanted to ask was why the business with Larry was taking so long.

"Alright," Bob said airily, continuing to needle Christian, "I'll just sit here and think about Lisa, and you guys can dream all you want."

"Some of us guys don't have to dream," Dharma said in an off-handed way, taking the *chillum* from Christian and turning his eyes to the pipe . . . but not before Christian read the flash of truth in his face.

A long, quiet moment of realization filled the room.

"What?" Bob asked slowly.

Dharma shrugged. "That night you stayed out with Julie, remember? The first night. Lisa knew, and she was mad as hell. I consoled her. We thought it best just to let it lie."

"You son of a bitch!" Bob narrowed his eyes at him.

"Anyway, after that, she went to Ananda Shiva, so it didn't seem to matter much."

"The hell it doesn't . . . *brother.*"

Christian settled back in the chair. So . . . that was the reason she'd taken a vow of celibacy, some form of atonement only she could understand. Bob was right about that part of her. With Lisa, every experience was a philosophical question.

Yet, he was also right about her passion. She had a hunger that lay close to the surface. He'd seen it, felt it, every time they'd been together. He understood for the first time what he should have known earlier—Lisa's passion guided her actions. From the beginning, she had been the one in control, drawing him into whatever held her interest at the time, and then setting conditions.

Okay, Lisa, I'm game. Let's see what we have to offer each other. You want to test me, I'll play. But in the end, I'll have all of you. And on my terms. Not just for a few weeks or months, but for a long, long time. For all the tomorrows. Not coming and going anytime you want and fucking with my mind.

The thought was a punch in the gut.

He stood and walked to the window, unable to hide from the truth, the hurt that had sent him on this journey. The fact was that Kathy hadn't cared about what he wanted, had walked out when he'd asked her not to go, hadn't given him the consideration of a single phone call.

He closed his eyes, his back to the room, his mind reaching out, searching, the effects of the *charas* strong.

None of this is like Kathy.

Suddenly, he was unsure.

The black phone rang, jarring the room. Dharma picked it up and listened.

"It's Rahool. He's got seats for us to Athens on tomorrow morning's flight. What do you want to do, Christian? You want to fly out with us? Or see Lisa and meet us in Kandahar?"

Christian turned to him, took a deep breath, and struggled toward reason, away from all his emotions.

"Let's get the business done first," he answered slowly. At this moment, he wasn't ready to see Lisa. "We'll be back in two or three weeks. I'll see her then."

"I told Julie you were all business," Bob smirked.

"Besides, that's a part of the world I've never seen before. Turkey. Iran. Afghanistan. Afterward, I'll have time to concentrate on Lisa."

Nothing was ever smoothly done in this business, and the trip east from Greece was no exception. True, the boat had arrived before schedule, but everything that had not been bolted down was gone from the Bronco—the radio, every tool, the jack and spare tire, even the ashtrays, floor mats, and the maintenance instruction booklet. Dharma said a silent prayer that they'd had the presence of mind to stash the important tools and acetylene torches in the false gas tank.

"Fuck!" Bob exploded from behind the truck. "You've got to see this!"

Dharma took one look at the two back wheels and roared with laughter. Two tires without tread that looked miniscule on the big truck had replaced the huge off-road tires in the rear. "Looks like they just needed something so they could roll it off the boat. Well, what now?"

"We're going to need four fuckin' new tires, that's what," Bob answered disgustedly, smashing his hand against the hood of the truck. "They need to match."

After two days of arguing and hassling, the tires were procured, and the long journey from Athens finally began. Up the fertile, warm peninsula to Thessaloniki they drove, the highways paved and easy, then on through the night, stopping only occasionally to eat. They crossed by ferry into Istanbul at sunrise, the yellow-orange sky pierced by silhouetted minarets, the prayers of the faithful echoing through the early morning streets.

Continuing east, they drove steadily across the great Turkish plain, through Ankara, until the mountains began to take them up. The weather turned cooler. The farther east they traveled, the worse the roads became. They crossed the summer snow line, driving cautiously along treacherous mountain cliffs. Here, all they could look forward to were rest stops with strong Turkish coffee and some respite from the intense driving. Each stop meant that the packs had to be taken inside, knowing from past experience that locking the vehicle was no insurance against theft. In Erzurum, high in the mountains, the truck skidded on ice, weaving helplessly for hundreds of feet before Dharma brought it under control, forcing it to a stop at the edge of a sheer cliff overlooking a cloud-filled valley.

I've already had to climb one misty cliff in my life, Dharma prayed, shaking. *Please, God, don't make me do it again.*

From Turkey, they crossed the border into Iran, driving to Tabriz and on to Tehran, the men appalled at the condition of potholed roads that forced a speed of fifteen miles per hour in some places and an absolute maximum of forty miles an hour on the good stretches. The bouncing and jarring managed to vibrate loose the back tailgate, the glove compartment door, and the fly windows. In Tehran, they realized that if the truck was to continue, the shocks would need to be replaced and the back door repaired. The price for the shocks was an old pair of Levi's, and the men were forced to watch uncertainly as a ten-year-old boy was ordered under the truck to make the changes, which, to their mixed relief and chagrin, were efficiently done.

From the mountains of white snow, they continued eastward again, catching glimpses of the desert sand awaiting them far ahead. Finally, they crossed the border into Afghanistan and found the welcomed American-built highway to Kandahar. The blacktop road stretched in a triangle, a gesture of good faith between Afghanistan and three foreign powers, the Americans, Chinese, and Soviets—Herat in the west to Kandahar in the south, Kandahar to Kabul in the northeast, and from Kabul back to Herat in the west.

As they traveled across mountain and desert, Christian felt the vastness of the world stretch continuously around him. Throughout the day, the sun passed overhead, changing the light and producing new sights of diverse color and nuance, people and terrain. Each morning and evening, he watched sunrise or sunset in a different place. The settled Berkeley lifestyle became stilted by comparison. He breathed into his body each new vision, becoming a part of it.

I've become too settled, he knew. *I've forgotten that the world is more than Berkeley.*

Images held him captive—the ancient fishing vessels in Greece, strong-armed men who farmed the sea, lines of Greek women wearing modest white scarves sitting to patch nets, the endless miles of carts pulled by donkey or horse in every country, countless white clay villages scattered across the Turkish and Iranian plains and foothills, nomads carrying children and bundles and walking with bent backs across narrow desert trails, camel caravans stretching across the sand, transporting goods as they had for millennia, sparsely covered mountains blanketed in white with occasional trees dusted in snow, and in Afghanistan the dark red morning desert with the turbaned Afghan and his family farming a living in land blown by fierce winds from the mountains.

The road they traveled had already been ancient in the time of Christ. Generations upon generations of tribesmen had used this trade route, and when Kandahar finally lay before them, Christian could already sense the wares she had harbored for centuries—carpets, fabrics, and drugs. On the outskirts of the city stood the tents of the nomads and camel traders, alive with the braying of camels, idle horses swooshing at flies with their tails, the cries of men trading their wares, barking dogs, women busy with gossip and cooking fires, and children chasing one another. The faces he saw told of a harsh, exacting life. Each man stood next to the other with a sense of equal value, head to head, his presence affirmed in a deeply etched face. The set of the shoulders, the antique musket guns with beautiful inlay work, the knives in evidence, all spoke a clear message. A man's story was alive, written in eyes of certainty.

Driving further into town, the rendered cinderblock buildings grew larger. Dharma wearily stopped the truck to get his bearings. The American construction crew had not only built the road, but had also constructed houses and dormitories for the workers, a great source of amusement to locals who watched the money, labor, and effort spent to build temporary quarters that were better than many Afghans could imagine.

"Yeah," Dharma muttered, remembering, "this way."

At last, they located a small house with a garage that was for rent at the old construction site. Exhausted from a week of driving day and night, they crashed hard, knowing that tomorrow would bring the first glimpses of the dark resin they had come to claim.

On the following morning, the men were up early, driving into town for breakfast at a café, and making plans while they ate.

"How do you want to handle meeting your contacts?" Christian asked, looking from Bob to Dharma.

Dharma shrugged, thinking. "It might be a good idea if I go alone to check out the scene. If everything's like I remember from last time, we can all go over."

"Alright," Bob nodded thoughtfully, "Let's hope everything's still cool. Take the truck, and we'll get a cab home. We'll meet you back at the house this afternoon."

All that day, Bob and Christian walked the streets of Khandahar, getting a feel for the city. Afghan women covered in blue *burqas*, with nets over their eyes, carried market baskets. Young school girls wearing uniforms and simple *hijab* headscarves walked together, laughing, books resting on their hips. Turbaned men followed Western women with their eyes, unable to comprehend their uncovered heads, sleeveless dresses, and sunglasses.

The blare of horns was loud and intense. Colorfully painted trucks with images of mosques jostled with cars on the roundabout. Christian winced as a cart driver smartly lashed a traffic policeman across the back with his whip for suggesting he wait to allow another vehicle to pass first.

As they explored, they perused small, open shops of brassware and leather, fabrics and scarves, herbs and spices, baked goods and tea. After a stop for lunch, they returned to bargain for several of the carpets they had seen earlier in the day, the conversation rising in tone and fierceness as Bob stood, wide eyed, as Christian raised his voice in equal measure to the tradesman. When the negotiations were over, Bob and Christian hailed a taxi and, loading their treasures, made for the bungalow, ready to hear what Dharma had discovered.

By five that afternoon, Dharma still had not returned. Shadows lengthened each time Christian watched from the window.

"What do you think?" he asked Bob anxiously. "You know your contacts."

Just then, there was a knock on the door. When Bob opened it, he saw a bearded man dressed in a turban, a knee-length cotton shirt, a *perahob*, baggy *tunban* trousers, and a vest of red and black. Over all, he wore an incongruous Western sport coat.

"Hyatollah has sent me to bring you into town," the large man told them.

"Be right there," Bob answered, wincing at the sight of the Mercedes in the driveway.

"Somewhat conspicuous," Christian muttered.

"At least it has dark windows," Bob whispered back.

The hotel owned by the Tokhis brothers reminded Christian of an ancient walled fortress, complete with towers at the rectangular corners. A large central door in the front wall passed guests into an inner court-yard, the hallway between lined with small shops and a smoke-filled cantina. In the courtyard, stairs led to a second story. Along the backside of the rectangle was an additional third story of rooms. Armed guards leisurely patrolled the perimeters of the different roof levels.

"This way, please," the driver gestured with his hand. "Second floor. Room thirteen."

Preceding them up the courtyard stairs, the man led them to a small, white room rendered in lime stucco. Christian breathed deeply as he stepped inside. Set in the center of the room was a huge hookah, with a piece of charcoal placed on top of a large mound of hash to keep the resin burning. On a cushion beside the pipe, next to a toasty wood stove, Dharma lay on a pillow, looking like a cross between the caterpillar and the Cheshire cat. To Dharma's right was Hyatollah Tokhis, the elder of the brothers, and to his left, Nazrula, the younger.

"No wonder you couldn't make it back." Christian grinned.

"Hey, I'm workin'," he muttered. "Tryin' samples."

Bob held out his hand to Hyatollah, smiling warmly. "It's good to see you again. Looks like everything's pretty tight around here." He gestured toward where Christian stood. "Christian, my close brother."

"Please," Hyatollah nodded toward the pillows, "let me offer you my hospitality."

At Hyatollah's encouragement, Christian took a seat, picked up a pipe hose, and toked on the huge hookah. From the edge of his vision, he could see that Hyatollah watched him carefully.

"Nice," Christian nodded. And it was.

With a grin, Hyatollah opened a small pillbox, placed a little piece of hash under his tongue, and offered the box to Christian.

The relationship between the broad Tokhis establishment and the

Brotherhood of Eternal Love was special. In exchange for both protection and the contract that brought the best hashish, the Brotherhood had brought bottles of multivitamins filled with different-color tabs of acid to turn on the East. Hyatollah and Nazrula had gotten off, and the two groups had bonded. A cupboard that members of the Brotherhood could use while passing through the country had been set up. From Southern California, travelers had brought an Acme juicer, a blender for smoothies, jars of peanut butter, protein bars, vitamins, books, extra blankets, and more. In exchange, the space that was left in their vehicles or suitcases or surfboards was filled with the superb hashish of the Afghans.

The color of the hash resembled the particular *Cannabis indica* plant that grew in the mountains, short bushes of five or six feet, hardy plants with wide, flat leaves, dark green, with blood-red veins. Afghans, loving the wild weed with its thick resin, were innovative and had made an art out of the production of hashish. Nothing foreign was added to bind the resin together—neither dirt, nor plant material, nor rancid oil—just a few drops of water to press the powder into shapes that resembled round moons, surfboards, rolled spaghetti sticks, or blocks. The samples Dharma had tasted that day were of many grades and colors, from pliable black-brown to dusk red. Most of what was shown to him was fresh, soft, still pressable with the fingers. By midnight, Christian could not remember being that stoned in a long time. And he knew that Nazrula and Hyatollah shared his headspace.

What's really cosmic about tripping, he realized, *is that no matter what the cultural differences or where you are in the world, you know you're going to the same place as the brother who trips with you.*

To one side of the hookah, Dharma began a slow, steady snore against his pillow. Bob kicked his foot. "Hey, tell me what's been goin' on all day."

"Huh . . . ?" Dharma answered, jerked awake, only to fall asleep once more.

"I will tell you." Hyatollah smiled. "Throughout the day, different samples were brought here to be tested. Dharma has been choosing.

Look for yourself. The best of what the mountains offer. See . . . " He picked up a slab and broke a piece off easily with his fingers. "Fresh."

"God, but I'm stoned," Bob said, trying to focus on the pounds lying in the corner.

"What causes the dark outer color?" Christian asked slowly, looking at one sample and comparing it with several green-gold chunks.

"It is from the fire. When the resin powder is mixed with water, it is placed on coals to bake—only for a few seconds—then turned to the other side. Heat binds the resin, plant oils, and water together, like a piece of dough. Then it can be shaped with the hands. Several times, it may be laid on the fire to achieve just the right consistency and bonding." He placed another slab into the hookah bowl. "Our garage is busy almost every day filling storage places. Americans. Dutch. Australians. English. We have your car there now. We thought it best to keep it out of sight. This way, we'll load you as it comes in."

"Keeping the truck off the street's a good idea." Bob nodded. "And a mechanic should look at it before we start the drive to India."

"How was your trip through Iran?"

"The roads were terrible. I mean, *really* bad. There should be something on a map that says you can only drive fifteen miles per hour over certain stretches."

"No, I mean politically. I have heard things. A movement is growing there."

"We didn't see much. But going through customs, we had to walk down a long corridor with display pictures of confiscated hashish. That was a first."

"Life imprisonment in Iran," Hyatollah informed them.

"Life?" Christian asked, suddenly jolted awake and feeling stupid for not knowing.

"The drug trade belongs to the Shah's family. And the Shah insists on all his revenue."

"Then we can thank God we won't have to cross those borders returning. We're shipping the car from Bombay back to Greece . . . "

And avoiding the prospect of life imprisonment, Christian thought, listening as Bob continued to explain their plan. Picking up the pipe hose, he sucked in his breath and blew billowing clouds of white smoke into the room.

"You know they've been sniffing around here." Hyatollah chuckled.

"Who?" Bob asked.

"Interpol."

Again, Christian focused.

"Looking for smugglers. It is amusing. We watch them. They watch us. We have men that watch them watch us. You must be very careful, my friend, especially once you leave this part of Afghanistan. While you are in Kandahar, you have our protection, but on the open road . . . you have heard the stories. Robbery. Sometimes murder. Arrest." Then with some quiet speculation, he murmured, "Should you have a problem with the police, always offer the best of what you have. If it is not accepted, then you are free to take whatever steps necessary to settle the matter. Never feel you must give up your freedom to appease an officer's pride. It is a price too high for one man to ask of another." His eyes narrowed sleepily, and as if trying to see something far away, remembering, he said quietly, "Once, a long time ago, when I looked like the dessert, an officer searched and found what I carried. I made a good offer so that I could leave with most of my goods and increase the wealth of the man. He refused and insisted on arresting me. He asked me to follow him to the jail cell. I made another offer, a better one. Again, he said 'no.' Then I had to look very carefully at this man who asked too much." He was quiet for several long seconds. "I had to make sure he did not take my freedom." He blew a large cloud of smoke into the room.

In the poignant silence that followed this story, Bob cleared his throat. "Um . . . did Dharma ask if you could get seeds?"

The room's mood changed and Hyatollah looked at him with interest. "Are you going to grow your own plants?"

"I'm going to try. Many people in my country like to smoke the flowers and leaves."

"Have you no seeds?"

"Yes. But it's a different plant. *Cannabis sativa.* I want to cross the characteristics of the plant that grows here with some of those grown in my own country. The *sativa* with the *indica*. The Afghan plant is hardy, but it smells. I'd like to combine the hardiness of your plant with the sweet smell of mine."

"Not all our plants have this smell you speak of. But the ones that do are very strong. Very powerful. Where do you plan to grow these plants of yours?"

"On a tropical island called Maui—one of the Hawaiian Islands. We have a valley with water and sun. The plants will be in remote areas. They need to be strong."

"When you have your new plant, will you return some of the seeds to me?"

"When I have them, they're yours."

"What do you think of what you have smoked?"

Bob grinned and looked at Christian for confirmation. "It couldn't get any better."

Four days later, Dharma, Bob, and Christian left the Tokhis hotel after breakfast, walking slowly, their eyes barely open from the hash they'd smoked all morning. The day was mild and fair—the exact reason they had chosen to travel in autumn. Dharma unzipped his windbreaker to let the breeze blow around his body.

"You know," he told Bob and Christian in a sleepy, stoned voice, "if we're going to finish the loading this evening, I see no reason to hang around much longer. What do you think about taking off tomorrow? We'll take a leisurely drive down to New Delhi, spend a couple of days so Christian can visit Ananda Shiva, and then go on to Bombay."

"Sounds good to me," Bob agreed. "I'd probably keep my six-week promise to Julie if we did that."

"Yeah," Christian nodded. "And there's no telling what problems or delays we might encounter."

"If I miss this baby, Julie will never forgive me, man."

Dharma looked at Christian. "When we get to New Delhi, you can decide to drive with us to Bombay or meet us in Greece. After Bombay, we've just got the flight to Athens, and once the car's on board in Greece, we're done. And if you get really hung up with Lisa, you can head back to the States on your own."

"Say," Christian told them suddenly, the idea just coming to him, "maybe I can talk Lisa into coming with us. Driving to Bombay."

"Crazy, man." Bob laughed, his eyes shining at the thought. "Can you see Lisa choosing to drive through India with the three of us?"

"Then it's settled? We leave tomorrow?" Dharma asked.

"I'd better get the shopping finished," Bob answered. "I need to stop at that dress shop over there. Pick up something for Kathy . . . ," he said without thinking.

Christian's eyes may have been barely open from the smoke, but he managed to fix them hard on Bob's face.

"Hey, man. Someone's going to have to pacify her," Bob tried. "What do you think she's going to do when you turn up with Lisa?"

12

MYLES CORBET AND CHRISTIAN
KHANDAHAR, AFGHANISTAN
OCTOBER 1969

Across the street from Hyatollah's hotel, standing in a small brass-ware store, Myles Corbet clicked his camera over and over again at the three men. Myles had spotted them days before, breezing in and out of the hotel in a Mercedes, looking very much like what he knew them to be—smugglers.

Myles had made quite the leap in the last years, from Berkeley botany student to informant to American agent working with Interpol in Germany. In the past months, he'd had remarkable success—profiling international smugglers, setting up a new computer system to centralize criminal data, closing down a bogus pharmaceutical company in Amsterdam, and currently studying the Tokhis brothers and their clients. But the year he'd promised Supervisor Bremer was almost at an end. He had to find a breakthrough case that would earn him the right to demand a return to Berkeley to pursue his career at the university.

Thoughts of returning to Berkeley also forced him to consider Jerry Putnam. Two years ago, he and Jerry had been best friends—in fact, more than childhood friends and academic partners. Each time he'd looked into Jerry's eyes, there had been a spark, one he had been afraid to explore. But even as he had decided to discuss what their relationship might become, their world had fallen apart. He'd been busted in ROTC with a small amount of marijuana, forced to be an informant or face a police record, and had set Jerry up for arrest to seal the deal.

The man in the store where he stood began to shout, eyeing him disapprovingly, knowing the camera was taking pictures of Hyatollah's customers. Myles sensed the disapproval long before the man started to argue, but the angle was so good, the image of the three men in the doorway of the Hyatollah compound such obvious evidence of their association, that he could not pass up the chance to continue shooting.

"Alright, alright," he finally said to the shouting owner and paid handsomely for a small brass hookah, calming the man.

The men being photographed walked into the clothing shop next door, and on impulse, Myles followed, pretending to look at merchandise, the small hookah protruding from his front shirt pocket.

"Hi," he said to the tall blond man. "American or Aussie?"

"American." Christian smiled. "How'd you know?"

"Seems like everybody I've met lately is either American or Australian. It's spring in Australia and a lot of people are traveling. Americans like us seem to be on permanent vacation."

"You from the States?" Christian asked, his blue eyes half closed, obviously very stoned.

"Berkeley."

"Well, that's a coincidence," Christian answered thoughtlessly. "So am I. You just traveling?"

"Yeah. I'm trying to get my visa extended. I really like it here. Only problem is I'm running out of money."

"Bring some of these shirts back." Christian grinned. "Start an import business."

"That's not the Afghan export that makes all the money," Myles laughed, "if you know what I mean."

Christian laughed with him.

"You guys just get in?" Myles asked, as relaxed as if he were in a Berkeley coffeehouse. "Say . . . here's one that's pretty nice," he exclaimed, holding up a shirt and pretending to inspect it closely.

"We've been here a few days."

"Need any help?" Myles turned back to Christian, still holding the shirt. "I'm pretty good at steering people in the right direction. I've got a great hotel, clean and cheap."

"Thanks," the dark-haired man interjected. "But we've got a place."

"Across the street?" Myles turned his attention to the man who had spoken, as if he were really interested in a rental. "Is it any good? What about the food?"

"Yeah, it's good. But we're staying somewhere else."

"Does it have the girls my place has?" Myles whistled long and low.

"So how *do* you intend to hang on here?" Bob asked, warming up to Myles.

"I'm trying to get Americans to change money with me," he answered, rolling his eyes to tell how difficult it was at times. "I give them the bank rate plus fifty percent, then sell dollars on the black market for twice the bank price."

"Interesting." Christian eyed him. "Is it a good scam?"

"I'm still here." Myles grinned.

The third man, sandy-brown curly hair, tall, a puka shell necklace just peeking from his shirt, joined the conversation. "We've been paying for things in dollars."

"I'll bet. The merchants turn around and sell the dollars on the black market and make twice the price of what they sell. Everybody wants US dollars."

"You looking for dollars?" Bob asked. "We'll take your exchange rate. Eh?" He looked at Christian and raised a questioning eyebrow. "We can do the rest of our shopping in local currency."

"Sure." Christian smiled easily and looked back to Myles. "If it means we can help a brother."

Myles faltered, suddenly brought up short. Brother? It had been a very long time since anyone had called him "brother."

From the other side of the shop, the merchant accidentally pushed over a pile of shirts. Cursing, he bent to pick them up, and Myles, grateful for a place to focus his eyes, turned away with pretended interest as the man folded and stacked.

"What do you think about this design?" he heard the man with the shell necklace ask.

"Nice," came the response. The man with dark hair. "Are you still going to pick up those rugs, too?"

"Yeah. I thought maybe I'd just pack them in the car."

"Are you crazy?" the dark-haired man cried. "They'd be gone before the steamer left Bombay Harbor."

"You think we should ship them?"

"I think we'd better damn well make time," Bob insisted.

Myles took out a pad of paper. "Okay," he said.

"What's that?" Christian asked, his mind wrenched away from the conversation between Bob and Dharma.

"Authorized bank form. You can't trade in your Afghani money when you leave the country unless you have proof you've traded with a legal money changer." He smiled easily. "I paid a dude working at the bank for his pad of forms. Seems, for the right price, you can get just about anything. Okay, I need to record your names and passport numbers here."

Bob was already absently reaching into his pocket for the cash for Myles. "I think I might just get an extra trunk. Fill it and ship it."

Christian watched the American briskly take a pen from his pocket. Something in his movements had begun to bother Christian. He tried to clear his head, leaning back to look hard at this man who had just walked into their lives. There was a reason for everything. What was the reason for his being here?

The man's shoes were neat, new sandals. Everybody on the street wore sandals, but these weren't lived in. His feet and toenails were clean; this was no dusty foot traveler. This guy had a scam and was making it.

Jeans, embroidered shirt. Young. Filled out in the chest and arms—three meals a day. He wasn't enjoying the cheap heroin. The pipe in his pocket was new, unused. He wasn't stoned.

No. This guy wasn't off the street.

His conversation was slow, friendly, but his eyes . . . He didn't seem able to directly meet Christian's gaze. His focus was on the shirts, then on his pad of paper. They were being hustled—and Christian wasn't sure for what—money, stash, what?

Suddenly, Christian was paranoid. The fear of it struck him hard and served to clear his head. The situation was out of control—Bob and Dharma were stone rapping as if they were in the privacy of their own homes. Bob handed Myles a hundred dollars, barely noticing his own movements as he continued to look at merchandise. Christian could see the money register in the man's face. He knew they had bucks and plenty of them compared with most Westerners.

Christian took a deep breath and tried to shake off his feeling. Even if something wasn't right, all the man would get was a phony name and a false passport number. The man waited, his face all innocence, looking like a young kid trying to make it on the street. Taking out a hundred bucks and his passport, Christian handed them over, but as he did so, a bad taste filled his dry mouth.

"How about you?" the man asked Dharma when he'd handed Christian his bank form and Afghan currency. The shopkeeper's eyes were wide with the money displayed in his shop. "Want to make an exchange?"

"Sure," Dharma shrugged, "why not?"

"So you're driving." The dude's delight was real. "That must be some trip. When are you leaving?"

"In a few days," Christian answered. He took Bob by the arm and said, "Let's get going. We don't want to be late."

Bob looked at him strangely. "Uh . . . sure." And to the stranger, "We'll be seein' you around, man."

"What's up?" Bob asked Christian just out of earshot.

"I just didn't like that dude. Too nosy," Christian told him, grinding his teeth. "Do you know what we just fuckin' did? We gave him our goddamned names and passport numbers!"

"Take it easy," Dharma said, looking back over his shoulder. "You think he was weird?"

"Look at the questions he asked. He wanted to know where we were staying and when we'd be leaving. You can bet he knows why

we're here. I can't believe what we just did! We gave him—*gave* him—
our passport numbers! We're too spaced, man. We've been smoking too
much. We've got to cool it with the smoke until we get that load back."

"Maybe you're right," Dharma answered, the look on his face clear
evidence that Christian's paranoia had infected him. "But tomorrow
we'll be gone. We just need to pack and come back in after dark to
load up."

Returning to his office late that afternoon, Myles telephoned the
Bureau of Narcotics Enforcement in San Francisco. "I've got some
names for you," he told Agent Phillips. "One of them says he's from
Berkeley . . . Christian Taylor Alden. I'm not sure about the other two,
Robert David Jones and Matthew Randolf Greene. You want to run
them through to see what you come up with?"

"Sure. Hold the line."

Within a few minutes, Phillips was back on the phone, excited.
"We've nothing on the second two names, but the Alden character's
hot. We've been picking up bits and pieces of 'Christian' over the years.
The guy's been around for a while. A recent tip just helped us put it
all together. We've got a file on the guy an inch thick. No pictures. No
evidence. But we know he's there. He's probably part of the Laguna
Beach Brotherhood. Stay on this one."

"I'll keep you posted."

Brotherhood. Alden had called him "brother."

*When these guys go down, I'll score points with Interpol, the FBI, and
with Bremer. They're well hooked. I've got them. All I have to do is reel
them in.*

*But where did he want these guys to fall. Here? Or back in the States?
At least in the States they won't be able to buy their way out.*

And if this bust was big enough, it would get him back to Berkeley.

That evening, the three men finished bagging the last of the hash, and with help from Hyatollah's crew, forced it into the hollow spare gas tank. Christian was uneasy as he worked. Something ate at him, causing his hands to shake until he finally sat down in a corner, closed his eyes, and tried to sort it all out.

"Okay, what is it?" Bob asked.

"That dude today. I don't know what it is, but I'm paranoid as hell. I have this feeling that won't go away."

Bob looked at Dharma, then glanced back to Christian. "You're not often wrong."

"I don't think he's seen this truck. Stashing it in the garage may have saved our asses."

Dharma had just put the finishing touches on the welding job on the bumper. He turned off the torch and set it with the rest of the tools. "I think you're right. I think it's serious."

"Interpol?"

"Very possibly," Hyatollah nodded, speaking slowly. "I told you they have been sniffing at my doorstep. Watching."

"Then we should get out of here," Dharma said.

"Leave tonight," Hyatollah advised. "Now. You're all loaded up, and the Pakistan border is only a few hours away. Once you are across, you can disappear."

"We knew we'd be leaving in the morning, so everything's here. Hyatollah," Dharma held out his hand, "the tools are yours."

"Then come upstairs. Have a quick meal and some strong coffee. That should get you to the border even at this hour."

To Myles's surprise, the three men did not appear at the Tokhis hotel the next morning, even though he had men watching early. A sliver of doubt began. Where were they? How much was it going to cost to find out where they were staying?

Another full day went by before he was able to locate the bungalow with the garage—a mammoth job in itself. The doubt spread to a sense of mild panic until, at last, his suspicions were confirmed. They were gone—with a three-day head start. The realization caused the blood to rush to his face. What had happened to his precise timing? They had been within his grasp. He should never have let them out of his sight, kept a man on them. But he'd been so sure. Embarrassed at his ineptitude, his failure soon exploded into anger. And fear. Fear that he had lost his ticket back to the States.

No! he assured himself. I have names and I have passport numbers. I'll find them whether they go west to Iran or east to Burma. This is a perfect opportunity to see whether the border guards are checking the lists we've compiled. Telephone messages can be sent with special instructions. What was it that spooked them?

Accepting the realization was hard. *Me, of course.*

Myles sat very still, all his concentration focused on replaying the meeting with the men.

The one with the light-blue eyes. Alden, the one who abruptly pulled them away.

Alden had spotted him. He knew it as surely as he knew the men were gone.

Alright, Mr. Alden, Myles sent a mental message. *Let's see if your intuitive powers are greater than mine. You're betting you can keep one step ahead of me. But I'm betting I'll have you at some border. Or Bombay harbor.*

KALI

VARANASI, INDIA

OCTOBER 1969

In early October, on the day Christian had cabled his plane would arrive, Kali's first waking thought was to wonder what time he would be at the ashram. She prayed he would come before the Master gave his daily afternoon teaching or certainly before evening *satsang*, convinced that once he knew the Master, he would begin to reexamine his life and make the changes that would bring him into the teachings. She lay in the predawn hours in a half dream, savoring old images of him.

The soft sound of sandaled feet in the hallway broke the spell.

With a muffled cry, she leapt guiltily from her bed, guilty because she was thinking of Christian in the old way, with the ardor she needed to forego to fulfill her promise to Padmananda. Hurriedly, she took a deep breath and tried to clear her mind by focusing on the Master's picture on her altar.

What was this mixture of feeling, this apprehension that only Christian could create? How could she love one man, while some part of her yearned for another?

As she dressed, she tried to imagine what she would say to Padmananda when Christian appeared at the ashram. On the first night in the garden, when he'd declared himself, she had tried to tell him that some part of her was still tied to Christian, that she had written to suggest that there might be a future for them if he accepted the Master's teachings. But after Agra, after Padmananda had put heart and soul,

bitterness and love into her, how could she tell him that Christian was
actually arriving? She had grown to love the boy, Nareesh, as well as the
disciple the boy had become, Padmananda. She had given a promise of
marriage. How had things come to this?

Clearly she needed to put Christian out of her life, but . . . didn't
she owe him the gift of the Master's teachings? The daydream intruded
again, a picture of Christian prostrating before Daya Nanda to receive
his blessing.

No, she thought, closing her eyes, ruthlessly honest, suddenly miserable and confused once more. *Not entirely true. There is something
about Christian that still lures me, a connection from the first moment
of meeting. Not what I have with Padmananda, but . . . an attraction I
can't deny.*

A bell rang downstairs, calling all to morning *puja*.

Shaking her head, she forced herself to accept the reality of this
awkward situation. The truth was that she and Christian were in different worlds. She was committed to the Master and the ashram. He, to
dealing psychedelics. His work was illegal. There was always the prospect that he'd be busted—or worse. Maybe killed.

From her altar, she removed a stick of incense, lit it, and tried to
push away the stories that were whispered about Nepal. Hash was legal
and could be smoked in the small, family owned and operated hash
shops. But if a big load was sought, a smuggler sometimes took to the
mountains, where he might be slipped liquid *datura* in an innocent
cup of tea. Tribesmen had been known to let a man wander blind and
abandoned, his money taken, eventually falling to his death from a
high ledge.

And what about the intrigues among travelers themselves? In places
like Goa, the introduction of ridiculously cheap heroin had turned
many a seeking mystic into a contented junkie.

Reports had been shared of previously unknown venereal diseases
in the Indian Himalayas, in places like Ladakh. Once Westerners had
discovered the peaceful villages high in the beauty of the mountains,
they had brought with them drugs and disease.

Farther north, in Afghanistan, she remembered hearing reports of robbery and murder as men ignored the risks and sought to buy the black-green slabs of hashish from unknown tribesmen . . .

Suddenly, Kali's breath stopped, and when she let it out again as a long sigh, she almost cried aloud.

Afghanistan! What a fool I've been! My ego's trapped me into thinking Christian was coming across the ocean to see me! Of course! It's the lure of Afghanistan's hash that draws him here! Bob and Dharma were on their way to score the last time I saw him. How could I not have suspected? He's not traveling halfway around the world to see an ashram or the Master . . . or me. I'm simply a stopover.

Put your illusions away, she ordered herself harshly. *Stop playing the fool!*

She glanced at the clock with a further sense of frustration. Once again, Christian had thrown her off schedule! She was already too late to get a seat near the Master.

In spite of her exasperation, she chose her favorite white blouse, one decorated with small embroidered flowers inset with tiny pearls and silk ribbon, the most beautiful, flattering garment she owned. She slipped it over her head and started out the door just as the conch shell blew, announcing the Master's arrival.

Kali waited for Christian all that day. And the next.

But, of course, India was different; traveling wasn't easy. Planes were delayed. Christian was who he was, always late. Nothing was predictable. So, optimistically, she shrugged it off and decided to give him a few more days. The waiting days passed into weeks, until finally, incredulously, she knew she had been stood up—again.

"Kali, what is it?" Padmananda asked as they stood in his office, preparing for the upcoming public health conference at Benares University. "You've been distracted for over a week now. What's going on?"

"I'm sorry," she answered. "I've had a lot on my mind lately."

He grinned. "Is it something to do with me?"

"Honestly," she smiled, "everything has to do with you." Then she shook her head. "But this is something I have to sort out for myself."

"There was a time when you trusted your problems to me."

"That was before your kiss at the Taj," she teased.

"You mean . . . before a kiss like this?"

Slowly, he pulled her against him, his mouth lingering deliciously near her lips, playing out the moment, savoring what was to come. When she closed her eyes, she felt the tender pressure of his mouth, his tongue softly searching, his arms tightening, his hands playing in her hair, ardor rising, leaving her legs weak, her body trembling and crying for more.

"Soon," he whispered, "soon we will know the full ecstasy of love."

His fingers still pulled through her hair.

"And if you truly have questions," he continued to whisper, "there are always others to counsel you. And Daya Nanda himself."

He leaned back on the desk and regarded the papers she had compiled. "I do not think I could have organized these meetings without your help. And I promise that once in Varanasi, you will love the Ganges River and the holy city of Benares.

"The Ganges," Kali whispered wistfully. "To bathe in the sacred river has been one of my dreams. How far is Varanasi from here?"

"A short thirty-minute plane ride. We'll leave early Friday morning."

Kali stepped back and turned away so he would not read her thoughts. In this, ironically enough, he reminded her of Christian. Friday. If she left, she could miss Christian. But then . . . Christian might never show up.

No more, she thought.

Turning back to Padmananda, she took his hands. "I can't wait to go."

"The Master's in Bombay until Friday afternoon. Krishna will assume my responsibilities until we return."

"Is there anything else I can do to help prepare?"

"Only the schedule is left. Will you have thirty copies made to give to each participant?" Then he was smiling again, reaching out to run a finger softly over her cheek. "You'll enjoy your time there, Kali. Even though I'll be busy, I'll make the time to show the city to you."

Benares, the ancient city within the modern Varanasi, was a holy city created on the banks of the Ganges. The site had been important for thousands of years. Devotees prayed to die here, to wash sin away in the waters of the river, to cleanse karma, to have their cremated remains carried away by the river's current.

Kali walked with members of the ashram toward the Golden Temple, along narrow bricked streets crowded with people, animals, and rickshaws. As fascinated as she was by the lively color and throngs around her, so did her golden hair fascinate those she passed. As though seeing a vision, craftsmen in their tiny shops ceased their pounding or drawing or weaving and watched until she was out of sight. Others stared rudely and whispered behind their hands. The Muslim women, with their black burkas hiding all but their dark eyes, followed her, clicking their tongues in disapproval, asking how a woman could go about so shamefully with her face uncovered, to be stared at by every man on the street—and with hair of gold that drew everyone's attention.

Ahead, Kali could see the dome of the Golden Temple. Padmananda was already reaching into his bag for *paise* for the ever-present beggars squatting in neat lines outside the temple doors.

A sudden haunting recall of Berkeley came to her, a night years ago, when she'd lived on the streets and was getting ready to sleep in a doorway on Telegraph Ave. She had not cared that night was approaching or that the doorway awaited her. Others were on the street, and she had been protected by their presence, one of the street people, part of the party at hand. All she could remember was feeling free—no possessions but the clothes on her back and a kilo of reg weed in a paper grocery bag. She'd been so stoned that she could hardly walk. God, but that smoke had blown her head off. And then Matt had come along, looking like fun for an evening . . . and of course, that's when she'd met Christian . . .

"You're smiling," Padmananda said, bringing her back to the streets of Benares.

"I was just remembering my own begging days." She grinned at him. "I'd almost forgotten."

"You? Begging?"

"Yes, after I left home." She gave a girlish giggle, and one of the ashram members turned with a stern look; they were at the entrance to the temple. She leaned toward Padmananda and grinned. "I'll have to tell you my stories about when times were tough."

Padmananda regarded her, unsure that he wanted to hear about those times, certain they would include stories of Christian. He had been working hard to give up any animosity he might still hold toward him, was even beginning to realize how easy it was to blame Christian for his father's death. The Master taught that karma was complex, pregnant with reasons no one person could understand entirely. He knew, too, that it was well past time to give up his attachment to destructive ideas. Christian needed to be an object of compassion.

But he was also certain that he wanted Christian far away from his world.

When the group emerged from the temple, the light was already beginning to fade in the narrow alleyways. The street rose to a slight crest, and at the top, where the land began to slope toward the shoreline, they had their first view of the Ganges, in the last hour of twilight.

"It's so quiet. So gentle," Kali murmured.

"At this time of year," Padmananda nodded, "yes."

Boats on the water appeared as dark shadows on a surface of golden glass. Across the river, the far shoreline faded, indistinct in the rising mist and haze.

"Shall we walk closer to the river?" she asked.

"Tomorrow morning, Kali. That's when you should see it. We'll come to the river every morning we are here." They stood on the landing, apart from the others, and in the dusk, he whispered, "You are beautiful. Even with the evening shadows on your face, your hair still glistens."

Modestly, Kali wrapped the shawl over her head and looked out over the vista with its thread of red-gold water. In the twilight, she murmured a thankful prayer, brushed her hand against his, a tiny act that spoke of seduction, love, ownership.

"For the first time since coming to India," she whispered, "I am truly content. I feel as if I've finally come home from a long journey."

14

CHRISTIAN
NEW DELHI, INDIA
NOVEMBER 1969

On the Friday afternoon when Christian walked through the gate of the ashram in New Delhi, Kali and Padmananda had already been gone for three hours.

Initiates and visitors strolled through gardens that were as beautiful as Lisa had described in her letter. If he had allowed it, he would have admitted to a feeling of peace and tranquility that only a holy place overseen by a living master can bring.

He ambled slowly, looking for her, around trees, over hedges, regarding benches, searching for the woman who had sat in the garden in Santa Monica, one foot tucked underneath her body, a book in her lap. When she was nowhere to be seen, he finally approached a group, and with his hands over his heart, bowed, and spoke softly. "*Namaste.* I'm looking for someone in the ashram from the United States. From California. Her name is Kali."

"Oh, yes," one of the women nodded right away. "That would be Padmananda's secretary. But she's gone for a week or two."

"Gone?" Christian asked, controlling his voice through a fierce flash of disbelief. "Where?"

"A conference, I believe. She just left this morning. Why not ask Krishna? He's a friend of hers from California and in charge of things until the Master's return. You'll find him in the office." She pointed. "That building over there."

Gone!

He could feel her anger now as clearly as the night he had brought the money for her trip to India hours later than planned. Okay, now he was a few weeks late . . . but, surely, she realized he had to move when it felt right.

At the door of the building, he stopped, poised on a precipice, teetering.

Should I accept this as a sign—just go home and square things with Kathy? All I have to do is walk away and never see Lisa again.

But he'd come halfway around the world and could almost hear Bob chuckling. The possibility of Bob's laughter decided him, and stepping through the door, he looked for the office.

"Excuse me," Christian said quietly, watching Krishna sort papers. "I'm looking for Padmananda."

"I'm sorry," Krishna answered in an equally gentle voice. "He's out of town. Is there anything I can do for you? Would you like to know something of the programs here?"

"Yes," Christian nodded, thinking that perhaps it might not be a bad idea to understand where Lisa was coming from. "But my business is really with Padmananda. When will he be back?"

"In a week or so. He just left this morning."

"I see."

Suddenly, Christian lowered his gaze, shocked. The man behind the desk was the same man he'd confronted in Santa Monica, the one who had always been extremely reluctant to allow him access to Lisa. If he was recognized before he knew where Lisa had gone, he'd never find her.

"Is he attending some program?" Christian asked humbly.

"In Varanasi," Krishna answered. "There's a medical conference connected with Benares Hindu University on public health care."

"Do you know where he's staying?"

"Why, yes . . . at the Mahabharata. A small hotel near the university. But it's a long way to Varanasi. Take lodging with us for the week."

Christian let out a slow breath. "I can't." He looked up at the man now. "I'm going back to the States soon."

"Where are you from?"

"Northern California. Berkeley."

Krishna squinted his eyes, as if beginning to remember. "Say . . . wait a minute . . . ," he mumbled, reaching within his memory to put pieces together. "Aren't you the one who demanded to see Kali in Santa Monica?" he asked incredulously. "You've cut your hair. You used to have a beard . . . "

"The same." Christian could not help but grin at the shock on his face. "Never thought you'd remember me."

"You're . . . you're really here for Kali, aren't you?"

"Not exactly here for her, just here to see her. Whatever she decides to do after that's her own business."

"Does she know you're coming?"

"Yes. But I'm late. I had a few problems."

"It seems that you're always late and always with problems."

"Actually, if you want to know the truth, she invited me."

"When?"

Christian hesitated. What would it matter? "During the summer," he answered.

"Ah." Krishna's body relaxed, his lips almost smiled. "That was some months ago."

Christian became wary. "What do you mean, 'some months ago'?"

"Look, why don't you give her a break and disappear. She has a chance to be happy. To do a lot of good for people."

The man was trying to separate him from Lisa once again, blocking the way, just as he had in Santa Monica. Why couldn't he let Lisa make her own decisions? Irritated, his voice rose. "I'm not going to take away her happiness or her goodness."

"She's gone, don't you see?" Krishna held out his hands, palms up, as if the answer might be written on them.

"I know she's gone."

"I mean . . . gone from you."

"What are you trying to say?" Christian demanded, angry now, his eyes hot on Krishna's face. "What makes you think you can speak for her?"

"Just disappear and leave her alone."

Suddenly, Christian's English public school accent returned. Using all the snobbery and elitism he had learned early at boarding school, he shook his head and said, "Not on your life, old man. Whatever the story is, I want to hear it from Lisa herself."

"You're going to ask her to leave the ashram with you!" Krishna cried. "Don't you ever think about anyone but yourself?"

The words stung. Christian believed he spent a great deal of time thinking about other people. He turned to leave without answering.

"Don't you see?" Krishna called after him. "She's with Padmananda."

"So you've said."

"I mean . . . *with* him. I . . . ," and Krishna faltered. "I think she's going to marry him."

"We'll see about that," Christian called over his shoulder.

"Who are you, anyway?"

Christian stopped, turned, and faced him. "My name's Christian Brooks. Thanks again."

Then he turned on his heel, walked through the gardens to the large wooden gate, and off the ashram grounds. His steps took him quickly down the alley, toward the main street. "Hotel Imperial," he sharply commanded a motorized rickshaw driver.

Sitting on the badly patched seat, he took a deep breath.

What's happening to me? he asked himself, rubbing his hands over his eyes. *Why'd I put out that kind of energy at the ashram? It's time to trip. I've got to get in touch with myself.*

A wind whipped through the open cab, and he shifted uneasily on the seat. An ominous feeling had settled over him that had nothing directly to do with Lisa. The feeling had been triggered when he'd given his real identity to Krishna. A picture was starting to form, but he couldn't capture it.

"You're back early," Bob said, looking up from the book he was reading. "Wouldn't she see you?"

"She wasn't there," Christian told him, sitting down in a chair.

"Yeah? Are you going back later?"

Christian was far away, distracted, trying to isolate the reason for his foreboding.

"Christian," Bob called.

"Huh?"

"Lisa. Are you going back later?"

"No," Christian said, his mind still preoccupied. "She's gone for a week. She went to Varanasi with one of her master's disciples."

Bob's expression was sympathetic. "You look spaced. Is everything alright?"

"No," Christian answered, standing up and beginning to pace, a routine that was becoming too frequent.

Bob glanced over at Dharma, and Christian felt them both watching him intently.

"Something's wrong," Christian told them both. "I can feel it."

"Alright," Dharma said slowly, channeling his own energy into Christian. "Let's put it all together. Is it Lisa?"

"She's part of my distraction. I guess I should have gone to see her when we first arrived. She's uptight. She went to Varanasi to spite me. But there's something else."

"Afghanistan?"

Christian nodded and sat down. "Can you remember our conversation with that guy—the Interpol agent, or whatever he was? Think back . . . both of you . . . go over every detail."

"We gave him money and passports," Bob said. "Not so strange in itself. Travelers do that for each other."

Christian closed his eyes. "A lot of money. Which says to him we're high rollin'."

"We looked at clothing. Did we talk about our old ladies?" Dharma asked.

"I'm not sure," Bob answered. "Maybe. We talked about rugs."

"Packing the car."

"Yes," Christian nodded, his eyes still closed. "He has names and passport numbers. He knows we have money and a vehicle. He made overt suggestions about smuggling hash. He knows our business. And something else . . . " Christian was silent for a moment, then opened his eyes. "Knowing we had a car and a load, he would have wanted to know where we were driving."

"He didn't ask," Dharma mused quietly, trying to remember.

Then it came to Christian. Everything fell into place. His body fell back into the sofa, weak. "He didn't have to," Christian answered. "We told him. Bombay Harbor."

"Jesus," Bob almost whispered. "You're right. I told him."

"We all gave him information." Christian's voice held a touch of incredulity. "Pretty smart dude. He isolated us, played each of us for our weaknesses. Me first, talking about Berkeley. I told him where I lived. Can you believe that?" He stood up, appalled, not believing it himself. "I should have known. I should have known," he mumbled. "He was hard. His voice was hard. We weren't thinking clearly. God, we were too spaced, acting like we were on the island."

Bob and Dharma stared in blank shock, stunned at the evidence of their carelessness. Christian resumed his restless pacing.

"Well," Dharma asked into the silence, "what now?"

"We have to find a new way home," Bob said disgustedly.

Dharma nodded. "Instead of going through the shipping lines, we're going to have to drive the car back to Greece."

Christian shook his head. "I don't like the idea of smuggling through Iran. The prospect of life imprisonment makes me more than a little nervous."

"We made it this far without being hassled; we can make it back again," Dharma assured them.

"It's going to add weeks to the trip," Bob warned. "The old ladies are gonna love that."

"True, but what other choice do we have if we're using a Greek vacation as a cover?"

"Alright," Christian finally answered, committing to the drive. "How long will it take to get the truck ready for the trip back?"

"Couple of days—three, four. What do you want to do about Lisa, Christian?"

"I'm going to Varanasi to talk with her. After that, we'll see."

"Look, it's okay if you don't drive back with us," Dharma told him. "If you really need to stay and get your life settled."

"Take three days," Bob added. "If you're not back by Monday at noon, we leave without you. I promised Julie . . . "

"I know. Six weeks."

"If you're not here on Monday," Dharma laughed, "we'll know you're in the middle of an outrageous affair."

"You sure about this, Christian?" Bob asked, suddenly serious. "Look what happened last time you were late, and that time, you were only a couple of hours off. You sure you want to get involved with a woman who's going to have you punch a time clock?"

"I'll know when I see her. It's something I have to finish. Once and for all." Christian picked up his jacket. "I'm going over to get my ticket from Rahool. And I think I'll give Allen a call from the travel office, let everyone know we're in New Delhi but behind schedule. Alan can call Keith about the change of plans. Let me have a few tokes off that pipe before I go."

KALI, CHRISTIAN, AND PADMANANDA
VARANASI, INDIA
NOVEMBER 1969

Darkness held the city as the taxi bumped against the rough brick streets, carrying Padmananda and Kali toward the Ganges. From the window of the taxi, Kali watched as the world still slept. Only when they began to approach the river, did people begin to stir, to quietly move about the streets, build a fire for warmth and food. Overwhelmed by a sense of human frailty in this time just before dawn, she settled closer to Padmananda and unconsciously placed her hand on his leg.

At the temple, hundreds of pilgrims gathered, the majority having saved for a lifetime for the privilege of making this *puja*, their joyous chants and singing heard far along the river. Padmananda summoned one of the disciples he knew well. "Take Kali to the boats," he said quietly to the man.

"But why, Padmananda?" Kali whispered urgently. "I want to bathe in the water with the others."

"Kali, take the boat this morning. Afterward, if you still feel you wish to bathe, do so with the Master's blessing."

"But these others . . . ," she began stubbornly.

"These others are different," he replied firmly. "Go to the boat first."

Sighing, she turned and followed the disciple down a narrow street to the *ghat*. As they drew near the river, people moved in the half-lit streets, their subdued voices calling through the night in the hushed, reverent tones of people preparing for ablution. Many of the beggars still lay asleep on the hard stone, an arm for a pillow, but others were already awake, waiting in orderly lines, ready to hold up their begging bowls.

Shame filled her. "The luxury of my hotel room," she murmured to herself. "The privacy . . . "

Memory tapped her shoulder, took a dream-like form, and she floated back to a time of whirling patterns. The notes of "White Rabbit" and Grace Slick's voice crept in one ear, filled her head, and crawled out the other. Color and sound fell across her body in tiny showers.

All I'll ever need, she had told herself as she lay giggling with Matt and Christian, *is air to breathe, food to eat, water to drink, and a space to lie comfortably. That's all anyone ever needs. Except friends*, she had thought, looking toward Matt and Christian. *Except love.*

She shuddered. What would it be like to live out that meager reality, trapped within it day after day? Generation after generation.

At the top of the stairs that descended to the river, the disciple stopped at a moneychanger sitting behind a low table. Before him, on a printed cloth, were dozens of stacks of five-*paise* pieces arranged in neat stacks. An invisible current passed through the line of beggars as they watched the transaction of a number of rupees. The disciple handed Kali a handful of coins. "It brings good karma to give *baksheesh* in the holy city."

"I'm supposed to have nothing, and yet I have so much," she murmured, staring down at the *paise* in her hands.

"Accept this as an act of humility," the older disciple told her quietly. "Accept the fact that *Brahma* works through you."

Walking down the steps slowly, Kali was careful to hit each of the raised bowls, listening to the jumble of soft words from the crouched figures as she did. The several stacks of *paise* in her hands would never be enough for every beggar on the *ghat*. She looked forlornly at the disciple as the coins evaporated quickly from her palms.

"You reach those you can. The others are destined to touch someone else," he told her. "Come. The boats are there."

Looking out toward the darkness, Kali knew that the river lay flowing like the sounds around her, smooth and solemn. A cold breeze blew off the water. She untied the scarf from around her neck and brought it up over her head. Small groups of Westerners arrived with guides, and even the haggling for boats, the words falling heavy and muted against the water and its thin, floating haze, did not disturb the intensity of the stillness.

At the boat, a small boy approached with a tiny candle in the center of a floating lotus. "Make an offering," the boy said, "make an offering." The light pierced the darkness. Behind him, another man approached, carrying leis of marigolds. "Make an offering, madam."

For the first time, in the dim light of a single exposed electric bulb, Kali saw the debris and gray-white foam spread near the shoreline. The disciple held out a hand to help her into the boat, and once seated, she found herself carried away from shore.

"There," the disciple pointed to lights on the shore. "The temple where Padmananda leads prayers. Soon, pilgrims will leave the building and come to the river to bathe."

Kali had no words. Instead, she was locked in private awe as she turned to the east, away from the city. Stars still sparkled. When would the first signs of the sun's rising appear?

Without warning, the thinnest of ruby threads began to stretch above the horizon, a glowing spider web that would not hold its form but continued to grow more complex, strength and thickness added in layer over layer in a deep crimson. Saying a silent prayer, she released the candle onto the inky surface of the water, its tiny beacon glowing in the night. Another whispered prayer, and the marigold lei fell to the river, floating downstream, as silently as the boat.

Like an anxious audience waiting expectantly for the second act of a play that has caught each of the senses, Kali turned back to the changing horizon. The far shore began to take shape, flat and dark against rose-colored water. One by one, the stars disappeared. The softness of pinks and violets vanished as the tip of the sun burst above the horizon, strong and piercing. A golden, ethereal light touched the earth, settling over all who witnessed the day giving birth to itself. Kali felt her heart soar in hope and purpose. Surely, humans must have been created to experience such beauty. Could there ever be any wonder why this was the sacred river and this place the holy city? The boat turned and headed upriver. Kali settled back, smiling in perfect peace.

Yet with the sun, things that the darkness had hidden became visible. The smile froze on her face as a wrapped body floated by some three feet away. On a sandy bank, a man worked alone, slowly trying to push the sacred flesh and bones of a bloated cow into the water, its stiff limbs sticking up toward the sky. Tiny bundles drifted by, once, twice—the bodies of babies, not uncommon in a land where infant mortality was high. As the boat drew closer to the shoreline, her eyes were drawn to a *ghat* and the flames of a cremation fire.

Along the shore, men gathered, squatting along the steps decending into the water to defecate, then stepping into the river to wash, dunking their heads, drinking, and cleansing their mouths and nostrils. Women joined with each other at a distance from the men, their sagging breasts peeking for just a moment from beneath their saris as they washed themselves and their laughing children. Atop a large, round boulder, a man stood in a white robe, his long hair streaked with wide bands of gray, both arms outstretched in prayer, a wooden staff held in one hand. A flute seller piped out a sweet and soulful melody of awakening. Dogs yelped at the river's edge. Birds floated softly down to the surface of the water, searching for fish. Showers of rose-tinted drops lapped at the sides of the boat.

Kali's smile returned.

I have reached for India's heart, she thought, *but this morning, I have touched its soul. As surely as I've witnessed death, I've witnessed rebirth and life. People are born and must die. What better way to meet death than openly, here, in the hope that dawn renews.*

"Are you ready to take the boat in?" the disciple asked.

Kali's eyes glowed with the happiness that comes from understanding the purpose of a gift, and nodding, said, "Yes. I'm ready for anything."

Shortly after nine in the morning, Christian's plane arrived in Varanasi. Dharma had told him of a guesthouse near the river, and after a brief stop to register and deposit his pack, he took a taxi to the Mahabharata Hotel, his eyes blindly passing over the streets while he considered what he was about to do. Lisa would be a different person now from the one he'd once known. A year had a way of altering people. India and living with a master were no small events. Yet he believed—had to believe—that what they felt each time they were together was real and unchangeable.

Paying the taxi driver, he took the steps up to the lobby door and nodded to the doorman. At the hotel desk, he approached the immaculate man standing behind it.

"Excuse me, sir. May I have a moment?" Christian asked.

The man cleared his throat slightly, elegantly, and picked a piece of lint from his three-piece suit. "As you wish, sir."

"I'm looking for a group from Delhi. From the Ananda Shiva Ashram."

"Ah, yes. The disciple and his initiates."

"There's a woman with them . . . blonde . . . "

The desk clerk understood immediately. "Yes, sir?"

"Can you give me the lady's room number?"

The man hesitated. Christian produced a ten-dollar bill. "Is she in?"

"Yes," the man nodded. "Room 241."

"And the disciple?" Christian asked.

"He left some twenty minutes ago."

"Thank you." Christian laid the money on the desk.

"The elevator is to the left . . . sir."

Comfortable on the floor, Kali had easily slipped into her mantra and was far away when she first heard the knock. Hadn't she asked not to be disturbed? Wasn't there a sign hanging from the doorknob? But the knock was gently insistent, and she wondered if it might be Padmananda. Perhaps he needed something last minute for his meeting. She stood, opened the door, and froze.

"Hello, Lisa," Christian said softly.

Kali's heart leapt, fluttering wildly. "Christian," she whispered out of a dry throat. "How did you find me?"

"At the ashram in New Delhi. They told me where you were staying."

Her legs were limp, and her heart continued its wild pounding. She was so painfully glad to see him that she had to force herself not to throw her arms around him. Instead, she asked, "Where have you been for the last month?"

"I got hung up." His grin grew broader. "You're staring."

"You've cut your hair."

"As short as I dared. May I come in?"

She hesitated. "I don't think that's a good idea."

"I've come a long way to see you. If we stand out here in the hallway to talk, the entire hotel will know our conversation before I walk down those stairs. Just for a moment. Please."

"Just . . . just for a moment."

Christian took a couple of broad steps into the room. "I'm sorry. I saw your sign. But what was I to do?"

"Christian, what happened?" she asked, closing the door. "Why are you just getting here?"

"We had car trouble. All in all, it took a little longer than we figured."

"We?"

"I'm here with Bob and Dharma."

Kali fought to keep the disappointment from being obvious on her face. So. He *had* come for business and she *was* a stopover, just as she'd feared. "Then what are you doing here in Varanasi? Is this part of your scheduled trip?"

"No. I'm here because you invited me. But you weren't at the ashram."

"I was in Delhi until yesterday. I can't spend my life waiting for you to show up."

He glanced around easily, then turned the full weight of his eyes on hers. "How are things with you and Padmananda?"

"They are . . . fine."

"So I've heard."

"What have you heard?" she asked with some alarm.

"Have you decided to marry him?"

How could he know?

"I wish you could know him."

"I haven't met him, but I think I do know him. As for love, I saw your feelings when you opened the door and saw me."

"Oh, Christian!" And in spite of herself, she laughed. "Love is more than what you see in my face. I invited you with all my heart to come and understand the teachings of the Master. I wanted you to feel the peace of the ashram, to understand a love deep enough to transcend all earthly matters. I thought that, perhaps, I could help with whatever it is you're holding inside."

Christian crossed to where she stood and pulled her against him. "God, do you know how long it's been since I've seen you laugh? You're so beautiful when your eyes sparkle." Before she could protest, completely surprised at his audacity, he kissed her softly on the lips, his mouth open, sharing her breath, feeling the warmth of her body, and looking into the eagerness of her surprised eyes.

Shakily, she moved away. "I . . . I think you'd better go."

"Not without you, I'm not."

"What's that supposed to mean?" she asked uncertainly, a seed of defiance beginning to sprout.

"I haven't come all this way to see you for five minutes. At least have lunch with me."

"I can't. It's no use. I just can't. I'm sorry you've come so far. I had so many things I wanted to tell you . . . share with you . . . but we're back to the same old thing."

"Don't you know why?"

"It's more complicated than . . . than what you see in my eyes. Please try and understand."

"Alright," his voice grew serious. "Have lunch with me, and I'll listen. I mean *really* listen. I do want to know about the last year. Please? Will you come?"

She turned away, considering. If they got out of this room to a public place, she could talk to him and keep him at an arm's length. In a restaurant, there would have to be less passion. "If I go, I have to be back at four."

"Four it is."

"I . . . uh . . . I don't have any money."

"I think I can handle it." Christian held open the door.

She stared at the empty hallway. There was nothing left to do but pick up her shawl and walk through the door.

Padmananda was still feeling fortunate to have had the meeting postponed for two hours. Taking Kali to lunch would give them some time together, and he'd promised to show her something of the city. As the taxi pulled into the driveway of the Mahabharata Hotel, he reached into his pocket, pulled out a handful of rupees, and was in the process of counting them when he glanced up to see Kali walk from the hotel, her gold hair ablaze in the midday sun, wearing jeans and an embroidered blouse, a shawl thrown casually over her arm, and behind her—Christian! Christian, almost exactly as he had once been, before the long hair and beard. Together, they looked young, happy, eternal.

Time froze for the longest moment in his life. The smile on his face died, and he sat rooted to the spot, void of all thought, his mind empty for a long, suspended, unbelieving instant.

So that's it, he thought slowly. *Christian. Christian Brooks here in Varanasi. Kali's distraction all these weeks. Dear God, of all people, why did it have to be Christian? And returned to India! Could one woman bring him halfway around the world? Somehow, I don't think so. Like me, he's too much involved in the responsibilities of life. And knowing, most certainly, what Christian's business is, I can guess his purpose. But how has he found her?*

Only one explanation was possible. Kali had somehow given him her plans.

For a few minutes, he allowed himself a feeling he had long ago resolved never to permit. His startled jealousy was allowed to slowly slip into an emotion very close to hatred. First, Christian had taken his father and his ideology from him, and now he sought the woman who held his heart.

I made a fatal mistake in not telling Kali exactly who left my father to the crowd. If I had, would she still be there smiling up at him?

"I'm . . . I'm sorry," Padmananda told the cab driver. "I no longer need to be here. Take me to the Krishna Temple by the river. There is a house nearby I need to visit."

Christian and Kali took a taxi to a small restaurant that Dharma had recommended near Benares Hindu University. As they waited for the food—a meal of naan, dal, egg and green pea curry, rice, and sweet lassis—Kali told Christian of her first meeting with the Master, of his aura and warmth. Several times, he brought her to laughter with stories of India and his travels, stories to which she could already well relate. He listened quietly, respectfully, made careful attempts to keep the conversation light.

At least until the meal was over.

"What time do you have to be back?" Christian asked.

She looked at him sharply. "Four o'clock. Or maybe a little before. I should be there when Padmananda returns."

"What does Padmananda know about me?"

Kali looked down into her lap. "He knows you gave me the money to come here. I simply told him I had once done you a favor."

"Does he know how I got the money?"

At that moment, she was sorry she had ever told Christian where he could contact Bob on that morning years ago at the Santa Monica ashram. But the journey he'd made from Berkeley had been far, and he'd looked so desperate . . .

She lifted her eyes to him. "I told him you were a dealer. Perhaps he's drawn his own conclusions. Don't worry. I don't think Padmananda's concerned about what you do for a living."

"Did you tell him you cared about me?"

"Christian, do we have to talk about this?"

Christian laughed. "Lisa, it's my guess that he's loved you from the first moment he saw you. Most men must feel that way about you. Look at Matt . . . or Bob . . . Dharma . . . "

Kali's face paled, aghast. Had Dharma mentioned the secret they held?

She closed her eyes against the truth in Christian's face, disgusted by the emotion the memory brought back.

"Bob was with Julie that night," she told Christian miserably, still a jealous edge in her voice. "He knew that I knew, but he went to her anyway. Dharma was . . . a comfort."

"But it didn't make you happy."

"No," she told him honestly, beginning to feel better with her answer. Suddenly, she knew exactly how to handle Christian—with absolute honesty.

"That was the push . . . but not the reason. I had been thinking about the ashram and the Master for many months. Try to understand . . . the Master's love is different from the love of an ordinary man."

"Is Padmananda an ordinary man?"

"He's special. You see. . . ." She took a deep breath and plunged. "I did speak with him about you before I left California. I couldn't understand why I was so distracted by you, why I wanted you. Why I was

jealous of the other women in your life, even of your business. I would
be so sure I'd gotten you out of my system, then I'd see you—begin to
dream of you—and all my hard work to control my emotions became
meaningless."

"Don't you think we should explore the passion that flares between
us when we're together?"

She thought of his arms around her, his mouth against hers, and
sighed. "Yes, there is passion. But there's more to love than physical
attraction." She tried to explain, "I'm also attracted to Padmananda.
If you'd meet him, I think you'd like him. But there's a difference
between the two of you. He sees a part of me you've never seen, still
don't see. Are you willing to put dealing aside? Meet the Master? Give
up drugs?"

"Sacraments," he answered. "Sacraments that teach people to trust
in themselves and take responsibility for their own actions. Surely, you
remember? LSD aligns us to a simple logic that stems from deep truth.
For the first time, religion's not just intellectual ideology, but ideas that
are intensely felt and understood.

"Look," he reasoned, "we're older now. We know which drugs are
teachers and which are destructive. I have enough money to do anything we want to do. If you come back with me, you can still be part of
the Berkeley ashram, continue your practice there."

"And what would you do?"

"I've got an acid lab going . . . "

"Christian!" she held up a hand. "I don't want to know! I don't
want that responsibility!" she cried. "I know it's a symbol of your trust.
But . . . please. Maybe if you knew the Master, you'd think differently."

"Is he anything like his disciple?" Christian asked in a voice tinged
with sarcasm.

"No one's like the Master," she answered, becoming angry.

Christian sighed. "Just let me know that you understand this
much. I'm offering you the same thing I've always offered you. Love.
And the freedom to be anything you want to be."

"I do understand." And she did believe him. But she also knew it was truly over between them. He would never give up his work for her.

After lunch, they had begun to walk, Christian explaining the things they passed—the shops and different jobs, the classes of people, the fabric of Indian society laid out before them. Now, they sat in the small showroom of a silk factory he'd insisted they tour, looking at bolts of the world's finest silks. A beautiful green sari of shot silk edged in gold caught her eye. Christian watched as she lovingly ran her hand over the fabric.

"This green one," Christian was quick to move, "you must have it. It matches your eyes." He held the fabric to her face, and she laughed.

"Do you think so? This is something for special occasions. What I need is a practical sari. Oh, Christian, I don't know."

"Well, I do. This green silk is the exact color of your eyes. No one could ever duplicate this if they tried."

Kali touched the material as she knelt on the padded mat of the showroom floor, turning it over and over in her hands. Shot silk, hand-woven, one thread at a time, first green, then gold. Each time she moved, each time the silk shifted, the light played on it. He was right. The green matched her eyes perfectly, the gold resembling the tiny flecks of gold within her own iris. The fabric was elusive, without a single color, a perfect representation of life.

"Madam," the silk merchant volunteered, "the gentleman is correct. The color is perfect for you. Come, madam. Try the sari on."

Standing, she began to wrap and fold the sari around her waist, making the graceful pleats in front that fell to the floor. Taking the remainder of the material, she pulled it up and over her shoulder, leaving a long portion to fall down her back. In the mirror's reflection, the green was cool and refreshing, reminding her of a spring forest floor shaded from the brilliance of sunlight, yet when she turned, it was as if the trees were parted by a breeze, allowing flashes of glittering, luminous sun spots to glow for a moment.

"It *is* gorgeous," she murmured.

Entranced with the dazzling fabrics in the room, she could not believe the price the man quoted for the garment in her hands. All the work, labor, and love that had created this precious hand-woven sari was being sold for pennies. But even that small amount was more pennies than she had. If she were to have this sari, it would be Christian who purchased it for her.

"We'll take it," Christian told the man, pulling rupees from his pocket. "A blouse to go with it?"

"It would have to be made, sir. But that is no problem. We'll take the measurements and have it done in a couple of hours."

"I'm sorry. I just don't have the time. Not even for the measurements, much less the whole blouse. I have to be back at four."

"Don't worry. We'll only be a few minutes late." Then, turning to the salesman, Christian said, "Take the measurements. I'll pick the blouse up this evening."

"But . . . ," Kali began to interrupt.

He held up a hand. "I want you to have it, Lisa. It's yours. It could never do anyone else justice. I'll bring the blouse by in the morning."

"Christian, I'm going to a special *puja* at the river in the morning. And honestly, I don't think it's a good idea for you to be seen coming to my room."

"Alright then. Come to my hotel. Tomorrow after *puja* is finished. I'll write the address for you. Just take a cab," he insisted. "You don't have to stay long. I'll be packing."

"You're really leaving?"

"Early the next day. We're driving back to Europe."

After he leaves, it truly will be over, she thought, turning to follow the woman who would take her measurements.

Suddenly, she wanted to weep.

From the hotel window, Padmananda watched as Kali stepped from the taxi, slammed the door, and leaned back to say good-bye to Christian.

Quickly, she ran up the stairs, lost a sandal, and hurried back to retrieve it.

Padmananda had spent the afternoon in meditation. But even in meditation, scenes of Kali and Christian together invaded his peace, ugly doubts about Kali's honesty, a renewal of the old questions about Christian's implication in the death of his father. He waited, giving her time to collect herself, then went up the stairs to her room and knocked on the door.

"Padmananda!" she cried, flustered, braiding wet hair from a shower she'd taken. "The papers . . . for the hospital fund. I'll get them."

"May I come in?"

She looked at him, startled by his intensity. She might never have moved if he had not shuffled his feet to show his impatience. "Yes . . . yes . . . come in."

Padmananda had never minced words with her, and he wasn't about to start now. "Will you tell me where you went this afternoon?"

Her face reddened. "How did you know I'd gone out?"

"I know something's been troubling you. Will you speak with me about it?"

She took a deep, wistful breath and then nodded. "Yes. Christian came here today. We do need to talk."

"How did he find you?"

"He said they told him at the ashram where we'd gone."

"The ashram? You were expecting him?"

"I received a cable from him not long ago. He mentioned that he was coming to India and would stop to see me. I waited, but . . . "

"But he didn't come until after we'd left."

Kali nodded.

"Why didn't you tell me he was coming?"

"I tried. But I never found the words. After all the things I told you about my feelings for him, and then after Agra . . . " She shook her head, flustered. "The truth is, I'm confused. He's so . . . distracting. He keeps insisting on what's best for me. He's so sure of himself . . . "

Padmananda almost smiled. "He must care a great deal for you if you asked him to come to India and he came."

"It wasn't only for me," she answered in a low voice. "He's leaving the day after tomorrow."

"So he will not see Daya Nanda."

"No." Her voice reflected her disappointment. "He's driving back to Europe with two other old friends from Laguna Beach."

"And you, Kali? What are you going to do? Are you tempted to go with him?"

Her eyes widened, until finally, she answered, "Yes. Tempted." But then she shook her head and smiled ruefully. "I'm going to see him tomorrow after *puja*. To say good-bye." Then with certainty, and clearly choosing her future, added, "I won't ever be seeing him again. I'm only sorry he's come this far and has no inkling of what the ashram is about. He'll never really know Daya Nanda."

"Perhaps there's still a way for the Master to reach him."

"Don't you think you could talk to him?"

Padmananda laughed. "Under the circumstances, that meeting might be awkward. No, I'd rather give him the Master's books. Will you take them to him? Will you tell him the books are from me?"

"Of course I will."

On the following morning, as the taxi bounced along the narrow brick street, honking its horn, Kali was still uncertain whether she was doing the right thing in visiting Christian, even to say good-bye. How had so much gotten out of hand? The peace and solace of the ashram, of her meditations, of the meritorious life she tried to live, was gone.

But there was something more. Something still bothered her about her conversation yesterday afternoon with Padmananda. His questions had been just as pointed as Christian's. The unsettling thought kept occurring to her that the men were pulling her between them.

"This is the place, madam," the driver informed her.

Kali looked from the window at the old building, still wondering if she was doing the right thing. Deciding, taking a deep breath, she opened the door of the cab, stepped out, and paid the fare. She had already turned away when she remembered the small briefcase Padmananda had given her with readings on the ashram and the teachings.

"Wait!" she cried at the driver and rushed over to retrieve the case.

Inside the gate of the rooming house, a woman sat on the steps, picking peas from their green pods. Kali gave her a hesitant smile, passed through an ancient door, and climbed a flight of stairs looking for the number of the room Christian had written down. For the first time in many years, she was alone. While she anxiously wandered through the darkened hallway, she reminded herself that she was a person who saw life as an adventure. Someone who made her own decisions. Who had come and gone at will, hitched around California, met new people. She wasn't afraid. She could do this.

But never in their entire relationship had Christian ever been on time. Why would she expect him to be here now?

She knocked.

At last, she heard footsteps. The door opened, flooding the hallway with natural light.

"Hi," Christian said casually. "You made it."

The room was full of sunlight from the tall windows that faced the River Ganges. Kali stepped inside and placed the briefcase near the door. Immediately, she compared the austerity of this old building with the luxury of her hotel. Embarrassed once again at her privilege, she walked toward the large, wood-framed window and watched the flow of the river not far in the distance, stretching its way through the crowded city, brown and uninteresting in the glare of mid-day.

"This room is almost like my room at the ashram," she told him, still watching the water.

He smiled and hooked his thumbs into the pockets of his jeans. "I guess I still have yearnings to be a monk."

"A monk?" she asked, turning around to see if he was serious. "What kind of monk?"

"Once, a long time ago, I'd thought of becoming a Buddhist monk."

"What stopped you? Sex and drugs?"

Christian reached for the only chair in the room and offered it to her with a gesture of his hand. "No." He took a seat on the bed. "My teacher was killed."

Kali's face fell, mortified. She brought her hand to her mouth. "Oh, Christian, I am so sorry."

"You didn't know. And sometimes I bring out the worst in you on purpose. Just so you'll remember you're human and not always a goddess. Kali." He picked up a brown bag next to him on the bed and passed it to her. "Here's that blouse and the sari. They included a slip. You should make sure it fits."

"Christian, I *am* sorry. It's just . . . I mean . . ."

"Open the bag," he said.

At first hesitating, she looked at the bag in her hands, saw what was inside, and lifted up the simple blouse. "This is beautiful," she said softy. "The color is perfect. You'd . . . you'd like to see it on me?"

"Very much. The bathroom's that way. While you're changing, I'll go downstairs and bring up tea."

"No room service?" She smiled. "Why *did* you choose the old part of town?"

"Because it's close to the river. I can walk there in the morning to meditate."

"I didn't know you still meditated."

"Come with me to Greece, and I'll tell you the story of my life."

Kali pulled the length of sari from the bag, ignoring the question.

"Not interested? That's alright. I'll get the tea."

But, in fact, she was interested. This confusion of spiritual values—how could he meditate, perform right action, and yet not care to meet the Master? What *was* his story?

In the bathroom, she unzipped the back of the blouse, pulled it over her head, and struggled to zip it up again. Then she wrapped the long length of green silk about her waist, tucking it into the slip, and threw the last length of the fabric over her shoulder. In the mirror, she regarded her face, the green of her eyes suddenly all important. Even braided, her hair was as gold as the gold thread. Smiling, she smoothed the fabric with her hand and felt the silk slide against her skin as she moved. Christian was going to like this.

In the outer room, he was just setting down a tray when she emerged. Feeling more than a little self-conscious, she turned around slowly. "What do you think?" she laughed.

The light in his eyes became blue fire. "I think you're the most beautiful woman I've ever seen." He took a deep breath and reached for the teapot. "Well, one of them, anyway. Tea? I was lucky. Water was already boiled."

"One of them, Christian?"

"Well, you know," he merely grinned while pouring tea into cups. "By the way, you missed a hell of a party. Woodstock Music Festival."

She accepted a cup from him and sat back down on the chair. "I read about it."

Christian leaned back against a pillow on the bed, sipping at his cup, telling her about the music, the Hog Farm, the acid, the storm, the laughter still in his eyes. She laughed with him, comfortable, just as they had in the Berkeley apartment when they'd first met. But then, no matter how much time passed, being with Christian was always as if she'd seen him just yesterday. Even when they argued, they never ran out of things to say to each other.

"When are you leaving?" she finally asked.

"Tomorrow. I have an 8:00 a.m. flight to New Delhi."

"You meant it, didn't you? You really don't have much time."

"Only until tomorrow morning. Have you decided whether you're coming with me?"

Kali stood and walked to the window, once again gazing at the river. "The Master insists on marriage." Casting him a teasing smile over her shoulder, she asked, "Are you proposing marriage?"

"Don't you know what marriage is?" he asked in return. "Marriage is wanting someone with every part of your soul so intensely that a fierce sort of joy fills you each time you make love . . . "

And Kali immediately knew there was someone in his life . . . or, at least, there had been someone. Someone who had taught him the meaning of love. That another woman had loved Christian during the last year filled her with an inexplicable longing.

I can't do this, she thought.

Standing, she placed the cup on the table next to the window. "I shouldn't have come."

Christian put down his own cup. "What do you feel? Right now?" he asked softly, seducing her with his voice. "Trust your feelings."

"I've given Padmananda my promise," she whispered.

"Yes, but you want me." He stood and slowly moved toward her.

"You only know my physical desire. Okay, I've always wanted you. But if I open myself to you and love you the way you want, I'll be making a commitment I won't be capable of reneging on."

"I would never ask you to. I would commit as well."

"And you're right. The nights do end, and then what?"

"I think I could fill your days."

"I'm not sure," she answered, turning away and once more looking from the window. "Your path is different from mine. Yours will land you in jail—or worse."

"Not if I'm careful. And I'm very careful."

"Do you realize what you're asking me to risk?" she cried, turning back to him. "I don't want to go to jail. And I don't want to put my life in the hands of someone who may end up there. Now you're asking me to drive halfway around the world with you . . . and Bob and Dharma—my God, what a pair—in a truck loaded with hash!"

"The truth," he told her just as forcefully, "is that I came to see whether you wanted to be my lady. Bob and Dharma had my money and their own contacts. I could have taken or left that bit of the trip. But the real reason is you, to see whether you're still afraid of the world outside the ashram."

"Afraid?" She thought of her fear in the darkened hallway just before she knocked on his door. Angry with herself, she cried, "What do you really know about me? Or what I've learned?"

He moved closer, afraid she would turn and run. "Lisa," he whispered. "Kali."

"You breeze into my life whenever you want, shake up my body with emotions I can well do without, then split." She stepped back from him, her voice still growing in intensity and volume. "You used to ask for my ideas, but you've changed. Telling me you're saving the world, when what you really love is money and adventure!" Her fists were clinched as if she was trying to hold to something. "You think you have all the answers?" Her voice was now a small roar, the beginning of rage. "Well, believe me, if you work very hard, you just might become worthy enough to be invited to hear the teachings of someone like the Master!"

He reached for her.

"No!" She pushed him away, starting to cry. "No, Christian! I'm so angry. Do you see what you've done? I am *never* angry—only with you!"

"Kali . . . don't . . . don't cry. Don't." Christian drew her slowly, soothingly toward him, holding her. He had never known what to do with crying women.

I should have tripped the other day when everything was crazy in my head, he thought. *Things would have become clear. What are the choices I've set up for her? To betray me, Padmananda, or her Master? What's she supposed to do? I've blown it. I've lost her.*

"Look," he wiped away her tears, "I was wrong. I'm leaving, stepping out of your life. I do love you. But I'll go and never return. Did you hear what I said?" he asked gently. "I said I was sorry." He stroked her hair as she sobbed on his shoulder. "Everything's alright. Go to Padmananda. I should have let you be. But once I was here and saw you . . . "

He kissed her forehead, still trying to hush her sobs, moving his lips across her face, tasting her tears.

"It'll be okay," he whispered. "Follow your path, your Master . . . "

Gently, he touched his lips to hers . . . and then . . . a shift. Her arms reached about his neck, her body pressed against his. Her face was beautifully distorted, a wellspring of tears and passion, her lips bright red, her mouth hungrily reaching for his.

When the yards of the sari lay at her feet and she'd stepped out of the new slip, when she'd reached her arms over her head to have him pull away the blouse, she looked as if she were a newly released bird ready to fly—tentative, excited, but doing what it was born to do. Christian lifted her gently and brought her to the bed. His hands slowly caressed her breasts, followed the outline of her hips, smoothed the sacred place between her legs, felt her hips rise to meet his fingers. His lips and teeth gently savored her neck, his tongue pulsed against her lips, his mouth tasted the hard nipple of her breast, his entire body hard and poised and considering the many different ways he could have her.

Kali's wet eyes looked deep into his while she undid the braid down her back. In the next instant, she was tugging at his belt, whispering in a raspy voice, "I've wanted you for so long."

Padmananda excused himself from the conference participants and went to the roof of the building overlooking the river. He sat down heavily, glad for the moment's respite. He had imagined that the day would be difficult, but he had not anticipated the strong sick feeling that filled his body.

Closing his eyes, he thought of Kali. She would have already paid her visit to Christian, and he refused to speculate on that meeting. All he knew was that, in a little while, it would be over. Christian would never again be a threat.

If it were so simple, then why was he despondent?

Searching for an answer, he finally knew with certainty that his anguish was beyond anything to do with Kali. Even with his eyes closed, he could not rid himself of the river's image, twisting and turning like his thoughts. And like the river, there was no stopping what he'd put into motion. He groaned aloud, a strange sound for a man so young, because it came from an old, old place.

Traveling inward, he began the rhythmical breathing, preparing himself for the recitation of the mantra. But instead of peace, he felt nausea and an anxiety approaching panic.

Then he was still.

As though breaking through a mist, he heard a voice. "This will destroy you." Daya Nanda's voice.

Rushed away in a whirlwind, Padmananda relived every second of the day he had first met Christian, each of the two children wide-eyed, trusting, immediately recognizing a kindred spirit in the other. Time sped through their years in the village, their boyhood ramblings, the help they gave to each other through heartache and sickness, the shared dreams on nights under stars and on lazy days beneath the aging tree near Ram Seva's home, their plans to bring more to the people of India. Their joint moments of spiritual awareness with Geshe-la and Daya Nanda, with Reverend Brooks and Ram Seva. Never once in all that time had Christian run from him or from responsibility. Why had he done so on the night of the riot?

A terrible doubt entered his mind. Had Christian run?

Fast, shifting visions took but a moment, but were a lifetime—the Master's death, his own followers, the son who would accept the teachings from him as he had accepted them from Daya Nanda and his lineage, the passing years to old age, his body slowing, a comfortable bed, a difficult breath, a last sigh, then, he was traveling toward the light . . .

"Nareesh," Daya Nanda's voice said gently.

Slowly, slowly, pulling himself back, Padmananda reentered his body. Almost as slowly, he opened his eyes to find that he still faced the water. For the first time, he truly understood what his father had tried to teach in his selfless act—each man was but a tile of an overwhelming mosaic, and that the highest act a man could achieve was charity—this was what made him important.

Where had he gone wrong? Why had he not understood that his

father's death was only a tiny act in the middle of a vast panoramic play, that Ram Seva had fulfilled his own role and his own karma?

"You cannot do this deed." Daya Nanda's voice again, with more certainty.

And Padmananda knew.

I love him. I love Christian more than myself. The pain I could not see past . . . I believed he had betrayed my love.

Abruptly, he stood. All he had set in motion had to be undone— and quickly. It was already late afternoon. Darkness would soon overtake the city. His feet took him to the stairs, then to the street, beginning his race toward the address Kali had given him.

Please don't let me be too late, he prayed.

Christian sat up on the edge of the bed and looked around for his jeans. One hand still held Lisa's leg. For hours, he had held her, touched her, been filled by her spirit. The sounds of her throat still resonated in that room, where they'd lost themselves in the intense passion that had seduced them for years.

"Christian," she laughed and nuzzled up to his ear. "What are you doing?"

"Looking for my pants."

"So that's it?" she grinned. "Are we finished?"

"I just want my pipe."

"Do you have to smoke around me?"

"Know where my pants are?"

"Look under that blanket. Over there."

As he leaned from the bed to pull at the leg of his jeans, his pockets emptied, everything scattering across the floor. "There's my pipe," he said, stretching to pick it up from where it had fallen. "Want some?"

"Christian, I don't want you to smoke around me."

"How about some tea? Are you hungry?"

"Starved."

"I'll go downstairs and see what the kitchen has. It'll just take a few minutes." He pulled on jeans and T-shirt, slipped on his sandals, kissed her hard, and went out the door. Kali could hear his footsteps on the stairs and smiled dreamily, floating in the almost forgotten rapture of love's aftermath. Pulling back her hair, she went to the bathroom to shower and dress. By the amount of light in the room, she gathered that it must be well into late afternoon. She was already brushing her hair by the time Christian arrived with a pot of tea and cold naan stuffed with vegetables.

"You're up!" he exclaimed.

"Look," she pointed to the window. "It's getting late."

"You're going back to the hotel?"

"Christian . . . you know I have to go back."

He set the tray down, and for the first time since he'd kissed her, remembered their conflict. "We didn't discuss it. You *are* going to leave with me tomorrow, aren't you?"

Gently, simply, she said, "I can't."

Stunned, he started to argue, stopped, then sat down on the bed.

"I still have time to spend with the Master," she explained quietly. "A couple of months before I return to California. That's important to me. You have to understand that I put him above myself. Can you? Can you understand that?"

He nodded slowly. "I think I'm beginning to."

"And I need to talk with Padmananda," she said softly. "I owe him some explanations."

"What are you going to tell him?"

"The truth. Everything. I believe you're right. I don't think he'll want to marry a woman who feels about another man the way I feel about you."

"If you won't drive back with me, what happens when you get back to California?"

Her voice changed, became certain. "I'm not driving around the world with a truckload of hash. I'm not doing drugs. And now it's your turn to think. If you want me, you're going to have to choose a new career."

Christian eyed her warily, poured milk and tea, and passed her a hot cup. He didn't like the ultimatum. After all, he had not insisted that she give up her spiritual practices or the ashram. He had even suggested the ashram in Berkeley to further her practice. Why should he give up his beliefs?

"We took so much for ourselves this afternoon," she said, coming to sit next to him on the bed, wrapped in the sari, leaning her head on his shoulder. "It's almost frightening. What will we have to give back? How will I tell Padmananda? He's had such a hard life already. And I . . . I was supposed to make it a little easier. Many of the things he's loved have already been taken from him. Now he'll lose another."

"I don't think he'd want your pity."

"I would never pity him, only give him my respect. He's a good man, Christian. Even when he knew I was coming here, he sent books for you on the Master's teachings. Over there. In that briefcase."

Gently, he touched her face. "I promise you I'll read them. And when you come back to California, we'll both know more about what we want from each other." He studied the softness in her eyes, a tenderness that spoke of love, of concern and wistfulness. "Come," he said. "Turn around. I'll brush your hair and braid it. Then I'll take you back to the hotel."

"Who taught you to braid hair?"

Sidestepping the answer that would bring him to Kathy, he asked, "Have you seen Srinagar? Or the beaches of Goa? Sri Lanka? The Taj? There are so many beautiful things to see in this part of the world."

"I saw the Taj with Padmananda. There was a full moon."

"Was it romantic?"

"Very."

"You slept with him?"

"Really, Christian? Of course not! There's more to romance than sex. We had . . . a kiss. But it was a kiss filled with all the love and sorrow of his past. You see, as a young boy, Padmananda went to an English boarding school here in India with a best friend. The friend's father was a Christian minister and decided to educate the boys together. As Padmananda got older, he'd planned to become a Christian minister as well. . ."

Absorbed in the telling, Kali didn't feel the hairbrush hesitate, then stop.

"But sometime near graduation from high school, there was a riot in Amritsar. Padmananda's father was a Brahman and felt responsible for the Hindu community. He went out into the night to try and stop the fighting. Not only his father, but my Master, Daya Nanda." She leaned against him, trembling. "When Daya Nanda was swept away by the crowd, Padmananda left his friend to take care of his father. Only long enough to ensure that Daya Nanda was safe. When he returned, his father had been killed. His best friend had fled to save his own life and to warn the Christian mission . . ."

"Lisa."

The word held a dread that forced her to turn toward him. His expression frightened her. "What is it?" she whispered, wide-eyed.

"His name. Padmananda's name. Did he tell you his boyhood name? Was it Nareesh?"

"Yes," she gasped, the word barely audible.

Christian slowly stood. "Nareesh." He exhaled the word, spoke as in a daze. "Nareesh here? Why didn't you tell me all these years that your Master is Daya Nanda?"

"Christian," Kali begged, trying to penetrate the stare, "what is it?"

"I'm the boyhood friend. It was my father who sent Nareesh to boarding school."

"Then you're the one who left his father to die," she said without thinking, her body shrinking away from him.

"That's not true!" he cried. "Do you believe that? Both Nareesh and I begged Ram Seva to get off the streets, but he wouldn't listen. The crowd was . . . terrifying." He covered his eyes with the palms of his hands. "Even after Nareesh left for help, I did all I could. Then the mob closed in and pulled me away. I couldn't get back to him." His voice was hoarse, close to tears. "Buildings were burning, men hurt and dying. My face, my hair—I was a target. I became trapped in an alley.

A man came at me with a knife . . . My teacher, Lama Loden, rushed into the space between us." The words were a sob. "He died in my arms. His life for mine . . . "

"Christian . . . ," she whispered, horrified.

"The next day, my parents sent me away. I wrote countless letters pleading with Nareesh to tell me where he was. He never replied. No one has ever told me Ram Seva died that night! But so help me, that was my part in it!"

"But . . . but he doesn't know!" she cried. "He blames you for his father's death!"

"Why hasn't he talked to me? Surely, he knows who I am. You must have told him enough about me so that he knows."

"I . . . I don't know," she stammered. "He never said anything. All he gave me were the books in the briefcase."

"The briefcase?"

The sudden sense of foreboding he had come to rely upon alerted him. Something didn't jibe. Taking a deep breath, he tried searching his mind for details, clues that should have warned him, but where Lisa was concerned, the facts were hazy. All he could remember was the distraction of his emotion. He jumped up, picked up the case, and threw it on the bed.

"It's locked," he said, his voice anxious.

"That's funny," Kali murmured.

"Not so funny." He pulled a pocketknife from his pack and began prying at the lock.

"Christian! I have to return that!"

"Oh, I don't think so," he told her, struggling to release the catch.

"What are you doing?"

With a final jerk, the lock popped open. Christian threw back the lid and pushed aside newspapers that covered the contents. What looked like five pounds of carefully wrapped hash lay inside. He pulled aside a corner of the covering, sniffing it.

"*Charas,*" he hissed. "I've got to get rid of this. And now."

Removing the pipe from his pocket and the small smoking stash he'd brought from New Delhi, he threw them both into the case. His ears caught the sound of voices downstairs, the pounding of footsteps ascending the stairs.

"Bloody hell!" he spat between clenched teeth.

Swiftly, he strode to the room's side window, away from the front of the room and the main street, dropped the open briefcase, and struggled to open the rusted latch. At last, the window gave. Grabbing the case to toss it, he glanced down to the alley below. Two men in army green uniforms smiled up at him. Before he could recover from his surprise, the door smashed open against the far wall. A half-dozen army officers stormed into the room, each carrying a drawn handgun or a rifle. Christian took a deep, resigned breath and dropped the briefcase to the floor, almost at the same moment that two of the soldiers reached him, each pointing a revolver at his body. Pushed hard against the wall, he raised his arms high above his head.

"Here it is!" said a third man, picking up the briefcase and replacing the contents that had tumbled from it.

A young lieutenant entered the room after the others and held himself apart. "There must be more," he said. "Where is it?"

"I've no idea what you're talking about." Christian's face and lips were white, his voice shaking from fear and adrenaline. "As a matter of fact, that's not mine either. I'm sure we can discuss this reasonably." He thought to switch to Hindi but decided the American passport might protect him.

"Of course," replied the lieutenant crisply, "it all simply appears from nowhere. But since it is here, you must have some idea of the whereabouts of the larger amount."

"Like I said, I've no idea what you're talking about."

"Search the room," he ordered his men in the same cool, dry voice.

While the men pushed through the room, emptying drawers, searching the closet, dumping the contents of his pack, moving the mattress aside, the lieutenant turned once more to Christian. "It will go easier if you give me the names of your partners and turn over the main consignment. Perhaps you can leave with your passport in the next few days. Wouldn't that be easier than a few years in an Indian jail?"

"Sorry," Christian told the man, shaking his head. He tried getting his voice under control, feigning confidence. "I don't know how that got into this room. Do I look like the kind of chap who carries a briefcase?"

"Money!" said one of the soldiers, throwing the contents of Christian's jacket onto the bed. Eyes in the room looked greedily at the dollars.

"How much?"

"Three thousand . . . four hundred . . . sixty-two . . . three . . . sixty-five dollars," the soldier answered, counting fast and with some glee because they would all have a share of it.

"Our information is quite clear. You are here to purchase a major shipment—far more than . . . how many pounds are there?" he eyed the briefcase.

"Five, sir."

"Five pounds? Really, Mr. . . . ?"

"Alden. Christian Alden."

"Do you really believe . . . Mr. Brooks . . . we can accept the fact that you've bought only five pounds? Come now, where is the rest of the hashish?"

"My name is Alden. I'm just here on vacation," Christian answered lightly, but beginning to realize the seriousness of his situation. Nareesh had given them his real name. He had to continue to insist on Alden, because that was the name on his passport.

"How do you suppose your government is going to take to passport fraud? Eh? Traveling under the name of Alden. I don't think they're going to be happy. Do you . . . Mr. Brooks?"

"I seldom find bureaucrats happy about anything . . . lieutenant."

At Christian's tone, the lieutenant's face grew darker, and when he next spoke, his voice was tight and menacing. "Then I will ask you once again while you have the time to enjoy the questions in comfort. Who are your partners? Where is the major consignment you have purchased?"

"And I will tell you once again, I don't know what you're talking about. Believe me, I'm more surprised than you to find this briefcase in my room. It was here when I returned after lunch. I'd just got around to opening it. Take a look. You can see I had to open it with a pocket-knife. I'm afraid you've got the wrong man."

"Bind him," the lieutenant ordered.

Christian had few moments to think. The lieutenant was look-ing over the rest of the papers in his pockets. What was he carrying? Behind his back, he could feel the rope tighten around one wrist, then the other, locking his arms together.

If only I'd known about the hash, even ten minutes before! I simply don't have a few days to spend in jail while I buy my way out. Bob and Dharma will be leaving at noon tomorrow.

"Wait a minute," Christian told the lieutenant. "I think we might be able to work something out."

"Yes?" The lieutenant turned to him, smiling.

"How much is it going to cost to get out of this mess? The amount of the fine?"

The smug police face lost its gay mask. "The names. I want the names."

Suddenly, Christian knew from the man's intensity that this bust was tied to something more. The lieutenant had a larger agenda. He was earning a reputation with the US government. Possibly Interpol. The money would come later.

"You're looking for a promotion," Christian told him, angry now, shaking his head, his voice tinged with British public school superior-ity. Something he knew would both humiliate and enrage the lieuten-ant. "I just thought you had some actual authority. That we could settle this here, like gentlemen."

The lieutenant nodded, and one of the soldiers reached long and hard to slap Christian full across the face, sending him reeling into the wall.

When the man's hand made contact, Kali screamed. All eyes turned toward her, and Christian found himself faced with a new danger. She would also be implicated. His confidence faltered. How many times had she told him of this fear? How many times had she made it clear that she didn't want to be responsible for his business karma?

One of the soldiers grabbed her, and Christian, his heart beating wildly, frantically pushed away from the wall toward the man who held her, only to find two soldiers tighten their hold on his arms.

They'll have to let her go, he thought in rising desperation as he strained against the men who held him. *They'll have to!*

"Look, she's just here for the afternoon," he cried. "I met her on the street. She has nothing to do with this. Let her go."

Below, at the bottom of the stairs, Nareesh had just reached the bungalow when he heard Kali's scream.

Oh, God! No! he prayed.

He flew upstairs and came to an abrupt halt in the doorway. Before him, Kali stood desperate and distraught in a green-gold sari that matched the darkened green agony in her eyes, her hair disheveled, shimmering against the golden silk threads. Beyond her, Christian struggled in the arms of two soldiers, his arms bound. From his protective stance and Kali's anguished, yearning eyes turned to him, Nareesh knew that they were lovers. Of all the things he thought and felt at that moment, he could only murmur to Kali, "You weren't supposed to be here."

"Not the girl," the lieutenant told the soldier. "She helped to get the information and keep him here."

Christian turned abruptly to look at her, his mind paralyzed. The soldiers holding him loosened their grip as the tension left him.

"You," he spat at an ashen Nareesh, finally finding voice. "*You* did all of this. I only learned this afternoon that Ram Seva died. You set me up without giving me a chance to explain." Planting his feet, standing squarely facing Nareesh, his voice rising in an escalating wrath he had never before known, he cried, "You think I would desert you? You think I would deliberately leave your father in danger? The mob killed him, not me. They killed him after pulling me away and dragging me through the streets. Don't you know?" his enraged voice collapsed again into a hoarse sob. "Don't you know Lama Loden died that night? And I almost died with him? He gave his life for me!"

Nareesh's breathing grew faster, his ragged breath trying to catch up to his accelerating heart, his mouth open and slack.

"My father sent me, beaten and half dead, out of India the following day. I waited for you at school. I wrote. You . . . you never even bothered to ask me!"

Arrogance had given way to betrayed fury. Even the soldiers ripping through the room stopped to watch as Christian abandoned himself to rage. Fighting once again against the hands that restrained him, he turned to Lisa who crouched against the wall. "And you," he spat. "You finally had to seduce me to keep me here!" The laugh he forced was harsh. "This afternoon might actually make the rest of this worth it. Kali, Goddess of Destruction. How aptly named you are!"

Kali stuttered from a white face, her eyes wide in terror, her body shaking badly. "N-n-no . . . no!"

"Take him away," the lieutenant ordered.

In a frenzy, Christian broke loose from his guards and lunged toward Nareesh. All he wanted was to inflict some pain, pummel the face of Lisa's lover, the face that had betrayed him. Flying through the surprised soldiers, his shoulder hit Nareesh squarely, sending them both sprawling backward through the door, landing on the floor in the hallway. But even as Christian tried to regain his feet, a rifle butt caught him full across the back of his head. The roar of pain gripped him for only a second, then the darkness.

Two soldiers lifted the limp body off the fallen Nareesh. One of them pulled back his head. "He's breathing."

The lieutenant waved an arm, and Kali saw only his back and the dragging soles of his sandals as they pulled him away and down the stairs.

Caught in a trance where time stood still, Nareesh tried to speak.

"No . . . no . . . ," Kali mumbled, trying to get her lips to work. Her hand grasped her throat. "No!" She looked up at the lieutenant, tried her voice again. "He didn't do it!" she cried, holding up her hands in supplication. "He didn't . . . "

Leaning shakily against the doorframe, Nareesh tried to stand as she rushed him. "Tell them!" She raised both fists to pound on his chest, her high-pitched voice filling the stairwell. "He didn't do any of it! Any of it! Don't you understand what he was trying to tell you?"

The crushing realization descended on him, everything falling into place. His personal torment for so many years had been based on a lie. He had destroyed the lives of two people he loved. Dear God, what had he done?

"How could you? You . . . " Kali stepped away with a sudden new look of horror, ". . . you used me. For your own revenge."

"I came to try to stop it," he whispered.

For a moment, Nareesh thought she would swoon. Her eyes closed, and she swayed to one side. But as he shook his head, tried to find the words to explain, she abruptly turned from him and bolted down the stairs.

"Kali!" he screamed after her. "Wait! Please!" Summoning strength from his shaking body, he started after her.

"One moment!" the lieutenant said curtly. A soldier stopped him. "I think we need to talk."

"No, not now! I have to catch her! I'll come to your office in a few hours . . . in a few hours . . . " Desperately, he looked down the stairs.

The lieutenant took a deep breath and glanced at his watch. Clearly unhappy at the turn of events, the look in his face suggesting a suspicion that he himself might also have been used, he nodded. "Very well. By eight."

Nareesh ran quickly, stumbling down the steps to the street. He looked left and right through the crowded mass of people. It was almost dark. He had to find her before night fell. Which way had she gone? Desperately, he ran left through the narrow, bricked streets, startling people who were settling down into the quiet of nightfall.

Kali had not stopped to consider where she was running. She simply ran as if driven by a demon, barefoot, her green sari flying behind her, her blonde hair disheveled and streaming.

Ahead, Kali could see the river, a gentle thread of wide red turning quickly to deeper and deeper shades of purple. She was crying, her tears blinding her, forcing her to stumble, to fall more than once. As she ran, choking on great rasping sobs, she fought for the breath that would keep her body moving, battled to keep the sound of the crack of Christian's skull from her mind, the image of him being dragged away.

Padmananda used me, the words echoed in her mind. *I loved him, and he used me. Used me.*

Oh, God, but I used him, too. I betrayed his love for an afternoon with Christian.

And she heard the sound of the crack of the rifle butt on Christian's head again.

No, she screamed, covering her ears as she ran, hearing the dull word travel down a dark tunnel.

The river was very close now, a long, darkening space at the end of the *ghat.* With a last frantic burst of energy, she raced down the stairs, unaware of shouting voices in the dim background. She didn't pause at the last step, but threw herself into the relief of the water. Seconds later, she was at the surface, breathless and swimming away from shore for what seemed a long time. The last thing she remembered before the darkness swallowed her was wondering how a thin, gold-green silk sari could become so heavy once it was wet with the water of the Ganges.

KATHY
NEW DELHI, INDIA
NOVEMBER 1969

When the Pan American flight from San Francisco touched down in New Delhi, the numbness Kathy had lived with for so many days gave way to a feeling of relief. Soon, she would be able to lay the whole nightmare at Christian's feet. She could already feel the strength that would make her whole, the ice, the hard place in her heart that was afraid to feel, would melt. He'd asked for commitment, for a partnership. She'd give him everything he wanted. Oblivious to her surroundings, she hurried through the airport, knowing that only a few miles separated her from Christian's arms. She carried her shoulder bag and strode with such purpose that porters and crowds parted for her as she moved toward the waiting taxis.

At the desk of the Hotel Imperial, she politely asked for the room number of the three American men, reached into her wallet when the man attempted to look confused, and then made her way to the elevator. At her knock, Bob opened the door to her and wondered whether his eyes lied. "Jesus, Kathy, what are you doin' here?"

"Alan told me where to find you."

Suddenly, Bob looked frightened. "Julie," he nervously asked, "is she alright? Shakti?"

"They're fine," she said, quickly searching the room for Christian. Then, looking into Bob's worried eyes, she said more gently, "They're fine." She set her pack down on the old couch. "But there is bad news. I need Christian. Where is he? Is he here?"

"Actually . . . no."

Then it was left for him to tell her the truth about Christian's plans with Lisa and his flight to Varanasi.

Kathy fell heavily into a chair, trying to fathom what this might mean.

"Something's happened," Bob said.

In the same small voice she had used for weeks, Kathy retold the story of cold and the desert and bodies in the light of the truck, of rip-off and murder, looking from Bob to Dharma, who were both shaken to speechlessness.

"Another brother gone," Dharma finally said into the pregnant silence.

Bob looked into Kathy's hollow stare, stood and pulled her to him, held her. "It'll be alright," he said softly. "It'll be alright."

And Kathy, finally giving in to the hours of flight and the pain of disappointment, stood sobbing against Bob's chest. Dharma put his arms around them both, and they held to each other for a long while, until Kathy's cries were no more than a strained gasp for breath. Afterward, they settled in with a pipe and some of the hash picked up in Afghanistan and talked late into the night.

Sometime during that long evening, Kathy left behind the helpless, wide-eyed child of misfortune and came back to herself.

"Christian and I had a disagreement about my going to Arizona," she told them, still stunned by the news of Lisa. "He said if I left that anything might happen. He mentioned that there was someone. But . . . I didn't expect him to move away from me this fast. I just . . . didn't expect it."

"If it's any consolation, it won't work," Bob told her. "Lisa's really into her guru. And Christian, well, you know how Christian feels about religion."

"That's not the only difference between them," Dharma added, placing a crumbled bit of hash into the pipe.

"What's she like? What does he see in her?"

Bob sighed. "Besides her beauty? I'm not sure."

"Well, I'm sure," Dharma told them. "He sees a hidden sensuality wrapped in a cloak of piety. You get glimpses of it just beneath the surface of her pure white robe. The contrast is irresistible, challenging. And she's smart. Christian likes smart women, especially those that are too smart."

"Is she an old lover?"

"No," Dharma shook his head. "That's part of it. They're into this long, drawn-out seduction that needs to be played out. Christian could have any woman he wants," he continued, looking pointedly at Kathy, "but he's got to get the fruit at the top of the tree. The fruit that's hard to reach. He likes a challenge, and we all know he likes to win."

"Why didn't you point that out to him before he left?" Bob asked.

"Tell Christian anything? Come on. You've got to be kidding."

Kathy gave a small, bitter chuckle, knowing exactly what Dharma meant.

"He'll learn," Dharma assured them. "If he plays the record enough times, he may start hearing the tune."

"Wasn't Lisa your old lady?" she asked Bob.

"And Dharma's lover."

"Well," she looked from one to the other. "I'm beginning to feel a bit excluded."

"Hey, no problem," Dharma edged closer. "Just slide on over here."

Kathy laughed. A turning point. The beginning of her healing, and indeed, she snuggled in next to Dharma, his body grounding her.

Even with the fatigue of traveling, Kathy could not sleep well in the few hours left to her before dawn. When Bob woke her to get ready for the airport, he asked, "You sure you really want to do this—go to Benares? You can come with us, you know. You'll see a part of the world you might never get to see again."

"Thanks, but I have to hear Christian say it. I have to hear him say he doesn't want to be with me."

"Come on, Kathy. How's any man ever going to say that to you?"

"Bob," Kathy put her arms around him and held him close, trying not to cry again, "you are such a dear."

"Here's the address of the guesthouse I gave Christian," Dharma told her. "If we don't hear from either of you by noon, day after tomorrow, we'll leave without you."

"Yeah," Bob added. "Tell that son of a bitch we can't wait any longer while he decides on a woman. And tell him . . . tell him he'll always be a brother. Tell him we'll see him back on Maui."

"Be careful," she prayed. "It's a long trip home."

"No problem. You'd better get going."

With a quick kiss for them both, Kathy left for the airport.

PADMANANDA
VARANASI, INDIA
NOVEMBER 1969

Leaving Christian's room and the scowl of the lieutenant, Padmananda raced down the stairs frantically searching the street in front of the guesthouse for Kali. If he had thought to ask any one of the shop owners or craftsmen if they'd seen her, he might have found her direction quickly. But he did not. Instead, he roamed aimlessly until long after dusk. Finally exhausted, he knew there were too many streets, too many narrow connecting alleyways to ever find her now. He leaned against a brick wall and covered his face. There was no longer any point in seeking. She'd vanished.

Suddenly remembering his appointment with the lieutenant, he glanced at his watch. He was already late and had to hurry. If there was nothing he could mend with Kali, at least he could concentrate on helping Christian.

The lieutenant's office was small and sparsely furnished, a desk with papers sorted into neat piles, a few chairs, a cabinet. The room had a brutal air. Padmananda sensed the agonies experienced in this room, the bitterness absorbed into its white-stucco walls.

"You're late," the lieutenant said, motioning Padmananda to a chair.

"I'm sorry. I was searching for the girl. I haven't found her. Perhaps she'll show up at the hotel later."

"Would you like to make some explanation as to what happened this afternoon?"

"All a terrible mistake." He held out his hands in a gesture that suggested the lieutenant should understand. "The man and woman at the lodging house are old friends. There was a small family disagreement and, somehow, a briefcase of contraband was mistakenly placed in the room."

"How did that happen?"

"Perhaps you can offer some suggestions," Padmananda asked, beginning the ancient bargaining game.

"I have a feeling the woman's involved."

"That sounds as if it might be a plausible explanation. You know how disturbing some of these emotional entanglements can be." Padmananda shrugged his shoulders and tried to smile.

"You make it sound like a simple matter."

"I assure you, it is very simple. I understand there will be a fine for your trouble."

The lieutenant stared briefly at Padmananda, then stood and walked around his desk.

"Unfortunately, what appears simple on the surface is often complicated beneath. Are you aware that the US embassy has expressed an interest in this case?"

Padmananda's heart sank, but he remained calm, never taking his eyes from the lieutenant's face. "No," he answered easily.

"Apparently, your Mr. Brooks—or Alden—was observed in Afghanistan. He is wanted for questioning not only on charges of passport fraud, but also for his involvement in a large hashish-smuggling operation."

"Surely, you don't think . . . "

"There will be an Interpol agent here to observe questioning on Tuesday at two o'clock—the day after tomorrow. I'm afraid your Mr. Alden has been quite tight lipped, refusing to answer any questions. The only time he opens his mouth is to say something he knows will make his situation worse. Both our governments—ours and that of the United States—are dissatisfied with his lack of cooperation. It may prove to be a difficult and unpleasant situation for him."

"What is it you expect him to answer?"

"The names of his partners. The men he was with in Afghanistan. The route they have planned to travel. The location of what Interpol believes is the main body of the contraband."

"And if he can't?"

The lieutenant sneered. "Mr. Alden looks like a smart man. I assure you, he will remember."

"Then the fine for his release?"

"I'm afraid there is no possibility of his release."

"If you could but name a sum," Padmananda pleaded, "no matter how exorbitant it might sound . . . "

"I'm sorry. Mr. Alden must be here to meet the agent."

"You don't suppose you could arrange for me to see him for a few moments?"

"A waste of time. Mr. Alden is still rather indisposed."

"Perhaps a doctor?"

"Sorry, no. Leave your address with the officer at the front desk and plan to make yourself available tomorrow."

Padmananda saw finality in the man's face, heard it in his voice. Standing, sick at heart, he placed his hands together over his heart and bowed. "*Namaste.*"

The lieutenant repeated, "*Namaste.*"

Outside the prison grounds, Padmananda stood dazed. Both of them—he had lost both of them. Little else could be done but return to the hotel and pray that Kali might be there.

His first inquiry was at the front desk.

No, the lady had not returned.

Nor was there an answer to the soft knock on her door.

Throughout the night, he waited, not daring to sleep. Several times, he rose to knock once again on her door. Early the next morning, she did not appear for *puja*. Entrusting the ritual to another, he sought Christian's room again. She was not there either. By afternoon, he was drained physically and mentally. All he could think was that Kali was gone, and tomorrow, the American agent would be arriving to question Christian. Returning to the hotel, he slowly walked to his room, opened the door—and found the Master waiting. He could not look at him, but collapsed at his feet.

"Daya Nanda, what am I to do? I've looked everywhere for her. I've such great fears. And Christian . . . I've tried with the lieutenant, to no avail. How can I reverse what I've done?"

"Come, my son." The Master touched his head. "You have done all that can be done for now. Tomorrow will show the way. Now you must sleep."

"But how can I sleep knowing I've changed nothing?"

"Tomorrow," the Master forced him to lie down, touching him on his head and shoulders as he had those many nights after Amritsar. Padmananda felt his tired body relax, his agitated mind fading into an uneasy peace.

"But . . . ," came his quiet, whispered voice as his eyes closed.

18

The tunnel was dark and long, but in the distance, Kali could see the light, still far away, but beckoning. She moved with unfamiliar motions toward it.

"Kali!" a voice called, forcing her to stop and look back.

"Master?" she asked.

"I am here," he answered. "Where are you going?"

"Why . . . toward the light."

"I need you."

"Master, I am worthless! I loved them, and they used me."

"Did they? Pain only teaches."

In the next second, a rough shaking and pushing intruded on her communion with Daya Nanda. A horrible rasping came from her throat. Disembodied voices, heavy with worry, drifted to her. She struggled to clear her lungs, gasping for air between vomiting and the hot rush of water out of her nose and mouth. Still gasping, she pushed her face away from where she lay in bile and water. Her world trembled, rocking from side to side. Long, wet strands of hair covered her face. An arm steadied her convulsing body. Shakily, she pushed her hair away so she could breathe easier and took in great, gasping breaths of air. She was in a small boat on a dark body of water with strangers—three men. One of them returned to the oars and began to row.

Slowly, everything returned to her—the afternoon with Christian, the police, Padmananda's face at the door, the Master's voice in the dark tunnel. Hadn't she agreed to return and make things right? But what had seemed clear in the dream was not so easy in reality. Shivering, her knees and elbows bleeding from where she'd fallen in the streets, every muscle hurting, she wondered what she could possibly do to help Christian or Padmananda.

The men in the boat spoke to her in a language she did not understand, and she could only shake her head, her teeth chattering loudly from shock and cold. The shoreline appeared and what looked like a small fishing village with a number of rude huts. As the little boat pulled up to the splintered dock to be tied among other boats, she noted that there were few lights, only a string of bare electrical bulbs growing brighter as the sun began to set. She looked back over her shoulder and could see the lights of Benares on the opposite shore and realized that she was on the eastern side of the Ganges.

That night, wrapped in a dry sari loaned by one of the women, huddled next to a fire, the haze in her mind began to clear.

She could not sleep. Instead, she crossed her legs in meditative posture and prayed throughout the night, prayed for Padmananda's torment and for Christian's life and freedom. How badly hurt was he?

Christian . . . Christian . . . the fault is mine. I knew before this afternoon that union with you would mean tragedy. The sexual energy between us began when I came to live with Matt. But it was delusion. How could we have played into it for so long? The feelings that seduced us were reinforced in only three small visits over the years—a prolonged mental foreplay that finally exploded into orgasm and disappeared, leaving nothing in its place but the same two very different people we always were. This afternoon, our sexual energy ran wild, sweeping us away. I forgot Daya Nanda's teachings. That energy is the lifeline to God, and we used it on ourselves in disregard of everything and everyone else.

Her body was as tired as her mind, and finally she curled up in a ball, like a child. But as much as she wanted to rest, to fall into oblivion, her mind raced on, open to the truth. Padmananda came to her again and again. She saw his failings, understood what Christian must have represented to him.

I complicated the situation, didn't I? I entered both your lives, formed the triangle, gave you a further reason for anger, jealousy, and revenge. Padmananda, what have you done? What have we all done to one another? I wish I could comfort you as I once did before, but would you want my comfort now—after I betrayed you and all you helped teach me?

And she wept, realizing she had thrown his love away.

On the following day, the same small boat carried her back to the city in the early afternoon, an act of compassion, because she had nothing to give them. She sat huddled on the boat's bench as she watched the dock approach, once again in the torn and dirty green sari.

Where can I go? she wondered, as she bowed to the two men and whispered, "*Namaste.*"

Where it ended. Christian's room.

Searching, she finally arrived at the guesthouse, and there she fell onto the bed to sleep for many hours.

The sun was well up before Kali woke the next afternoon from a heavy sleep filled with dreams. The clock showed that she had slept for almost twenty-four hours. As she stood and began moving, every part of her body hurt. Her throat and mouth cried for water. The tea Christian had brought from the kitchen two days ago was still there, cold and bitter, but it helped bring life back to her body. She surveyed the shambles of the room and was still eating leftover naan when a knock on the door startled her. She froze. She wasn't ready to face anyone yet. But at the second insistent knock, she pulled on her jeans and one of Christian's T-shirts and reached for the doorknob.

"Hello," said the dark-haired woman who faced her. "You must be Lisa."

"Do I know you?"

"I'm Kathleen—Kathy. Bob and Dharma gave me this address. I'm looking for Christian. Is he here?"

Suddenly, Kali was paranoid. She didn't know this woman or what she might want. What if she was working for the police? What if she expected information about Bob and Dharma? "He's not here," she said cautiously.

"Do you know when he'll be back?" Kathy asked. "I've come a long way to see him."

"Who are you?" Kali eyed her guardedly. "How do you know Bob and Dharma?"

"Julie and I are old friends. I spent time with Bob and Dharma in Hawaii."

"And Christian?"

Kathy hesitated. "Christian and I are friends."

"I'm sorry. Please excuse my bad manners. I'm . . . paranoid. My name's Kali. Come in."

Kathy's lips curved into a tight smile, "Well, if you know Bob and Dharma and Christian, you have every right to be paranoid." She stepped inside and looked about the room. "I know Christian's never been terribly neat, but . . . "

"The police made this mess. Christian's in jail."

"Jail?" Kathy spun around, the world suddenly stopped. "My God, why? What happened?"

"He was set up. They found five pounds of hash in a briefcase in this room."

"Set up by who?" she cried.

"By . . . by an old friend."

"Friend! So what's being done? How long ago?"

Kali tried remembering. Time had become hazy. "In the afternoon. The day before yesterday."

"Have you been to the prison?"

"Me? No. I . . . I'm not sure what to do. The only person I can ask . . . set him up." Kali brushed the hair away from her face as she spoke, spaced, trying to pull her mind together.

"You mean, you've left Christian in jail for two days without doing anything?" Kathy asked angrily. "Who else knows he's there? Why are you just hanging out in his room?"

Kali saw the way Kathy held her chin, found herself responding to the woman's anger. She shook her head, becoming angry herself. "Who are you to Christian?" she demanded. "He's never mentioned you."

"I'll bet."

A rising jealousy burned with Kathy's anger.

So . . . Christian's moved me out to come for this woman. I'm not impressed. If he's decided to pick someone who'll clean house and be his ornament, I'll gladly walk away.

"What happened?" Kathy insisted. "Start at the beginning."

She began to furiously pick up Christian's clothes while she waited for Kali to speak, folding them as she had dozens of times before, setting them in a pile next to his pack.

"How well do you know Christian?" Kali asked, watching Kathy's practiced hands.

"Apparently not well enough."

In the silence that filled the room, Kathy finally glanced up. Kali had sat down heavily on the bed, stubbornness still in her posture, but also something more. Kathy read both pain and realization in her eyes.

She sat down next to Kali on the bed, and sighed. "I'm sorry." She did not want to play this old game of jealously and possessiveness, did not want to fight this woman for Christian. But Kali also deserved to know the truth. "Christian and I have been living together for about a year. Christian's business sometimes takes him away. So does mine. He was unhappy when I left on a business deal. By the time I got back, he'd split. This trip to India is his way of telling me how hurt he is."

"I should have known," Kali murmured.

"What?"

"Christian always comes to me when he's broken up with someone. I'm always second choice."

"Sister," Kathy said to her forlorn expression, "tell me what happened."

"It's a long story."

Kali explained the tumultuous relationships that had caused this tragedy. Padmananda's belief that Christian had deserted his father, his bitterness, the jealousy that had been stirred by Christian's visit. She told of the arrest, the surprise of the pounding footsteps on the stairs. Her terrible shock at Padmananda's confession, her panicked run through the streets, the night in the village across the river. As she spoke, Kathy's shock was matched only by her anger.

"Oh, Kathy, the pain I've caused everyone," Kali cried. "This is all my fault!"

"Hey, will you get off it?" Kathy answered impatiently. "Padmananda and Christian are two big boys. You had an affair with Christian because you both wanted it—not just you. And Padmananda knew exactly what he was doing when he set Christian up."

"What do we do now? I don't know anything about how the prison system works here."

"We're going to need to go see someone who has connections in this country. Padmananda, if he's sincere about helping."

"If anyone can help, he can," Kali said.

"Get dressed, and we'll get something to eat. That should help put your head back together. You've been through a lot."

With a grateful nod, Kali disappeared into the bathroom, and while she waited, Kathy started packing Christian's clothes.

Goddamn it, Christian! You fucking bastard! she screamed silently. *Damn you! Damn you! Wherever the fuck you are, damn you! You couldn't wait a few goddamned weeks?*

Her anger kept her moving, fighting the tears she wouldn't let Kali see. She picked up the blankets lying on the floor and pulled them over the mattress. Coins and a key fell out and lay scattered on the wooden boards. And something else.

"Oh, my God!" Kathy grinned, holding up the prize. "Kali! They overlooked his passport! How do you suppose they left this behind?"

"It wouldn't be hard," Kali answered, coming from the bathroom in a blouse and jeans and braiding her hair. "Not with the confusion around here, with Christian claiming he didn't know a thing . . . "

"What was he supposed to know?" Kathy asked cautiously.

"The lieutenant wanted the names of his partners and the location of the larger stash." She stopped, clearly wondering whether she'd said too much.

"Yeah?" Kathy prompted.

"Christian just kept repeating that he didn't know what the lieutenant was talking about, grinning like it was nothing. The man wasn't very happy about Christian mouthing off to him. One of the soldiers hit him across the face."

Kathy nodded. At the moment, she wouldn't mind slapping his face, either. Maybe a little jail time would cool him out a bit.

"There's more. When Padmananda came to the door, Christian went for him. One of the soldiers knocked him out with a rifle butt. He was unconscious when they dragged him down the stairs."

"Oh, Kali, why didn't you tell me this sooner!"

Dear God, she prayed, feeling the sickness return. *Please don't let him die. Whatever happens, please don't let him die. I don't ask for anything—even for him to love me—just let him live.*

"Are you okay?"

"Yeah." Kathy opened her eyes, blinked. "But if he's hurt, we need to get going."

19

CHRISTIAN
VARANASI, INDIA
NOVEMBER 1969

At first, Christian could not place the sound—a bizarre combination of moan and heavy breathing. Then he realized it was his own labored breath. His face lay pressed against something cold. With tremendous effort, he opened his eyes to find himself on the brutally hard floor of a dank prison cell.

Slowly, feeling came back to his arms and legs. He inched his arms up, trying to push his face off the concrete. The agonizing pain that shot through his head almost caused him to lose consciousness again.

Just take it slow, ol' man, he told himself. *It doesn't look like you're going anywhere.*

With a deep breath, he tried again and managed to get an arm under his head. With his free hand near his eyes, he studied his torn wrist and offered thanks that they had untied him.

Was it worth it, he wondered? Was knocking Nareesh down worth what he was feeling right now?

No way.

If I had used my wits, I might have turned the tables, accused Nareesh, and pointed to Lisa. If I had just stuck to my story, I might be free. But I let my anger betray me.

He pulled his knees up under his stomach, the movement of his legs sending pain roaring through his head like a train in a tunnel. He lay still until the torment subsided, then reached behind his head with his free arm. There was no blood—only a lump the size of his hand.

Jesus, he thought, *they sure as hell got me.*

He clenched his teeth, opened his eyes, and pushed himself to a kneeling position. Swaying with dizziness, he was almost blinded by the throbbing pain. A quick survey of the room showed no chairs or beds, only four concrete walls and a small window set high in one wall. The room's only item was an earthen jar that filled the room with the smell of urine and feces. Judging by the light that showed pale pink, he thought it must be either early morning or late afternoon.

Slowly, nauseated and disoriented, he crawled toward the wall and propped his back against it. He forced himself to take his mind away from the gagging odor of the jar. With what will he had, he kept his eyes open; when he closed them, the pain took over, and everything whirled. He continued to swallow to keep from vomiting, his body shaking hard from both cold and shock, the searing throb in his head intensifying with his shaking.

Deciding that he had to get off the cold concrete, he pushed off from the floor by leaning heavily against the wall and straightening his knees. Again, pain shot through his forehead and eyes, and he reached up to grab at his head. To his left, he noticed the door for the first time and moved along the wall toward it. He reached out, tried pushing on it, half expecting it to open.

"Guard!" he tried yelling in Hindi, but the word came out flat and soft, without strength, and again his hands reached up to hold his head. "Guard!" he yelled louder, this time summoning the courage to pound on the door.

Speaking only served to establish that his throat was thick and dry. He desperately needed something to drink. Once more, he tried calling and pounding, but the effort brought back the nausea and dizziness. He slid back to the floor, knowing he would just have to wait. The patience he had not used in the guesthouse, would have to be practiced today.

The light from the window was brighter now. Morning. A square patch of sunshine moved slowly across the floor. On shivering hands and knees, Christian crawled to the light and forced himself into lotus. If any time needed prayer, this one did, and with the first few lines of the Tibetan chant, he began to feel the nausea subside and his shaking diminish.

All that morning, he moved with the sun, chanting his mental prayer to keep the thought of time, pain, and thirst at a distance. But by midday, weakness overtook him, and he lay down across the path of light and slept.

When he awoke, the light had faded again. Gratefully, he sat up without the nausea. The ache in his head had lessened, and the shaking was gone, although he knew the room would get even colder with the darkness. An erection reminded him he had to piss. To his surprise, the door suddenly clanged open. A turbaned man entered, carrying two buckets: One contained lukewarm tea; the other carried the smell of curry.

"I want to see the lieutenant," Christian said in Hindi.

But the prison worker looked neither right nor left as he ladled tea into an aluminum cup and the curry onto a plate.

"The lieutenant! Tell him I want to see him."

Still silent, the man turned and walked back toward the door.

There was but a split second to think. The open door decided Christian, and he jumped faster than he thought possible. He reached the door before the prison worker—only to see a sneering guard outside with a rifle, daring him to leave the cell. Stopped, he tried to recover quickly from the surprising sight of the gun. He shaped his voice into an authoritarian demand. "I want to see the lieutenant."

The prison worker idled slowly past him. Once he was in the hallway, the door slammed shut, loudly, the sound echoing down the empty hall, and Christian was left standing in the deepening darkness. The allure of years of adventure, work, and love called to him from the tiny, sky-filled window. The humiliation of his capture suddenly overwhelmed him. Hadn't he just told Kali this would never happen, that he was very careful? Alone, staring at the door, for the first time in a long while, he began to question his abilities.

His legs gave way, and leaning against the wall for support, he slid again to the floor. The aluminum cup of tea sat near his hand, and he greedily drained the bitter brew. One look at the curry, and he knew he would be sick within the hour. Better to fast.

Everything had started slowly, imperceptibly, he reflected—experimenting with pot, the thoughts and revealing visions, the power of the acid experience, sharing with friends, the knowledge that others might benefit from the experience. Each time he passed a dose to someone, he'd felt as if he were sharing Loden Rinpoche's teachings.

At first, the money he made wasn't really his. It belonged to the business, to getting the work done, to helping brothers who were in need. But as his business grew, it couldn't operate without capital. Money was needed to purchase chemicals and equipment, rent buildings, provide transportation. Albert and Doug were counting on him. So were a dozen others. Slowly, the money had become his, because he had the ability and knowledge to use it. But in exchange, it had seduced him—slowly, subtly. It gave him mobility, license, and freedom, and he had come to rely on it, often thought of it as the means to an end.

Somewhere, he had lost his way. Somewhere in the challenge of the next deal and the excitement of handling large quantities of product and money, he had been lured from the humble life he had once contemplated. He was egoless each time he tripped, subject to the power of the universe, to God, reduced to the very cells that made up his body, but each trip also served to increase his vision of himself. Only a handful of men in history had seen and understood with the depth acid bestowed. He had known he was among them. He had become egoless, only to take more pride in knowing his greater abilities because of his visions.

Caught between living in the world or remaining separate from it, he had made his choice. Wasn't that the argument he and Lisa had always had? He had insisted that he needed to use the world to create a vision for others, while Lisa was determined to leave the world to find peace for herself. In Mahayana Buddhism, one chose rebirth to Earth out of compassion, to teach others how to achieve enlightenment; in Hinayana Buddhism, one worked to liberate oneself from the karmic cycle of rebirth. The choice was a fundamental part of being human, the sacred birthright of each human soul. Only now did he know with certainty that he and Lisa had chosen different paths in their expression of the Divine.

Lisa. Her name burned across his mind in a blaze of newfound shame. A clear image formed of her distraught face as he'd accused her of deception, and in that face . . . he recognized her innocence.

She's been a dream to me, he thought, *a beautiful, seductive jewel. Unavailable. Irresistible. A dream that I should have awakened from long ago. Someone with great empathy, whose emotions I manipulated each time I needed a place to put my hurt.*

He hugged his knees and laid his head on his arms as he recalled his pursuit, lust blinding him to his inability to accept her spiritual path, just as she could not accept his. Neither could change the course of their lives, which left them with nothing in common except the mutual needs of their bodies, their dangerous play with the root chakra.

The room darkened, only a hint of dusk still at the window. "Lisa," he whispered, raising his face to the dimming sky, "I'm sorry. Please forgive me."

Overwhelmed, his chest hurt, causing him to take several deep breaths against his welling tears. And suddenly, he was crying, low sobs shaking his body. He buried his face in his arms again, crying not only for Lisa and his lost freedom, for the hurt of his body, but also for Nareesh's bitterness, for his father's sorrow, Lama Loden's gift, for Ram Seva's loyalty, and for Kathy, who, by now, surely knew she'd been abandoned.

He suddenly imagined he could hear Kathy's voice, the harsh truth of her words.

Tears? You're acting like you didn't know what you were doing. You get your hands slapped and you cry like a baby. Wake up! You know the penalties for smuggling and manufacturing, and you know why you take the risks.

The moon must have risen, because a silvery sheen brought a new low light to the room. The air was getting colder; the night ahead would be long. He wiped the tears from his face and pushed away from the wall, to stand, to pay attention to Kathy's spirit, to pull himself together. He began the ritual that was his, the steady pacing that helped him put his thoughts together. As he walked, he tried to remember Nareesh's face at the door of the guesthouse. It was hard to remember. He'd been so out of control. Nareesh had not expected to see Kali, of that he was certain. Why had he come at all? To revel in his revenge? To gloat?

No. His eyes had held sorrow and regret. What would he feel—or do—once he realized his vengeance had been a terrible mistake?

Perhaps, Christian thought, with a flicker of hope, *perhaps Nareesh will find a way to get me out.*

The temperature continued to drop, and Christian continued to walk the cell, his arms wrapped around his body, wondering when he had ever been this cold.

Maybe the night on Haleakala, he thought. *But how different—the stars in the darkness, colors behind my closed lids, Kathy's body beside me, her warm breath. If they sentence me to prison, it may be a long time before I see her again.*

For the second time, tears flooded his eyes. He fought with himself, battled the self-pity. *If only I'd stayed in New Delhi to drive with Bob and Dharma.*

With a sudden surprised rush, his thoughts flew to Bob and Dharma. How could he have forgotten? What day was it? If this was Monday, they should have left at noon. But what if they'd waited a day, hoping he'd be back to take care of business? Even if they left tomorrow, they'd still need a good day to get through India. That's two days until they split the country. They might even need three.

Why's the lieutenant so sure I have partners and a larger stash? Why does he keep insisting on names? How much does he know, and how much is guesswork?

Answer the questions while it's still comfortable to do so, he'd threatened.

Under severe questioning, can I hold out for three days?

Whatever they did would be painful. He'd heard the stories—men beaten on the soles of their feet, the damage so pervasive that they would always walk with pain, beatings with fists and thongs, other unimaginable tortures. He was already surprised he wasn't in with the general population, subjected to appalling conditions, to bullying and beatings by the guards and attacks from the other inmates.

Okay, Bob, Dharma, he promised silently. *You've got three days. If it gets bad, I'll try to hold out for three days.*

In the hours before dawn, tired and sick at heart, he lay on the cold concrete floor, an arm for a pillow, and tried to remember the meditation Lama Loden had taught to warm his body. But thoughts crept into his mind, distracting him. The rest of the night passed in fitful snatches of sleep, attempted meditation, and the ever-pressing cold seeping from the damp floor, until at last, with welcomed relief, Christian saw the lightening of the sky behind the window and prayed for the warmth of the little square patch of sunlight.

Not long after the day had dawned, there came the sound of voices and feet in the corridor, the sound of a key in the lock. Christian hoped this time the tea would be hot.

As the door swung back on its hinges, two soldiers entered the room, and a third stood at the entranceway. Christian's already lacerated wrists were cuffed together tightly in front of him, and he was pushed toward the door.

"Step out," the man with the rifle said. "You're wanted upstairs for questioning."

"So," the lieutenant began as Christian stood weakly in front of his desk, "how are you feeling?"

Straightening his back, Christian smiled slightly, the English public school voice back, sure to irritate the lieutenant. "Quite well, thank you. Although I must admit the accommodations are a bit sparse."

The lieutenant's eyes narrowed. "Then you won't mind standing."

"I'm quite comfortable."

"Your government has become very interested in your case." The lieutenant eyed him. "They are interested in a certain group of criminals engaged in smuggling operations."

"Lieutenant, I'm sure that, by now, you have reason to realize that this has been a terrible mistake. I haven't the faintest idea what you expect from me. I just hope that you are not severely reprimanded for your treatment of an American citizen."

"You dare to threaten me?"

"It's not a threat. I'm simply aware of my rights."

"You would not care to elaborate on your smuggling operations?"

"I don't think you understand. I tried to talk to you yesterday. My name is Christian Alden . . . I don't know who this Brooks is . . . and, unfortunately, I was set up by a jealous lover in a dispute over a woman. The briefcase wasn't mine."

"So the man has tried to tell me," the lieutenant answered, his eyes fixed on Christian for response.

Christian faltered. "When?"

"Sunday evening. After we brought you in."

"If you had his testimony, why didn't you release me then?"

"Because something doesn't fit," the lieutenant said, standing. "I believe you are involved in some kind of familial dispute with . . . the *holy man* . . . " His voice contained a stab of sarcasm.

Christian felt his mouth tighten at the attack on Nareesh's character, but he was alert now, because the lieutenant's mind was concerned with something more than Nareesh and religion.

"Yet there is more. Your government sent an agent to work with Interpol in Afghanistan. I believe you were in Afghanistan, yes?"

Christian's smile froze on his face. His passport would contain the visa.

"While he was there, the agent was able to record certain activities. You and your friends were observed with a particular pair of Afghan brothers well known for their activities in hashish circles." The lieutenant walked around his desk and stopped in front of Christian.

"When you were first arrested, I took the liberty of checking a special list of traffickers for your name. It's there. Alden. And whether the name is Brooks or Alden is unimportant."

Christian's voice lost any amusement, and in the tone well practiced by the privileged of his school, said, "I admire a man with ambition."

The inflection of his speech struck the lieutenant with the same force a strong backhand might have. Rage curled the lieutenant's lips, made fists of his hands.

Surprisingly, he sat back on the desk and caressed the pleat in his trousers as he attempted to regain his composure. "You know, Mr. Alden, an Interpol agent is due to question you, but once he leaves, you are my prisoner. If you cannot give suitable answers to relatively simple questions, I'm afraid I might have to . . . extract the answers." At the moment, the pleasure he would take in hearing Christian's screams was written on his face.

"And when is the agent to arrive?"

"Today. At two."

"And this is . . . Tuesday?"

The lieutenant nodded. "Enjoy your morning, Mr. Alden. It might be your last enjoyment for a while. Unless, of course, there is something you would like to say?"

"I don't believe we have anything to discuss."

At a signal from the lieutenant's finger, one of the guards pushed Christian toward the door. At the last moment before leaving, he turned back to the desk. "There is one thing. The woman who was with me. What happened to her?"

"I can well understand your interest," the lieutenant smiled, "but the fact is that she has disappeared."

"What do you mean 'disappeared'?"

"After you . . . lost consciousness . . . she ran down the stairs to the street. The disciple tried to stop her but couldn't find her. To my knowledge, she hasn't been seen since. Too bad—such a beautiful woman."

Stunned, Christian could not answer. The guard pulled him from the room.

Christian once again sat against the wall of his cell, alone, his wrists still handcuffed. The interview with the lieutenant had not gone well. Ironically, the US government—the very source of his problems—was also the source of some comfort. The coming meeting with the official had probably saved his ass; the lieutenant couldn't afford to produce a tortured American prisoner, regardless of how relevant the information might be to his gaining a promotion. They had done everything to begin to break him—solitary confinement, no mat or blanket, rancid food, handcuffs selectively gauged to rub against his wrists that were already raw.

But none of these things bothered him as much as the information he had just learned. He closed his eyes. His mind, honed by a growing sense of danger and heightened by the lack of food and sleep, began to search through the lieutenant's conversation for clues.

Two thoughts were clearly dominant. Where was Lisa? And was it possible that Interpol had the license plate number of the truck?

He prayed that whatever they did, he could hold out for one more day. That was the promise. Three days for Bob and Dharma.

20

NAREESH, KALI, AND KATHY
VARANASI, INDIA
NOVEMBER 1969

Padmananda's dreams were disturbing. He tossed uneasily. "No . . . ," he cried to a running figure far in the distance. But the golden hair flew in the air and the face fled away from him. "No!" he cried aloud.

Then, his eyes opened. A sharp breath escaped his throat.

"My son," a voice said gently.

Padmananda turned from the tangle of his sheets to see Daya Nanda sitting quietly in a chair near his bed. "Master, did I sleep? But . . . how could I? . . . Kali . . . "

"Kali has returned. She is in her room. She waits for you."

A desperate anxiety filled him. How was he to face her? What could he possibly say? He could barely breathe.

"I have something for you," the Master said. "A gift."

"A . . . a gift?"

"It is a name. You spoke with the lieutenant, did you not? And he told you that Christian was to be imprisoned?"

"I am caught in my own trap. The lieutenant cannot be bribed by money. His motivation is his ambition. And Christian is a catch that gives him credence in diplomatic circles. Perhaps another time, money would do. But now he thinks of position and power."

"The name I give you is a superior to the lieutenant. For the right price, doors may be left unlocked, chains removed. It is for you to determine what price you will pay."

Padmananda's face took on a spark of life. "Anything. I'll pay anything to undo what I've done."

The Master shook his head. "You may be asked to pay only part
of the price. Others may have to pay the rest. Do not decide someone
else's fate too rashly. Here is the name of a colonel at the prison."

When Kali opened the door to Padmananda, she could not raise her
head to him, simply stared at his feet as he stood there, unmoving.

Alarmed, desperate, she asked, *will he enter? Will he refuse even
friendship?*

Finally, taking the courage to look into this face, she saw that his
eyes were shining with unshed tears and filled with emotion—longing,
regret, embarrassment, and deep sadness. Her initial impulse was to
take him into her arms, to comfort, to explain the joy of his presence,
to confess the deep wellspring of love that grasped her body. Instead,
her actions were tempered by memory. She'd taken to Christian's bed
with abandon, left the conference she and Padmananda had worked so
hard to direct, had forgotten the sick, the poor, the abandoned. How
were they to bridge this gap? How could he ever forgive her?

"Padmananda . . . ," she whispered, and began to softly weep. "I'm
so sorry. So sorry."

"No," he said softly, tears falling quietly down his face. "Not Padmananda. Nareesh. For the moment, only Nareesh. I must go back to
the boy and earn the right to become the man."

He held out his arms and she walked into them. "I betrayed your
love. I . . . "

"And what I did? How can I even ask for forgiveness. I tried to
destroy the two people who mean most to me. Don't cry, Kali," he
begged. "We are all in danger because of my actions. Me alone." Then
he lifted her chin so that she looked into his face. "And in the future,
will we not understand more about the weaknesses of others we counsel? Knowing our own?" His lips bent to gently touch hers.

Kathy stepped forward. She had been standing near the window, so still she was almost invisible. Kali stepped away from Nareesh, wiping her eyes as she reached for Kathy's hand. "This is Kathleen Murray. She's a good friend of Christian's. She's here to help."

Suddenly serious, Nareesh nodded. "We must combine all our strength and abilities to get Christian released."

Kathy exhaled. "I was worried," she said, looking directly into Nareesh's eyes. "Prepared to dislike you." Then, more softly she added, "But now I see that everything will be alright. You love Christian."

"All is not lost," Nareesh told them. "We have Daya Nanda to guide us. And he has given us a name."

"Now let me see," the colonel said, looking down again at the papers on the desk. "Christian Alden. Yes, he's still here. And I do recall a visit from an old friend last night."

Colonel Janata was a man in his late forties with the darker skin characteristic of southern Indians, raven-colored eyes, and dark hair touched by isolated gray strands. He was huge, big-framed, with marks of dissipation on his face, and his bulk so dominated the room that it was easy to overlook the shrewdness in his eyes. Janata, rumor held, had a logical mind in solving cases, a reported ruthlessness, and a generosity in sharing bribes that ensured the loyalty of his men.

Nareesh sat between the two women, and Kathy saw that he waited patiently—too patiently—for Janata to finish his perusal of the papers. "There will be a price," Nareesh had warned them in the hotel room. "But I will pay whatever it takes."

Kathy moved restlessly in the chair where she waited, repelled by the heavy belly resting in his lap, and impatient with what she considered his slowness.

How much? Just tell us how much!

She noted the colonel's pudgy fingers as they worked through his greasy hair then dropped back to the papers on the desk. Occasionally, the narrow, amused eyes would glance up toward Padmananda, turn to linger on Kali's face, then turn to her own.

Why, the bastard's studying us, she thought.

"It seems this arrest is one of a sensitive nature. Apparently, Mr. Alden was seen in Afghanistan with certain persons of ill repute. Unfortunately, the men with Mr. Alden disappeared before the license number of the car they drove was recorded."

"Why would someone want to take down the license number of Mr. Alden's car?" Nareesh hedged.

"The information was taken by an Interpol agent working in Afghanistan on international drug trafficking."

"Surely an error."

"This same agent believed the car was on its way to India. To Bombay. But so far, the car has not appeared where it was expected. The American officer involved in the case would like to ask Mr. Alden the location of the vehicle. I understand that he will be here at two this afternoon to question the prisoner." Kathy winced at the news, and Janata added for emphasis, "It will not be easy for him."

"What can we do?" Padmananda asked. "Surely, now that you have heard the details of the case, you must understand that this has been no more than a small family disagreement. I'm sure you know about family disagreements, yes?"

The colonel laughed, quivering the jowls around his neck. "Quite right, sir. Quite right. We all fall into family arguments. If only this were so straightforward. Why, Mr. Alden could pay the fine and be on his way. But with the US government and Interpol involved . . . well, you can see the problem is not so straightforward. There will be many questions and inquiries. There is even the possibility of a small international incident. I'm sure you understand."

"There must be something we can do," Kathy said impatiently, sitting forward in her chair. "Surely, you know a way."

Padmananda gave her a hard look, his eyes telling her to sit back and keep quiet.

Swallowing her next words, she pushed herself back in the seat, but her eyes held the demanding tone of her voice.

"You must understand," the colonel said to Padmananda, "it is a very difficult position for one such as I. To have to answer to the US Embassy . . . well . . . " He shuddered.

"I realize," Padmananda answered agreeably, "that the discomfort must be offset. It is a great task indeed."

"It will probably mean many meetings and inquiries at all levels," Janata explained, looking across the desk, "and at each of these levels, there will be those called upon to give an account of their actions."

"I understand perfectly. Each level of involvement must be satisfied."

"A large factor is the problem of time. We have, perhaps, three hours before the meeting between Mr. Alden and Interpol. Once this meeting takes place, I will no longer have any control in the matter whatsoever."

"What is it that will open doors and satisfy the distress of all involved?" Padmananda asked directly.

"Probably five thousand US dollars," Colonel Janata said in a flat, even voice.

Padmananda recoiled slightly—a small gesture, but it told Kathy that he had never heard of such a fee for this service before. He hesitated.

"It'll take time to raise that kind of money," Kathy said. "It will have to be wired from the United States."

The colonel smiled.

Padmananda shot Kathy a warning glance that told her she'd blown it, although she wasn't quite sure how. Five grand was small enough payment for Christian's freedom.

"What is it you can afford to pay now, in the next hour?" the colonel asked her directly.

Kathy considered for a moment, not sure she understood Padmananda's signals. She'd come with four thousand dollars, most of which she still had in the pack with her. If she offered him two, she'd still have enough bucks to get herself and Christian out of the country. "Two," she said at last. "I can give you two grand."

"But, my dear, that may help our guards and prison workers, but what of me?" he laid his hand on his breast, his eyes wide with the question. "What will be my reward for my trouble?"

"Colonel Janata," Padmananda jumped in, "two thousand dollars is a very generous offer. Very generous," he added, with another look toward Kathy.

"Perhaps for some cases, but for an international incident? What do I tell my superiors? The US Embassy? The American agent? The Afghan government? Surely, you see the seriousness of the matter?"

"There's only two thousand dollars," Kathy told him bluntly, "and time's getting short."

The look Janata gave Kathy told her the game had changed, and for the first time, she felt fear—not for herself, but for Christian trapped in this unknown system. The same desperate feeling she had felt pulling Jose from the gully swept over her. Anything . . . she would do anything to keep Christian from getting hurt.

Before the colonel could speak, she shook her head. "I'm sorry," she told him in a quiet, frightened voice. "I seem to have been extremely rude to people over the last few days. A lot has happened in a short span of time." She could no longer lift her eyes to the colonel's. "I just need Christian back. I hope you'll understand."

The apology took the tension from the room and softened the colonel's voice, if not his words. "Two thousand dollars in an hour . . . and your personal favor," he said calmly, looking at Kathy. "Or yours," he cast his eyes toward Kali.

Padmananda stood abruptly, but Kathy continued to stare into Janata's eyes. Something there told her the offer was good—and firm. There was a risk the man had to take to order Christian freed, and this was the price that risk was worth to him. Kathy had seen that look a hundred times before, in almost every business deal she'd undertaken. An exchange had meant risk for someone, and each had named his or her price. Janata's eyes told her this was a straightforward business deal, a proposition she could understand. But she had never sold herself before.

"A very interesting offer," Padmananda said. "I'm sure you can appreciate that this is not a decision I can make alone. If you will excuse us, we will give you our answer shortly. Good day."

Padmananda, held out a hand to Kali, who grasped it, stood, and left the room without looking back. Kathy started for the door. At the last moment, she turned to look into Janata's eyes. "Thank you for your help," she told him, meaning it.

The colonel smiled graciously, standing. "May I again stress the importance of time?"

"We understand," Kathy nodded. "Good day."

Padmananda closed the door behind him and walked in angry silence through the prison and out the small front door in the high gate to the waiting taxi.

"My God!" Kali was first to speak as they took seats in the cab. "Can you believe what he asked?"

Kathy looked at her, perplexed. "We were the ones asking. He was simply stating the price of a business arrangement."

"There will be no consideration of this offer," Padmananda interjected. "The price is unacceptable."

Kathy sat back in her seat and stared out the window.

"What will we do then?" asked Kali.

"We'll appeal to the American Embassy, explain that there's been a mistake. The Master has friends in secure government positions who will help. It'll just take a little more time, and we'll need to hire a good attorney."

"How much longer?" asked Kali.

"We'll have to wait and see."

"What about the agent coming from Afghanistan?"

Padmananda said quietly, "That's something Christian will have to face. If he values the freedom of his friends, perhaps he can hold out."

Kathy's head suddenly whipped toward him. "What do you mean 'hold out'? What kind of questioning are we talking about?"

Padmananda tried to shrug the question off. "I'm not sure. But it will be intense, and if he's already hurt . . . "

"You mean you won't say."

On the way back to the hotel, Kali and Padmananda gave words to their fears, questions, and proposals, while Kathy continued to stare out the window, involved with her own thoughts. Every once in a while, she would tune into the conversation between the two of them, slightly shake her head, and refocus out the window. The terror Padmananda tried to conceal in his voice told her he understood as completely as she did what the situation involved.

Why are they hesitating? she wondered. *It's so simple. Two grand and a fuck. God, what could be more clear? And there's only two hours to put everything in motion.*

When they reached the Mahabharata Hotel, Padmananda and Kali stepped from the taxi. "Coming?" he asked when Kathy didn't move.

"I need some time alone," she answered, looking down at a hole in the floorboard. "I think I'll go out to the river for a while."

Before Padmananda could protest, she raised her eyes to his and watched as he slowly realized, began to shake his head, started to speak . . . then she reached out to pull closed the taxi door.

Leaning forward to the driver, she said simply, "Let's go." Reassured by the pack beside her that held the money, the key to Christian's release, she directed, "Take me back to the prison."

Just a straight business deal, she reminded herself. *Just business, like every other deal. Only this time, the product's different.*

"My dear, so good of you to accept my offer," the colonel spoke in a syrupy voice. "I was hoping to see you again."

"You said there wasn't much time," she answered, putting the two grand down on his desk.

"It is done. He will be released."

Kathy shook her head. "I want to see him. Once I see him safely outside the walls, I'll pay the rest."

The colonel's eyes narrowed.

"I'll pay. I swear it," she whispered.

He smiled placatingly. "Of course, my dear," he answered soothingly, reminding her of a fat old tomcat toying with a mouse.

"I have a taxi at the front gate," she told him. "Please see that it waits at whichever gate you intend to use."

Opening the door, Janata barked an order that shook her further—hard, commanding, threatening. A man came running within seconds. A brief dialogue was exchanged while the man stared wide-eyed with curiosity at Kathy. At some point in the conversation, he smiled, surely feeling the increase in his income. The colonel's furrowed brow spoke more to Kathy than his words to the man. He was worried. After a last vehement sentence, he turned back to her, the cat again.

"My dear. If you please. Follow this man. I will meet you at the gate. The agent has already arrived. You must hurry."

Kathy took a few steps forward, then turned back to face Janata. "You . . . you wouldn't want to take an extra grand instead of . . . ?"

"Of you? My dear! I thought we understood each other!"

She nodded, then followed the guard down an isolated corridor, reeking of urine and damp with cold and slime. The sounds of the guard's shuffling footsteps and the clink of the metal keys vibrated within the littered corridor. Low, flat voices, intermixed with an occasional muffled outburst from some unseen place, filled the hallway.

"Here," the man said, stopping before a door.

Kathy held her breath as the jailer fit the tarnished old key to the lock, stepped back, and motioned for her to enter. She hesitated. Janata could arrest her and take everything he wanted without releasing Christian. Why hadn't she foreseen this possibility? Was this one of the things Padmananda had feared?

"Quickly!" the man ordered, causing her to jump.

Gasping at the fetid odor, she stepped gingerly into the dim cell. Christian appeared to be sleeping, sitting in the corner with his head thrown back, knees drawn up, his handcuffed wrists tight around his legs. Her heart broke at the sight of his short, disheveled hair, the growth of beard, the filthy clothes.

"Hurry!" the guard spat.

She tried to still her shaking and knelt beside him. "Christian . . . Christian, my love . . . ," she whispered in his ear, crying softly, kissing him gently. She felt him stir.

Far away on a welcomed flight from reality, Christian heard someone call his name. Kathy's voice. He could feel her hair fall over him, a gentle kiss upon his mouth, wondered if it was morning, tried to remember what appointments he'd made for the day. He reached up to put his arms about her and had some difficulty moving. The pain of his wrists cut through the dream, and he found himself wholly awake and looking into Kathy's tear-brimmed eyes, the soft feel of her hair floating about his arms.

"Kathy," he whispered, his voice rasping.

"Hurry!" the man at the door hissed again.

"Are you alright?" she asked in a low voice. "Can you walk?"

"What are you doing here? What's happening?" Struggling to his feet, Christian leaned unsteadily against the wall.

"Take these off," Kathy demanded of the jailer, keeping her voice low.

He grunted and held out a key to Christian's waiting arms. The chains fell to the floor, and Kathy touched Christian's raw wrists.

"This is the best deal I've ever made," she mumbled.

"What's that?" he asked.

"Hurry, hurry," the man repeated.

The guard put the handcuffs inside his shirt, then the three of them were outside the door, listening to the lock click. They moved quickly and quietly down the hallway, upstairs through corridors, along the side of an open courtyard, to the privacy of a small side door in the high wall where the colonel waited.

"There's a taxi outside," the colonel told Christian, looking furtively around. "The driver will take you to your friends."

Christian nodded and started through the door, then turned back to Kathy. "Let's go," he told her.

"Go on," she said evenly. "I'll meet you. I have a few details to clean up."

"Come with me now!" Christian demanded, looking from her to the colonel.

She pushed him gently, firmly through the door. "Christian, my love, for me . . . you've got to get going."

"You'd better hurry," the colonel added. "The US agent is already here. You should have been long gone by now."

"Soon," Kathy told him, "I'll see you soon." And before he could speak, she quickly closed the wooden door.

Leaning against the door, Kathy opened her eyes to see the colonel watching. He walked forward and placed one arm on the wall above her.

"You can't back out now," he said with satisfaction.

Kathy met his gaze, thinking of all the men she had loved with her body. "I won't. This is the best deal I've ever made."

"This way, please." The colonel smiled and gestured with an arm. "Just one more thing. I'd like to enjoy it."

21

MYLES

VARANASI, INDIA

NOVEMBER 1969

Myles Corbet was ushered into the lieutenant's office with all due respect. As a representative of the US government, he had learned to enjoy the power he had in foreign countries. People sought out his favor, ingratiated themselves. There was always a dinner party, an open consulate door, or an important meeting that was only important because he was there. He was no longer the frightened botany student who had turned informant to protect his name and his future position with the university.

"Good afternoon, lieutenant," Myles greeted him. "It's good of you to receive me so quickly. I came right from the airport."

"I'm pleased you are here," the lieutenant answered cordially. "Unfortunately, I don't think you will be satisfied with the attitude of our prisoner."

"Alden? What seems to be the problem?"

"He has not only been totally uncooperative, but he has tried to threaten me with your government's disapproval for the way he has been treated."

Myles chuckled. "I have a feeling Mr. Alden thinks too much of himself. Perhaps if I were to speak to him . . . ?"

"Shall I have my man bring him now?"

"First, explain to me the conditions of his arrest."

"Several nights ago, I received a visit from a well-respected man of this community. He apologized for the lateness of the hour, but he had heard, on good authority, that a young man traveling in this country had a supply of hashish. He felt it his duty to inform me and give me the address of his lodgings." Here the lieutenant hesitated.

"Go on."

"I'm afraid the case is a bit muddled. I have reason to believe the quantity of hashish we recovered from Mr. Alden's room was, indeed, not his. It is his own karma, of course, to be punished with the very thing that is his sin. But from your information, he should have had a larger supply."

Myles was confused. "How much of the drug did you find in Mr. Alden's room?"

"Five pounds."

"Five? I expected a hundred. Possibly more. The other men whose names I telephoned?"

"Their location is unknown. My fear is that these men and the contraband you seek may leave the country, or that the hashish may be hidden until a more appropriate time to move it. If you wish to recover the cache, it is imperative that Mr. Alden give you the information you need. And quickly. We've already had him here three days, and I cannot see that his attitude is weakening." The lieutenant gave him a measured look. "We do have the means of extracting information, but we were unsure of your government's policy . . . " And here he shrugged, allowing Myles to use his imagination.

But Myles had no imagination in this area. "Explain."

"To start . . . belts or canes on his stripped body. If that does not produce results, we can dislocate bones, especially the hips. Of course, we can put them back, but your Mr. Alden might find some difficulty walking for the rest of his life. Electric shock on the genitals. Other methods."

Myles took a deep breath. "Why don't you let me talk with Mr. Alden?" he said in a flat tone.

Jesus. He's asking me to condone torture.

"Very well," the lieutenant nodded, giving the order. "There is another possibility," he continued after the soldier had left. "There is a young woman involved in the case. It appears that Mr. Alden was set up in a dispute over this woman. We may be able to use Alden's feelings for her as leverage."

"Possibly." Myles gave a curt nod.

"Let me offer you some tea, sir."

"Thank you," Myles answered.

As he sat in the lieutenant's office, outwardly calm, sipping his tea, his thoughts went back to the suggestion of making Alden give them some quick answers. For the second time in his life he faced an impossible moral decision. The first time, he'd been nineteen years old, startled by the appearance of big men in the ROTC commandant's office and the words that had shattered his life. "You're under arrest, Corbet."

"You've got to be kidding!" he'd cried. "For two joints!"

But the supervisor of the Northern California Bureau of Narcotic Control, Dolph Bremer, had not been kidding. In fact, his outburst had appeared to solidify Bremer's interest in him.

"I'm sorry, Corbet," the commandant had further admonished, "but we're going to have to make an example of you."

That day, he'd been forced to betray a friend, Jerry, the man he believed he loved. If not, he would have been arrested, fingerprinted, given a record. His name would have been headlines because his father was the renowned head of the biology department at UC Berkeley.

Now, as a maturing agent for the federal drug bureau in Washington working with Interpol, he was being asked to condone a man's torture. For a brief moment, in that shirt shop, he and Alden had actually liked each other. They were the same age, from the same place, recognized the same intuitive instincts in one another, both far from home, and but for two joints a long time ago, they might have been friends.

Myles shook away the thoughts.

I've got to get home, take up my life again, make it my own. I can't take much more of Bremer using me as he pleases. I just can't let this chance get away from me.

As he had before, Myles hardened himself to the situation. The choice wasn't his, but Alden's. He desperately needed answers to questions, and if Alden refused to supply them, the price was his to pay. Besides, how long could a privileged young American hold out? And for a load of hash?

The lieutenant was beginning to pace the room. A look of relief crossed his face at the opening door, only to quickly turn to dark anger when he saw the ashen face of the soldier. "Sir, a moment with you alone, please," the man asked.

"Speak it now," the lieutenant's voice was dangerously quiet. "What is it? Where is the prisoner?"

The man turned from the lieutenant to Myles. Myles felt his stomach turn.

"He's gone, sir," the soldier said.

"Gone? What do you mean?"

"Disappeared. I've looked everywhere. The cell is locked . . . and he is gone."

Myles stood abruptly. "Are you trying to tell me that you have misplaced the prisoner?"

The lieutenant turned toward his desk for a moment, then turned back to Myles with a great measure of control. "No, sir. Not misplaced. The man is gone."

"Do you mean disappeared?"

"Exactly, sir. Disappeared. Gone."

Myles abruptly rose to his full height, and in a well-trained diplomatic voice, said, "My government will be extremely annoyed. They will, of course, demand an immediate and full investigation."

"Your government," the lieutenant answered angrily, "can demand all it wants. But the fact is that the prisoner is gone."

Myles regarded the man's defeated eyes and realized the full extent of what this disappearance meant to him. "Can't you make inquiries?"

"I can inquire all I want. No one will have seen anything. It appears your Mr. Alden has . . . influence. There will, of course, be an investigation."

Myles had to accept the fact just as bitterly as the lieutenant. "You will send me word when you have news?"

The lieutenant nodded. "When the investigation is complete."

"Then I bid you good day, lieutenant," and he turned to leave the office.

"One moment, Mr. Corbet. Another fact that may be useful. I have reason to believe that Alden's true name is Christian Brooks. I hope this will be of some help."

"It means all the passports are fraudulent. Thank you, lieutenant. Perhaps it was worth coming to Varanasi just for that information."

22

KATHY
VARANASI, INDIA
NOVEMBER 1969

Closing the door to his office, the colonel sat comfortably in his big chair and demanded that she undress. Leaning back, he lazily watched while she began removing her clothing in front of the cot that rested against the far wall. She could already see the bulge in his pants.

Kathy had not tried to imagine what the afternoon might mean, what the man would demand. She could never have imagined his power over her. A simple possession of her body, the release of his lust, skin against skin, and it would be over. Only several hours later, after humiliation, rape and oral sex, a beating and sodomy, did she know Nareesh's fears. For he had heard the stories and knew that in every war, every dispute between men, the victor would always take the woman in a show of power. The colonel, Nareesh had known, would long to inflict himself on what he considered Kathy's insolence and arrogance.

In the end, when the man finally unlocked the cuffs from around her wrists, she was unable to move for many minutes. Slowly, she found her hands and pulled the gag from her mouth, wondering what would come next, no longer caring. To her surprise, the man was already dressed and sitting on the edge of the cot.

"I want you to know, I did enjoy the afternoon," he told her, humor in his voice.

Kathy closed her eyes against him and said nothing.

"When you dress, open the door, and the soldier will show you out. Thank you again, my dear." With a bow, he left the room.

Kathy looked around for anything to wipe away the tears she could no longer control, the saliva and mucous that smeared her face, the anal blood between her thighs. She took a long, painful time to dress. When she finally gained some control over her heaving chest, she opened the door and found herself quickly on the street, the guard anxious to be rid of her. Stepping into a taxi, she could not bear the thought of going to the hotel to face the questions and looks in the faces of those who waited for her. How could she hide the extent of what had happened?

Instead, she went to the river, to a quiet, solitary *ghat* and, sitting with difficulty, focused her gaze on the water. There, she watched the river until the sun went down, sitting through the night, moving only long enough to put on the jacket she carried in her pack.

Her thoughts carried her back to the beginning, to her school days in Baton Rouge, and how, with laughter and courage, she and Marcie had set out on a journey they believed would better mankind. Retracing her steps along the highways as they had hitched, she shuddered now in fear of what might easily have happened on that Texas night with a dozen frustrated and drunken cowboys roaring by them in pickups.

The poverty of her first days on Haight Street touched her, the lights that played on her eyelids as she danced behind Felix and his band, the needle puncturing her vein with the wild rush of methamphetamine, the nauseating downer of heroin. The weakness of hepatitis. The birth of Marcie's baby. The high tension of every deal passed through her body like a wave. The faces of the men she'd loved. The tribal friendships bound together by the insight and visions of shared psychedelic experiences, the moment of ecstasy, touching the face of God.

She remembered the nights she and Carolyn had bedded Larry, his smile and passion, the bloodstained body, still and dead, Jose's agony.

All these weeks, she'd held her memory of Larry at bay. Now she wanted to feel him and touch the pain. She wanted to look at it, to let the hurt pass through her body, change her, then fly from her hands like a newly released bird. She replayed touching his straight raven hair, knew his kindness and arrogance, sensed his mind. Larry held all the essentials of the New Age: beauty and health, compassion and strength, morality and idealism. Now he was gone forever, would never touch her again. It was hard to believe that existence could be such a thin line—life on one side, death on the other.

As if in a dream, she remembered the first time she'd seen Christian's face in the light of Bob's window, remembered him trying to crawl into her womb on Haleakala, pulling her from the riots in Berkeley, teaching yoga at Woodstock, moving hundreds of grams of acid around in a shopping bag, rolling over in the morning to pull her to him.

On through the night, she remembered every detail of the last three years.

She had gone to Larry because he had called her, and now she had to face the fact that Christian had felt abandoned. He had come halfway around the world to look for a woman who could offer him the stability he yearned for, a woman to care for him, to have his children. Yes, she had bedded Larry. But that was one afternoon, the special touch of a brother. Christian had moved her out, had gone to Kali to ask her to be his lady. He had committed to this woman. And that made the difference.

Hurt and angry, she wasn't sure she would ever recover from this new scar in a place already open and raw. Hadn't she promised herself long ago never to chase a man who did not want her?

Sitting in the dark, shivering with cold, the welts burning across her buttocks, she reminded herself that she and Marcie had planned to change the world. But what had they changed? She had never understood that the world was so large, filled with so many people and so many needs, so many motivations. She had never known the world held such evil. How did you touch all those people? How did you give them the dream? Where was she to go from here?

The answer came to her as a soft whisper, but quick and sure.

Only into myself, into my own strength, as I always have.

At some point during the night, she must have slept. She was awakened just before the first rays of light by dogs sniffing at her prostrate figure. The sun rose and ascended, and in that new dawn, she knew she was on her own.

Time to go home.

But before I leave, I'll have to see that Christian has the money and his passport to get back.

Suddenly, she remembered that he might be sick or hurt and wondered whether it were serious. No matter. Others would certainly have cared for him by now. That is . . . if Christian had done what he was supposed to do. How often had that happened?

A small fear pushed her to stand.

I just need to make sure he's alright, and then I'll be on my way.

For those along the Ganges, the sun rose in a perfect fiery ball, red and mesmerizing, full of hope. Around her, people stepped into the water with prayers and chants. She turned and cast one long look at the sun, put down her bag, and performed an *asana*, the Salutation to the Sun.

Some of her strength returned, and she promised herself that she would not submit to self-pity. She would go on.

But she also knew, even in the beauty and joy of this awakening morning, that youth and innocence had completely died, just as sure and final as the body being cremated nearby.

23

CHRISTIAN
VARANASI, INDIA
NOVEMBER 1969

Christian and Nareesh had spent a sleepless night, talking, remembering, catching up on the lost years, sharing all the emotions and fears and secret dark places of the soul that had consumed them since the night of the riot. Once again, Christian recounted the story of Lama's death, and Nareesh relived the overturned cart, the trampled, lifeless body of his father. They spoke of the cremation of Ram Seva, his ashes taken to the Ganges, of Lama Loden's cremation and the hundreds of orange and maroon robes of the monks who had attended, the drums and horns and Tibetan prayer flags surrounding the bier. Nareesh told Christian about his role at Ananda Shiva, the clinic he was building. Christian explained why he had committed to distributing sacraments. Without even realizing it, they had slipped into the roles they had always played when with each other, had become the same two brothers they had once been.

Throughout the long evening and night, they watched the door, waiting for footsteps in the hallway, a tap on the wood, any sound that would tell them that Kathy had returned. What they would not do is count the passing hours aloud, put into words their worst fears, speculate on where Kathy was and what the colonel might have done to her. They both took full responsibility, and they both agonized over why it had to be Kathy who paid for their mistakes. Not until early morning did Christian finally put words to his fears, and several times, Nareesh had to caution Christian to patience. Christian wanted to return to the prison to demand her whereabouts. Surely, he would be arrested. Would he give away all that Kathy had bought?

When Kathy finally did appear at the Mahabharata, the sun was well up, and Christian had already roused himself from the chair where he'd fallen asleep near the window. With the knock on the door, his mind stopped, his body afraid to move for several precious seconds. When he finally tore open the door, Kathy stood there, a bag slung over her shoulder. Nareesh murmured a thankful prayer and, fearful of looking into her eyes, had excused himself, closing the door quietly behind.

Christian reached for her, but she turned away from him. "Please," he pleaded, "let me hold you."

She shook her head and threw the bag on the bed.

"Have you been at the prison all night?" Christian asked in a voice that feared the answer. "Are you hurt? Please, Kathy, speak to me."

Kathy unfastened the straps of the pack, refusing to look at him. "Hurt? No. I just needed some time to think. I spent the night sitting on a *ghat*. I must have fallen asleep."

Incredulous, Christian cried, "Why didn't you come here! You knew I was waiting! Why didn't you come?"

"I've just come to give you some money. And your passport. I found it cleaning your room."

"The deal with the colonel . . . you don't know the danger . . . "

"Don't I? It was the only deal in town," she said, cutting him off.

"I wouldn't have let you do it," he told her with a tearful hoarseness. "I could have handled anything they threw at me!"

"Sure you could have." And to Christian's further anguish, he watched her shudder. "You're the one who apparently doesn't know the danger. They want the truck and the hash, and they want you and Bob and Dharma on ice. You think we can afford to lose all that? There's Julie's baby. The land. Who'll run the lab? Christian, it had to be done. And . . . " Now she sat down on the bed, suddenly looking tired, defeated. ". . . And I just didn't want you tortured."

"Kathy, please. Look at me . . ." He took a knee on the ground to be at eye level, raising his hands in supplication. "Please don't turn away from me. If we ever needed each other, it's now."

"Don't ask me to be with you just now, Christian. I can't. You came here to ask Kali to be your lady. I would imagine you had a real good time. I . . . I just can't." She reached into the pack. "So, here's your passport. I found it on the floor of your room in the guest house. And here . . . a grand to get you out of India. You'd better leave as soon as you can."

"This isn't about me anymore. What can I do?"

"You can take yourself out of danger." Throwing the money and passport on the bed, she stood. "You owe me three grand. I'm leaving as soon as I shower."

Lifting the pack, she brushed past him, ambling into the bathroom. Christian heard the turn of the lock.

Completely devastated, fearful, he stared at the closed door. Exactly what had they done to her in that prison?

Standing, he moved toward the door, knocked gently. "Kathy, please open the door. You can't do this on your own. Please talk to me."

There was no sound.

Sensing something terrible she would not share, he knocked louder. "Open the door."

Only silence.

Exasperated, he slammed his shoulder against the cheap door, cracking the lock.

At first, he only registered the shame on her face . . . and then he saw the rest. Starting at her eyes, he worked his way down, gradually realizing the extent of what she'd had to endure—the bright purple bruises on her neck and arms, the teeth marks cut into the flesh of her breasts, the reddened and lacerated wrists, the long angry welts, half-open across her hips and buttocks.

Kathy raised her hands and buried her face in them, finally sobbing.

And Christian . . . Christian fell to his knees at her feet, to hold her, to place his face into her soft belly and cry with her, and even as she stroked his head, telling him not to cry, he was ripped in two—wanting to believe in Lama's teaching on compassion and the value of an enemy, but he also wanted nothing more than to kill Janata with his own two hands.

24

CHRISTIAN
JALANDHAR, INDIA
NOVEMBER 1969

A thousand memories touched Christian as he reached the mission compound in Jalandhar. He slipped through the small iron gate at the back of the yard, struck by the scent of roses. The old gardener was still there, just as Christian had left him three years ago, busy at work with his straw broom. He noted the new wire fence around a coop in one corner of the courtyard and smiled. The chickens were finally out of his mother's garden. From the other side of the tall stone wall surrounding the property, goats bleated. The tangy odor of cooking food, of cardamom, turmeric, and cumin, wafted through the screened door that led to the kitchen.

In a few minutes, he would see his father again. The thought terrified him. What would he say after all these years? How would Reverend Brooks make him feel for the hurt he'd surely caused his mother?

At the back porch, he took the stairs, then knocked on the sill of the open kitchen door. Dasa, the old housekeeper, was busy shaping bread. She gave him a passing glance, clicking her tongue disdainfully. "Another one begging," she told the kitchen girl in her own language. "He should be ashamed."

"It is you who should be ashamed for not recognizing me," Christian answered.

Stopped, turning swiftly, she eyed the young man at the door. His hair was falling to his shoulders, a week's growth of beard covered his face, his clothing was bright, a colorful vest of Afghanistan over a cotton Indian shirt. He wore American blue jeans and carried a pack slung over his shoulder. His face was . . . older, touched by sadness. But there was no denying the eyes, the blue eyes she'd looked into for many years. The old woman cried aloud and, wiping her hands on a towel, rushed to take him in her arms. "The Lord has answered our prayers!"

Christian picked her up, and spinning her around, suddenly smiled bright and true at her girlish giggles. He put his finger to his lips for silence, lifted his father's lunch tray, and walked down the highly polished hallway to the library, hands shaking with emotion. So many questions he had to ask. So many things he had to hide.

The library, with its hundreds of books, had been his father's sanctuary, his place of retreat, his home within his home. Without knocking, Christian quietly entered the room and set the tray on a table. Reverend Brooks stood near the window, reading, the morning light highlighting one side of his body, his right hand pointing to a passage.

His priceless books, Christian thought. *More precious than gold.*

As his eyes became accustomed to the dim light, Christian studied the profile of the man against the window. His father had not been a young man when Christian was born. The tall man he remembered towering at his pulpit was now a slight, stooped, gray-haired man in his late sixties, still wearing the same white shirt and cleric's collar, dark pants and jacket, he'd worn all his life.

"Just set the tray down, Dasa," he said, his voice strong and rich, his eyes never lifting from the page.

"Father," Christian spoke softly.

Reverend Brooks turned, startled, his eyes wide. "Christian?" he murmured.

The two men started toward one another, almost touched, then stopped short. The time passed had been too long, the bridge too wide. Reverend Brooks took a long, hard look at Christian, raising himself to his full stature. "So, this is what you've become. That school, that Berkeley." The voice was mocking. "The hair. Your clothes."

Christian tried to gain control of his quivering voice. "I just cut my hair." True, it fell over his shoulders, but it was no longer to the middle of his back. Were they going to get stuck on appearances?

"I see," said the older man. "Then you have not come to India to return home. You have come seeking the cheap thrills that others of your kind come here to find. Have you any idea what kind of reputation the West is developing in this country because of the exploits of the rabble who pass through here? Women, half-clothed. Sleeping not only with the white men in their groups, but with Indian men, thinking they are being open-minded. Young people looking like skeletons, begging on the streets for a few coins for food and their drug habits. Can you imagine what people who barely manage to feed themselves think of a young, healthy man begging on the street after spending more money to get here than most villagers see in a lifetime? I can't tell you the number of children I have fed. Children with glassy eyes and staggering gaits consumed by opium and heroin . . . "

"Father . . . "

"Are you one of them, Christian? Is this why you have written three letters in five years? Is this why you've come to India? Is this the image you wish the Indian people to have of Western Christian nations?"

"Father, please . . ."

Once again, the man was in the pulpit—tall, dark, overpowering, his voice honed from a lifetime of practice. "There's a small colony of . . . what do you call yourselves—hippies, is it?—hippies who live near here. They live in unbelievable filth . . ."

"Father!" Christian's voice exploded, his body shook. "I've come to tell you I've seen Nareesh. I want you to explain about Ram Seva!"

Reverend Brooks looked at Christian as if he'd been struck. His voice faltered midword, his eyes widened, his breathing became shallow and fast, his finger still frozen to the passage in the book. Slowly, he turned back to the window, but not before Christian had seen the events of the night of the riot play across his eyes.

"Why didn't you tell me about Ram Seva? Why couldn't I stay for Lama Loden's cremation? Your life is supposed to represent the Christian ethic. Have you no compassion for me? Do you think you're better than an Indian? Or Tibetan?" The pitch of his voice rose, accusing, frustrated, demanding. "You sent me away not to protect me, but so that I would become what you thought I should—a carbon copy of you!"

The light from the window still played against one side of Reverend Brooks's body, and again, there was only the small gray man held by the morning light.

The outburst shocked Christian. He had never raised his voice to his father, had promised to bring the face and spirit of Lama Loden into the room with him, but the words, once they were spoken, could not be taken back. Now, in the deep silence, he was filled with remorse.

"I can see I have not made the last years easy for you, either," his father replied, his face gray and drawn. "You ask me why I did not tell you of Ram Seva, why I forced you to leave so hastily? I'll tell you, Christian." Reverend Brooks closed the book, put it carefully on the desk, and sat heavily in the nearest chair. "Because I was wrong. And right. It is exactly as you said. I hoped you would take my place here. You were to be the continuation of my work. My life. I was so proud of you. I could see you had all the gifts necessary for the ministry.

"But I also sent you away because I wished to spare you pain. I believed you had suffered all one could suffer at your age. What happened that night should never have happened," he said sadly. "Afterward, I looked everywhere for Nareesh. Amritsar was too large, our village too small. The rumor that Christians had something to do with the tragedy was too pervasive. People turned from me. Suddenly, I found myself suspect after all my years here."

He looked around the room as if his beloved books could give him an answer. Then, gathering strength, he continued, "Christian, have you any idea what a ministry really is? The number of families I've consoled over the years? The deaths and burials? The illness and trauma I've overseen? When people are miserable, they bring their misery to the church, to God. Only the exceptional remember God when they're happy. I derived strength and purpose from my usefulness, but also frustration.

"I believed, son, when I was your age, that I would make vast changes in this country. I knew I could change poverty and suffering. Dasa was a symbol of the best I had done. Yet, even with many of the poor and dying reborn in Christ, their poverty and suffering remain unchanged. And I've worked hard to make it different."

He looked down at the swollen hands bent by age that had succored and soothed and blessed so many.

"When I learned you were going to a Buddhist monastery, my world stopped. My dream of Christianity being India's salvation died. How could I expect to make conversions when my own son had turned away from Christ?"

A long pause, and finally, Reverend Brooks looked directly at Christian for the first time. "Then the riot. Yes, I knew of Ram Seva's death. As well as Lama Loden's. Christian, tell me—should I have let you stay to see the lama's body burned? To witness the cremation of one you loved? The act is so final. I wanted to spare you." He clasped his hands in his lap, his fingers tightly woven together. "I attended the ceremony in your place. Now it seems I was wrong. I should have given you the opportunity of making your peace and letting go of your lama. If you wish, you may still visit with the Geshe. His remains have been taken to Nepal and placed in a reliquary, a *stupa*. I'm told many pilgrims visit there. You are free to be one of them."

Christian finally knelt beside his father, picked up his hand, and began to cry. He'd expected his father to be more than a man, to be perfect. What had he told Kathy only days before? *I'm just a man. I make mistakes.* How many more would he make in his life?

"I'm sorry. Forgive me. I'm sorry that I hurt mother . . . "

His father's eyes softened, and he wiped the tears from Christian's face. "I give you my love, son. But I'd like to give you a good bit of the devil, too. What have you been doing for five years? And this hair?" He gave it a tug.

"Thomas," they heard as the door quietly opened. "Oh! Excuse me! I didn't know you had a visitor."

"Jeannie!" called her husband. "This is a visitor I think you would like to meet."

Quickly, Christian wiped away his tears and stood. "Mother!"

His mother swayed against the door, and in the next instant, she was in his arms.

25

BOB, DHARMA, AND MYLES
GREECE
NOVEMBER 1969

From New Delhi, Bob and Dharma traveled west, crossing the
Indian border to Multan, traveling across Pakistan to the Indus
River. At Quetta, they turned south, paralleling the Afghan border,
finally reaching Iran and the long, arduous, slow road to Esfahan.
Here, they decided to continue west rather than head north to Tehran.
The mountain roads were treacherous and narrow, winter imminent,
and it was with more than a little relief that they reached the broad,
flat, potholed roads of the Iraqi desert.

In Baghdad, they traversed the Tigris River and then the Euphra-
tes, driving a road that paralleled the watercourse for many miles.
Again, they had to decide whether to veer north through Syria for the
Turkish border or to cross Syria to rest for a few days in the resort city
of Beirut in Lebanon.

Bob's promise to Julie decided them. They turned north, toward
Turkey.

At the border, they were waved past with a brief glance at their
passports and a single stamp. Onward, they crossed the great Taurus
Mountains and the wide breadth of land beyond, then north toward
the Black Sea and the minarets of Istanbul. For all this distance, they
had not stopped, driving night and day, fearing both for the safety of
their cargo and for their lives.

"Dharma," Bob called to him, "wake up. We're almost to the Greek border."

Dharma mumbled and looked into the dimness of the vehicle. "What time is it?"

"Almost 4:00 a.m. Jesus, but I'm tired of traveling."

"No shit. Hawaii's lookin' pretty good about now." Dharma stretched and sat up. "Man, I am so burnt. Damn Christian anyway. He could have helped out with the driving instead of lying in bed for three weeks. You want to place bets on whether he's with Kathy or Lisa?"

"I wouldn't bet against Kathy. And if she catches Christian with Lisa, Lord." Bob whistled long and low.

Dharma looked once more at his watch, as if to make sure it could really be four in the morning. "What do you think—want to pull over and wait until light or roust the guard awake?"

"Let's keep going and rest for a day when we get to a good beach. I'll feel a lot better when we're in Greece and the truck is delivered. There's the border ahead." Bob pulled the truck to the side of the road. "You want to get out and walk across . . . just in case?"

"Nah. Let's just find that beach."

The border between Greece and Turkey at this point was the Evros River. Bob parked near the small customs and immigration office, stepped down from the truck, and knocked until a weary official sauntered out. Bob handed him their passports.

"One moment, please," said the man. He took the books inside.

When he returned to the truck, he held a flashlight. "Do you have anything to declare?" he asked.

"Not really," Bob answered with a tired yawn. "Just the few things we picked up traveling. Nothing expensive." God, but he was tired. He should have wakened Dharma sooner. He glanced up at the sliver of moon setting on the horizon.

"Would you mind opening the back door and showing them to me?"

Startled, it took Bob a few moments to move. The glance he gave

Dharma said, *Fuck! Four in the morning and they're going to shake us down!*

In a few moments, they were joined by another official. The new officer turned on a large spotlight on the side of the building. An unearthly glow flooded over the truck. Bob felt his hair bristle. One of the men was pawing through their packs in the back; the other was too interested in the details of the bumper.

"Watch that guy," he whispered to Dharma. He began to sweat and walked to the customs official going through his stuff at the back of the car.

"As you can see, there's nothing much here. We just wanted to drive across Asia and the Middle East before returning to school. Not everyone gets an opportunity to do that once they've settled down, eh?"

"One moment, please." The man walked forward to confer with his partner.

"What do you think?" Bob asked Dharma under his breath.

"I don't know. Something's up."

The second guard took a knife out of his pocket and pried at the green-colored epoxy they had used to weld the bumper to the truck. Bob turned to look at Dharma. The look that passed between them said everything.

It was over.

The border guards knew the hash was there and would search until they found it. Somehow, they were waiting for them.

Unknown to the two travelers, a list had been taped to the wall of the guardhouse, the names of three Americans underscored in red ink. The guard had almost forgotten it in his rush to return to his bed. But the red ink had caught his eye at the last moment, and he had roused his partner.

Bob desperately surveyed the options. The choices were few. They could dash back across the bridge and hope the Turks would accept drug smugglers into the country without passports, or they could go over the side of the bridge, stumbling in the dark over river rock, trying to find a way into Greece while being pursued. Neither option was feasible.

He thought of putting his bandana into the gas tank and igniting it. In the confusion of the truck's explosion, perhaps they could escape. Except that this wasn't the movies, and if someone died, the consequences would be painfully karmic. The price would be his life, rather than the few years for smuggling.

One guard had the bumper off and was pulling out the wrapped bags while the other walked to get the soldier from his post at the center of the bridge.

"What's that?" Bob asked the guard opening the bags.

"Perhaps you can tell me," he answered indignantly. "You are under arrest, prisoners of the Greek government."

"Why?" Bob asked, all innocence.

"This, if you really need an answer. Smuggling and transportation of hashish."

"Hey, I have no idea how that got there. It must have happened when we had the shocks fixed in Tehran," Bob told him.

From the center of the bridge, the soldier and the customs agent were getting closer.

"Look," Dharma tried with the man, "there's been a big mistake. We're willing to leave the contraband here and pay you for your trouble in removing it from the vehicle."

The man only sneered. "This is Greece. I have principles and morals."

For a fleeting moment, Bob wondered what Hyatollah would do. No doubt, he would use the handkerchief and blow the truck and the evidence. Encouraged, Bob reached into his right pocket with one hand and found the handkerchief. His left hand felt for his lighter. Slowly, his feet inched toward the gas tank. He tried convincing himself of the logic of this possibility. They had made a righteous offer to the man, but the guard wanted their freedom, a price too great for any man to ask of another. He pulled out the handkerchief. Only minutes were left to perform the task, the soldier from the bridge almost upon them. Bob stood on a precipice, balancing, looking right and left at two options from his height. Torn between worlds—the logic of the East and the scruples of his Western childhood—he faltered.

In the end, his early conditioning was too firmly rooted, the act too outrageous and out of character.

The soldier pointed his gun toward them, and they raised their hands. Frisked and cuffed, they were left to stand on the bridge while the guards pulled apart the vehicle and everything in it. The sun was rising. The day would be beautiful. They leaned against the stone bridge in the rose-colored light of dawn, arms behind their backs, and watched their lives come into focus—the destroyed vehicle lying in sections on the road, their packs and clothes and books and personal items strewn in the wreckage,.

Bob felt himself sinking through strange layers of despondency, as if he were stirring from a nightmare to find that waking reality was no different. What was this going to mean to all their lives? To Julie and the baby due in a few weeks? To Keith and his family? Where would they go with the small children if the land was lost? The growing despondency solidified into sharp terror. Would Julie still love him when he returned? How long would it be? Months? Years?

The anguish that gripped his body was beyond anything he had ever experienced, the physical pain of it, the way he found his life force consumed. The conscious world stopped. From a tiny place that still held reason, he watched as his psyche fractured, watched it crack into shards and then break into thousands of pieces. He floated in a meaningless space without reference, only the pieces of his shattered mind surrounding him.

Perhaps the only thing that kept him sane at that moment was the thought of Julie. Taking a deep breath, he struggled to come back to himself, and with a huge effort, made the beginnings of reintegrating his life, using the shards to reform a reality.

Anguished, the full weight of his capture on him, his soul reached halfway around the world, touching her and praying she would wait for him.

The door to the small room that served as a cell opened, and a well-dressed man entered, carrying a briefcase. He held a card out to Bob. "I am told you are in need of legal representation," the man stated matter-of-factly.

"No kidding," Bob answered, standing up, walking the few feet he could. "They won't even wait to hold the trial until we can call our lawyer in the States. We only got popped two days ago."

"My rates are very reasonable," the man told them, "and it seems you need someone today."

"What are our chances of getting off?" Dharma asked.

The lawyer smiled gracefully. "Not very good, I'm afraid. After all, seventy pounds of hashish is a great quantity of contraband."

Bob wondered what they would say if they found the other thirty pounds stuffed into the fat roll bar. "How much time do you think we'll get, realistically?"

"It will depend on the mercy of the judges. In all honesty, it would be futile for me to hazard a guess. Anyone who told you differently would be lying."

"Alright." Bob looked at Dharma for confirmation. "How much do you want?"

"Two hundred US dollars."

Two hundred dollars was an exorbitant price to pay, especially when he would do no more than give them lip service and perhaps an hour of his time. But at least someone would be able to answer questions and translate. The trial was scheduled for that afternoon.

Myles Corbet had spent his first two days in Varanasi nursing a rising fury that threatened to break into panic. At the prison, not only had

Christian escaped, but the passport Myles had hoped to examine for forgery was also missing. Even the woman the lieutenant had mentioned had disappeared, returned to New Delhi with a religious master of some kind to a closed retreat. No one would violate the ashram.

One thought offered hope. Alden's vehicle had to be somewhere in Asia. Borders had to be crossed, and the passport names of all three men could be tracked.

Moving to New Delhi so he could be close to a large international airport if he wanted to travel quickly, Myles made calls to every country the vehicle might travel through, east and west, giving the passport names. He called repeatedly, checking and rechecking, pressuring them with the importance of his position and the commanding tone of his voice. Then he sat by the phone, waiting for the call that would be his ticket back to the university. Myles did not leave his hotel room in New Delhi for seven days.

Ten days, he'd given himself. Ten days before he returned to Germany.

On the morning of the eighth day, the call had come. The system had worked. An alert guard in Greece had compared the passport names to the list Myles had pushed in every country. Two of the men had been located and about seventy pounds of hashish confiscated.

"Which two?" Myles asked anxiously. "Was there a Christian Alden?"

"No. Robert Jones and Matthew Green."

Where was Alden? Myles wondered. *Maybe still in India?*

God, how he wanted that man! Myles had made a bet with the dude—about whose intuitive power was strongest, his own or Alden's. But for the moment, there was nothing he could do.

That evening, he boarded a plane for Istanbul, then traveled by small prop plane to the Greek border town.

Just before the court session began, Myles slipped quietly into the back of the courtroom and silently eyed the two prisoners awaiting the judge. The dark-haired man, Robert Jones, had eyes that continually traveled the room, almost as if he expected help to come from some quarter. Myles saw recognition in his surprised glance. In the next moment, he nudged his partner.

Myles returned the steady gaze.

Let them know, he thought. *Let them know who won.*

Walking toward the prosecutor's table, Myles shook hands and presented his credentials. A few more whispered words, and he went to sit next to Bob and Dharma.

"The name's Corbet," he told them. "I'm a US agent assigned to Interpol."

They gave him a frozen stare.

"In a few moments, you gentlemen will be put on trial for smuggling. Without friends, that may very well mean a lengthy sentence. Some cooperation on your part, and you may find an ally in the US government."

Still, the two prisoners said nothing.

"If you can give me the whereabouts of Christian Alden, then perhaps I can be of some help to you."

Nothing but stormy silence.

"Gentlemen, time is running out."

Bob turned to Dharma, looked into his eyes, and smiled. In that glance, thoughts were exchanged, decisions made. Myles felt their complete disdain for his presence, a contempt that made him unworthy of their attention. He was struck by the power of that glance. There was no one in his life with whom he could share any part of himself. His struggle had not been to share, to confide, or to console, but to outwit and to prove his superiority. In that process, he had isolated himself.

Shaken, he rose abruptly to his feet, regaining control. A warm anger crept through him. He turned on his heel.

"Just a minute," Bob called after him. "There is one thing I have to say to you. Something about brotherhood. The strong love of one friend for another. I'm willing to go to prison so that my brother can continue the struggle. I know that the Brotherhood is more important than I am. They'll take care of my family."

Using agitated hand movements, Myles whispered something to the prosecutor the men could not hear.

The court proceedings were a surrealistic nightmare conducted in Greek, no questions asked of them, nothing explained.

"What's happening?" Bob asked the attorney desperately. "What's he saying?"

"The judge is telling the court that hashish kills hundreds of people a day in New York City. People all over your country die from the drug."

"That's crazy!" Bob reeled from the lie. "From hash?"

"He also says your government would consider it a favor to remove undesirables from the United States, and because our governments are bound by friendship, we can accommodate you in our prisons here," the attorney whispered.

"Wait!" Bob demanded, trying to keep his tone civil. "Don't we have a chance to produce counterevidence?"

"What evidence?" the lawyer looked at him incredulously. "You were caught smuggling seventy pounds of hashish into Greece."

In less than an hour, it was over. The gavel came down. Bob and Dharma looked questioningly at the attorney.

"Seven years," he told them, avoiding their eyes, picking up papers, and shoving them into his briefcase.

"That's . . . that's impossible," Bob whispered hoarsely. "Seven years?" He was twenty-five years old. Seven years was a lifetime. Shakti, his daughter, would be nine years old. His unborn child would be seven. A slow sense of horror overwhelmed him. He stood rooted to the spot, unbelieving. There had to be some mistake. Maybe a mistake in translation. He turned toward the judge to be sure, looked wildly around for escape, but soldiers carrying American-made Thompson submachine guns covered the doors and windows.

"This is just the first trial," he heard the lawyer say. "You may be able to appeal, have the sentence reduced. I would be happy to represent you if you wish to try for a second trial."

"Don't worry," Dharma said to Bob's anguished face. "We'll create our own reality. We have our tools. Meditation. Yoga. Good US attorneys. We'll make it."

Bob felt the handcuffs tightening on his wrists. The despondency returned, settling over him like a lead cloud. He wasn't sure he could walk, but a soldier pulled his arm. As they were taken from the courtroom, only the sound of the sentence echoed in his ears.

Three days later, Myles was in his office in Hamburg when the cablegram arrived.

> Congratulations. Good work. Come home.
> —Bremer

26

MARCIE
BERKELEY, CALIFORNIA
OCTOBER 1969

Because Alex was sick, Marcie was doubling up with Richard to help with the tabbing, using gloves and a mask, hoping to avoid the intense, disabling stone. Where once it had been fun to spend a couple of days tabbing and tripping, these days, it was only another task to complete. She didn't have time to trip anymore.

"Have you talked to Alex today?" she asked Richard. "How's his flu?" Whatever Marcie felt about Alex, she knew he was needed to keep things going.

"Not good," Richard answered, wrapping tape around the box he was getting ready to mail. "And he won't take his nose out of the coke bag, even when he's sick." He took the scissors from the table and snipped the tape. "Did you see the last acid crystal he wanted to sell?"

"I saw it," Marcie replied. "It looked like shit."

"It was shit."

Marcie collected the tabs as they fell from the hopper, weighing them, four thousand to a bag.

"I think I've figured out where he's getting it," Richard said quietly.

Her hands hesitated. "The acid? He hasn't told you?"

"I think it's from David." Richard focused on the box, pretending to inspect it.

"David? David who tried to blacklist you when you cut him off after the People's Park demonstrations?" Then with some anger, added,

"David, who preferred coke and really young girls to his wife and daughter?"

"Yeah, well, I'm pretty sure that's where Alex is copping his coke, too."

"So what now?" Marcie asked impatiently.

"I've been asking around." Richard's voice had a resigned quality to it. "We're supposed to be partners, right? Fifty-fifty. Well, it seems that Alex has been turning pounds of coke behind my back."

"He knows you don't approve of coke. Too many people strung out and some really bad decisions behind it."

Richard set the box on the table near the door and gave her his full attention. "Marcie, it wasn't just to spare my feelings. He's making bucks. Maybe a couple of hundred thousand dollars' worth of bucks. Using our customers. And cutting me out."

"Are you sure?"

"I'm sure. He's using my name—our partnership—to turn pounds. God only knows whether he's selling quality flake or garbage."

Marcie took off the surgical mask, turned off the machine, and sat down next to him. "Do you really think he'd cheat you like that? I just can't imagine it."

His face was pale, his fist clenched, knuckles white. She was slightly stoned and his subdued violence frightened her. "Richard," she whispered uneasily, putting her hand over his fist. "What's going on?"

"He's been doing up that dirty acid I refused to sell and sending it to Canada."

"Why?" Marcie asked incredulously. "He has all the money he needs!"

"To spite me."

When he spoke again, his voice was sad. "I always thought that if someone loved and cared about him enough, he'd come around. But he hasn't. He's gone out of his way to betray me."

"Are you sure about the acid?"

"Peter verified it in Vancouver. Mailed me some of the tabs. I got them today. It's our machine, our tabs—just another color."

"What are you going to do?" she whispered.

"He fucked me, Marcie! He went out of his way to deliberately fuck me! I'm going to do what I should have done long ago—dissolve the partnership. I figure he owes me at least a hundred grand, so I'm taking the machine in payment."

"The machine!" Marcie cried. "Richard, he'll be so pissed!"

"Tough. He gave up his right to the machine when he put out shit acid. As soon as we finish getting this order out for Peter, I'm moving it to a new factory. I called Merlin early this afternoon to come down and help."

"It's all pretty heavy."

"Yeah," he put out his hand to rub her neck. "Heavier than you think. We have to move again, too. I don't know how crazy Alex will get."

"Oh, Richard," Marcie groaned, "moving was okay when we had a mattress, a few boxes, and tapestries. But we've got a house full of furniture. John's crib and dresser. Just . . . so much stuff. And think about what another move will do to John."

"John will be alright. I'm going down to rent a truck before Merlin gets here. Can you finish up?"

"Where's Christian, anyway?" she asked disgustedly. "And Kathy? When will they be back? Why haven't we heard from anyone?"

"They probably decided to spend some time seeing the country. Making up. You know Kathy. Once she's away from here, she never gets back when she says she will."

"*I* would like to go to India. I would like to study with a holy man."

"Someday. I promise."

Marcie's irritation rose. "When? When you stop working? How many times have you quit? I'm sick of counting the times. Every time you get paranoid, you quit, only to run into a deal you can't pass up."

Richard picked up the box he'd wrapped, ready to take it to the post office. "Don't forget Peter's flying in tonight," he reminded her. "He wants into Merlin's crop. Everyone's beginning to say he grows the best weed in Humboldt. Can you make dinner?"

"Sure." But she turned away from him in frustration. How wonderful to be able to eat one of the lovely pink tabs, she thought, just lie down and laugh, like the old days when she could trip anytime she wanted, when she and Richard could be together twenty-four hours a day, before John, before the bucks were really big, before all the responsibility.

Carefully covering her nose and mouth with the mask, she ran the buffed crystal through the machine. It would take a couple of hours. Then she had to get those leaflets xeroxed for the annual peace march and rally, pick up John at Debbie's, shop, make dinner, hassle the bedtime routine, and start organizing a move.

Oh, Richard, she thought again miserably. *Where's this all going to end?*

Marcie lay John down in his crib, covered him, and stood listening to his soft breathing while she gently rocked him. Then quietly, she tiptoed from the room. She had just closed the door, when she heard Richard come in with Peter and Merlin.

"Marcie," Richard called, "we're here."

"Hey," she said walking down the stairs to the living room. "Hi, Peter. How's it goin', Merlin?"

"Is dinner ready?" Richard asked, pulling off his jacket.

"I'm just getting to it," she answered tiredly.

"Jesus, Marcie, we're starved. We've got a long night ahead."

"Come on, Richard. Give me a break. I've put in a long day too."

"How long till it's on the table?"

"Not so long," Marcie tried to control her voice, "because, for once, you're going to help. Merlin, you know where the rolling box is. And the stereo. Help yourself."

Richard was on her as soon as they were in the kitchen. "Do you have to get on me the minute Peter and Merlin walk in the door?"

"If they don't know me by now, Richard, they never will. You have got to start taking some responsibility around here."

"I do my fair share," he retorted gruffly. "Without my business, there's no money for food or rent."

"Well, right now, you can keep the trip afloat by washing lettuce," Marcie returned irritably. "And don't forget I help you with your business. I handle all your phone calls and coordinate your appointments. I cover for you when you need someone to make deliveries or run the machine or pick up money. I put people up when they need to spend the night, cooking, washing sheets and towels, and making conversation. And it goes on twenty-four hours a day! We never have any privacy anymore or a chance to talk to each other. When am I supposed to tell you what I'm thinking or how I feel about something?"

"You don't have to start the minute Peter walks in the door. By the way, did anyone call while I was out?"

"There's a list on the table." She nodded toward it.

Richard glanced quickly down the list. "Marcie, look," he sighed, eyeing the phone hanging on the wall. "I've got to call Dale. Can you tear up this lettuce for me?"

While he talked into the receiver, Marcie avoided the lettuce and put the rice on. She began slicing eggplant, and when she'd finished, she found the metal grater for the mozzarella.

"Dale may stop by after dinner," Richard said, hanging up the phone. "You need any more help? I should really talk to Peter."

"Do the salad." Marcie pointed to the lettuce and said irritably, "And how about spending a few minutes talking to me?"

"You still uptight about moving?"

"Yes. I'm getting tired of a lot of other things, too.

"Like what?"

"Like not being able to sit down and smoke a jay. Or do yoga. Meditate."

"You think I don't work?" he asked, his own voice becoming tight. "You think I have a lot of time for myself?"

"You work. I'm just saying I want a little more space for myself. And some private time with you."

"You can have me anytime you want," he answered, putting down the knife and pinching her tit.

"You do have two ladies, don't you?" she said, slapping his hand away. "One for fucking and the other for wooing, for play. Your business *is* your other lady. I get fucked, and she gets wooed."

"Now . . . wait a minute!"

"And you want to know what?" she continued angrily. "If push comes to shove, you'll always choose her over me, because she's more fun than an hour's fuck!"

"Marcie!"

"It's true! You have your male-dominated world, where you get to wheel and deal for fourteen to sixteen hours a day. When you get horny, you come home and give me an hour of your time. You're all the same—all you men with your tribal rituals! Your contests to divide the spoils! I don't ever want to hear about how greedy Alex is anymore. You're all greedy. All of you. With your ideas of revolution and your big capitalistic bucks and your hot dicks at the ballrooms in the evenings."

"That's . . . enough!"

"You want to know something else, Richard? I've been writing again. You wouldn't know because it doesn't make money. You wouldn't know because you're never around long enough to listen to what I have to say. Listen now, because I'm telling you that when I write, I feel powerful, because my writing's good. I feel a tremendous resource lying within me. But you want to know something else? It's the only time I feel powerful. The rest of the time, my energy's all spent picking up behind you. Well, I'm sick and tired of it! You can go screw your other lady!"

Richard stood in the middle of the kitchen, shocked, his face pale, his hands trembling with anger and hurt.

"How's dinner coming?" Merlin asked, barging into the kitchen.

"I . . . I have to fry up this eggplant." Marcie almost gagged on the words. "It won't take long. Merlin, set the table, will you? Please. Richard, help Merlin with the table, and I'll finish the salad."

The swinging door between the dinning room and kitchen was still swaying when she heard Merlin's low whisper from the next room, "They all get like that sometimes."

Before Richard could respond, Marcie pushed open the door. "One more thing. Do you think you can watch John one night a week while I attend a poetry workshop?"

He cleared his throat. "Sure, Marcie, I'd be happy to. If I'm here, of course."

Dinner was over and Marcie began clearing away plates, deciding what to do with the remaining food on the table.

"Marcie, I'd help with the dishes, but I really do have to talk with Peter." His eyes pleaded with her.

"Go ahead. I'll put water on for tea."

She felt bad about her earlier outburst. Richard was a good husband and father. What she felt was subtle, confused. She even wondered where the storm of words had come from. Just so many little things, and a feeling of—of being hedged in—a question of free time and a growing need for creativity. Where before she had played her guitar with regularity, she hadn't even removed it from the closet since the last move. Nor did she sing, as if her happiness was somehow waiting for the right moment to be released from her heart.

The dishes done and tea in a teapot, she placed cups and spoons on a tray with honey and oranges and carried the tray into the living room. The air was already thick with smoke.

"Here, Marcie," Richard passed her a joint.

"Nice," she said, feeling the lazy hum working within her.

The day began to slip away, the change in consciousness taking her beyond dishes and work. The mellow flute of Jethro Tull played softly in the background. Colors in the room intensified, brightened. The beautiful *Bukhara* rug looked as if it had an inner glow. The dull, yellow light of the lamps was golden.

Somewhere through the music, Richard's voice came to her. The words, taken alone, were soft and congenial, but their meaning was sharp and to the point. As Marcie listened, she heard what she'd always known was there. The wooing. Richard was enticing his comrades with logic and statistics. They countered with their own logic, their own way of seeing things, their own offers. In the moment, she saw clearly the private, personal ego each revealed to the others. A masculine sensuality filled the room, their psychic nakedness embarrassing in its intimacy.

She had come to realize that a cold reasoning governed Richard's business decisions. He had a grasp of economic laws she would never have. With a reputation based on integrity and strength of character, he had beome a master game player. Other men deferred to him, respected his opinion, made him powerful.

And in that moment, it was clear to Marcie that Richard liked both power and money. If there was moral purpose in acquiring both, so much the better.

"Uh, Marcie," Peter's voice broke into her thoughts. "Listen, I hate to ask, but do you think you could give us a few minutes?"

"Huh?" Marcie tried to focus on him.

"We're going to get down to business now, the details of the smuggle. Do you think you can give us a few minutes?"

"You want me to leave the room?" she asked, trying to keep the incredulity out of her voice.

"If you don't mind." Peter smiled obligingly and shrugged slightly. "You understand. A need-to-know basis."

Marcie shot Richard a quick, furious glance, watched the mental groan in his eyes. But he said nothing.

She waited.

Still nothing.

"Sure, Peter." She finally stood up. "I'll just finish this cup of tea upstairs."

"Thanks, Marcie. There's really no reason for you to know any of the details. In case you're ever asked, you're uninvolved."

"Hey, safety first, eh? You don't have to tell me. I'll just be . . . uninvolved." The last word she spoke to Richard through tight lips as she left the room.

She worked very hard to quietly close the door to her bedroom, avoiding the drama she would have preferred—a loud, slamming door to tell everyone how she felt.

How dare he ask me to leave my own living room? she screamed silently, pacing the floor. *After I spent the better part of my day getting his order out! Uninvolved! I couldn't care less what the fucking details of the smuggle are. All I want is a few minutes with my old man, a pleasant stone, and a cup of tea.*

She was still pacing twenty minutes later when Richard appeared at the door. He took one look at her face and said, "He couldn't have picked worse timing, could he?"

"Why didn't you say something?"

"I didn't want to blow the trip. We stand to make fifty grand on this one."

"We, Richard? We? So now I'm in again! A half hour ago, I was out! You tell me. Is this your business or ours?"

"I did build it from scratch."

"But what about my time and my energy?"

"You're right, Marcie," he held up a hand. "It's our business."

"Then why didn't you speak up?"

"You don't want to lose your half of fifty grand, do you?" he asked, grinning.

"Fuck you, Richard."

"Listen," he said, picking up his jacket, "I have to leave. Peter has a guy named Frank flying in on a plane at eleven o'clock."

"I want to talk to you for a minute."

"Tomorrow, okay? In the morning. You can ride around with me for a while."

"I don't want to fucking ride around with you just so I can talk to you. I want you to give me some of your time. I want to know if you'll take care of John on Wednesday evenings from seven to ten."

"I can't promise that. You know how quickly things come up. I have to go when I get a phone call."

"Richard, we have plenty of money to let a few slip by us. I need a commitment from you. I need to hear you say that if someone calls at six thirty, you'll tell them to wait until ten thirty."

"I need to be available to my clients," he protested.

Marcie was beginning to feel desperate, shackled by something she didn't understand. "Your son needs you. I need you. We should come first."

"Marcie, please. Be patient. We'll discuss this tomorrow. I have to leave."

"Can't you let Peter pick this guy up by himself?"

"It's important. Frank has access to some ET. I'm anxious to meet him." Ergotamine tartrate. The basis of lysergic acid.

"ET?" Marcie sighed, resigned. "Alright. For ET you can do it. What about the movers?"

"I didn't have time to call. Could you take care of it in the morning?"

From the first meeting, Marcie didn't like Frank, but she kept her intuition to herself. At the moment, Richard was so disgruntled with her that nothing she said could influence him. And Frank was one person Richard wanted to court. The sample of ET had tested pure. The negotiations for five kilos had begun.

Moving was tiresome, but the whole process took only a couple of days—one day for the actual packing, a few days for unpacking in the new house. Then Richard and Merlin moved the machine in the dead of night.

Don't get too settled this time, she reminded herself. *Don't get caught up in possessing the space, or even in possessing a feeling of being settled. Buy only what's necessary. Be prepared to jam everything into a small mobile truck. In a few months, or in two weeks—perhaps even tomorrow—we may have to move again on an hour's notice.*

Marcie could not shake the feeling that something about Frank just didn't fit. He was of medium height, large-boned, with sandy hair and brown eyes. He wore black-framed glasses. Odd, when everyone was wearing Lennon glasses. His most distinguishing feature was a mustache. Although he was quiet and polite, there was something rigid about his body, with none of the fluid easiness she'd come to recognize in the people who were a part of her world. And his eyes—they appeared preoccupied, hard, without light or laughter. She had the sense that he was constantly watching.

Frank had walked in on the first night of his arrival wearing a cowboy hat and boots and a tan jacket with a sheepskin collar. Richard had dropped him at the house with Peter, introduced the man to her, and had asked her to make up some beds and see to their comfort. He'd whispered to her ear that he and Merlin had an errand. They were off to check out the neighborhood and the traffic around the new house where they would move the machine. They wouldn't be long.

Later, after Richard and Merlin had returned, she'd tried to sleep but couldn't. The four men were still downstairs, talking. She longed to go down to tell Richard everything was alright between them after her earlier outburst and her anger over being forced to her room. She wanted to snuggle up to him for a few minutes. But walking into the living room scene would have been like walking into a men's locker room.

So she stayed in bed, listening to their voices float upstairs, heard Frank say he'd been a student at a university in Germany, studying botany, and it was there that he had met the connection that had access to German ergotamine.

Peter was trying to convince Richard of the value of selling coke, arguing that the big bucks helped finance other trips.

Then Merlin was asking Peter to lay him out a line or two. Marcie could even see Merlin's smile in the darkness of her room, knew the only time he'd do coke was on his business trips to the city.

She closed her eyes and tried to force herself to sleep. If coke was on the table, they'd rap until dawn.

On Wednesday morning, Marcie reminded Richard about the poetry class. As evening approached, she bathed and got John ready for bed, then waited for Richard to arrive. By 6:50, she knew he wouldn't show. With stark realization, she knew, too, that he'd never put the time aside. For some reason, he was threatened by her interest in the poetry workshop.

The thought astounded her. His insecurity was subtle, but this one small step in her own direction made him ill at ease. He wanted total control. He would deny it, feel insulted if she accused him of it, but nevertheless, the truth was there.

At 7:30 she put John to sleep, walked downstairs and took a seat at the dining room table, understanding a dynamic she should have known months ago. In fact, she realized, it had started when they'd left the Haight. The business was Richard's life. Tonight had shown that the time he spent with it was more important than her time or needs. And if she expected to be part of his trip, she would have to follow.

With a melancholy sadness, Marcie realized that the final link with the Haight had been severed. The Summer of Love would always be her cornerstone, a touchstone for her life's energy. When things became complicated, she would look back and remember that time without economic class or racial barriers, when men and women could pick and choose each other freely, when she could come and go at will and answer to no one, when being holy and recognizing the spiritual worth of each man and woman was a reality. But the days in the Haight had been a fairy tale, a shining moment, and it was time for her to grow up and put the fairy tales away. She was a mother with a toddler who was growing into an active little boy.

From a far corner of her mind, she took out the young woman who had stood on the highway in Louisiana. Maybe she hadn't felt sure about hitching without money or direction, but she'd been courageous, ready for direct action, ready to believe that her involvement could make a difference. Now she felt as though she were looking over castle walls, and the world loomed huge, varied, and interesting. Time to step back into it rather than hide behind crenellations, afraid to meet anyone unless they were introduced, secrecy the mode of living.

The years between hitching from Louisiana and moving to her newest home in the Berkeley hills had slipped away in a haze. What had she done during the time? Most of it had been a commitment to the family and the business. A lot of it had gone into personal learning—yoga, organic foods, herbs, natural childbirth, child rearing—things she shared directly with the family. The rest of her creative time had been spent in psychedelic meditation.

Sitting alone, waiting for Richard, Marcie had hours to think. She'd reached for the rolling box, had the neatly wrapped smoke sitting before her in a thin joint. She stared at it, knew that if she smoked it, the evening would fade into the same haze as all the other evenings.

Those thoughts, she cried silently. *Those thousands upon thousands of insights that have filled me over all the years. Where have they all gone? Why didn't I write them down?*

No, she thought, *still staring at the joint. Not tonight. I've been stoned every minute of every day for three years.*

Instead, she took out her journal and began to compose a love poem to her mother. The words welled up inside, bursting to appear on paper like fireworks waiting to fill the sky. The phone did not ring once during the evening, and her spirit soared with the unusual free time. Hours later, she critically reread her poem. Good in some places, rough in others, unstructured and stumbling where she tried to connect some ideas, but it was a good start.

Near midnight, when Richard returned, he found her still at the dining room table, pen in hand.

"Hi," he kissed her cheek softly. "How's it going? Any messages?"

"No," Marcie answered, closing the journal. "It's been very quiet."

"Have you been writing?" he asked, sitting down.

"In lieu of going to class tonight."

"Tonight? Oh my God! I spaced! Are you really angry?"

"No."

"Are your feelings hurt?"

"Somewhat."

"Marcie, I'm sorry. I promise I'll be here next week."

"Unless you have a better offer," she said softly. "You know the real shame, Richard? You're the one who'll ultimately lose. You'll miss your special time with John and all the memories that time would bring."

"Look, I'm really sorry. We made ten grand this evening."

"When you talk like that, what am I supposed to say? How can I equate my class to ten grand? Don't you see? It all comes down to the same thing. Money becomes more valuable than anything else—more valuable, even, than time with your son."

"There'll be plenty of time to play with John."

"Now is when he needs you. Have you seen how fast he's changing?"

"Sure I have. And I do spend time with him. Anyway, Frank needed those tabs first thing in the morning. He has an early plane to catch to Seattle and some chick on the line who's going to run it across the border with the midmorning tourist flow."

"You sold to Frank?"

From the way he quickly looked away, she knew. He hadn't meant to tell her. Knew she didn't like the dude.

"Yeah. You still feeling uneasy about him?"

"What did you sell him?"

"Ten grams of L."

"First time?"

"No," he admitted. "I sold to him early last week. A thousand dollars a gram."

"That's an awfully good price. He'll quadruple his money across the border."

"He has additional expenses. He has to pay his runners. Look, I know he doesn't have a lot of social skills, but if he's going to sell me ET, he has to be okay."

"Did you turn it hand to hand?"

"Jesus, Marcie, I'm a little stoned, and I don't feel like getting paranoid."

"Did you?"

"Yes."

"I just want you to think about what you are doing. If you get popped, it's not just you who's affected. It's all of us. What about John? He'd be grown before you even knew him. What about the families who depend on you for their income? Not to mention the people you support outright. Like Honey, since she's had the courage to leave Alex. Or the money you loan out. Mary Ann and Keith could never have put together the organic food store without you. What are we all going to do if you get yourself busted?"

"Just calm down," he said slowly and emphatically. "I'm being careful. Frank rented a garage near Oakland Airport so we could have a stash. Believe me, I know what I'm doing. Let's go to bed, okay? I need to lie down with you for a while."

"No," she pouted.

"Alright," Richard answered quietly. "Oh, by the way, I saw Alex today."

"You did?" Her interest was immediate.

"I told him I moved the machine. And I told him why. I think, for the moment, he's in a state of confused embarrassment. He thought he was so smart, really pullin' one over on me. He's going to have to think about this one."

"Is he angry?"

"He feels I cheated him. By tomorrow, the story will float through the scene that I ripped him off and cut him out of the partnership. That's why I've got to get out of here early and explain my side. Both stories will float around, and people will believe what they want."

"Do you think he'll try to hurt us?"

"Maybe. But he doesn't know where we live. I halved everything else right down the middle—money and product. I think he'll at least be satisfied with that."

"But maybe not?"

"He's always wanted something he was missing within himself. Something none of us can give him."

Richard stood and turned toward the door. Then he stopped, looking back toward her. "As I was leaving, he threw something else at me. He's been skimming off the top. He started by taking a few hundred hits off every gram and selling them to David. Then he began to juggle the books. Gave David thousands of tabs that didn't show up in the accounting. That's how he originally began the Canadian market."

"It's been a pretty rough day for you, hasn't it?" she murmured.

"Yeah. I'm really tired. I'm goin' to bed."

"Richard, ask me again."

"What?"

"Ask me again if I'll come to bed with you."

His smile shattered her last hesitation. "My lady," he bowed, "will you allow me into your boudoir?"

"Yes," she whispered.

RICHARD
BERKELEY, CALIFORNIA
NOVEMBER 1969

Four days later, Richard bought a kilo of ET from Frank.

"Wait until Christian sees this!" he told Marcie gleefully. "And there's four more kilos."

Marcie had just climbed into bed, thinking Richard might be out for a good part of the evening, and now she turned on the lamp so she could better see.

"I wanted you to take a look before I take this over to Allen," he told her. "He needs to get this to the lab right away." Allen was not only living with Christian in the Berkely Hills house, but with Christian in India, Allen was taking care of things.

Marcie glanced at the clock. "It's 1:00 a.m.," she murmured, her brow knotted.

"Better not to have it around here. And Alan can take the first plane out in the morning. I'll be back in an hour."

"When's Christian coming?" Marcie didn't seem especially pleased to be holding the jar.

"What's the matter with you?" he laughed. "That's magic in your hands."

"I'll feel better when Christian gets back from Asia."

"Well, I'll admit Frank's not the most sensitive guy in the world. But he's no mojo. This proves it."

"Have you talked to Frank about Christian or Albert?"

"There's no reason to."

"Don't. Richard, just go with me on this one. Please," she added earnestly. "Did you tell him we were connected with a lab?"

"What would he expect we'd do with the ET? It has to be going to some lab."

"You could just be passing it on. That's all he needs to know."

Richard pressed the automatic garage opener to the rented house they had dubbed "the factory," drove inside the garage, and pushed the button to close the door. Two weeks ago he and Merlin had set up the tabbing machine in the back room.

Man, was he aggravated! His mood was sullen, his mind silently grumbling.

Marcie! What's her trip, anyway? Why's she feeling so insecure?

No one in the world was more important to him than she was. Her job was the most valuable he could imagine. Sometimes he felt like a mule—simply moving goods from one place to another—but Marcie had control, held the entire network together. She was the central switchboard, coordinating people and times. Always had good food for fuel. Spent her days with John, forming him into the person Richard wished him to become.

What more does she want? Recognition? Prestige? It's not my fault being a housewife's not a particularly prestigious job. Not my fault she works so hard without getting paid for her labor. Don't I give her a part of every cent I make? And whenever she asks for it?

Inside the kitchen, Richard opened the refrigerator and took out a small brown jar with ten crystal grams and tried to decide what color dye to mix with them.

Purple, he decided. *Purples are selling well.*

Instead of getting to work, he set the jar down on the kitchen table and stared at it without even knowing he was spacing, still distracted over the latest argument with his wife.

He loved her, loved being married. The closeness, their mutual concerns, talking late into the night, listening to her opinions, her insight. He even loved the arguments, how they seemed to draw apart like two independent electrons circling some philosophic nucleus, only to be attracted to each other again. Sometimes he feared that the magnetism between them might break and that she would fly away to circle some other nucleus. But the bond never broke. Their marriage had lasted through three unbelievable years. The trips of ego death and rebirth had given them lifetimes together. Their mettle was tested, fired, hard. In three short years, Richard already had a sense of what it might be like to share a lifetime with her. What would he feel for Marcie in ten years? Or twenty? Or fifty? The thought staggered him. Fifty years! All those mornings of waking up to her smile and sharing the day. Endless nights of lying down together, feeling her rub her hands along his thighs, looking forward to life because Marcie was there, and it was wonderful to be alive.

In that moment, he recognized that there were things about his lifestyle he wanted to maintain—a clean home and the things in it he'd acquired over the years, the artwork, rugs, and furniture. He enjoyed having two cars, especially cars that were fun to drive. In fact, he was becoming more and more aware of the benefit of living in a society where he was able to act in accordance with his beliefs. He recognized that American society did allow for dissent. It was indeed possible to stand on any street corner and leaflet against the war with sheets printed from any press. True, he still couldn't practice his religion openly, but he was working toward that end. He'd even begun to appreciate the idea of a free enterprise system.

"So how are you any different from your father now, huh, Richard?" Marcie had screamed at him that morning.

Damn! he thought. With a single question she had provoked him beyond belief! How could she stay uptight for so long about missing a dumb class?

Richard found that he was still staring at the jar of crystal and tried to bring himself back to the job at hand. Carefully, he picked it up, broke the seal, and lifted the lid.

Without warning, into the stillness and quiet of the house, he heard a loud pounding on the front door, a garbled shouting, a crash as the door fell away from its locks and hit the wall behind it.

"Jesus!" he whispered aloud, knowing immediately what was happening. He closed his eyes, frozen. "How?"

His body shook with an internal coldness.

Don't move, he warned himself. *Don't give them an excuse. There's nowhere to run.*

Slowly, and with great regret, he replaced the lid and set the jar back down on the table. In the next instant, a man was through the kitchen door, pointing a pearl-handled chrome .45 in his face.

"Alright, freeze!" the man shouted. "Thinking of running, asshole?"

The man kicked the chair from under him. Richard fell backward, hitting the floor.

"That's it! Go on! Think of running!" the man growled.

Richard stared into the glinting eyes behind the gun. The man's mouth was salivating as he spoke, and he was shaking as badly as Richard himself. Sweat beaded the man's forehead. Richard watched his finger squeeze slightly on the trigger, release it, squeeze, and release again. For what seemed a lifetime, Richard stared into eyes filled with a hatred so intense that he asked himself what he had done to cause this man to want to kill him. Slowly, he tried to stand, holding his arms up high.

"Easy," Richard said quietly, his voice quivering. "Take it easy. No one's going to hurt you."

The sound of the soft, sure voice infuriated the agent. He swung the gun and connected with Richard's face.

Richard felt a great stabbing pain race inward at his ear. He reeled sideways, crashing into the back door. In the next second, his heart stopped. The sound of the fired .45 filled the room and echoed through his head, on and on and on. He waited for pain or darkness. He waited until he heard the sound of another man's voice.

"Sorry about that, Bremer. Looks like I stumbled coming into the room," the second cop told his wild-eyed, white-faced colleague.

"Damn it, Hanson!"

Slightly to the left of where he stood, Richard could see the hole in the wall that could just as easily have been in his body. Quickly, he stood up straight, holding up his arms, knowing the room's dynamics had changed. That stumble was no accident.

"The bastard was trying to get out of the back door!" Bremer accused Richard, furious.

"I'm not going anywhere," Richard answered, his voice still soft, blood streaming from temple to jaw line, his head pounding from the blow. "I'm stayin' right here."

"Better hold still," Hanson told him, pointing his own gun at Richard's face. "You're lucky. You'd be a dead man if I hadn't tripped coming into the room. Turn around slowly. Hands against the wall . . . legs apart . . . "

Bremer took the wallet from Richard's back pocket and pulled out his phone list, only to recognize a list of coded names.

"You'll want to see this, Dolph!" a third cop called excitedly, joining Bremer and Hanson in the kitchen. "The back room has a tabbing machine!"

"Wilson," Bremer nodded. "Search him."

Wilson stepped forward, frisking Richard, running his hands through his hair, along his chest and belt, his crotch, down his legs, while Bremer continued looking through the papers in Richard's wallet.

A fourth agent brought in a briefcase he'd found in a closet. "This place is hot!" he laughed. "Man, there's at least a hundred thousand hits back there!"

"You want to give us the combo, asshole?" Bremer asked, shaking the briefcase at him, malice heavy in his voice.

"Six-nine-six-nine," Richard answered.

"Cuff him," Bremer nodded to Wilson, turning the combination numbers. "Put him in that chair."

"What's this?" the new cop asked, picking up the jar that sat on the table. He opened it. Tiny bits of crystal fell on his hands and onto the table. He put his nose close to sniff at it. "It's not coke."

"Careful, Phillips, that's acid," Hanson said. "Crystal. Wash your hands and the outside of the jar. Get it into a plastic bag for transport down to the lab."

Too late, Richard thought, stifling a grin. *He can wash all he wants; that guy's dosed.*

Bremer opened the briefcase. "Not bad." He emptied the contents onto the table. "Ten little packages. Ten grand."

From where Richard sat in the kitchen, his hands cuffed together tightly behind his back, he heard agents moving through the house. "There's some smoke here!" The words drifted toward him from the back. They'd found his primo stash of Panama Red. Furniture was being ripped, hammers tapped on walls. Every once in a while, there was a crash, laughter, and wild, party-like bantering. He sat very still, alert.

It could have been worse, he tried telling himself. *Marcie could have been with me. Or Merlin. Allen. Even Albert.*

He shuddered. Albert was Christian's chemist. If the alchemists went, all was lost.

"Who else works here?" Bremer demanded, turning on him, finding a place for his real anger. "Come on. You're in for about twenty years. If you cooperate, we can start taking some of that off. Who works here? I said, give me some names, fucker!" Bremer hit him open handed and heavy across the face, knocking him out of the chair again.

Phillips picked him up, slammed him into the wall.

"Where does this come from?" Bremer asked, holding up the plastic bag with the brown jar of crystal. "Let's have some names, asshole."

Phillips punched him hard in the stomach. Richard gasped for breath, doubled over. His knees hit the floor hard as he fell.

Phillips and Wilson pulled him up again. He stood unsteadily, still gasping. They went to work on his ribs and stomach. When he hit the floor this time, he tried to press his chest to his knees to protect himself, just like years ago during the marches in the hot Mississippi summer. Black-toed shoes caught him under the left armpit and so deeply into his side that a heavy cloud covered his mind. Closing his eyes, he realized how merciful things would be if they'd just push him a little more past consciousness.

Retching, he was once more lifted and held against the wall.

"The names, asshole. Where'd you get the crystal? Where's the lab? Answer me!" Bremer pulled his hair so he was forced to lift his face. The gun was against his temple. "Answer me!"

The pain and humiliation only made Richard obstinate. He tried to focus his eyes on Bremer, the others in the room. Then his attention finally synthesized on one man standing near the doorway, a thousand questions answered at once.

Frank.

Relief began to crowd his obstinacy. At least now he knew the extent of the penetration. He knew where Frank had come from and who he'd been introduced to. He was in big trouble, but the rest of his family was safe. Marcie was uninvolved in a business sense. Merlin was safely tucked away in the mountains. Only Peter had a problem. Frank had met no one else.

Marcie had been right once again. Thank God he hadn't mentioned Christian or Albert, not even when he'd felt like swaggering at Frank's subtle questions.

"Doesn't look like there's a lab here," said yet another cop, this one wearing an FBI badge.

Bremer stepped back. Phillips and Wilson looked at each other and released their hold on Richard. He swayed, trying to stay upright.

"Nice haul, though, Bremer. You state boys did a good job for once," the fed said, watching Richard carefully as he stood gasping for breath.

"The base," Frank demanded. "Where's the base?"

Richard was beginning to understand. Frank must have been convinced the lab was here and had expected to recover the kilo.

"Sorry, Frank," Richard muttered hoarsely. "I don't know what you're talking about."

"The kilo you picked up this morning," Frank demanded.

"What kilo?" Richard managed a grin.

"You think you've won, asshole?" Frank stepped toward him, faced him squarely. "You tell me that after you've been shoveling shit for a couple of years with the prison work program. You like sewage treatment plants? The job's yours. You like lying on a cot every evening for the next ten years, watching your face grow old and wondering who your old lady's fucking? Your kid'll be a teenager before you ever throw him a ball. Still think you win, asshole? Yeah, you win."

Bremer nodded to Phillips. "Get him out of here," he ordered, unexpectedly pleased with Corbet. The year away had matured him.

But Phillips was starting to come on to the acid. He simply grinned and looked like he was having a hard time finding the floor with his foot.

"Lucky you," Richard told him.

28

KATHY

LONDON, ENGLAND

NOVEMBER 1969

A week in a London hotel room had not put Kathy in any better frame of mind. When the rain was not steadily beating against the windowpanes, she looked out at a gloomy, gray sky. Wild gusts of wind rattled the window and clawed at her raw nerves. All the while she sat, her spirit was drawn to New Orleans. Simply put, she wanted her mother.

But she couldn't return with scraped wrists or open welts on her buttocks, so she stayed in London while she healed, using the comfrey leaves she'd purchased at a local herb store. Occasionally, she would make visits out to some destination, the British Museum or the National Library or the National Portrait Gallery, and although awed by objects that were cornerstones of Western civilization, everything was viewed through a thin curtain of gauze, as if she were not actually present.

On the day she thought she could make the trip home, Kathy anxiously called the old phone number from her childhood. At the sound of her mother's voice, she wanted to cry out the story of Larry, her love for Christian, and the horror with the colonel. Tightness clasped her throat. She forced her lips to stop quivering. "Mom, I want to come home."

"Is anything the matter?" Irene asked.

"I'm okay. Will you pick me up at the airport? I'm planning to stay for a while."

There was a moment's hesitation on the line. "Your room's ready. We haven't changed it much. Kathy, have you finished your degree? They desperately need a teacher at St. Mary's."

"Not yet, Mom. I had to take the quarter off."

"Well, when are you coming?"

"Day after tomorrow. I arrive at 6:00 p.m. on Eastern Airlines. From New York."

"New York? What are you doing in New York?"

"Long story."

"Kathy, do remember to dress nicely for your father. None of those hippie clothes or hair. Okay?"

"Why . . . sure. I'll look . . . neat. See you in a few days."

Kathy replaced the receiver and felt the blood drain from her face. Everything was the same as she had left it. Her room. Her parents. Teaching at St. Mary's? How would her mother ever be able to console her about Larry or understand her relationship with Christian?

Between two pictures in her wallet was a blotter of acid. Within thirty minutes, she was coming on. Like a flood, visions of the last weeks engulfed her. She began to smile despite herself, laughing as great bolts of tightening and releasing flashed up her legs.

In the middle of all the sensations, the one overwhelming reality was Christian, his presence close, real, her mind intermingled with his. His mouth moved along her neck, touched each part of her body. On that hotel room floor where she lay in a bed of paisleys, she made love to him, knew she could always touch him. As long as he was in her mind, he was hers, alive and present. Freedom wasn't about making love to any man she wanted anymore. Freedom was choosing to love Christian with a devotion so ancient that it embodied the very essence of life. Now she saw with complete clarity that walking out on him in Varanasi was a way of paying him back. A part of her had wanted to see the devastation on his face as she'd left the hotel room, to hurt him for not being there when she'd needed him. For making it with Kali.

She began to cry huge, deep tears from a place of love and shame and joy and grief. How could she have hurt him when he was so vulnerable? How could they have hurt each other?

I should have done this in India—tripped with him! Oh, God, how different everything would have been! Acid cuts through all the ego games. What's important becomes immediately recognizable. Where else am I to find the goodness and compassion I've found in this man?

For a long time, London did not exist, just laughing play, tears, more laughter, and the sense of him. Kathy lay against her blanket, every pore open, each cell a tiny tingle singing the story of its own life, her body a giant orgasm pressed on and on and on into ecstasy, wishing Christian were there, knowing he was both present and absent.

As she began a yoga asana, her consciousness expanded, up and outward, spreading over all the things she was trying to grasp and knowing that the events of the last weeks were greater than her own actions. From this height, she could see a larger pattern of cause and effect. She knew the colonel's mind, what motivated him, became him . . . pitied him. He was only part of a system that fed off of what Christian had always called the *afflictive* emotions—anger, greed, lust, jealousy, and hate.

Her people—her brothers and sisters, the people of the tribes— had wanted to give a new vision to the world, a future that sustained the planet and its life, one of right action and thoughtfulness for all living things. When she tripped, the vision was here again! She bowed her head in humility, knowing in the deepest part of her soul that her knowledge was old and hard won.

A few days ago, she'd told Christian that her dream of a better world had been destroyed, that she'd lost too much. Instead, the people of the tribes had been scattered. Her friends and loved ones forced underground, dubbed criminals because they wanted to get in touch with the Spirit. Her brothers and sisters imprisoned. Kevin murdered by a man with a badge. Larry killed trying to fill his peace pipe. Christian tortured.

But now she understood that the mistake was not in the dream, but in thinking it would be easy to accomplish. Whoever promised that the struggle would be easily won?

Someday, if we hold to our beliefs, we will make a difference. Christian has to get home. He and Albert and Doug and all those others need to continue to distribute the ideas that will change the world. Ideas all bound in a tiny pill.

She sat in lotus, her body perfectly still, her breathing deep and regular, her mind swirling around revealed truths.

So where do I start again? How do I make permanent change without having to drive out into a desert in the night?

She smiled. The thought that had been teasing her came to the forefront.

Law school.

The knowledge stood before her, a visceral reality.

I'll merge with the system, become one with it, use it. Isn't that one of the lessons of acid, that all things are a constant merging to become one? The next quarter begins in January. When I return to Berkeley, it's time off for Danny and nights with my books.

She prostrated herself on the floor, in humble thanksgiving for the gift of insight.

"Mom?" Kathy said softly over the phone later that evening, still very stoned.

There was a silence, then Kathy heard, "You're not coming."

"I don't belong there anymore. I simply don't fit. But I needed to tell you how much I appreciate every moment, every effort you've given me. I promise to try to make you proud. You may not always understand what I do or why, but I'll always lead a moral life. I'll always work to help others."

"Kathy . . . " Her mother began to cry softly. "I love you. It'll be so hard to lose you again. Why aren't you coming?"

"I need to make a life in California. That's where I belong. I've got to finish my classes at Berkeley. I'm going to apply for law school."

"Law school? Kathy, talk . . . talk with your father."

"Is it true," her father asked, "what I just heard?"

"Hi, Dad. I called to ask whether you'd just give me a little more time. I still have a lot of growing to do. Somehow I don't think we're as far apart politically as appears on the surface. I know you long for peace in the world, just as I do."

After a moment of silence, he responded, "It's hard for me to really understand what you want."

"The most important thing is my love for you. If I could only tell you how many times you've been with me over the years! There were times when I touched your memory so deeply that I thought you must surely feel my love, even from a distance."

"Just hearing you say that gives me some peace of mind. And a little more patience." He paused. "This time, keep in touch."

"I will, Dad. I promise."

"By the way, Marcie called for you today. She said she was looking for you and thought to try here. Where have you been?"

"Traveling. But I'm going home now."

When Kathy hung up the phone, she felt her heart sing. *Oh, to hear Marcie's voice!*

With a great deal of concentration because she was getting spacey, she focused on the number she had written down to give to the operator.

"Marcie!" Kathy cried into the phone, once the operator had connected her. "How did you know to call Mom?"

"Christian. He said you might be going home."

"Then he's back? He made it?" She closed her eyes and whispered, "Thank God."

"Kathy . . . "

The word electrified her. "What is it? What's happened?"

For a moment, there was no sound, just hoarse breathing.

"Is it Richard? John?"

"Richard," Marcie answered slowly. "Richard's been busted."

"When?" Kathy asked, beginning to shake.

"A few days ago. The same narc that killed Kevin took him out. A man named Bremer. We're trying to get his bail reduced."

"How much did he have on him?"

"The whole wad. The factory went down. A hundred thousand hits and the tabbing machine. He's been charged with manufacturing. Among other things."

"Oh, Marcie! I'll be right there! Tomorrow."

"And Kathy . . . I'm pregnant again."

29

CHRISTIAN AND LANCE BORMANN
BERKELEY, CALIFORNIA
NOVEMBER 1969

Christian sat impatiently in the outer office, waiting to see his attorney, Lance Bormann. He glanced at his watch. Eleven forty. His appointment had been for eleven. He stood and walked across the room toward a secretary he'd never seen before.

"Is he with a client?" Christian asked.

"No, sir. I'm sure he'll be with you in a moment."

Christian found it hard not to pace the floor. Something was up with Lance. He was being power-tripped.

The man needs to turn on, he told himself angrily. *We've given him our confidences and our secrets, thinking he would join us, but he hasn't. As time passes, our differences are becoming more obvious. He needs to have the acid experience. It's time.*

The secretary avoided his eyes and was visibly relieved when the buzzer on her desk sounded.

"Yes, sir?"

"Send Mr. Alden in, please."

"Thanks." Christian nodded to her.

"Christian." Lance smiled and stood, holding out a hand. "How's it going? I haven't seen you in months."

"Things are . . . complicated."

He looked Lance squarely in the eye, gathering messages, and Lance's gaze wavered.

What's happened to him? Christian wondered.

"Sorry about the wait." Lance shuffled papers on his desk. "I had to clear up a few things before this afternoon. Please sit down."

Christian leaned back in the chair, still studying him, wondering how much the man was to be trusted. Lance was changing. They all were. They were being bent and bullied by life and circumstance, forced to live underground or go to jail, tested to their limits. Bad things were happening to people like Kevin . . . Larry . . . Bob and Dharma . . . Richard. Kathy. He sighed and looked through the window to a white cloud moving slowly across blue sky. Even though he'd only been back a few days, India already seemed like a long time ago.

Even before he had time to set his pack down on arrival from the airport, Marcie took his arm. "Where's Kathy?" she asked expectantly. They were meeting at Danny's, unsure about the amount of heat on Richard's house.

"I think she's in New Orleans," he answered, affecting indifference. "She said something about stopping in to see her parents."

He turned quickly to Richard, noting the bruises on his face, a cut on his forehead still healing after two weeks. "What's the story of your bust? Start from the beginning."

They sat on the rug, close, sharing a jay. Christian could feel Richard's fear. Every once in a while, Marcie threw out her own questions about Kathy's visit to India.

Yes, she'd found him. Yes, they'd talked. Yes, she seemed to be doing okay.

"Christian!" Marcie finally exclaimed. "What's going on?"

Facing the inevitable, he told her. "She walked out on me. I wanted to be there for her, but she no longer trusted me."

Marcie looked at him strangely. "Didn't she tell you why she'd gone to find you? Why it couldn't wait? Didn't she tell you about Tucson?"

"What do you mean? What happened in Tucson?"

Marcie's intake of breath was sharp and quick. "Christian . . . Larry's dead. And Steve, an old friend of his. Jose was wounded. Shot on a back road making a new connection just north of the border. That's what took so long."

Marcie told him the story of Kathy finding the bodies, pulling Jose from the gully, the drive to Mexico so there wouldn't be any heat on the ranch.

"So she stayed on to help, to care for Jose's wounds, to deal with the police. When she did manage to get to a phone booth, there was never an answer at your house."

He closed his eyes, the room spinning, the ground falling away from him.

"What happened in India?" Marcie demanded.

Then he told his own story, about Kali and Nareesh, Lama Loden and Ram Seva, about jail and the lieutenant, the American agent and the possibility of torture, how Kathy had walked into it with her weakness and her love, had taken control, buying him out with her money and her body, how she'd spent a night on a ghat instead of coming to him, how she'd walked out of the hotel room without looking back.

He told how he'd knelt at Daya Nanda's feet, and, finally, taking Daya Nanda's advice, had gone to visit his parents.

When his story was done, the room was quiet. Marcie put an arm around his shoulders, and he leaned into her, sinking, sinking. Drowning in too many emotions—guilt and fear, sacrifice and honor, love and compassion—the realizations rushing at him in pounding waves. And still so very vulnerable, he had wept.

"What's wrong?" he heard Lance ask.

"I'm thinking of a brother who just bought it in Arizona trying to put together a weed deal."

"Dead?"

Christian nodded. "It was hard news."

"Things are warming up in that area. The bodies are beginning to pile up—mostly kids."

"Yeah, well, let's just keep marijuana illegal so more people die trying to buy and sell," he answered bitterly. "And there's more. I received a phone call this morning from a sister in Hawaii. Two men I was with in the East went down in Greece with a truckload."

"Hash? How'd it happen?"

"I'm not sure. But I know Interpol was on us even before we left Afghanistan. The border guards were waiting for them."

"So that's where you were. Where are they now?"

Christian's body was tight. "They've already been tried and sentenced. Seven years. God, seven years! It was maybe two days from arrest to sentencing. Here's the name of the prison they were sent to." He passed Lance a piece of paper, and Christian watched as his eyes gleamed at the prospect of international recognition.

He's hooked, Christian saw with satisfaction. *But do I want him? Seven years of Bob and Dharma's lives are at stake. Taken day by day, that's a long time.*

Alright, Lance. I'll go one more round with you. Let's see what your colors are.

"I want you to do everything possible to get these two men out. Spend whatever it costs. Make whatever bribes you have to make. But get them out. This guy," Christian leaned over to touch the paper, "Bob. His old lady's going to have a baby soon. If you can get him out and back for that baby . . . "

"I'll see what I can do. I'm going to ask Bert, my partner, to go with me on this one. You covering expenses?"

"Whatever it takes."

"I think I might call a press conference. It's time the public became aware of Americans locked up in foreign jails. It may bring some pressure to bear on the Greek government."

And it certainly won't hurt your career, either, Christian mused.

True, Lance was a brilliant attorney, but there were others now who were specializing in drug cases—maybe younger and untried, but dedicated and smart, not as greedy. Christian had paid Lance a large retainer and additional fees over the years for emergencies such as this one. Now it was time to collect, and he could feel Lance opening his hands for more. It was important that the energy he'd worked to develop be used. Money was going to be tight now—the hash lost, Bob and Dharma in prison, Richard popped and too hot to work.

"I have another problem," Christian told him. "You read about that tabbing machine getting busted?"

"A few weeks ago?"

"I want you to talk to the guy about taking his case."

Lance looked at him for a long moment. "You've really had your share of it, haven't you?"

Christian's grin was sickly. "That's only half of it."

"What's the guy's name?"

"Richard. Richard Harrison. Besides the machine, he went down with about a hundred thousand tabs, twenty-five grams of crystal, some smoke, maybe some odds and ends."

"Just a few small things, eh?"

"He's in really deep. He sold to the agent twice, hand to hand. And he bought a kilo of ergotamine from the guy on the day before he was popped."

"When does he want to come in and talk?"

"Soon. Before you leave for Greece."

"Tomorrow morning?" Lance asked, glancing at his calendar.

"Tomorrow's fine."

"Will you be covering his bill?"

"From here on out, it's his own case. I need to put some distance between us."

Lance gave him a quizzical look. "Are you friends?"

"We're tight."

"And he can take care of his own bill?"

Christian nodded.

"You know anything about his politics? How he's connected?"

"When are you going to trip?" Christian asked.

"When I have time." Lance brushed the question aside. "Listen, try staying out of trouble for a while."

"It only takes one evening."

"I'll get around to it one of these days." Lance stood and started around the desk. "By the way, do you have any coke?"

Christian shook his head.

Was that it? he wondered. The game this morning, the cold aloofness—where was the dedication and sense of moral purpose he'd once felt in Lance? Was it gone? Right into the heart of coke and alcohol? Had those had become Lance's fast-lane wheels?

"You want to meet me around five thirty for a drink?" Lance asked him. "You can tell me all about your trip."

"Actually, I'd like to know when you're going to make the time to trip."

"Persistent." Lance cleared his throat. "Okay. When I get back from Greece. I'll make it a priority. Now what about this evening? You want to meet for that drink?"

Christian considered for a moment. "I think I'll wait for you to get back."

Lance got the message. To know Christian or his secrets, he would have to pass the acid test.

"I'll ask Elaine to put Harrison's name on the calendar for tomorrow morning."

"Elaine? Is that the new secretary?"

"Yeah." Lance grinned at him knowingly. "I got a little too close to Georgia."

Christian could only stare. Georgia had been with Lance for years, had always watched his back.

"Are you coming in with Harrison tomorrow?" he heard Lance say.

"No. It'll be just him and his wife." Christian stood abruptly. "Here." He took an envelope from his Indian bag. "Twenty grand. That should cover your tickets for Greece, lodging, and bribe money. If not, you know I'm good for the rest."

30

DOLPH BREMER AND MYLES
BERKELEY, CALIFORNIA
NOVEMBER 1969

Dolph Bremer sat at his desk, touching the edges of a file with his fingertips, his eyes only skimming the words of the page. His real attention was focused on the time and the immanent meeting with Myles Corbet.

Myles was his best agent and his worst. He was extraordinary in his intuition, abilities, and ambition, but he was unpredictable.

And this last incident.

Bremer picked up a pencil and tapped nervously at the desk.

Myles had come back from Germany by way of Canada, and as soon as he was back in Berkeley, had walked confidently through the office, shaking a few hands, and slipping into Bremer's office. Even Wilson and Phillips had regarded him with a new kind of respect. He was thicker in the arms and chest, confident, more arrogant than usual, and clearly a man used to wielding his authority. When he'd finally taken a seat in the old chair in front of Bremer's desk, he'd leaned back easily and told Bremer what he wanted the department to do.

Told him.

"Corbet just came in," Phillips announced.

"Tell him to get up here."

Bremer straightened up, the chair groaning with his shifting weight, anxious to get some quick answers.

"Morning, Bremer."

"Sit down, Corbet."

Bremer took a long, hard look at Myles. "You want to tell me what went wrong? You know what kind of flack I'm getting? A kilo of base. Gone. Disappeared."

Myles frowned. He didn't want to admit to letting Richard . . . or Marcie . . . slip by him.

Everything had been played and replayed in his mind dozens of times. He'd put the base in the garage late in the evening, and had called Richard to confirm the drop. Richard was supposed to have picked it up the next morning. Only he hadn't. Clearly, he'd decided to pick it up just after Myles had called. That could be the only explanation for its disappearance. Richard had gone to the stash sometime after midnight and had brought the base somewhere. But true to form, he hadn't mentioned it when Myles had spoken with him the next morning, would never have talked about it over the phone.

That next morning when Richard was supposed to have picked up the base and left the money, they'd staked out the garage. Once the package was in his car, they would follow him.

But on that morning, Richard had driven by the garage without stopping, and oddly, had simply made a U-turn at the corner and driven away. At that point, they had followed him as planned, and he'd led them to the factory. A few hours after busting Richard, they'd gone to his house in the hills, looking for the base. The place was clean as a whistle. No base. No drugs of any kind.

Marcie had stood in the middle of the room, shaking, her lips white, holding the baby close to her breast.

"I thought so," she'd told Myles, her eyes bright with anger and fear. "From the first moment I saw you. Why, Frank?" she'd cried. "You're young. You're one of us. You have everything to live for. Why join the side of hate?"

Yet her eyes had told him she hated him. Bremer had laid it out hard and heavy how Richard had gone down.

Even as she'd hurled the accusations at him, Myles had remembered the night Peter had brought him over. Obviously tired, Marcie had graciously fixed tea and snacks and made up the beds, saying it was no problem, her voice gentle, putting their needs before hers.

I protected you, he'd wanted to tell her. *I put all the heat on the factory. We wouldn't even be here now, except that I need that base back.*

Truth be told, he was a little impressed to find no smoking stash in the house, knew that Marcie's intuition had been on target. She'd cleaned up.

"I don't know," he finally answered Bremer. "I've been through it all a hundred times. I think your men must have missed something."

"Missed what?" Bremer narrowed his eyes.

Myles threw his hands into the air. "It was so simple. Foolproof. All you had to do was follow the base."

"Let's take this from the beginning," Bremer said acidly. "Up north, in Vancouver, you talked them into 'loaning' you a kilo of base. I had to sign for that. I feel like some monkey's ass, and I want an explanation! Not an accusation!" Bremer's voice was picking up speed, becoming a small roar.

Myles answered complacently. "I put the jar into the garage in a brown paper shopping bag. Were your men on surveillance through the night?"

"Some of it."

"Some of it?" Myles asked in a quiet, incredulous voice, his eyes widening.

Bremer couldn't hold his gaze.

"You said he was going to pick it up in the morning, right?"

Myles slowly nodded his head.

"We had a man out there from 6:00 a.m. on. Harrison showed the next morning, as expected. We followed him. So, where's the base?"

"It's obvious, isn't it?" Myles asked, furious and trying not to show it. "He had to have come in the night to pick it up, then passed it on. God knows where it is if you've let it get away."

"Well, you'd better come up with some ideas for finding it," Bremer ordered, standing abruptly, almost knocking over his coffee cup. "And quick. I've got a report to write."

Myles looked at the sloshing liquid in the cup and the file underneath it.

"Are those the details?" he asked, staring at the file.

"No. Something we thought might be connected. No chance of finding out now. This one will have to wait."

Bremer's voice sounded hungry. Myles looked once again at the thick file. "What is it?" he asked.

He watched as Bremer tried to smother a smile. "This file is a four-year running record. I'm not sure this is a case you'll want to take."

"Four years?" Myles asked. "Something connected to Richard Harrison? Why haven't you mentioned it before?"

"It was incidentals. A word here. A name there. A rumor somewhere else. It just started to come up with more frequency in the last year. Even the rumors started to make a pattern. A dealer involved in everything, connected to the Laguna Brotherhood. Possibly manufacturing LSD. When the Harrison case popped up, I thought I'd find something. Here. Take a look."

Myles took the file and read the name printed across the top. *Christian Alden.*

"The man in India who got away!"

Jesus! he thought to himself. *This is it! I've been waiting for over three years for this!*

Barely breathing, he tried to control the expression on his face. "You think Alden is connected to Harrison?"

"It was the manufacturing rumor that first tempted me to pull it out. It makes for interesting reading. About a month ago, some kid we'd busted here two years ago got popped with a half ton of weed in Miami. Name's Wade Tillich," Bremer told Myles absently. He opened the top drawer of his desk and pulled out his pearl-handled Colt .45. Slowly, he began to polish it with a soft cloth, fondling the piece. "I think it was before you went big time, Corbet."

"What happened to Tillich in '67?"

"He was arrested, then jumped bail. On Marvin Nelson. You know Marvin—Lance Bormann's good buddy. Anyway, Tillich sang long and sweet. Told us Alden was responsible for all the hash that came into Berkeley that summer. That he was bailing people, helping them disappear. Not only dealers, but draft evaders. Deserters. He fouled up a couple of busts for us. He liked acid, was moving plenty of it."

Myles opened the folder and started reading.

1967 September: Rumor of fifty pounds of Afghani hash brought into Berkeley by "Christian."

"Afghani." Myles almost sighed the word.

"I thought you might be interested because of your recent travels." Bremer watched him read down the page. "There's plenty more. Keep reading. There's years of tidbits."

"I tell you what." Myles moistened his lips with his tongue. "I think it's time we talked."

Bremer narrowed his eyes again. Each time he thought he understood what motivated Myles, the kid changed color. Unpredictable. Dangerous.

"I'll bring down this Christian Alden for you," Myles promised, "and I'll find the base. I have reason to believe it's all one and the same."

Bremer's hands stopped abruptly.

"In exchange, I want my freedom. I want my private record that you have tucked away destroyed. Everything about the work I've done for you, for the government, Interpol. Nothing about me—either arrested or working as an undercover drug agent—will be in any file. After this case, I want to retire, finish school, and become a nice, bored Berkeley professor."

"It won't be as easy as you think," Bremer told him, an edge of smugness putting Myles on alert. "Read on. Start about June of '69. You'll find an old friend of yours."

"Jerry! Jerry Putnam!" Myles exclaimed. "What does Jerry have to do with Alden?"

"Seems they're acquaintances. You'll be walking a fine line on this one. Trying to penetrate a scene where you're known."

Myles paged through the file, ideas, thoughts clicking into place, possibilities spinning off. What could Jerry have to do with someone like Christian?

Unless Jerry was dealing?

"So, is it a deal?" he asked Bremer. "One last case and I'm off the payroll?"

"And if you fail?"

"Then I'll continue working for you," he answered with assurance. There was no doubt in his mind—he was getting the base back, and he was going to locate the lab. He'd have his record destroyed and move on to the next phase of his life.

"We can begin this case by amending your files. Christian Alden is an alias. His real name is Brooks—Christian Brooks. I know him. I'd recognize him anywhere. I have pictures of him I took in Afghanistan in front of the Hyatollah brothers' compound. Somehow, he disappeared in India. My first job will be to find out whether he's back in the US."

"How will you do that?"

"I'll start with my only lead. Jerry."

"There's a couple of other things I want you to do," Bremer told him.

"Yeah?"

"I want Bormann. I want him in jail and off the Harrison case. I'm going to push to have that trial as quickly as possible, and I don't want Lance Bormann's mouth to interfere. Work with Hanson and Wilson," Bremer ordered. "When Bormann gets cracked, I'll be somewhere else. It might seem inappropriate if I'm involved, considering the way we've clashed over the years."

"How do you think you're going to get away with arresting Bormann?"

"Jesus, are you kidding? I've been tailing him for three months. I have eyewitness reports that confirm he's been partying hard with his clients. Smoking dope. Snorting cocaine. Accepting drugs in lieu of cash payments. Did you see those headlines when he went off to Greece?" Bremer's voice was louder now, his hands more excited. "What audacity! We know for a fact he's giving advice on how to pack shit and which borders to use."

Myles looked at the gun. "You're going to rub right through the shine."

Bremer became even more agitated as Myles looked at his pistol. "And I'm sick of this stupid psychological idea that guns are phallic. Used by people who need to get off. Guns are used for protection by police officers who put their lives on the line every time they put on a uniform or stick a badge on their chest to take out some punk."

"What else do you want me to do?" Myles forced himself to ask.

"This man," Bremer tapped the file, "this Alden or Brooks, I want him for myself. I don't want you talking about this case with Hanson. You'll report only to me. I'll assemble the team when it's time to move. Got that?"

Myles glanced once more at the polished metal in Bremer's hand and nodded.

"Good," Bremer said, settling back into the chair.

31

RICHARD
BERKELEY, CALIFORNIA
NOVEMBER 1969

Richard numbly heard Lance Bormann's secretary tell him to go in. He glanced first at Marcie, then at Kathy, and gave them a weak smile.

"Take it easy," he said to Marcie's worried face. "It's like a giant chess game and it's our move."

Lance stepped from behind his desk to shake Richard's hand.

"This is my wife, Marcie," Richard said, introducing her. "And this is a close family friend, Kathleen Murray."

For a long moment, Lance looked hard at each of them, then, "Let's start from the beginning," he said to Richard. "Tell me what happened."

"Start with the night Frank came over," Marcie suggested.

"A friend of mine from Canada brought over a man who claimed to have some base. ET. It's the base used in manufacturing lysergic acid."

"Go on."

"We talked. I sold him twenty grams of tablets. I bought the base. He busted me. Pretty simple."

Lance laughed, breaking the tension in the room. "It's never simple. Now start again. How did Frank get into your house? Was it at your invitation?"

Richard knew exactly how Frank had come at him. It was because of the brown crystal Alex had sold in Canada.

When Alex had first tried to form an association on a visit to Canada, Peter had turned him down. But one of Peter's customers, Jack, had slipped Alex his phone number, and they'd connected. Jack was busted with Alex's tabs and had fingered Peter.

So Frank had come to Peter, made a buy, and was ready to make the arrest when he heard of a lab. Richard could imagine what that must have meant to Frank. A lab was a whole new ballgame, not merely a sales rap. Richard pictured the argument Frank must have used to manipulate the Vancouver Narcotics Department: The manufacturers can be lured with base as bait, and the lab can be located by following the base.

"I suppose I invited him in," Richard murmured. "He came with a friend."

"Who's that?" Lance asked, taking notes.

Richard hesitated, had difficulty getting the words past his lips. It was a sacred trust among his people—one never named names.

"Does it matter?" he asked.

Lance looked up. "Believe me. If the agent came in with your friend, they already have his name. It might be nice if I had it too."

"Peter. From Vancouver."

"Do you know his full name?"

"No."

"Where is he now?"

"Out of reach. I have a way to get ahold of him if I need to, but it takes a day or so."

"Okay, so Frank comes over with Peter. What happens then?"

"We talk. Start bargaining."

"Did Frank do any drugs with you?"

"He smoked. Didn't do any coke. I liked him for that. Where I made my mistake was in not tripping with him, but he was always about to catch a plane for somewhere."

"I see. You remind me a lot of Christian Alden. The two of you good friends?"

Richard glanced at Kathy, who stared at her shoes. She hadn't seen him since returning to Berkeley.

"We know each other."

"Alright. Now Frank's in your house. You're smoking together. Talking. What do you decide?"

"He tells me he has five kilos of base. I'm ecstatic. Then he sells me one."

"How?"

"Frank rented a garage near the Oakland Airport. He said we could leave each other goods there. That way, each of us could make pickups when we felt comfortable."

"Did you sell to him before you bought the base?"

"Twice. Ten grams of LSD both times."

"Where did you sell him the LSD?"

"We met on a street corner and transferred in my car."

"Hand to hand?"

"Yes. He paid cash."

Lance shook his head. "Tough. I'm sure the money was marked. Is that what was confiscated in your factory?"

Richard nodded.

"What happened to the base?"

"He left the base in the garage. Late. I told him I'd pick it up in the morning because it was near midnight. Frank was going to return for the bucks sometime the next afternoon. But I was too excited, so I just drove on down there about 1:00 a.m. And a good thing I did. There was no heat on me. It was all waiting the next morning when I went back to drop off the money. But . . ." and here he glanced at Marcie. "Something didn't feel right. I decided I'd give Frank the money the next time I saw him. They saw the car drive by and followed me to the factory. It was all very smooth. The department money they found in the briefcase went right back to the department. Then they took more bucks off me when I bought the base. The dude was covered. The operation would have been perfect, if they'd recovered the base."

"But he didn't get the base back."

"No." Richard grinned.

"So you have it?"

Richard shrugged.

"And where is it now?"

"Gone."

"Okay." Lance looked down at his desk, thinking. "There's a lot going on here. We'll have to take it apart and analyze everything. Do you know whether you were served with a warrant when they entered your factory? Did you let them in?"

"They had a warrant." Richard laughed. "But the only thing they served me was a blow to the head with a gun, a couple of fists, and a few kicks to the ribs. That guy, Bremer, blew a six-inch hole in the wall where he expected my body to be. If it hadn't been for one of the other cops hitting his arm, I'd be another statistic."

"The cop who hit Bremer's arm, was it Hanson?"

"Hanson? Yeah, that's the one. How'd you know?"

"Before you do anything else, I want you to go get pictures taken of those bruises. That cut on your forehead."

"He's yellow-blue underneath his clothing," Marcie told him, her voice soft and trembling.

Lance looked worried. "Who bailed you?" he asked.

"Marvin Nelson."

"Okay. You know you're in big trouble? Manufacturing's a heavy rap."

"I know. Big trouble."

"But there's a lot we can do." Lance played absently with the pen in his hand for a moment, thinking. "I'm concerned about Bremer's shootings. I want to hire an investigator to do some work for us. The information may be very useful, may even save a life. But it's going to be expensive."

"I expected that."

"If you don't have the money yourself, perhaps your parents would be willing to help?"

Richard looked toward Marcie. "My father's already done enough.

He put up his house as security for my bail. I'll be responsible for the rest of my bills. I'll pay whatever it takes."

"Good. I know Joe will be effective."

"Just one thing," Richard added. "I want a religious defense."

"Then you're looking at five to ten, easy," Lance answered without hesitation. "The religious defense has been tried many times. Half the people who come in here ask for it. No judge is going to be responsible for making pot or LSD legal. Take my word for it, they'll find good reason, with everybody's blessing, to say no."

"Why can't my religious conviction be my defense? Am I protected by the First Amendment or not?"

"Not if you consider the use of LSD your religion."

"Why?"

"Because judges are responsible for voicing opinions that are usually a statement of a society's needs and attitudes. Only when people change do laws change. Quite frankly, American society hasn't changed enough to permit the courts to reflect the beliefs of an elite minority."

"You mean I haven't turned enough people on?" Richard asked with mock seriousness.

"That's one way of looking at it."

"God, where'd all those millions of tabs go?" He held out his hands.

Marcie gave him a look that insisted he play this one straight.

"Richard," Lance continued, "freedom to believe may be considered absolute. You can express the view that LSD and marijuana are beneficial. You can advocate the repealing of the laws against their use. But according to the law, you may not use LSD or marijuana or hashish. And your arrest record shows you in possession of all three. Not only possession, but you had a hundred thousand tabs packaged for sale. Try to remember that, will you? And a true religion has to have form, structure, ceremony, *history*."

"How can we have form?" Richard cried, exasperated. "They won't allow us to legally incorporate so we can make form. Go ask Timothy Leary about making ceremony. He tried to establish the League for Spiritual Discovery. I mean, what do we have to do to be accepted?"

Lance settled back in his chair. "Even if you can establish your philosophy, you'll have to prove that you cannot attain your personal type of communication with a supreme being by any other means. The court will call your use of LSD 'reliance on an artificial aid.' It'll suggest that there are other ways to achieve apperception."

"You're right. I suppose I could flagellate myself into agony and ecstasy. Or pierce my flesh with arrowheads after fasting for a week to experience the death–rebirth cycle. At least I wouldn't be using an *aid*. God forbid that altered consciousness be a simple organic process."

Kathy laughed aloud, her voice trailing off gleefully through the room.

"Okay," Lance answered, casting her a look. "Supposing you prove that LSD or marijuana is essential to the practice of your religion."

"It is."

"Then the state has a right to claim a 'compelling state interest.'"

"Now what does that mean?"

"It means that if it's in the state's interest to make marijuana or LSD illegal, your First Amendment rights may be abridged."

"Just taken away?"

"Right. For instance, if a group of people decided that human sacrifice was an essential part of their religious belief, the courts would be allowed to outlaw the practice in the interest of society at large."

"So I go to prison for wanting to talk to God."

"Like I said, if you use a religious defense, you're looking at five to ten."

Richard turned to Marcie and passed a thought to her through his eyes.

"There's more," Lance continued. "You'd better hear me out. There's also the problem of gain and profit. If you're achieving financial gain by your sales, the court would consider your use of LSD as something other than a religious practice. You cannot use the claim of religious immunity as a cloak for illegal activities in which you profit."

"To maintain production, I have to make money. Dealing supports the tribes."

"That's known as gain."

"Any religion passes the collection plate."

"Richard," he countered with some small exasperation, "there are other things we can do with your case. I'm telling you, the religious defense will frustrate you. You're trapped until society changes its mind on what constitutes religion, until the research on marijuana and LSD is reevaluated."

"But that might take fifty years!"

"We should look instead to areas of entrapment and your Fourth Amendment right to privacy, see just where Bremer's going to lie."

"Entrapment? You think there's a chance the warrant's illegal?"

"No," Lance answered honestly. "Not with two hand-to-hand prior sales. But we'll make a pretrial motion, take a stab at it. We'll start stirring things up. What I'm really worried about is the shooting. It's time we nailed Bremer before someone else gets killed." He paused. "After Kevin, there were two other deaths, all 'furtive gestures.'"

"I'm willing to explore whatever it takes to get that dude," Richard told him. "For Kevin. For the others." He gave Marcie another look, sending the same message as before. "But the religious defense has to be part of my trial. To deny my experience with LSD would be to deny myself."

"Alright," Lance nodded, resigned. "How do you want to go about setting up your religious defense? You'll have to have expert testimony."

"You could talk with Benjamin Miller in the botany department at Cal," Kathy told him.

"If you can get him to testify, bring him in," Lance told them.

"There's Ron Hughes in sociology," Kathy added. "Meyerson in comparative religion. It'll come together. But Mr. Bormann's right. The most important thing right now is staying out of jail."

"Please," Lance shook his head and looked directly at Kathy, "call me Lance." Then, standing, he told them, "Why don't you have a cup of coffee in the waiting room while I call Joe O'Brian, my investigator. Let me find out what his schedule is. And don't worry," he added encouragingly, "not everything's stacked against you."

"Thanks, Lance," Marcie said sincerely. "I'm more hopeful."

32

CHRISTIAN, LANCE, AND BERT PARKER
BERKELEY, CALIFORNIA
EARLY DECEMBER 1969

Lance and his partner, Bert Parker, left for Greece among a flurry of reporters, decrying the abuse of Americans in foreign jails and smiling for the cameras.

One week passed. Two. Then they returned—alone.

"There wasn't much we could do," Lance told a disbelieving Christian, who sat stunned in his office, listening to the verdict. "They'd already been found guilty and sentenced."

"But didn't you try to bribe anyone? Surely, there was someone who would have taken a payoff."

"We contacted one of the best attorneys recommended to us. We did our best to understand what our alternatives were."

You bungled it! Christian wanted to scream at him. *It could have been done—quietly, surreptitiously, without fanfare. Easy in, put down big bucks without all the words, and easy out.*

"Apparently, they made the front page of Greek newspapers," Lance was saying. "The attorney told me about the hundreds of letters Greek mothers had written to the courts praising their quick action. I'm sorry, but they're in. They made the choice to carry the load, and they got popped. There's nothing more I can do. I gave the attorney a retainer, and he's started the appeal process."

"But that may take months. Maybe years."

"Maybe. But it's all that can be done. Believe me."

"His lady needs him now. She's going to have a baby in a few weeks," Christian cried, making no attempt to hide his distress. "How are they, anyway? How are their heads?"

"Great," Lance answered, seeming to relax as the pressure shifted from his own actions. "Dharma said whenever he felt boxed in, he'd just send his spirit over the walls to touch the people he loved. They're meditating, doing yoga. We did haggle enough to get them vegetarian meals. We told the prison it was part of their religion. The only real hang-up seems to be Bob's concern for his lady—Julie, is that her name? He's sick with worry, terrified of losing her. If you can get her to write and let him know everything's okay, it would relieve a lot of pressure for him."

"How long until we know about the appeal?"

"If they agree to hear the case, about six months."

"Six months," Christian murmured. "It's not like being in jail here, you know. And here is bad enough."

"I know."

Christian stood up, tried to pull himself together. "What's happening with Richard's case?"

"We're going to go to work on it. A pretrial hearing date's already been set—December 20. If we do wind up going to trial, it'll be the last week of December. They're not wasting any time. They want him convicted quickly, but we can push the date back," Lance shrugged, "if he wants a few extra months of freedom."

Christian looked up at him sharply.

"Look," Lance told him, "I know you're upset about the Greek trip, but I didn't choose to smuggle or to manufacture LSD."

"You really don't get it, do you?" Christian spat at him, openly angry now. "You really don't understand that Richard did it for you—for all of us."

Lance swallowed, looking at the papers on his desk. "Take it easy, will you? I think we might have this one. I'm getting some interesting stuff from Joe O'Brian."

"When's your next meeting with Richard?"

"Tomorrow. We're going to start taking his story apart."

"I'll talk to you in a few days," Christian said coldly, knowing he had the task of breaking the news to Julie. "I'll have Julie give you a call. Can you take the time to explain the trip to her in detail?"

"Sure. Bob said a lot of things she might like to hear." He stood up and walked with Christian to the door. "My secretary has a bill for additional expenses."

"How much more than the twenty grand?"

"Our hours," Lance answered in a flat voice. "Figure eight hours a day for fourteen days."

"I'll want an itemized list of your expenses, plus the Greek retainer fees."

"I'm not sure I can do that. I didn't keep receipts. You should have told me you wanted an itemized list before we left."

In a voice that held the same British public school tone he'd used with the lieutenant in India, Christian said. "That should be fairly standard practice . . . for professionals. Give it your best shot, will you?"

Clearly annoyed by the insinuation, but feigning nonchalance, Lance added, "By the way, I met a woman just before I left. She was here with Richard Harrison and his wife. I believe she's a friend of yours. Kathleen. Is there anything between you? Or would you mind if I asked her out?"

"You'll find that Kathy has her own mind," Christian told him, furious again. Lance could not have picked better bait. "You'll have to ask her what she wants to do. Not me."

"Great. I think I will." And he smiled as if he were already tasting her.

Christian nodded angrily and left the office.

Once he was on the street, he forced himself to stop and regroup his thoughts. Lance and Kathy. Last night, he'd almost asked Richard to talk to her for him. But Kathy knew where he was if she wanted him.

And Greece! How much had Lance really tried to achieve? Christian had expected him to leave no stone unturned—to try avenue after avenue until the job was done. For this, he would have paid anything. But to support Lance's party . . .

Several days later, he learned from Richard that Lance had told Kathy stories of Greek wines, expensive restaurants, the beach along the Aegean Sea, sightseeing, and women.

It's my fault, Christian told himself over and over. *I knew something was off center. I gave him the job anyway. I should have gone to oversee the project. If I hadn't decided sleeping with Lisa was more important than joining the drive back, maybe we would have crossed the border at a different time. Or a different border. Maybe my presence would have made a difference . . .*

There were a thousand maybes.

And Kathy seeing Bormann.

Christian began to look for another attorney to represent Bob and Dharma. This time, he turned to long-established firms, walking into sedate, dark-paneled rooms where men reflected their surroundings without flash—instead, with a low-key presence that represented money and influence. His interrogations took him through four separate firms, carefully questioning men experienced in international law, paying large fees for an hour or two of consultation until finally he was assured that a certain part of a very old and very influential law firm in Paris had the quiet connections he sought with the Greek government. Money would do the job, but it would still take time—not seven years but some time to satisfy the Greek mothers who had read the story on the front page of their newspapers.

Then, quietly, telling only Richard, Albert, and his housemate Allen, and swearing them to secrecy lest Bormann hear, Christian left for Paris.

Lance and Bert sat around a small table at the Irish pub, drinking whiskey and reflecting on their partnership. They had been back from Greece for almost two weeks.

"Have you heard from Christian?" Bert asked.

"No." Lance shook his head. "I don't think I'm likely to, either. Not for a while. Richard says he's out of town. Something's up. I'm not sure what, but I have a suspicion it has to do with his buddies in prison. You think he'd be foolish enough to try and get those guys out himself? The last time I talked to him, he looked as if he was going to put together a commando team."

"That's not his style," Bert answered emphatically. "His leaving probably has something to do with his lab."

"You think he operates a lab? You think he's a chemist?"

Bert shrugged. "I'm not sure."

"By the way, what do you think of Kathy?"

"Nice. How's it goin'?"

"Not good. I thought I was getting it together with her when she called to meet me. Seems she only wanted firsthand info on the duo in Greece. She's involved in some way."

The waitress set down another round of drinks. Lance held up two more fingers to her.

"We're heading into a hangover tomorrow," Bert warned him. "You sure?"

"Yeah. You know, I don't think Christian's going to pay us the remainder of the bill for our expenses. He seems to think he's given us enough money."

"But if we'd been here, those hours would have been paid for by other clients," Bert argued.

Lance nodded. "You don't have to sell me." Reaching inside his pocket, he removed a safe deposit box key and the letter giving him power of attorney. "I think it's time to use this and put an end to the case."

"Is that Bob's key?"

"I've thought about it, and I think we should just take our fee from the cash in the box. Bob asked that we send the money to Julie and someone named Keith. Something about money due on a land payment. But we need compensation for our time. Fair is fair. If you play and lose, you have to pay."

"Alright," Bert said slowly. "Why don't you go to L.A. tomorrow. Need me to cover anything for you?"

"No."

The cocktail waitress put two more drinks on the table.

"I figure a thousand dollars a day for the two of us should cover it," Lance told Bert. "That's fourteen grand. Bob said there was twenty in the safe. I'll have a cashier's check made out for the remaining six thousand sent to that post office box on Maui."

"Here." Bert reached for his wallet. "Let me buy this round."

"Thanks. I'm going to the men's room. I'll be back." And he fingered the small glass vial filled with coke in his pocket.

33

RICHARD
HUMBOLDT COUNTY, CALIFORNIA
MID-DECEMBER 1969

A fire was blazing in the fireplace, filling the crowded room in Merlin's cabin with too much heat, but fire was essential. The flames would draw a drifting mind to color and warmth. Primitive, comforting, it would be the group's powerful focal point. From where he sat on the hearthstones, Richard looked at each face in the semicircle of a dozen people who had gathered to give him both love and courage as he faced trial.

To his right was Danny—sixteen when they'd first met, eighteen now, and always a man with an acute sense of responsibility.

Beside him, Mary Ann and Keith, older by a few years than the others, partners through four children and powerful social and spiritual changes. Thanks to a substantial loan from Richard, they managed one of the Bay's first organic food stores.

Next to Mary Ann, sat Debbie. Richard's heart tightened, because it had been Debbie's old man Kevin who had been killed by Bremer in a raid. Kevin had been an amazing artist. His work was now gaining traction, the prices for his canvases rising by the week. Debbie herself had started back to school in fashion design and had opened a shop selling her beautiful embroideries. Having Debbie in this circle also meant that Kevin was with them.

Seated beside her was Honey, who had finally had the courage to leave Alex and a relationship of emotional abuse. Now, she worked in Debbie's store.

Albert and Doug sat opposite the fireplace, chemists, men responsible for millions of doses of LSD.

Next to them, Christian, one of his closest brothers, whose ideology of wisdom and compassion matched Richard's own beliefs.

Beside Christian, Jerry: quiet, reserved, deep, who spoke of spirits and shamans and his travels in Africa, South America, and Mexico. Richard had never tripped with Jerry, but he hungered to know the man who had grown such beautiful mushrooms.

Merlin, who lived in this farmhouse, who was proud and strong in his accomplishments, gentle with his children, tender with his wife. Merlin wanted to enjoy a salad from his own garden and eat from a table he had made. In his lap, he held a small hound puppy—a gift from Neil Bolton, his neighbor. Rumor had it that Neil burned hippies out. But no more. Merlin was teaching Neil to grow weed. Together, they were going to bring some bucks to the economically depressed county. The pup was a contract between them.

Next to Merlin was his wife, Greta, who had blossomed into a beautiful woman, working hard to maintain family and farm, and who was happily pregnant with her third child. Her flower garden had become a local showcase, and she had begun classes in herbal lore and the distillation of herbal essences.

Finally, there was Marcie, his sensitive, beautiful, sad-eyed wife, who needed to trip to understand patience, to know that in time he would be given back to her. Marcie, who could not trip because she was carrying their second child.

Only Kathy was missing. She had pleaded schoolwork, but they all knew it was to avoid intimacy with Christian, especially here, where he had told her the story of his lama. Even Marcie, her oldest friend, had pleaded that she talk to Christian, find a way to meet with him in friendship. The entire family had gathered for this ceremony. Even the kids. Everyone but Kathy.

And Lance Bormann, who had also been invited, but who had once more made an excuse.

The room was quieting down. Incense smoke floated toward the draft of the fireplace. Candles were lit, the lamps turned low. The music was easy.

Christian reached into his pocket and pulled out a plastic bag full of tabs. "We made these up especially for this evening. They're 200 mics apiece."

And so saying, he poured about a dozen tablets into his hand. One he pinched between his fingers and ate. The others he passed into Jerry's hand.

Around the circle went the tabs, each person, except for Greta and Marcie, eating one. Then Merlin was moving, turning up the music while everyone sat back quietly, waiting to come on.

"Richard, come over here," Christian called. "You've got to listen to this one Doug and Albert have going."

It was near morning, and everyone was on the down side of the trip.

"Yeah," Doug told him excitedly, "you know how ticked off we are about your bust, right? Especially about this guy Bremer. We've figured out a way to get even."

"Okay," Richard grinned, "let's have it."

"Why not set something up? You've got this house, right? Call in a tip so the cops expect a big buy. When they bust in, give them ten seconds, then explode a small DMSO bomb with LSD. Soaks right through the skin."

Richard laughed but shook his head. "You can't do that. That would be casting your pearls before swine."

"I'm serious," Albert insisted. "It wouldn't be expensive at all. The rental on the apartment would be the largest expense. And we'd only

have to rent for one month." He pushed his glasses up onto the bridge
of his nose.

"Actually," Doug turned to Albert, suddenly in private conversation, "we wouldn't need a bomb at all. Just a time-release valve on a
metal cylinder."

"A tip-off by phone," Albert added, "open the front door, and
they're dosed."

"Wrong, guys," Christian interjected. "Bad karma."

Albert looked as if he were surprised Christian was there. "Jesus,
Christian, why not?"

"It's almost dawn," Merlin announced. "Let's walk up to greet the
sun."

The sky was beginning to lighten in the east as Merlin led the way
up the road toward one of the higher hills. The pace was quick, and it
was good to walk, to breathe the clear, fresh air, stretching, massaging
faces sore from smiling. To the west, the tips of high, snow-capped
mountains had already caught the color of day and were rose tinted.

At the summit of the hill, they stopped, breathing heavily, and
waited. Into that sacred space created by their presence, the silence
punctuated only by birdsong, Merlin's voice whispered, "It shouldn't
be long now."

They formed a circle, holding hands, and minutes later, the sun
crested over the mountaintops, their faces bathed in a warm golden
glow, their vision still filled with patterns, spirits holding to the sense
of peace.

"I need to say something," Richard said solemnly. "I will be leaving you soon. I think it's pretty clear I'm going to do time. Only the
amount is still in question." He lifted Marcie's face so that she looked
into his eyes, and he smiled. "We have to face it with courage. Without
shame or regret."

With an arm still around her, he touched every soul in this beloved
circle, sending a wave of emotion, gathering the energy, each mind
bound to his.

"When I leave, hold to each other in the brotherhood we have built. Keep the tribe strong. It is only in each other, in our shared ideas, in our understanding of the power of peace, that we'll find a measure of true humanity. We have a right to our lifestyle. A right to know ourselves and each other in new ways, to learn the possibilities of the human mind. In truth, the very future of humanity lies in our ideas."

They had come to him, those hard-faced men wearing gray or black, inquisitors, and had promised a deal for his cooperation, a lighter sentence, and all he had to do was give names and take away someone else's life.

"They'll try to chip away at us," he told them, his voice wavering. "Try to turn us from each other. Divide us with threats of long sentences if we don't give up a brother or a sister. In time, we may have to hide our colors. Cut our hair. Pretend we're like them to survive."

Merlin looked at him, pity and sorrow on his face; he knew what Richard had been asked to do. Knew what he was giving up by remaining true to the brotherhood.

"I'm not glad to go to prison, but I go in the love you have all given me tonight. And I go alone, so that the body of our tribe can continue."

They formed a line to the east, facing the sun, their arms around each other. In the vast stillness of the valley below, mists rose in slow curling wisps. Christian began to *om*. The sound was low, breathed deeply and rising from the bottom of his *manipura* chakra, the solar plexus, then a higher oscillation was joined to it from another in the circle, until each member had found his or her own vibration to became part of the harmony.

Once again, they were one person, wrapped in the timeless beauty that only love and caring brings.

34

Myles
Berkeley, California
Mid-December 1969

Myles sat in front of Bremer, waiting for him to put down the phone, and mentally rechecked his plan. It had been fairly simple to locate Christian. He smiled. On several occasions, he'd even worn a disguise.

"I know where Brooks lives," he said to Bremer when he had his attention. "You were right. He knows Jerry. He knows Richard Harrison. And if the rest of the rumors are true, he is your Mr. Big and connected directly to a lab. Whatever he is, he's heavily involved. I don't have any doubts he's connected to the Brotherhood. I'm reasonably sure he put up the money for Bormann and Parker to go to Greece."

A flash of anger crossed Bremer's eyes at the mention of Bormann, just as Myles had expected.

"He's also known to be associated with weed, mescaline, hash, and psilocybin sales."

"What about cocaine?" Bremer asked. "Amphetamines?"

Myles shrugged. "Doesn't fit the profile."

Bremer looked impatient. "Maybe it was different at one point," he told Myles, unwittingly defending himself, "but I've had hard evidence in the last months that members of this so-called Brotherhood are starting to sell a lot of coke. And you know why? Money. Big bucks. We're also getting our first statistics on the rise of coke-related deaths.

So much for the principles of the Brotherhood and their idea of a psychedelic religion."

"I suppose my next question," Myles said, "is whether you want the whole trip or just Brooks."

"What do you mean, 'the whole trip'?"

"You know. The lab and chemists. Along with the return of the base."

"Our deal was for Brooks *and* the base. Remember? You said you could deliver."

Myles held up a hand. "I'm asking if you want the lab as well. If you do it'll take a little more time, but I have a plan."

"Let's hear it."

"First, we need a good operator. I mean, really good. Someone new, who'll put in a large order through Jerry Putnam. I can arrange an introduction. The order has to be large enough so that Brooks either has to visit the lab for product or has to receive it from a courier. A courier who can be followed."

"Go on."

"Second, we need fresh faces on the streets for surveillance. Fresh cars. A nice Berkeley van or a VW bus. O'Brian will have you pegged in minutes if you don't."

"O'Brian?"

"Looks like Brooks has been working with both Bormann *and* O'Brian."

Tiny foamy bubbles appeared at the corner of Bremer's mouth. Myles could always measure the level of Bremer's internal anger by those bubbles.

"I have plans for Bormann," Bremer told him. "In the meanwhile, find out what O'Brian's up to. He's much too quiet these days."

"Alright. When can you get me that operator?"

"I have someone in mind. She's supposed to be very good."

"She?"

Bremer nodded. "I'm putting twenty-four-hour-a-day surveillance on Brooks's house."

"Be careful," Myles warned. "I mean, any moves must be discreet. If he suspects anything, you'll spook him, and he'll run. He's not your ordinary space case. He's clever, seems to sense when there's danger. He spotted me in Afghanistan and ran."

"We can bring some boys in from Los Angeles for this one," Dolph agreed. "Fresh faces."

"There's something else I want to be absolutely clear about," Myles went on. "I can deliver Brooks to you with a sales rap in a couple of days. Going with surveillance and trying to track down a lab means there's a risk of losing him. I'm asking you again, do you want Brooks? Or do you want to run the risk of spooking him, maybe losing him in order to find a possible—probable—lab?"

Dolph licked his lips unconsciously. Without hesitation, his voice came out short and excited. "Go for the lab."

35

L ance looked at his watch. It was late, just after eleven o'clock at
night.

He'd sat in his living room all evening, trying to read a prepared
brief, one of the few quiet evenings he'd had recently. But each time he
picked up the report, his mind wandered.

*What's Christian doing right now? If I'd really wanted to learn some-
thing about him and about myself, why didn't I go to the farm with him
this morning?*

Because you were afraid, the answer echoed back.

Lance knew he didn't want to come face-to-face with himself at
the moment, even if doing so meant discovering what was right about
his life.

What's disturbing me?

Had it been the matter of explaining things to Julie about Bob?
And about the money from the safe deposit box?

Julie had come to see him as soon as her new daughter could travel.
Lance closed his eyes, remembering Julie's childlike, trusting face, her
tanned skin and blonde hair, the tiny infant fumbling for a breast heavy
with milk. With true sincerity, she had thanked him for his help, taken
what was left of the money, and flown back to Hawaii.

Or perhaps it was Marcie that Lance wasn't prepared to face if he
were to trip that evening. Like a fool, he'd made a play for her, had even

visited her on a day when he knew Richard wouldn't be home, only
to learn she was pregnant, had never had an affair with anyone since
meeting Richard, and never intended to.

There were other mistakes—countless and embarrassing ones.

The silly power games with Christian—deliberately creating a rift
over Kathy, charging him for expensive restaurants and women on the
Greek trip, putting Richard off for a week after he'd already been paid a
huge retainer just to teach Christian a lesson about his attitude.

Perhaps he couldn't face thinking about his wife, Rachel. Even
now, she was with her mother and hadn't returned. What did she have
to think about anyway?

The thought that Rachel was on to him was the final blow to his
concentration. Lance closed the folder and turned off the light on the
table.

Eh? he thought. *Someone on the porch?*

Another noise. Then a heavy knocking on the door.

Oh, God, he thought, disgustedly. *One of my drug-crazed clients.
Thank God Rachel isn't here.*

"Okay," he called, looking again at his watch. 11:15. "Take it easy.
I'm coming."

Opening the door, a startled Lance faced the forbidding figure of
Agent Phillips brandishing a gun.

"We have a warrant to search the premises." Phillips flashed the
paper and his badge before rushing past Lance.

"Please step into the main part of the living room and sit in that
chair without moving," another agent told him.

Lance was pushed firmly into the living room while ten men with
guns veered out into different parts of his house—tearing through
drawers, closets, the refrigerator, small wooden boxes that might hold
stash, dumping the contents and spreading things across the floor and
tables for a better view. It happened so quickly and was so unexpected
that Lance was unable to speak.

Finally, white-lipped and dry-mouthed, he demanded, "By what
right did you secure that search warrant?"

God! I've got to get control of my shaking, he thought, surprised by the unaccustomed fear and adrenaline rush.

Watching the chaos around him, he knew at last what his clients had tried to describe—the shock of the first loud pounding, the broken doors, shouting, the aggressive force of the first rush, the destruction that followed. Even here, where they were playing by the book, Lance still felt the hard, brutal violence.

"How did you secure the search warrant?" he asked again, louder this time, looking directly at Phillips.

"On the affidavit of a confidential reliable informant."

Lance's breath grew tight, and he went through the house in his mind. The small stash of smoke he'd had upstairs for weeks: Had he locked it in the hidden safe? The coke was finished, but the crumpled paper: Could he have left it—with residue—in the wastebasket of his study? When did the cleaning people come? Which day? He examined every room, adrenaline clearing his mind of tiredness.

Lt. Hanson came from the kitchen. "Looks like the kitchen's clean," he said matter-of-factly.

"Keep looking," Phillips answered testily, tiny beads of perspiration forming on his forehead and temples.

Something was wrong, out of place, Lance decided. A few more minutes went by, agents coming and going into the room where he sat, when he realized what it was. Bremer was missing. Hanson was the senior officer and should have been in charge. Clearly, he was not. Wilson had control of this mission and acted as if he were on some personal vendetta. Grim. Determined. Driven. Hanson kept in the background, seemed embarrassed, gave Lance a look that said if you're not clean, then you're simply stupid. Bremer had sent faithful Wilson to do his dirty work.

Everyone had warned him, but he'd laughed. Bremer would never come at him. He'd never do anything so blatantly obvious!

Men were regrouping in the living room, talking in quieter tones, giving him sidelong glances, tense, cynical. In the face of each man, Lance could see the clients he'd once represented. Heard the dull, flat

tones of the narc voices as the agents answered questions on the witness stand. Saw them blink and stare straight ahead when they lied.
Listened to their hazy recall to pertinent questions.

For a single dizzying moment, he thought he would vomit. All this
time, he thought he'd been playing an intellectual game around the
law. At one point in your life, you were a defense attorney, at another,
maybe a prosecutor, someday, perhaps a judge. It was all the same game.

But Christian had told him over and over—and Joe had, too.
Decide, they'd insisted. With some other branch of law enforcement,
it might be different. But not with narcs. They were a different kind
of cop. You had to decide which side of the fence you were on; you
couldn't straddle.

He wondered again why Christian took the risk. What was it about
his experiences that kept him going? No wonder Christian had refused
to share his personal life with someone who was untried, who still
didn't understand the personal conviction involved.

Lance took a deep breath to try to settle his nausea. It wasn't the
intrusion that was causing his contracting stomach, but the realization
that once they had made so bold a play, they couldn't afford to lose.
The ante was too high. If they found a clean house, something would
be planted. *What would it be?* he wondered, listening to drawers still
falling against the floor. Acid? Coke? Heroin? Pot?

"Maybe you'd better check the study again," Wilson told Phillips.

"Yeah," he answered, leaving the room.

Within minutes, Phillips was back, a grin covering his face. "Good
guess, Ed. In the back of a drawer under a file, pretty well hidden. A
lid of grass."

"Alright, Bormann," Wilson shouted, visibly relieved. "You're
under arrest. I presume you know your rights. On your feet."

At once, a great joking conversation erupted in the room as men
congratulated each other on a job well done.

Lance, speechless, perhaps for the first time in his life, felt Phillips pull him out of the chair and push him face first against the wall,
spreading his arms and legs. Wilson stepped forward, patting his hands

intimately over Lance's body, then cuffed him roughly, tight enough to stop his circulation. Another arm pulled him toward the door, and through the melee of laughter and jokes about whether he knew a good lawyer and his own relief that they hadn't found his real stash in the hidden safe, Lance could hear Wilson talking excitedly on the phone to some anonymous listener.

"We got him!" he was yelling. "Boy, we got him!"

36

MYLES AND BREMER
BERKELEY, CALIFORNIA
MID-DECEMBER 1969

By noon on the day after Lance Bormann's arrest, Myles was summoned back to the Berkeley drug enforcement office.

Myles watched as Bremer paced the floor while he talked, his hands uncontrollable, tense. Myles felt a twinge of fear. Bremer's emotions were building into a frenzy, out of control, like the emotions of a crowd at a hard-fought championship game. His passion disturbed Myles. Without control, anything could happen. A nervous move might blow the case, and with it, his own chance for freedom.

". . . out within four hours, if you can believe that," Bremer's voice reached him. "He didn't even have a chance to piss in that cell! Just calls the judge. At home! And arranges to be released on his own recognizance. Didn't put up a dime for bail!"

"You knew Bormann had connections. Why does that surprise you?" Myles asked. "You should have told me this was part of your plan. It was a mistake. Bormann will never do jail time for a lid. Even with a conviction, he'll see six months of probation at most."

"He didn't even fucking suffer!"

"I'm not even sure you can get Bormann disbarred," Myles continued. "Not for a lid. If you really wanted to get rid of Bormann, you should have bided your time. Set him up at some landing field with a plane coming in. He might not have been put off the Harrison case, but eventually he would have been put away for good."

"Well, there's one saving grace in all of this," Bremer told Myles as he paced. "At least the jury's confidence in him will be shaken because of his arrest. He won't be as effective. I'll make sure the information is leaked." Massaging the back of his neck, he took a deep breath and tried to steady himself. "By the way, have you picked up anything on O'Brian?"

Myles nodded. "Looks like you're safe there. I found out why he's been so quiet lately. He's been out of town. Oregon. And up at some Indian reservation in Northern California."

Bremer stopped pacing and turned to look right through Myles. As if he'd been punched hard, his shoulders slumped and his arms hung lifelessly at his side. He was, Myles recognized, stunned.

"Is it something to do with this case?" he asked.

Bremer didn't respond, stared blankly at the opposite wall.

"Should I know about it?" Myles tried again.

Bremer shuffled slowly to his chair and sat down. "No. I was just reminded of something."

Myles sighed and rubbed his eyes. "When do I get to meet that operator?" he asked, uneasily.

"Three," Bremer answered in the same monotone voice. "Three o'clock this afternoon."

"I'll be here."

Myles stood up to go. Bremer didn't seem to see or hear him. What was wrong?

"Three o'clock," Myles said again, and without getting a response, turned and left the office.

Bremer remained motionless at his desk for a long time.

So, he thought. *Bormann's upped the ante.*

He'd never before known the fear of being stalked, the hunter breathing close on his neck. He knew what information O'Brian sought. Something he had learned at the Indian reservation. And he knew it was to be used against him in the Harrison trial.

I'll kill you with my ideas, O'Brian had said.

The thought magnified itself in Bremer's mind. He could still see O'Brian's intense face, the deep-set hazel eyes, alive, sure.

I'll kill you with my ideas, the words echoed again.

Bremer began to see and feel things his agitation had hidden.

Christian Alden/Brooks and Richard Harrison had put up the money for O'Brian's investigation. Bormann had given O'Brian the specifics of the job. This was no ordinary trial. This confrontation was the apex of his career, a battle to either win or lose everything.

Slowly, he began to regroup, breathing deep, slow breaths. A strange catharsis settled over him. There could be no more mistakes. Each obstacle would be overcome logically, systematically. O'Brian had to be dealt with. Brooks's lab must be found and brought into the court as evidence. Lance must be discredited. Harrison convicted.

Standing, he took his jacket from the wall hanger and put it on.

The first obstacle had to be met immediately.

Opening the door, he left to find a man he used to know but had not seen in many years.

37

A midmorning patch of sunlight picked up the exquisite red in the carpet of Lance's office. Joe sat in the chair in front of Lance's desk, waiting for Lance to finish reading the report he'd just handed him.

Lance concentrated on the papers, his brow tightly knit, his mouth set in a straight, grim line.

Last night's bust had personally revealed to him the enormous power of the narcotics bureau. Clearly, they operated on perjured testimony and befuddled judges with evidence for search warrants that was untrue and unjust—all ostensibly in the name of the law and the fight against drugs. Whether he wanted to admit it or not, Dolph Bremer had done him a favor by putting him on the receiving end of one of those warrants.

"I think we've got him," Lance said, looking at the sworn statements before him. "Without this we'd have wood, kindling, and paper but no matches. Good job, Joe. It takes a special kind of talent to get people to sign these statements."

"It wasn't easy. But this is just the surface."

"What more do we need—wife beatings, drinking problems, racism, illegal use of his weapon . . . Shooting out the windows of his own home in broad daylight!"

O'Brian shook his head. "You knew all that. You heard it months ago without the affidavits. No, the real story is the shooting of the Indian kid. You remember. Bremer picked up two drunk kids several years back, then released them. Later in the day, one was found shot in the back, and the other kid disappeared. That's the one extra piece that fell into place on this visit. The disappeared kid showed up recently."

"Was he a witness to the shooting?"

"Saw Bremer shoot his buddy in the back."

Lance gasped. "Why didn't the boy say something at the time?"

"An Indian? Accuse a police officer?" Joe asked with mock disbelief. "There's this vigilante group . . . "

"But in the back?"

"Bremer ordered him to stop. The kid kept running. The weird part is that Bremer never copped to it. If he had brought the body in, he probably could have gotten away with it. Cited some necessity. Furtive gesture. Something. But he panicked. Seems he was off duty. That's when he went on that huge binge and shot out the windows of his house."

"So where's the evidence?" Lance asked, looking again through the papers. "Did the other boy sign an affidavit?"

"Black Elk finally helped him to see reason, but only after I'd left. I just got the call. The affidavit should be here this evening by special delivery. I'll pick it up at the post office after four."

Then Joe smiled, and Lance knew what was coming next. He couldn't blame Joe. How many times had he been warned?

"By the way," Joe asked innocently, "what's going on with your bust?"

"Bremer hoped to make me less effective at the Harrison trial," Lance answered honestly, his ego no longer involved. He'd been wrong about a lot of things lately. "I have no doubt he'll 'leak' news of my arrest to the press and any potential jury members. But before he does that, *I'm* going to make the announcement of my arrest. And I'm going to make it clear to the court, to the press, and to anyone reading a newspaper why I was arrested."

"You're going to accuse Bremer of setting you up?"

Lance nodded. "To get me off the Harrison case. I'll make it seem that our guilt or innocence is locked together."

"Doesn't Harrison want a religious defense?"'

"Yeah. He'll get it. But he's going to get the rest of it, too. I'm not losing this case."

"You want to meet later? After I pick up that mail?"

"Not tonight. I need to get some sleep. I was up pacing in a cell all night. How about first thing in the morning? Nine o'clock? The pretrial hearing starts the day after tomorrow."

Lance woke early the next morning, put on his running shoes, and began the slow pull up the steep street toward the running paths in Tilden Park. Without his morning jog, he wasn't sure he could handle the mounting pressure of his job. Running through the thin mist, he looked up at the eucalyptus trees.

Perhaps Rachel's right, he thought. *Perhaps it's time to move to some quieter place. Maybe even quit playing around and start a family.*

Lance had a queasy feeling that Rachel knew more about his extra-curricular activities than she was letting on. For the first time in their years of marriage, he was beginning to understand her great strength of character and loyalty. She'd been visiting her parents when the narcs came to his door. Now she was staying there until the Harrison trial was over. Still thinking things over.

After the trial, we'll take a long vacation and decide about the future, he assured himself, taking the trail smoothly.

At nine o'clock, Lance walked into his office, expecting to meet Joe, and found, instead, an ashen-faced secretary.

"Lance," Elaine said quietly. "Jennifer called this morning. Early. It's Joe . . . he's dead."

"Dead?" Lance asked stupidly. "Dead?" he asked again, looking to his secretary for confirmation.

"She says they killed him," her voice was deep, despondent, repeating words she could not believe.

Lance, blinking away quick tears, was torn between grief and rage. He knew Jennifer was right. Bremer had removed Joe. It was incomprehensible, but true. Somehow, he'd learned about the new evidence.

Unsteadily, he picked up the phone to call Jennifer. His legs felt as though they might crumple under him. He placed an arm on the desk, leaned against it for support. For a fleeting second, he thought he should give it all up. Everything had gone too far; the stakes were too high. Had he known they would go this far, he would never have bet Joe's life. It was stupid not to have considered this as a possibility! It was his fault. He gave the orders. He should have known.

"Jen, Jen, I don't know what to say. I just don't know what to say."

"About four o'clock yesterday afternoon," she began weakly. "Joe was just leaving for the post office. He got a phone call. That's all I know. Said he had to meet a man and that he'd be home about eight. We could have a late meal."

"And?"

"He never showed. Eight o'clock came and went. I didn't think much about it. He often stayed out if he was onto something. Working. Then at about eleven o'clock, I received a phone call." Her voice trembled and broke into a guttural sob. "The coroner's office. I knew. I knew right away. But I hoped it wasn't him. I just stood there hoping."

"Jen, I am so sorry," he said quietly, searching for words.

"They asked me to come down and identify the body. I went and stared at him for a long time. There was this piece of glass between us, like they didn't want me to get too close. Just look. I stared, waiting for him to wake up. There was only this small cut on his nose. I wanted to touch him!" Jennifer cried. "God, Lance, I would have given anything just to feel him again, but I could only stare at him through that piece of glass! Then they asked me to leave. I told them I wanted just a few more minutes with him. The man insisted. 'There's never enough time,' he said."

"How?" he whispered.

"His car crashed. They said he drove it off a cliff in San Francisco. They measured the alcohol content in his bloodstream. He was legally drunk. There were witnesses. He just didn't make the curve . . . "

"The papers Joe picked up at the post office. Did you get them?"

"They brought me the contents of his pockets. A small lock of his hair. Everything that was loose inside the car." Her voice hardened. "There was no briefcase. No papers."

"Jennifer," Lance cried aghast, feeling the sickness spread from his stomach. "I need you to go back to the Indian Reservation."

"You need that affidavit, don't you?"

"Yes. If you'll go, I'll brief you."

"I'll do anything."

"Just give me a half hour. I'll be right over."

"Lance!" Bert called across the waiting room of their office later that afternoon. "Where've you been? I need to talk to you. Elaine, hold all calls."

"I've been with Jennifer. Come on in," Lance answered, opening the door to his office. "God, you can't imagine the kind of day I'm having. With the details of O'Brian's death, Jennifer, the Harrison pretrial tomorrow . . . "

"I need to talk to you about something," Bert interrupted. "I guess I'd just better say it."

"Okay, shoot," Lance said, reading quickly through the messages on his desk.

"I'm going to take a vacation."

Lance froze, astounded that he would even think of such a subject at a time like this. "Do you have to talk to me about this now?"

Bert didn't move, didn't speak.

"When?" Lance asked impatiently.

"Today."

"Today? Are you crazy?" Lance shouted. "You know what's going on around here!"

"I do know. And I know it's gotten out of hand."

"What are you saying?"

"I'm saying I don't want to wind up in jail, especially on some phony charge. I don't want to be disbarred. And I don't want to end up mysteriously dead."

"Now just a fucking minute." Lance walked around the desk. "We took every case together. We made joint decisions based on a joint ideology. You knew the risks of playing with fire."

"I don't really think I did," Bert answered with a cold, overly controlled calm. "I don't think I knew the burns would be so deep. I want a future. I don't see it in this partnership."

"What about our responsibility to the clients we already have? We've taken money from most of them."

"I have a feeling that when the news of your arrest gets out, we won't have as many clients as we thought we did. They'll find other attorneys who'll give them a chance. With any luck, you can hope the news of your arrest gets out later rather than sooner."

"Wrong, Bert." Lance walked closer to confront him at eye level. "I've called a press conference for this afternoon. By this evening, my arrest will be front-page news. Not only my arrest, but the precise reason I was arrested."

Admiration touched Bert's eyes, prompting Lance to try a different tack.

"Look, don't freak. Hang in there with me. I need you. I can beat this one. Just a little courage, a little patience."

But Bert stepped back.

"We blew it, Lance. We went for too many headlines. We became too visible. We set ourselves up for all those idiots who love to shoot people down. When I heard about O'Brian, it was like getting slapped in the face. It suddenly occurred to me that some people play for keeps. I want a future, a career. I want to stay alive."

"Can you at least see me through the Harrison case? I need some backup."

Bert shook his head. "You know it's the Harrison case that's become the contest. I'm sorry. I can't."

Very late that night, for the first time in over a year, Lance called his father. Michael Bormann was an attorney with a long history of work with sensitive cases. But those cases had not extended to drug arrests.

Lance was scared. Really scared. He practiced what he would say, hoping not to give himself away.

"I watched the evening news," his father said. "Are you a madman?"

"I hoped you would have thought I had courage."

"Lance . . . " His father had a hard time finding the words. His reply was forced between tight, frustrated breaths. "If you're not a madman, then you're certainly a fool."

Lance heard the click of the receiver.

38

LANCE AND AGENT FRANK HANSON
PRETRIAL HEARING, BERKELEY, CALIFORNIA
MID-DECEMBER 1969

The next morning the first round of the contest began. The courtroom was unexpectedly filled with a large contingent of reporters and with freaks wearing all their colors—flowered shirts, beads, feathers, bells, some carrying flowers.

Lance knew his best chance of beating the Harrison case was going to be today, in the pretrial hearing. If he could get the search warrant thrown out, all the evidence collected at the factory would be inadmissible. In his confidence that Richard had a manufacturing site or a lab at the house on Stanford Street, Bremer had made a fatal error. He had secured the search warrant based on a lie. Richard had never entered that garage on the morning of his arrest. But expecting to recover the base at the factory, Bremer had sworn that he had seen the base leave the garage and had followed it. Bremer had secured the subsequent search warrant based on Richard entering the garage. True, Richard would eventually face charges on the hand-to-hand sales, but perhaps there was a way to discredit the informant as well. One step at a time. Right now, Lance had to get rid of the copious amounts of evidence taken from the Stanford Street address with its tabbing machine and everything that went with it.

Suddenly, he was aware that everyone was waiting, looking toward him—Judge Crowley, Richard, Marcie, Kathy, the spectators, the reporters at the back, Bremer, and McKinley, the district attorney.

Lance stood. "Good morning, Your Honor. I'd like to call as my first witness Lieutenant Frank Hanson, Berkeley Police Department."

"Lt. Hanson, do you swear to tell the truth, the whole truth, and nothing but the truth, so help you God?"

"I do."

"Lt. Hanson," Lance began, "why did you go to 2203 Stanford Street on October 17, 1969?"

"We secured a search warrant for those premises based on the affidavit of one of our undercover agents. We had the reasonable expectation of finding a drug manufacturing site at that location."

"Tell me, Lt. Hanson, how often have you used that agent before?"

"Many times."

"And how often has his information been reliable?"

"He's running well above ninety percent."

"In Mr. Harrison's case, what information did he give you?"

"Our agent was in possession of twenty thousand tablets of LSD bought from Mr. Harrison."

"In the search warrant for the premises, Supervisor Bremer claims to have seen Mr. Harrison enter a garage in Oakland on the morning of October 17th and remove a pound of ergotamine tartrate. The search warrant is issued on this observation. To your knowledge, is it correct that Mr. Harrison did enter the garage?"

"Yes."

"Whose idea was it to sell Mr. Harrison a pound of ergotamine, Lt. Hanson?"

"Ours. We felt the base would lead us to an illegal lab."

"And did it?"

"No. Instead, we found a tablet-producing machine and contraband."

"How did you arrive at the Stanford Street address?"

"Three officers watched Mr. Harrison pick up the ergotamine from a garage we'd rented and followed him to the house on Stanford."

"How did the officers know he was driving base? Did it have a sign on it?"

"I was not there, but I know we packaged it in a shopping bag. Supervisor Dolph Bremer, and two of our agents watched as Mr. Harrison backed up to the garage, got out of the vehicle, and walked into the garage. Then Mr. Harrison returned to the car. The ergotamine was gone when they checked. It is reasonable to assume that he took it."

"Reasonable?" Lance stepped toward him, an eyebrow raised. "When you say shopping bag, are you speaking of a plain brown bag like those you see in any grocery store?"

"Yes."

"And where did you say this bag was placed?"

"In a garage located on Edgewood Drive in Oakland."

"Did your team ever lose sight of that bag?"

"Well, yes. While it was in the garage."

"Did you ever lose sight of the building where it was stored?"

"Yes," Hanson admitted reluctantly. "We didn't have an officer on surveillance until 6:00 a.m. on the morning of October 17th."

Lance's tone suggested this type of police work was inconceivable. "Are you trying to tell me that you have a pound of ergotamine tartrate capable of being made into . . . ," and he referred to the paper on his desk, ". . . millions of doses of LSD—at least that is the charge—and you didn't keep surveillance on it? How could this happen, Lt. Hanson?"

"He . . . Mr. Harrison . . . was supposed to have picked up the base in the morning. We had no reason to believe he would be there any sooner. It was already midnight when our agent left the garage."

"So between the time you left the bag, around midnight on October 16th, and when you had surveillance in place, at 6:00 a.m. on October 17th, anybody could have entered that garage and picked up this supposed bag. Is that true?"

"Yeah. But you'd have to know it was there. There were no signs of burglary."

"Do you know if anybody else had the key to those premises other than Mr. Harrison?"

"No, sir, I don't."

"Could there have been?"

"Yes."

Lance paused, walked to the defense table, and casually looked at his notes. "Lt. Hanson, did you find the base at the address on Stanford Street?"

"No, sir."

"Did you find it anywhere?"

A pause. "No."

"You didn't find it in Mr. Harrison's home or on his person?"

Another pause. "No."

"Well then, isn't it likely that Richard Harrison didn't pick up this supposed base at the garage on the morning of the 17th?"

"Again, I wasn't there that morning, but I believe it very likely that he did."

"Likely?" Lance changed tack. "Lt. Hanson, can you tell the court how long you have known the supervisor of the Northern California Bureau of Narcotics, Dolph Bremer?"

"About four years."

"And during that time, you have worked closely with Supervisor Bremer?"

"Yes."

"How many times would you say Supervisor Bremer has used his gun in making an arrest?"

"Every time. We all use guns."

"Let me rephrase that, Lt. Hanson. How many times would you say Supervisor Bremer has fired his gun?"

Lt. Hanson looked wary. "I don't recall. In four years, Supervisor Bremer has been responsible for scores of arrests. He's used his gun— and fired it—when the situation warranted it."

Lance glanced at Bremer, who was sitting at the prosecution table. He was alert, listening. Lance could see his pinched eyebrows. "Lt. Hanson, on the day of Richard Harrison's arrest, you were in the kitchen with Mr. Bremer when he fired his gun, were you not?"

"Yes."

"Would you tell the court what happened in the kitchen when the gun discharged?"

"It was . . . very confusing. I simply don't recall very much until Mr. Harrison was in handcuffs."

"You don't recall?" Lance repeated. "Lt. Hanson, have you ever known Mr. Bremer to drink alcohol before a raid?"

Hanson quickly glanced at Bremer, and McKinley was immediately on his feet. "Irrelevant, Your Honor."

"Overruled. I'd like to hear where this line of questioning is going."

"Please answer the question, Lt. Hanson. Has Mr. Bremer ever had alcoholic drinks before a raid?"

"Occasionally." Lt. Hanson looked toward the floor.

"How occasionally?"

"I haven't kept a tally."

"Lt. Hanson, is there a departmental policy on the use of alcohol when an officer is on duty?"

"Yes, sir."

"And what is that policy?"

"You don't do it."

"You don't do what, lieutenant?"

"You don't drink on duty or before going on duty."

"And why is that?"

Hanson shrugged his shoulders, annoyed. "Because alcohol clouds your judgment."

"Have you ever reported Mr. Bremer's drinking habits while on duty to any of his superiors?"

"No, sir."

"Why is that?"

"Because each person handles the stress of the job differently."

Lance looked Lt. Hanson squarely in the eye. "Do *you* believe that alcohol and firearms mix when you are working in a professional capacity?"

Hanson looked toward McKinley for help. "No, sir."

"Why not?"

"Objection, Your Honor." McKinley jumped to his feet. "The methods of our officers are not on trial here. Mr. Bormann has no right to steer this trial away from the accused by trying to place guilt on the very officers who enforce the law."

"Overruled. I believe the law is exactly what we are about here, Mr. McKinley. And how it is used. Given the testimony so far, Counsel is allowed to explore the breadth of the officer's state of intoxication or lack thereof."

"Would you say, Lt. Hanson, that guns and alcohol don't mix?"

His mouth in a tight, straight line, Hanson answered, "No, they don't mix."

"But Mr. Bremer drinks before a raid, along with other members of his team?"

"Yes, sir."

"Do you drink before a raid, Lt. Hanson?"

A sigh. "No."

"Would you say that Mr. Bremer was drunk on October 17th when he entered the home on Stanford Street?"

"I've never seen Supervisor Bremer drunk."

"Lt. Hanson, when you walked into the kitchen and saw that Mr. Bremer was prepared to fire his weapon at Richard Harrison, what did you do?"

"I don't recall. There was a lot of confusion."

"Did he scream 'run' to Mr. Harrison?"

"I don't recall."

"Are you aware, Lt. Hanson, that on April 23, 1966, Mr. Bremer left work early, went home, and drank to such an extent that he used his regulation firearm to blow out every window of his house?"

"Objection, Your Honor!" McKinley screamed into the startled courtroom. "Mr. Bremer is not on trial here!"

"Well, I'm not sure about that yet, Counsel," Judge Crowley declared. "Proceed, Mr. Bormann. I must tell you that I'm interested in your line of questioning."

"The police were forced to intervene. His neighbors were evacuated. Thankfully, Mr. Bremer was peacefully relieved of his gun by his captain. A slap on the wrist, a hushed cover-up, and Mr. Bremer found himself supervisor of the Northern California Bureau of Narcotic Enforcement. And out of Eureka."

Bormann reached down to the table and held up papers. "Confirming these facts, I have the sworn affidavit of Mr. Bremer's former partner, who resigned his position in disgust. He now works for the Medford Police Department in Oregon. I also have the sworn testimony of several of Mr. Bremer's former neighbors, who claim that when Mr. Bremer drinks, he viciously beats his wife."

The noise in the courtroom rose sharply. Judge Crowley banged a gavel to bring order back to the court. "We are beginning to wander here, Mr. Bormann," the judge told him. "We are interested in Mr. Bremer's state of mind when he entered the house on Stanford Street."

Hanson had tried to keep his face and tone neutral, but those affidavits startled him. Things were beginning to click. He recognized for the first time that Bremer was an alcoholic, surprised he'd never put it together before, remembered the quiet anger when Bremer drank, his insistence on meeting in a bar before a raid.

He looked over at Richard. The kid was watching him keenly. He knew what Harrison hoped for. The truth. Once again he saw the image of that other kid, Kevin, choking on his own blood. He'd pushed Dolph's arm in that kitchen because he didn't want to see it happen again. Not if he didn't have to.

"Your Honor, the facts speak for themselves," Bormann continued through the courtroom noise. "You have before you Supervisor Dolph Bremer. A man who represents the law. An alcoholic who becomes vicious under its influence. A man who drinks before an arrest. A man who has shot and killed more than one unarmed man because of a 'furtive gesture.' Three, in fact." Bormann held up another sheet of paper with the details.

"This same man maliciously beat my client, pushed him toward the door, and fired at him. If it had not been for Lt. Hanson," Bormann pointed toward where he sat in the witness chair, "Mr. Harrison would be dead at this moment! I'd like to ask you again, Lt. Hanson, what did you do when Supervisor Bremer raised his gun to shoot?"

The courtroom murmurs stopped. An expectant hush covered the room.

Hanson saw that Lance waited. He sifted through and discarded possible answers, weighing what each would mean, his eyes wandering from side to side, focused on the floor. He was finally getting it. Bremer had taken the job he thought would be his. Supervisor Bremer had come to the Bay with a covered-up record. He was dangerous to the department because his practices put both men and cases at risk.

A light suddenly flared in his eyes. A new understanding slowly came to him. He looked up and into Bremer's face. Bremer had lied about the evidence to get the search warrant. Had to have lied. He couldn't have seen Harrison pick up the base. If he had, it would be sitting in the courtroom as evidence. But that fact would be overlooked. Explained away. They had the sales rap on Harrison. But . . . how many other cases had Bremer lied about?

With a great deal of reluctance, he pushed his insights aside. Bremer was his boss. A fellow police officer. There was only one choice at the moment.

"I . . . I simply don't recall," he finally answered, his voice barely audible. "There was a lot of confusion."

"I see. Thank you, Lt. Hanson. I have no further questions."

Again, the courtroom murmurs rose, and the judge used his gavel. "Mr. McKinley," he called, "would you care to question the witness?"

"Yes, Your Honor." McKinley stood immediately, talking fast. "Lt. Hanson, in the four years you have worked with Supervisor Bremer, how often was he late for work?"

"Never." Hanson's voice was sullen.

"Did you ever see him drunk in his office?"

"No."

"Was there ever a time when he put in hours overtime?"

"Daily."

"Do you feel Mr. Bremer has the respect of his coworkers?"

"Almost reverence among the younger men."

"I ask the court to consider the work of a dedicated man, a man responsible for enforcing the law in dozens of cases. This hardly appears to be the picture Mr. Bormann would wish for us to accept—an irresponsible alcoholic. It is Mr. Bremer's job to use a gun, his job to walk into frightening and overwhelming circumstances demanding split-second decisions. The public trust must be with him to make the judgment to use his weapon when the situation calls for it. I request, Your Honor, that we return to the issue at hand, not Supervisor Bremer."

"Mr. Bormann." The judge glanced at him. "Do you have any further questions of the witness?"

"No, Your Honor. I believe the affidavits speak for themselves." Lance was now sitting quietly at the defense table, scanning his notes. He only looked up briefly.

"Very well. Thank you, Lt. Hanson. You may step down."

Lance stood, watching as Hanson sulked past him. "Your Honor, I'd like to call to the stand Agent Ted Phillips."

"Agent Phillips," Lance asked after he had been sworn in, "where were you on the morning of October 17th?"

Lance listened as Phillips told how he had watched Richard enter the garage, return to the car, and drive off. How Phillips had followed him to the house on Stanford Street where the machine was located. How he had notified waiting officers to rendezvous at the address.

"And you showed the search warrant at the door?" Lance asked.

"Yes."

"What was the basis of the warrant, Mr. Phillips?"

"That Mr. Harrison had in his possession the ergotamine from the garage."

"Mr. Phillips, you have testified to watching Richard Harrison arrive at the garage on Edgewood, leave, drive to the Stanford Street address, and make no stops. If all this is true, where is the base?"

"I don't know."

Lance tilted his head in a quizzical manner. "You don't know. You followed Mr. Harrison directly to the house on Stanford Street. And yet you lost a kilo of base?"

"It simply disappeared," Phillips answered tightly.

"Yet you filled out a search warrant based on the integrity of watching Mr. Harrison enter the garage. You have just now sworn under oath that you saw Mr. Harrison pick up that base."

Lance changed tactics. "What happened when you entered the kitchen at the Stanford Street address? Where did you find Mr. Harrison?"

"Trying to flee from the back door."

"Did you beat Mr. Harrison?" Lance turned to stare directly at Hanson.

"Objection," from McKinley.

"Did you in any way lay hands on Mr. Harrison?"

"We were forced to wrestle him to the ground."

"Is kicking a man while he is lying on the ground considered wrestling?"

"Objection!"

"Your Honor, pictures of bruises on Mr. Harrison's body taken by his doctor after he posted bail—two weeks after the incident." He handed the bailiff a folder of photos. "Did he receive these bruises from being wrestled to the ground, Agent Phillips?"

There was no answer.

Lance turned to face the bench. "I submit, Your Honor, that this is the type of law enforcement the Bureau of Narcotics Enforcement under Dolph Bremer is executing. By a series of lies and terrorism, officers representing the law randomly harass political activists or those who practice their religion. In fact, anyone who might think differently from Mr. Bremer and his thugs. It is time to make visible these secret police tactics that we so loudly denounce in foreign countries.

"Judge, my client was approached by the police themselves to purchase ergotamine. They made that purchase contingent on my client selling LSD to an agent, a substance Mr. Harrison considers sacramental.

"It is obvious that Agent Phillips lied to secure the search warrant in his fervor to please his supervisor, because of the 'reverence' that Lt. Hanson spoke of earlier. These lies, I might add, happen with regularity, including the planted evidence in my own arrest. The truth is that Mr. Harrison never entered that garage on the morning of October 17th. Nor did he carry out a bag. If he had, it would have been found at the Stanford Street house or in his vehicle.

"In fact, I have to seriously question whether there was any base at all. Look who they've paraded up here to tell us that there was. Lt. Hanson, who would like us to believe that he can't remember anything. Mr. Phillips here, who lied to get the search warrant for his superior. Supervisor Bremer, an alcoholic who drinks on duty, gets excited, and shoots unarmed men in the back!"

"Objection, Your Honor," McKinley cried with real outrage. "We are not here to try or defend any of the arresting officers. Nor are we here to discuss Mr. Bormann's problems with the law!"

"Yes, we are," Lance retorted quickly. "My arrest is directly connected with Mr. Harrison's. Like my client, I was set up for political reasons—to keep me out of this trial! So that their Gestapo tactics could not be exposed!"

Judge Crowley banged his gavel and called firmly for quiet in the courtroom. "Mr. Bormann, have you any further questions for the witness?"

Lance took a long, outraged breath. "No, Your Honor."

"Mr. McKinley, have you any questions?"

"Yes, Your Honor. Agent Phillips, how long have you been on the narcotics force?"

"Almost four years."

"So you have been there since Supervisor Bremer took control of the office."

"Yes."

"How many times have you performed surveillance during that time?"

"Dozens."

"In your professional opinion, is it always easy to see what enters a car and what is taken out of it?"

"It is often impossible."

"Your Honor, we heard Agent Phillips report that the base was placed in the garage, that Mr. Harrison knew of and entered that garage. Even if Mr. Harrison did pick the bag up at some other time during the evening, I think it is quite reasonable for Agent Phillips to assume that the base was in the car. The search warrant was issued in good faith and without malice."

"Judge, I don't believe anything Agent Bremer does is in good faith," Lance retorted. "Consider his practices of lies and intimidation. In fact, I have to question whether there was any ergotamine at all."

Now was the moment.

"I submit, Your Honor, that the warrant in question, the warrant allowing entry onto the premises located at 2203 Stanford Street is based on a premeditated lie. In the interest of justice, I ask that the evidence used to secure the search warrant be deemed inadmissible."

Judge Crowley paused for a moment and regarded the gavel in his hand. The noisy courtroom suddenly became quiet.

"Mr. Bormann," Judge Crowley said thoughtfully, "I believe you are correct in your objections to the search warrant. This issue of the missing base is confounding. Also, lies, if they can be called such, to secure a warrant, are disturbing. You also claim that such practices by this law enforcement agency are routine. This, too, if true, is deplorable.

"But I believe that Agent Phillips acted in good faith when he

signed the affidavit to secure the warrant. He had more than enough
reason to assume that Mr. Harrison was heavily involved in drug trafficking. The twenty thousand tablets purchased by the undercover
agent is indisputable. The evidence from the house on Stanford Street
also proves as much.

"Your request to suppress the warrant is denied. Mr. Harrison will
be bound over for trial."

39

RICHARD
BERKELEY, CALIFORNIA
LATE DECEMBER 1969

When the day of the actual jury trial arrived, Richard was unprepared for the crowded courtroom. Marcie and John were in
the front row behind him, with Kathy and Danny. Behind them,
in the second row, Dr. Miller sat talking with Jerry Putnam. Greta
and Merlin had just arrived and had found seats alongside Keith and
Mary Ann. Many of the people in the courtroom Richard had never
seen before—outrageous-looking friends of friends dressed in colorful clothing, and their friends in turn, who had come for support and
idle curiosity. Toward the back of the room, a half dozen reporters
from various newspapers and television stations jotted notes or drew
pictures.

Lance walked up and put a hand on his shoulder. "We're just about
to begin. You ready?"

Richard nodded.

"Hear ye, hear ye. The Superior Court of the State of California is
now in session, Judge Whiton Burgess presiding."

"Good morning, Mr. Sorenson, Mr. Bormann, ladies and gentlemen of the jury."

Judge Burgess looked around the courtroom. His eyes scanned the
members of the jury, turned to the spectators, and finally lingered on
the reporters.

"Mr. Sorenson, are you prepared with your opening statement?"

"I am, Your Honor. The prosecution will show that the accused, Richard Harrison, did willfully and with complete knowledge of his actions, conspire to, and did manufacture LSD, or lysergic acid diethylamide, in violation of the law. Furthermore, he possessed certain controlled substances, including psilocybin mushrooms, mescaline sulfate, and marijuana. And furthermore, the evidence will show that he did sell twenty thousand doses of LSD to a government informant on October 30th and another twenty thousand doses on November 10th of this year."

"Mr. Bormann?"

"The defense will show, Your Honor, that Mr. Harrison's civil and religious rights as guaranteed by the Constitution, were violated, and that Mr. Harrison's arrest is part of a system of fraud and deliberate perjury on the part of certain individuals representing the government of the State of California."

Judge Burgess paused, then, "Mr. Sorenson, you may proceed."

"Your Honor, I'd like to call to the stand Dolph Bremer, field supervisor for the Northern California Bureau of Narcotic Enforcement."

"Mr. Bremer, can you tell us what happened on the morning of November 17, 1969?"

"I can," Bremer nodded. "Based on information given to us by our undercover agent, we followed Mr. Harrison from a marked garage near the Oakland Airport to a house north of the Berkeley campus. We were reasonably sure that we would find a manufacturing site. Carrying a search warrant, we knocked loudly, called the defendant's name, identified ourselves, and entered the house. Once inside, we found a number of items we believed were controlled substances."

"Did the defendant answer the door?"

"No. We had to enter forcibly."

"What was the reaction of the defendant?"

"He tried to escape through the back door. I was forced to fire a warning shot to stop him."

Richard listened through the morning as evidence was produced— the tablets bought by Frank, the marked money found in his briefcase, the laboratory reports analyzing the grams of acid crystal, marijuana, hashish, mescaline, and mushrooms. The tabbing machine.

When it had all been labeled as exhibits and sat in a pile, it was overwhelming. Suddenly, he knew. He lived in a dream world of what he wished reality to be. On the other side of the line were people who didn't understand, would never understand, because they'd never had the psychedelic experience, were fearful of it, believed the propaganda against it.

He saw in the faces of the jurors both quiet resignation and amazement at the scope of the evidence. From time to time, one or another would regard him, and he was glad he'd refused to cut his hair, because it made no difference. He looked down at the table, his head falling toward his chest. How had he ever expected to beat this?

The first three days passed quickly, and all too soon, on the morning of the third day, Richard heard the prosecution rest its case. Now it was time for Lance to begin his defense. Richard looked on without much expectation, knowing time was running out.

Lance stood to speak. "Your Honor, ladies and gentlemen of the jury . . . " His tone was sure, confident. Richard wondered whether he was really feeling that way. Under the circumstances, he could think of nothing Lance might say that the jury would understand.

"I submit that the motives of my client in this case are spiritual, that his use of psychedelics is his desire to attain a oneness with God. I submit that he has the right—indeed, the moral responsibility—to follow his conscience in the use of these substances. I submit that his arrest has violated his First Amendment rights in the exercise of his religious freedom.

"Now I understand that the use of hallucinogens is a complex problem—so complex that the attitudes of our own legislative and judicial branches of government are inconsistent and confused.

"For instance, in February of 1967, the President's Commission on Law Enforcement published findings that marijuana should not be classified as an opiate-like narcotic. Indeed, the Commission recommended an inquiry into the wisdom of the marijuana laws themselves. Yet, in May of that same year—three months later—the United States Senate ratified an international convention outlawing the possession of marijuana." Lance paused for a moment and walked toward the jury.

"It is estimated that millions of Americans have tried smoking marijuana. Other statistics have shown that three-fourths of all servicemen in Vietnam smoke marijuana, some even under combat conditions.

"That means that as a society, we are faced with enforcing a law against mass violations. What happens when so many members of a society disregard a law? We are faced with two possibilities. Either the law is not enforced, or it is enforced . . . selectively." Lance pronounced the last word clearly, eyeing the prosecution table.

"One might ask—indeed, one ought to ask—why does this confusion arise?

"It is a source of continued amazement to me each time I step into a courtroom to defend one of my young clients, that the United States government has no end to the number of 'experts' it can bring forward to expound the antidrug position.

"It is equally amazing to me that, under questioning, the only expertise these 'experts' have is their title and position with the government. Why," Lance's voice was filled with sarcasm, "that would be like asking—say—someone like Mr. Bremer here for his opinion on hallucinogens. After all, isn't he the field supervisor of the Bureau of Narcotic Enforcement, and therefore, one would assume, he must be knowledgeable about the drugs for which he makes countless arrests.

"But Mr. Bremer knows nothing about hallucinogens," Lance frowned. "Yet Mr. Bremer is exactly the kind of person the government uses to relay information to the American public. A man who holds a title and an opinion. An opinion without substance.

"So you can see how frustrated I become each time I find I am forced to defend my clients on charges of abuse which have never been established by men of science. Where were the medical doctors, the psychologists, the sociologists, the ministers, rabbis, and priests when these laws were placed on the books? Where was the calm, objective examination of facts by experts? Not opinions. Not hearsay. Not anecdotes. Not that silly movie *Reefer Madness*. Facts.

"Of course, everyone is entitled to his own opinion. We have heard the phrase countless times that this is a free country.

"But opinions have no place in a court of law. Especially when our youth, the very spirit of our future, are sent to jail, often for long terms, for trying to achieve oneness with God, a right guaranteed by the Constitution."

Richard watched Lance take a deep breath and walk the length of the courtroom before continuing.

"Drug use touches the Bill of Rights at numerous points," Lance told the still courtroom. "At the First Amendment, as an issue for the free exercise of religion. At the Fifth, in the nature of unreasonable classification. At the First, Fourth, and Ninth, in regard to the right to privacy. At the Fourteenth, as a matter of the denial of equal protection of the law. The use of peyote is legal for the American Indian, but psychedelics are prohibited for other groups. At the Eight Amendment, as a question of cruel and unusual punishment."

He paused and slowly looked over the jury, allowing them time to consider. Then he turned to the spectators and nodded to Dr. Miller.

"At this time, I would like to call Dr. Benjamin Miller of the University of California, Berkeley, Botany Department. Dr. Miller will give us some perspective on the history of man's use of psychoactive plants.

"Dr. Miller, will you please take the stand?"

"Judge Burgess, I object," interrupted Mr. Sorenson. "I'd like an offer of proof as to the appropriate value of this testimony."

"Yes, Mr. Bormann," the judge agreed, "I'm interested in the appropriate value of the testimony also. Could I see counsel in chambers, please."

"Judge, I'd really like the jury to hear this," Lance argued.

"In chambers. Now, Mr. Bormann."

It seemed only a matter of moments to Richard, a dream-like nightmare of Lance's raised voice coming from the closed door of the judge's chambers and then the judge's voice, and then Lance was back beside him, his face pinched in anger, his eyes cloudy.

"The son of a bitch won't allow the testimony," Lance muttered under his breath. He shook his head at Dr. Miller, who had taken a seat in the front row next to Kathy while waiting for the decision.

"The court thanks you for your time, Dr. Miller," Judge Burgess confirmed.

"Your Honor, I would like to call as my next witness, the Reverend Doctor James Booker."

"Judge," Sorenson cried with obvious frustration, "again, I'd like an offer of proof out of presence of jury!"

This time, the wait while the three men were in chambers was longer. This time, Richard heard not Lance's raised voice but Sorenson's.

When the judge took the bench, he announced to Lance, "Counsel, you can proceed. Let's hear your religious defense."

"Reverend Booker, can you tell the court where you have your ministry?" asked Lance.

"I am a chaplain at the Graduate Theological Seminary in Berkeley."

"And can you tell the courtroom in what aspect of religious thought you are an expert?"

"Mysticism."

"Mysticism," Lance repeated. "Can you define the word *mysticism* for us?"

"To put it simply, mysticism is a study of man's most intimate experience, the moment of his union with God."

"And you consider this experience a reality?"

"A very well-documented reality."

"Do you believe it possible, Reverend Booker, for one to achieve the mystical state through chemical means?"

"Yes. William James, the great American philosopher, is a good example. After experimenting with nitrous oxide, he wrote that, for the first time, he understood that waking consciousness is but one type of consciousness. Surrounding waking consciousness are other levels, other potentials, separated only by what he called the filmiest of screens. Many people describe the psychedelic experience as a lifting of this screen or a veil, as if they see for the first time what has never been seen before.

"This new awareness within James was perception at an intuitive rather than a rational level, gained by direct experience. Afterward, he was able to write with complete comfort and knowledge of both the unsolicited mystical experience and the systematized methods developed to achieve oneness."

"And this is important? Oneness with God?"

"Absolutely. It is usually so real and so profound that a person's life attitudes are altered. St. Theresa wrote that once a person is returned from God, it is wholly impossible to deny that you have been in God and that God was in you, even after many years have elapsed."

"Reverend Booker, can you describe the mystical experience? What are its aspects?"

"The literature is voluminous, but there are four aspects of the mystical union that we can consider universal, regardless of how the experience is induced . . . "

Richard sat spellbound, listening to his beliefs in the words of the minister. As Dr. Booker explained to the courtroom the process of achieving mystical union, he sensed a change of time and space, knew the sacred. Boundaries slipped away. His sense of self expanded. Richard closed his eyes and felt his lips start to tingle, his mind climbing the ladder to wholeness, and he subtly marveled—he could relive the psychedelic experience anytime he wanted, just by playing it back. His very thoughts, his brain waves, could produce the chemical that started him on his way.

"The fourth aspect of the mystical experience," he heard the reverend say, "is the awareness of a great energy pervading all existence. Many believe this to be the substance of God. Religions, in their various forms, are an expression of man's desire to understand this mystery.

"The intimate moment of unity with this single energy, this place beyond duality, beyond death, this place of singular oneness, is the captivating moment of the mystical experience. It is a place of total knowledge and peace. A place that exists as clearly as this courtroom . . . "

"Judge," Sorenson interrupted impatiently, jumping to his feet, "give us a break. How much more of this is the court and the jury going to be forced to listen to?"

"Mr. Bormann, don't you think you've made your point? We are beginning to drift a little, are we not?"

"Judge, just a few more minutes. I'd like to tie all of this up."

"Then do it, counsel."

"In your opinion, Reverend Booker, can you tell us if you believe there is a difference between the sacramental use of peyote and the sacramental use of LSD?"

"Many people who use psychedelics do so for religious purposes."

"And is there documentation to support the mystical experience through the use of LSD?"

"Quite a bit."

"Reverend Booker, in your opinion, as a question of religious experience, does it matter whether a religion has been practiced for thousands of years or whether a religion has been in existence for ten years?"

"All religions were once only ten years old. All of them were young, searching for ways of consolidating their theology, adjusting themselves to human beings with human needs and to existing political and economic systems. A church is people. It forms from the pressure of their needs."

"Thank you, Reverend Booker. Your Honor, I believe I have no further questions at this time," Lance announced.

"That's good, Mr. Bormann. Mr. Sorenson, your witness."

"Reverend Booker, do you need LSD to have this religious mystical experience?"

"No."

"No further questions."

MARCIE AND KATHY
BERKELEY, CALIFORNIA
LATE DECEMBER 1969

Late that day after trial, an exhausted Marcie followed Richard and Kathy to her front door, carrying John in her arms. Once inside, Richard simply stopped and stood in the middle of the front room, spaced and silent.

"If you'll excuse me," Marcie said testily, moving around him, taking a sleeping John upstairs to his crib.

Laying John on the bed and covering him, she quietly closed his door, then went into her own room next door. The force of her own door slamming shut created a sound louder than she had intended, but at the moment, she didn't care what anyone else thought. She was tired of pretending, tired of acting as if everything would work out, because after today, she knew it would not.

Drained, she could do nothing but sit on the bed and stare, her blue eyes large and troubled. A soft knock echoed from the door.

"You look like you're not going to make it," Kathy said softly, closing the door and sitting down next to her. "What's happening in your head?"

"It's not going to work," Marcie answered, her voice dangerously husky. "No matter how good Lance Bormann's supposed to be, he's not going to get Richard off."

"What are you saying?"

"I want to split. Go underground. Do something."

"Did you talk to Richard about this?"

"Of course I talked to him," she cried, casting Kathy an angry glance. "He says Lance told him he'd serve eighteen months to five years max. That he can do the time. If we run, we'll never have a future."

"There's the issue of his father's house."

Marcie's shoulders finally slumped, all the fight gone, the anger holding fear and sadness at bay, dissolved. "You're right" she whispered miserably. "We could never let him lose his home."

"Then it sounds like Richard's decided."

"But what about me?" Marcie's voice finally broke, her face crumpled, and she began to sob, her words forced from a dark, hidden place. "Everyone's so concerned about Richard. But I'm the one who's going to have to give birth alone. I'm the one who's going to have to find the means to take care of two small children. What do I say to John? How will this baby know his father?"

"You'll never give birth alone. I won't leave you. Not for a minute."

"You can't imagine what's its like to have the Gestapo raid your home. Over a sacrament. The heavy pounding at the door, the intrusion into every corner of your life, looking at personal papers . . . my writing . . . and . . . and the underwear in your dresser, even the soiled tissue in the waste bin. Their gleeful destruction, deliberately breaking whatever they can. The displaced power. Their demand that I stand in the middle of the room, shaking so hard and holding to John and trying to protect him from that evil . . ."

"Marcie . . ."

"And you . . . you're one of the people going on with your life while Richard goes to prison. You're not dropping out. You're back in school in a week. You've turned your back on your people . . ."

"Please listen . . . "

"They're taking Richard. And you . . . you couldn't even make Richard's ceremony!"

Kathy's face was white. Gently, she took Marcie's hand. "I couldn't," she whispered softly. "You see . . . I'm pregnant. I couldn't let Christian know why I wouldn't trip."

All the air seemed to leave the room. Marcie gasped.

"I need you," Kathy pleaded.

Marcie threw herself into Kathy's arms, holding to her, a dam bursting, finally crying in long, hard, gasping breaths. "I'm so sorry . . . so sorry. It's just . . . I love him so much. What will I do alone with two small babies?"

How could she explain the hole that was building inside, the place where her soul should be? How could she explain this fear of time, the sense that she was moving toward disaster and there was no way to stop it?

"You'll show your children what real strength is," Kathy answered firmly. "You'll teach them to be independent, to think for themselves. We'll give to our children all the beliefs of this new age. And instead of moving up to Merlin's, stay. Get involved here. Go on with the women's poetry collective you've started. I'll pass you weed, and Christian will pass you acid. Sell enough to old friends to support yourself and the children."

"You're still going to stay in business?"

"Not like before. But yes. It's going to take money to get through school. I'm on my own and don't have many choices." She sighed and looked at Marcie with sad eyes. "Things are . . . changing. The sacramental aspects have become secondary to greed. The innocence of our intentions is gone. I'll just have to be careful."

"I must have been blind." Marcie wiped her eyes. "How many weeks along are you?"

"My doctor says this is probably a Woodstock baby. So . . . I'm about four and a half months. I might have been pregnant even before Woodstock. My breasts were already tender."

"And you haven't told Christian?"

She sighed, holding tightly to Marcie's hand. "Being pregnant isn't the only thing I haven't told him. You see, I slept with Larry on my first afternoon in Arizona. It's . . . all so complicated. I immediately knew it was a mistake. Christian had made a commitment to me. But now I know that Larry was on his way out. I feel like God gave us this moment of love in a holy place as a way to say good-bye." She looked up at Marcie, and their eyes met.

"Oh, Kathy, I'm so sorry," Marcie whispered. "All I've been able to think about is myself. I should have been there for you. Understood. The rape in India . . . "

Kathy shook her head. "I'd wondered even before I arrived in India if something might be different about my body. I'd been nauseous in the mornings. I'd skipped a period. But I thought with all the stress surrounding what happened in Tucson . . . well, it wasn't stress. After all those nights with all those men in the last years, I'd begun to wonder if I'd be able to have children."

"So when I asked you to come up to Merlin's . . . "

"I couldn't. How could I expect Christian to understand all that's happened? I'm still trying to understand it myself. I slammed him for sleeping with Kali. Walked out on him. What's he going to say when I tell him about Larry?"

"Kathy, this is Christian we're talking about here."

"I'm just getting back on my feet emotionally. I can't go through it. And I don't think he can either. After what he's been through, he shouldn't have to."

"How will you manage school?"

"Day by day. I don't have any illusions about how hard it'll be. But I've discovered something recently. It takes tremendous courage to live. But then, we're given blessings along the way to make it bearable. Like this baby."

Marcie wiped the last of the tears from her face and pulled at a wad of tissue. "Christian has a right to know," she insisted.

"Not now." Kathy's voice took on a pleading quality. "I'm not ready. I can't give up everything I'm finally putting in place to be Christian's old lady."

"If you love him, do you have to?"

Suddenly, the doorknob turned, and Richard was standing there, his eyes darting nervously between them.

"You heard?" Kathy asked.

"Everything," he nodded. "From the beginning. Things I needed to hear."

"If you breathe a word of what you heard about me to Christian, you're a dead man. Understand?"

"Yes, ma'am," he mumbled sheepishly.

41

LANCE
BERKELEY, CALIFORNIA
LATE DECEMBER 1969

Once he was back in his office after court, Lance closed his eyes and took a deep breath. Where had he left his running shoes? Were they in his car? Or at home? He had to run. This evening, he would run until he felt his heart strain and then keep running, searching for the moment when everything but his breath and his heart had any meaning, waiting for it all to slip away—Joe, his bust, Bert, all those women, Marcie's face at lunch, Kathy's teasing smile, Richard's faith.

For all his trying, Joe slipped back into his thoughts. Joe . . . Joe was gone.

Lance's mind tumbled, and he laid his head in his arms. There had not even been time to grieve. The police report he'd asked for and received was sitting in front of him. How could he learn what had really happened? Where was Joe with all his magic to investigate his own case? Where was the briefcase with the evidence against Bremer?

Raising his head, he pushed the button on his desk. "Elaine, have you heard from Jennifer O'Brian?"

"No, sir."

Lance paused. "Nothing? Not a phone call?"

"No, sir. Nothing."

BREMER

BERKELEY, CALIFORNIA

LATE DECEMBER 1969

Bremer waited in his office for Myles early on the morning of what would be the second day of defense testimony. Anxious, he knew the defense would have to rest soon. What more could Bormann say? That meant there was not much time left for Myles to produce the evidence on Christian Brooks and the lab. Bremer wanted that base back as a sign of his credibility, and he wanted to shovel shit all over Bormann, especially after what Bormann had alleged about him in the pretrial hearing.

When Myles came into his office, Bremer was ready for him.

"How was court yesterday?" Myles asked.

"It's a goddamned zoo. There's an audience, reporters. Bormann put this minister on the stand as a so-called expert. You can't imagine how boring it was. What did you think of Susan, the operative you met yesterday?"

Myles hesitated, so Bremer answered for him. "She's consistent," he said. "I can trust her to do exactly what she says she'll do."

"I hope so. All of a sudden, we both have a lot riding on her. Make sure she only contacts Jerry. Make sure she doesn't meet Brooks."

"Why?"

"Brooks would see right through her." Myles shrugged. "And it sounds better if she's paranoid and doesn't want to meet anyone. Cops want to meet people."

"Have you arranged the introduction to Putnam?"

Myles nodded. "Yes, it's done."

"When are they going to meet?"

"Sometime this morning. She's going to ask for ten grams, forty thousand hits. With Harrison no longer tabbing, Brooks may have to contact his lab—if he has one. How's the surveillance going?"

"We've had Pacific Bell telephone workers on a pole outside his house for two days."

"Are you tapping his phone?"

"Not with Bormann on the trial."

"Who's following him around town?"

"A VW van with two officers in it."

"Make that one," Myles said automatically. "Cops work with partners. Put another vehicle on the street, one that will pick up where the van turns off."

Bremer didn't like Corbet's unguarded tone, the orders he was giving. But he held his peace.

"Can you get a woman to drive the van?" Myles asked.

"Not a bad idea."

"I'm meeting with Susan after lunch, after she talks to Jerry. By that time, she'll know when the drop can be made."

"Good," Bremer nodded. "Be here after court. At four."

"All rise. The Superior Court of the State of California is now in session. Judge Whiton Burgess presiding."

"Good morning, ladies and gentlemen. Mr. Bormann, continue."

"Yes, sir," Lance answered. "I'd like to call Dr. Ronald Hughes, professor of sociology at the University of California, Berkeley."

"Could you be so good as to tell the court the reason for Dr. Hughes's testimony, Mr. Bormann?"

"Certainly, Judge. Dr. Hughes currently receives a grant from the United States Government to study drug abuse. His testimony will clarify many points I intend to raise in this trial."

"Your Honor," McKinley argued, playing the frustrated prosecutor, "once again, we are not here to question the laws of the State of California or those of the federal government. I see no proof that this would be valid testimony."

"At this point, I quite agree with you. Mr. Bormann, we have already heard the expert testimony for your religious defense. I don't think we need a repeat of yesterday."

"But Judge, Dr. Hughes's testimony touches the aspects of drug abuse that this court should know. Particularly in relation to alcohol. You and I both know that Mr. Bremer's alcoholism is at issue here."

"That's quite enough, Mr. Bormann. You've already discussed these matters in pretrial hearings."

"Judge, Supervisor Bremer lied to get that warrant. We shouldn't even be here. I think the jury needs to know that Mr. Bremer fired at my client after drinking in a bar before the arrest."

"Objection!" McKinley screamed into the shocked courtroom, the noise level steadily rising. "Mr. Bremer is not on trial today!"

"Any man who shoots out the windows of his own house when he drinks should be on trial," Lance continued, his voice rising, knowing he was infuriating the judge. But he had the jury's attention. "Especially if he's trying to put people in jail for drug abuse."

Judge Burgess's face was bright red. "Mr. McKinley's objection is sustained! Another word," he roared, "and I'll hold you in contempt of court, Mr. Bormann. Both counsels will see me in my chambers. Immediately! Court is recessed for ten minutes."

"Mr. Bormann," Judge Burgess spluttered behind the closed door, "I've never seen anything in a courtroom like I've seen today! You already made a pretrial motion to suppress the warrant and it was denied. Supervisor Bremer is not on trial. Nor are any of the other officers. Neither is the law on trial."

"But Judge, they should be. We are seeking justice here."

"I will see you off this case if you don't stick to the facts at hand!"

Without another word, Judge Burgess strode back to the bench, his robes flying behind. He banged his gavel heavily. "Mr. Bormann, your request for Dr. Hughes's testimony is denied. Dr. Hughes, we thank you for your time." Again, he angrily used his gavel. "Court will recess and resume after lunch."

Lance sat down at the defense table and let out a long, controlled breath.

"Things look pretty bad, don't they?" Richard said as the entire court moved toward the large double doors and the hallway.

Lance looked squarely at Richard. "You understand that your religious defense is dead?"

"But . . ."

"What you believe is unimportant. I told you. No judge is going to legalize psychedelic use—not if he wants to get reelected—especially since he personally abhors the thought of religion through drugs."

"Sacraments."

"Richard, do we understand one another? Look at what's happening, the stakes that are involved. They busted me a few days before this trial began, hoping I'd give up this case. Joe's dead because we hired him to help us. Don't you see that if you fall, I fall?"

Lance looked toward the doors Bremer had just left through. "And something's up. I feel it. I don't know what it is, but Bremer's much too calm. Listen, I want a chance, too," Lance told him emphatically. "Will you give me a goddamned chance?"

"What chance do we have?"

"The information about the Indian boy. If we can get that in the court record . . . "

"Will the judge allow the testimony?"

"No. But if the jury hears it, it might make the difference. Apparently, lying, brutality, and alcoholism aren't enough. We need Joe's evidence. Will the jury close its eyes to murder?"

Richard looked hard at him. "It's all or nothing, isn't it? For both of us."

"It was always all or nothing," Lance answered quietly. Then, so that only Richard could hear, he lowered his voice, "Unless, of course, you wanted to cooperate and tell them where the base went . . . and about Christian. Then you'd have a bargaining chip."

He watched Richard's uneasiness, his quick glance at the floor, averting his eyes.

"I'm not asking you to do it," Lance assured him. "I'm just making it clear that it's the same chance you've always had."

Lance watched Richard consider, saw both hope and fear cross his face, knew he thought about his wife and children, his dread of going to prison, the loneliness of the long days and nights ahead, the temptation to have it all go away.

"Lance," Richard finally answered, his voice equally quiet. "I can't

step over that line. I can't secure my freedom by taking someone else's."
He stood. "Marcie's waiting. I'll be back after lunch."

Toward the back of the courtroom, Lance saw Elaine wave to him.
"Let me see what's going on," he muttered.

He pushed his way through the small crowd that still stood near
the courtroom doors, offering a hello, promising a few words later to a
reporter, then took Elaine to one side. "Did you hear from Jennifer?"

"She says she's still waiting."

"Waiting for what? She's been gone for days."

"The boy's disappeared again. They're looking for him."

Christian had a favorite phone booth he liked to use that was set back from the noise of the road. He didn't expect Doug or Albert to be home at two o'clock in the afternoon. But schedules were erratic. Perhaps he could reach them.

The phone rang again and again. On the tenth ring, Christian was tempted to phone the lab. But the sacred agreement was that the lab phone was to be used only as a warning system. That rule was never to be broken. As much as Christian wanted to reach Albert, as much as they needed the money from the sale, it would have to wait. Suddenly, unexpectedly, a voice answered.

"Hello?"

"Doug? You're home."

"Yeah."

"How's it going? You okay?"

"Just groggy. I was asleep. I had a small accident yesterday. Got my hands dirty. I've been up all night."

"Where's Albert?"

"Albert?"

"Is he in the house?" Christian asked calmly.

"No."

"Is he working?"

"In a manner of speaking. We were saving it as a surprise for you."

"Surprise?"

"Well, you know those plans we made while we were at the farm?" he asked, sudden glee in his voice.

"Plans?" Christian tried to remember. They'd talked about so many things. "What plans?"

"You know. With the gas cylinder. Albert went down there yesterday and put it together. We thought our friend prosecuting Richard should understand a little more about his subject matter. I was going to go down and help him set up, but I got too fucked up."

Oh, my God! Christian's mind exploded. *They're actually going to try and dose Bremer!*

"Doug, I thought we'd talked about this. You can't do it, not to someone like that. To trip, your intention has to be righteous. He'll wind up in the hospital, freaking. They'll put him under heavy sedation. His mind will still be active while he has no control of his body. For him, it *will* be a psychotic experience. When he comes down, he'll be even angrier and more determined. It's bad karma, Doug. Everyone has the right to choose."

"Yeah, I know . . . but . . . "

"But what?" Christian asked, fighting to keep his voice calm.

"We thought . . . well, who knows, maybe he'll enjoy it. After all, how much more vengeful can he be?"

"Doug? How'd you go flying?"

"One of the canisters I was tightening let out an unexpected burst of spray. All I had to do was breathe. We were pretty pleased. The system works."

"So, where's Albert now? Like, exactly where?"

"He should be back here at any time."

"I want the address of the house in Berkeley."

"Hold on. Let me see if I can find it."

Christian waited, shoving quarters into the phone. He didn't dare hang up.

"Here it is," Doug said at last. "We rented an apartment for one month."

"What's the number?"

"1612 Henry Street. It's a duplex. We have the downstairs. When Albert finished, he was going to leave a tip by phone."

"Doug, I need ten tickets for that concert. Do you have them?"

"I think so."

"I need those ten as soon as possible. When Albert gets back, tell him I'm sorry, but he's got to turn around and bring them up here this afternoon."

"What are you going to do about our plan?" Doug asked.

"I'm going to think about it."

"Christian, if you go over to the apartment . . . "

"Yeah?"

"Don't open the front door."

45

BREMER
BERKELEY, CALIFORNIA
LATE DECEMBER 1969

B remer was quiet on the way back to the police station. The men
with him kept their distance. Even with O'Brian out of the way,
Lance had dropped those tidbits about his drinking like small bombs.

*A man can't even take a drink without it becoming public news!
Tomorrow, my personal details will be in every newspaper, and I'll have to
make a public apology. Humiliating, but not crippling.*

*At least Joe O'Brian will never cause problems again. That smug, arro-
gant bastard who promised to destroy me.*

He smiled faintly, thinking how the department had cheered at the
news of Joe's death.

When he entered his office, he found Myles waiting.

"What's happening with Brooks?" he asked, taking a seat behind
the desk.

"We're on hold, waiting for a courier," Myles told him. "Brooks is
sticking close to home. Something has to happen soon. We've given
them a deadline."

"When's that?"

"This evening. We told them we had to catch a plane. If they
couldn't make the sale by seven, we'd cop from someone else."

"Start thinking. I need some leverage on Brooks. I want him to
testify against Harrison. I want him as my star witness tomorrow
morning."

"You're not going to get him to talk," Myles warned.

"Find a way," Bremer snapped back.

"*You* find a way. There are methods. They had them in India."

"Don't get smart with me."

"I'm not," Myles countered coldly. "You can find a way to make him hurt without leaving marks. There are drugs. I figure you have at least two days until you have to get him up on that stand."

"What happened in India?" Bremer avoided Myles's eyes.

"He wouldn't talk after three days without food and with a head wound. They held him in chains. He knew he'd be heavily interrogated. I don't know how he would have held up. The opportunity to learn never presented itself. I'm just saying if he wouldn't talk under those conditions, he's not going to crack under your kind of interrogation."

Bremer was still, his face hardening. "Alright." His voice was harsh, the word delivered in a cold monotone, his eyes flat, hooded, the decision made. He reached to pull open the desk drawer and lifted the polishing rag with the pearl-handled Colt .45 wrapped inside.

"Alright, what?" Myles asked, his eyes on the gun.

"We don't need his testimony. Harrison's gone. But I'll tell you what I do want. I want Bormann busted again before he comes to his own trial. I want him approached by one of our agents on laundering money and, from there, a developing friendship that will offer him half a million bucks in a smuggle. Let's see Bormann turn that down. I want him there at that landing strip."

Myles watched Bremer polishing his gun until it became a caress, a look of security softening his face. For the moment, Myles wasn't going to remind Bremer that this was his last case. "What about Brooks?"

"We'll give that fucker twenty years. We'll try him on his own mistakes. It doesn't have to be with Harrison. Ladies' man, eh? He'll be a man's lady in the joint."

"The timing has to be perfect this evening." Myles brought him back to the assignment at hand.

"Let's hear it."

"When the courier comes in, I want him identified. I want to know that he's here. Shortly afterward, we should get a phone call from Susan with a time when the delivery will be made. The exchange is on at Jerry's house. Brooks will make the delivery and is expected to leave before Linda gets there. It's Jerry who's making the final sale. We'll take them when Brooks walks through the door."

Myles could not take his eyes off Bremer, looking first at his face, then his hands, as the cloth slid across the chrome slide of the pistol. Bremer never glanced up. Except for occasionally wetting his lips with his tongue, his absorption was complete. Even when the heavy metal gleamed, the cloth still moved soothingly back and forth.

"Uh . . . Dolph," Myles began, hesitantly.

At the use of his first name, Bremer lifted his eyes to Myles, as though surprised he was still there.

"This evening with Jerry," Myles spoke softly, "when you make the arrest . . . make sure he doesn't get hurt."

For a long moment, the two men understood each other—a rarity for two men who seldom let anyone touch them. Bremer searched for something to say, was visibly relieved when the telephone rang. He reached for it, listened. "Courier's in. Just pulled into Brooks's driveway in a rented car from the airport."

"We could take him now."

"No," Bremer shook his head. "I want to follow that fucker. I want that lab. I want the base. And I want Putnam."

"Alright then," Myles answered slowly.

"Are you going to be in on the raiding party?"

"If this is going to be my last effort, I need to oversee the job."

"Not quite your last effort. You're testifying tomorrow in the Harrison trial. Here's your subpoena." Bremer withdrew a piece of paper from his inside pocket and threw it toward Myles.

"Why do you need me?"

"Just to sew it up. If the jury is indecisive about the validity of the search warrant, we need your testimony that he sold you forty thousand tabs."

"But the judge told them to ignore the remarks."

"I don't want to risk a hung jury. I'm not taking any chances. Get some lunch and be here in half an hour for tonight's briefing."

Myles picked up the summons and started toward the door, then stopped. "By the way," he turned back to Bremer. "A tip came awhile ago. The desk asked me to take a look at it. Seems pretty straight-forward. House on Henry Street in Berkeley. Someone's uptight and wants to bust the occupants. I cruised by there. It's an open space, the lower flat. Pretty easy in and out. It might be fun—just like old times. A parting memory. You want to go for it?"

Bremer thought a moment or two as he carefully rewrapped the Colt in its polishing cloth. "Let's do it. Bormann's asked for a recess until tomorrow. He's stalling, but it works for me. Being occupied might take the edge off things around here."

46

CHRISTIAN
BERKELEY, CALIFORNIA
LATE DECEMBER 1969

The bright afternoon glare bounced off the Bay and reflected into Christian's living room like an ignited mirror. Occasionally, a dark cloud of birds would disturb the purity of light, but to Christian, who stood at the large window, watching, the contrast was a lesson in perfect harmony. In his hand, he held a small pink tablet. He lifted it, letting the clear afternoon light fall across his palm. When he swallowed, a tingling touched his lips. A slight queasy giddiness filled his stomach.

Linda came into the room with her beadwork and made a place for herself near Allen to complete the peyote stitch she was making along the length of a cigarette-lighter cover.

"What possessed you to do such a thing?" Christian asked Albert. "Setting up a spray bomb in an apartment? What a waste of good acid."

"We just thought if Bremer had the experience, something might change for him."

"I thought we'd discussed this at the farm."

"We had. A little. It was just too good an idea to pass up."

"You simply can't use other human beings in your experiments, Albert."

"Bremer's human?"

Christian shook his head. "For acid to be effective, you have to have high moral purpose. This experiment's a waste of time. You already know what the outcome will be."

Albert only shrugged. "What do you think of the tabs?" he asked, playing for time.

"Compact. Tight. They should travel well. Who did you find to do the tabbing?"

"People we know at Cal Tech. They're actually in the Physics Department."

"Too bad Richard's machine's down," Christian murmured. "He could use the bucks."

"Richard's machine is a little more than down," Albert chortled. "Isn't it on display in the courtroom?"

"That's what I hear."

Christian blinked. His eyes were beginning to alter their visual patterns. His voice sounded flat to his ears and, at the same time, seemed to come from everywhere. "I'll be able to tell something about the dosage in an hour or so," he mumbled. "I'm already starting to come on. If it's a nice hit, we'll send them out. How's Doug?"

"I think he's just coming down. He really got gassed. I had to peel him off the floor."

"Yeah . . . you know . . . we have to do something about this Henry Street house," Christian eyed him, his face breaking into a smile.

"You have something in mind?" Albert raised an eyebrow, grinning in return.

"Albert," Christian had a hard time moving his mouth. "I'm getting ready to sit down and sign off for a few hours. No mojo. What are you going to do?"

"Alright," Albert sighed with resignation. "Can I make the phone call from here?"

"No," Christian shook his head. "Allen can drive you down to a phone booth."

"We'd better do it now, before it's too late. I phoned in the tip early this morning."

Two hours later, Christian was certain the dosage was good. When he began to have the tingling sensations that opened him, he took to the rug that had arrived from Afghanistan, stretching and breathing, feeling the tightness dissolve in muscle and mind. He performed his yoga for hours, letting his thoughts carry him, going through events in his life, the people he knew, trying to honestly understand why he hadn't approached Kathy. Ego? No, he simply couldn't touch a hot stove just now. Kathy burned him each time he came close.

Lifetimes later, he felt his eyes begin to clear. His body became controlled. Once again, he felt ready to move, alert, perceptive, able to gather a much broader range of information and internalize it.

"It's good, eh?" Albert asked Christian's flushed, smiling face.

"Great," Christian replied. "You ready to head back to the airport?"

"Yeah. I've got a lot to do. We're in the middle of a reaction."

"Will you drop me at Jerry's?"

At six o'clock, Christian and Albert left the house carrying a bag of forty thousand tabs under the watchful eyes of two overtime Pacific Bell telephone workers.

47

Three unmarked police cars had sat scattered on Henry Street for about half an hour, waiting for someone to enter or leave the address that had been phoned in as an anonymous tip. The flat was an old, slightly dilapidated, low-rent building with an unkempt garden and lawn. Bedspread curtains covered the windows, downstairs and upstairs.

"We'll give it five more minutes," Bremer spoke into the microphone of the car.

The upstairs flat was busy. People in street dress and long hair were coming and going every ten or fifteen minutes. Street dealers, Corbet knew after ten minutes of surveillance. Maybe they should just take the whole house. The lower flat still appeared lifeless. Dead.

"Corbet, get up there and see what's going on," Bremer ordered. "If no one answers, take a look in the windows."

Myles nodded, but he had an uneasy feeling. He hesitated, unsettled because he could find no reason for his premonition. As he walked toward the corner, the entire building came into view. Pacing himself with the loose, easy gait of one who might be stoned and had nothing better to do, he approached the house warily, knowing he would be talking to people entering or leaving the second floor.

"Hey, man, how's it goin'?" he called to a young kid who had walked quickly down the stairs.

"You here to see Jody?" the boy asked.

"Is he here?"

"Yeah. But there's too many people around now. I'm comin' back later."

Out of habit, Myles made a mental note of the name. He knocked on the door of the lower flat. Nothing. He shrugged his shoulders to loosen up, trying to get in tune with what he felt. There were a lot of mixed vibes.

The energy of the upper flat's throwing me off, he decided. *Concentrate on the lower flat.*

Walking around the house carefully, he found a back door. With one hand, he tentatively turned the knob. Locked.

He walked back to try the front door. The smell of marijuana drifted from upstairs and floated across the front porch. Hoping no one from the upper apartment would surprise him and ask what he was doing, he reached for the doorknob. It turned. He pushed open the door, peered inside, and took a few tentative steps across the threshold, debating whether to search the rooms or go for backup.

"Hold it!" someone screamed commandingly at him.

Myles spun on his heel, his heart in his mouth. Shaking, he stared, white-faced. "Phillips!"

"It's a trap!" Phillips shouted, standing back. "The house is wired with some kind of LSD bomb set to go off when you open the door!"

Myles jumped to the porch and glanced at the open door with horror. Tasteless, colorless, odorless, the manuals said. Had he already breathed it? Was it too late? Would he get stoned? His heart pounded unbearably. He jumped from the porch to the sidewalk, running some distance from the house.

"The bomb squad's on its way down here to dismantle this room. You alright?"

"I . . . I don't know," Myles answered. "I'm not coming on yet if I breathed it. I mean . . . I don't feel stoned . . . yet . . . "

In the police car, Bremer watched Myles's shaking hands. A few more minutes and they would have all been dosed. Who'd done it? Did they have other plans? Bremer began to respond to that fear. He felt unsafe, swallowed hard. He needed a few drinks to get it all together. From his car, he watched the bomb squad arrive. Anxious people quickly left the upstairs flat.

"You feeling anything from that stuff?" he asked Myles.

"No . . . I . . . I think it's going to be okay. It's been at least a half hour. I'm . . . I'm going to walk back to campus. I've got some work to do. I'll call you later. You've got surveillance on Brooks?"

Bremer looked over his shoulder and regarded Myles in the backseat. Any trauma and the kid returned to the womb of the university.

"Right on his ass," he assured Myles. "Be at the station at six. The transfer's on for early evening."

48

JERRY PUTNAM
BERKELEY, CALIFORNIA
LATE DECEMBER 1969

J erry looked at his watch as he walked toward the door of Benjamin Miller's office. The afternoon was quickly slipping into evening. His arms were full of books, and one hand held a manila envelope. He fumbled with the key, glad when it turned. Only a few seconds were needed to put the proposal on Benjamin's desk. A quick run to the library, and he'd be on time for the meeting with Christian.

"Oh!" he exclaimed in surprise. He had not expected to see anyone in Benjamin's office, especially at this time of day. Especially Myles Corbet.

Two years. It's been over two years since I've looked fully into that face.

Behind him, the door closed with a quick, even click. A deep silence fell between them.

"What are you doing here?" Jerry finally managed to ask.

"Making some notes for Benjamin," Myles responded.

Jerry read an entire story in Myles's stance—twitching facial muscles, his body poised for flight, fear parading across his eyes, resignation, and finally, defiance.

"So how's it goin'?" Jerry asked.

"Not bad. Yourself?"

"Still managing," Jerry nodded.

Silence again filled the room, the weight of it heavy between them.

Their ears ached for sound, any sound to break the tension that held them mesmerized. Finally, Myles spoke. "Benjamin's not here," he mumbled.

"I didn't expect him to be. I have some papers for him." Jerry flashed a manila envelope.

"Another grant?" Myles asked, sudden interest in his voice. "Where are you off to now?"

"Guadalajara. To study the Huichol."

"The peyote eaters?"

"Something like that."

"What are you going to do when Benjamin leaves the university? He's taking another teaching position, you know."

Jerry's eyes hardened. "You seem to know a lot about what goes on in this department."

"Probably a remnant of my father's day." Myles shrugged. "You heard I was accepted into the graduate program?"

"Congratulations." Jerry's voice was flat. "That's what you've always wanted, isn't it?"

Myles hesitated and turned his face to the window. "Yes. But I never thought it would be without . . . him."

Surprised, Jerry's voice softened. "I'm sorry about your old man. I mean it. He was a mentor to me for many years. Always had time to talk plants when we were kids. Maybe I know how you feel. You remember when I lost my dad, don't you? That was a tough time." Then he couldn't help but add, "Almost as tough as some of the stuff that's come down in the last years."

After all this time, Jerry realized, he still wanted an answer, wanted Myles to tell him why he'd sent him to prison, tried to ruin his life.

But Myles wasn't really listening. Instead, he was backed off somewhere within his own thoughts, looking through venetian blinds while oblivious to the world outside.

"He never disliked you," Myles mused aloud. "It's just that he always felt so much responsibility to his work. To the honor and prestige of this department. If it came down to it, he would always choose what he thought best for the university. He wouldn't compromise his principles for anyone. Not even for me."

Something in his tone made Jerry waiver. Some great sadness that Myles could only have felt here in this first home of his—and perhaps only now, as the fading pink sky spoke of day's end.

"How do you know, Myles?" Jerry finally asked him, warily. "How do you know what he would have chosen? Or what he would have given to you?"

"Oh, I know, alright." Myles laughed bitterly. "Things were either black or white with him."

Jerry cringed at the sound of Myles's laughter, knowing both the admiration and fear with which Myles had regarded his father. "At any rate, he's gone," Jerry answered. "And he'll never be tested."

"Tested?" Myles turned to look at him. "It would have been the supreme test, don't you think?"

Jerry tilted his head to one side. "What test are you talking about?"

Myles narrowed his eyes, then he relaxed and laughed the bitter laugh again before turning back to the window.

Nothing is to be gained here, Jerry told himself. He glanced at his watch and reached for the library books, only to freeze at the sound of Myles's thin, stifled voice.

"Do you hate me, Jerry?" Myles asked, barely above a whisper.

The words drove a cold dagger into Jerry's stomach. For years, he'd waited for just this opportunity, had waited to tell him exactly how he felt.

Then suddenly, he was back in the jungle with Maria Guadalupe, the *curandera*, wondering why it was that hatred perpetuated itself. The answer had been given to him in the mushroom *velada*. Peace lay in forgiveness. Life was a continual reaching out, a union made between things. Death occurred when things were no longer connected. And here was Myles, building a bridge out to him. This man who had ruined so many lives had certainly also ruined his own. What terrible price had he paid to become the withdrawn shadow standing before this darkening window?

Sighing, Jerry said softly, "I'm remembering another time in the late afternoon. We were about ten. We both still had our fathers then. We were standing in that river collecting lichen from the rocks. Remember? The light in the canyon had already begun to fade, and the water was freezing our balls off. But we wouldn't get out until we'd collected that bright green lichen to see under a microscope. You got up on my shoulders. Working together was the only way we could reach it." Jerry paused for a moment. "Where'd you go, Myles? What happened?"

Jerry could hear the silence. Myles still faced the window, unmoving. Jerry waited and then broke the stillness with a deep exhalation of breath. "Whatever you think, I don't hate you." And without expecting an answer, he turned to leave.

The squeaking of the opening door was loud above Myles's hushed voice, but Jerry still heard the words, felt the explosion in his chest. He wondered whether he'd heard correctly or whether his ears were playing tricks. He glanced back at Myles, his face dim in the fading light.

"Don't make that meeting with Christian tonight," said the quiet voice.

A thousand questions flooded Jerry's mind. But every answer pointed to one thing: Myles had set him up again.

Jerry walked over to stand behind him, raised a hand to touch his shoulder. "It's haunted me from the beginning," he said. "Why? Why me? What made you do it?"

Myles turned to face him. "You were the first. They found a couple of joints on me in ROTC. I was supposed to be an example. That meant an arrest and some jail. Front page newspaper headlines because of my father. I was terrified of what my father would say. What he would do. I was terrified of . . . the test."

Jerry wanted to cry. "Maybe getting busted with those joints was like seeing reality for the first time. You were vulnerable. You were like everyone else. It might even have been good for your father. He might have been easier on others. On me."

"I didn't know," Myles moaned, clutching his head in his hands now. "I didn't know what I was doing. I couldn't imagine what I would become without this department. I didn't really mean to bust you. You were simply the only person I knew who could get a kilo of smoke. I said yes to Bremer; you said no. On the basis of that one decision, we've become what we are now. God, I had no idea how important that decision would be. It's become my life! I panicked. Made my choice. Only, then I was trapped."

"About tonight. How much do they know?"

"Everything." Myles dropped his hands from his face and looked up at Jerry. "They know the courier's in. They know Brooks is tied to Harrison. They expect to follow the courier back to the lab. They want the base that was lost. They want to produce it for the Harrison trial."

"Jesus," Jerry whispered. "How do they know?"

"Some kid Brooks bailed out of jail a few years back got busted in Florida with a half-ton of weed. He fingered Brooks so he'd serve two years instead of eight. That was about six months ago. Since then, Bremer's followed up every lead, every rumor. He has a file on the man like you wouldn't believe. But no direct evidence. He means to get that evidence tonight."

"I see."

"Not quite," Myles answered, his voice hard now. "It's more than just a job with Bremer. It's a passion. He knows Brooks has foiled any number of arrests he's tried to make, often after months of investigative work. There are probably three people he hates most in all the world. I believe you know them all. Lance Bormann, Joe O'Brian, and Christian Brooks. O'Brian is no longer with us, but Bremer means to get Bormann and Brooks. Not for the law, but for himself."

"What do you mean?" Jerry asked, confused.

"I see it in his eyes. In the smirk on his face."

"What?"

"I see it when he cleans his gun. Do you understand? He has this pearl-handled .45. Sometimes I watch him clean and shine that piece and there's a look on his face like . . . like maybe he's thinking about fucking. But it's with the gun, you understand?"

"Are you trying to tell me he's planning to shoot Christian?" Jerry cried in disbelief. "Or Lance Bormann?"

"A year ago, he shot a naked man in the back and killed him. Over the last eight months, he's fired at people on four separate occasions. Two of those men died as well. Hanson from the Berkeley office stopped him from killing Harrison. Bremer's made sure Hanson won't be with us tonight. You understand? Hanson won't be there."

"Will you testify to that in court?" Jerry asked, shaking.

"No. And one other thing. When I left, he was heading for a bar."

Feeling sick, his face pale and slack, Jerry looked down at his watch. What if Christian were early for the meeting? "What are you going to do when Bremer finds out you told me all of this?" he asked Myles fearfully.

"I've always gotten past him before."

Jerry read the time on his watch again, then paused. "What can I do to help you?"

Myles shrugged. "Nothing."

49

CHRISTIAN
BERKELEY, CALIFORNIA
LATE DECEMBER 1969

"You can just drop me here," Christian told Albert.

Albert pulled the airport rental car over to the curb near the Shattuck Avenue Co-op. An old green VW bus braked hard behind them, hesitated, then curved around them and entered the co-op parking lot.

"I have a few minutes, so I'll just take a slow walk on up there. Listen, thanks for making that phone call about the apartment today. You'll probably rake up some good karma."

Albert shrugged. "You gonna be okay if I let you off here?"

"I've already peaked. Great acid. You're a special man, Albert." Christian gave him a hug.

"That's what my teachers have always told me," Albert answered, embarrassed at the way Christian always hugged both the men and women in his life.

"Not only in your head. You've got a good heart."

Suddenly, Christian fidgeted in the seat and turned to look at the road behind.

"Sure you're okay?" Albert asked.

"Yeah. I . . . uh . . . I don't know. I have this kind of uncomfortable feeling. I'm trying to pick up on where it's coming from. I've had it since we left the house."

"What kind of uncomfortable?"

Christian turned around again as if searching for something. "I'm . . . I'm getting paranoid."

"Why don't I hang with you for a while?"

"It's okay. I've got it under control. I think it's this trial of Richard's. It's got everyone sitting on the edge."

"Are you sure?"

"Yeah. Yeah, I'm sure. I'll call you tomorrow. Have a safe trip."

Christian got out of the car, waved a last farewell, and shouldered his pack. He watched Albert pull away from the curb and continue down Shattuck Avenue. The old green VW bus hustled out of the parking lot and roared across on the yellow light. Christian registered the information with all the other bits of information he was processing.

Same VW bus that was behind us when we stopped, he thought.

Again, he twisted his neck, the twinge of paranoia touching him. Where was it coming from? Why would a woman in an old VW bus be following Albert's rented car?

Christian was remembering, his mind clear, images forming. He isolated facts from his consciousness that had been buried until this moment.

That woman in the VW bus—he'd seen her yesterday—twice—and once the day before. It couldn't be coincidental.

What else? he asked himself. There had to be more. His mind kept searching.

His house. There were men in front. Not just all day but late into the night.

As if in slow motion, he could see the men and each nuance of their behavior. Too much of their vision was focused on his house, not enough on the work at hand. The workers had an intense look, wore sunglasses. Why were they there? What were they doing?

Not only Pacific Gas and Electric uniforms, he remembered, but Pacific Bell. He'd seen them two, three times. There was too much energy. Too many things in front of his house needed repairing. It didn't compute. His sense of paranoia grew.

Jerry was selling to a friend of a friend—a new customer, someone who needed the tabs right away. Impatience. With the need for cash, he'd made an error. Even though he would never meet the person, he should have checked her out better, asked more questions.

Less than two blocks from Jerry's house, he felt tremendous energy centered on him. He was picking up on thought waves.

The energy. It's not from behind, his senses told him. *Ahead. It's there ahead.*

Of course. He smiled. *No reason to follow when they know exactly where I'm going. It's Albert they're following now. A lone woman in an old green VW bus. They'll pick him up at the airport. Or in L.A.*

The lab! Of course! They wanted the lab!

Where was the heat coming from? Christian went through his customers and friends methodically as he continued walking slowly.

Richard? Had Richard freaked? Turned him? Marcie? No.

Peter? Peter had disappeared into Canada. *Was Peter ready to make a deal to rid himself of a fugitive warrant?*

Allen? Linda?

With each name, he could feel the essence of the person, but there was no one he could sense who would roll over.

What mistakes have I made? he asked, analyzing his motives and behavior. *Have I been righteous with my brothers, kept my intent pure?*

Without missing a step, he walked into a dark yard around a tall hedge and slipped off his pack. He removed the brown bag with the acid and forced it into the center of the dark, thick leaves. If things turned out okay, he'd come back for it later. Maybe he was unduly paranoid.

Christian shook his head.

No. He wasn't paranoid; something was up.

He stepped around the hedge, watching carefully, using his sensitive hearing to pick up sound, his face tense with concentration.

There was still nothing behind or around. It was all ahead.

Yes, they were waiting at Jerry's.

In an instant, it all came together. What was happening was not spontaneous but the result of careful detective work, months of investigation.

My entire family's in danger, he thought, beginning to tremble.

A nagging doubt that he might be in the middle of a grotesque paranoia trip remained. He had to be sure.

At the corner where he would turn toward Jerry's house, he gazed down the street. Cars were parked in the next block. Among them, a green Ford, a white Ford. Streetlights reflected off windows fogged by vapor. People sat in these cars. He closed his eyes, picked up on the mental energy, tuning in to the frequency like a radio beam.

Certain there were more cars nearby with other men, Christian became convinced. Afraid now, he knew he had to move fast. How long would it take him to get to a phone? Jerry needed to be warned. Allen and Linda. Albert and Doug.

Turning with the same steady gait, a walk that would not betray his thoughts if he were being observed, he began to retrace his steps, following the sidewalk back toward Shattuck Avenue, where there were lights and crowds he could blend into, phones.

As he neared the corner, he felt an enormous surge of energy focused on him, intense and physical. His adrenaline pumped, preparing his legs to flee. A car cruised toward him down the dark, dimly lit street. For a moment, the headlights startled his sensitive eyes, then the car slowed. The hair stood up on his arms. Prepared to run, he felt for a path without resistance. The car stopped opposite him.

"Hi," a voice called quietly to him. "Need a lift?"

"Jerry!" Christian walked to the driver's window looking full into his face, anxious, trying to find a way to explain.

But Jerry said, "Bremer's waiting for us."

"You know?"

"I just learned," his voice was filled with fear. "I came to warn you. Thank God I got here in time. Get in."

Christian walked around the car with the same smooth, unhurried gait, opened the door, slipped off the shoulder bag, and threw it into the center between them. Everything would be all right. He just needed to get to a phone.

The feeling of safety disarmed him. He was unprepared when the quiet street turned into a stampede of racing cars, screeching tires, and shouting men who quickly surrounded the car.

Jerry looked briefly at the bag and closed his eyes, fingers tightly gripping the steering wheel. "Jesus!" he whispered. "We're busted!"

Broad searchlights from the police cars blinded them. Christian froze in the intensity of the attack.

"Police! Get out of the car! You're under arrest!"

Christian, very stoned, shaking uncontrollably at the violence, swung open the door, put two feet on the asphalt, and stood, lifting his arms above his head.

"Hold it right there!" a harsh voice shouted.

Then shots. The windshield of Jerry's car shattered into spider web patterns.

"Jerry!" Christian screamed, afraid to move, holding his arms high in the glaring light from the surrounding cars, fearing his knees might collapse.

A new car drove up one side of the street. "Move it!" one of the cops shouted to the driver.

Christian, barely able to acknowledge anything that was happening, taking in everything and nothing, was pushed hard against the car, his arms and legs spread. Probing hands quickly covered his body. Across the top of the car, he could see two men pulling Jerry from the seat of the vehicle. He held his breath, listening to his heart above the noisy confusion of the street.

"Against the car!" a throaty voice ordered.

Jerry stood up, dazed and spread eagle against the door.

Christian closed his eyes and lowered his head, weak with relief. When he lifted his head, it was with a thankful prayer and a smile that Jerry could not mistake, even in the harsh, surreal light.

"I'm glad to see you're enjoying this," Jerry mumbled with a sick grin in spite of his shaking lips.

"I thought for a moment . . . "

"Quiet!" a voice ordered.

The hard muzzle of a gun tapped Christian's ear. His grin faded quickly. Whoever was holding the gun was shaking uncontrollably, the smell of alcohol penetrating the air.

"Dolph! Here it is!" someone called, picking up Christian's pack.

The car that had stopped still waited. "I said move it!" one of the cops ordered the driver.

The driver rolled down his window.

"Hanson . . . what are you doing here?" the man with the shaky trigger finger asked, his surprise palpable.

"I got an anonymous call. Someone gave me the time and the address. Shots, Bremer?"

"He dropped something."

"A furtive gesture?"

"Phillips, open the bag," Bremer ordered.

Hanson got out of the car to watch, walking closer, his eyes on Bremer.

"There's . . . nothing . . . couple of books, newspaper."

"Look around," Bremer told them. "Check the car. Search the street. It has to be here somewhere." He turned to Christian and screamed near his ear. "Where's the stash, punk? Don't make me have to beat the shit out of you for an answer."

"I'd be careful," Hanson told him, nodding to a Shattack Avenue crowd that had gathered. The Coop grocery was just a half block away. "They're called witnesses."

Christian merely shrugged, a gesture that pushed Bremer over the top, and crowd or no, he brought the back of his hand up hard against the side of Christian's face.

"That's enough, Bremer," Hanson said coldly.

Bremer turned to him with an angry snarl. "Who the fuck do you think you are, giving me orders?"

"I think I'm a police officer. And I've had enough. You hear that, Bremer? I'm taking myself off this detail and going back into a section that contributes something to law and order. I'm sick of the macho brutality and indiscriminate lack of law in your group. But before I do that, Bremer . . . before I do that . . . I'm going to see my way through this one last case."

Hanson turned to one of the men on the squad. "Have you found anything?"

"No, sir. Nothing."

"What about the car?"

"Nothing," Phillips answered. "Not even a goddamned roach in the ashtray."

"The men?"

"Clean."

"Okay, boys," Hanson looked at Christian and Jerry. "Take off."

"Are you out of your mind?" Bremer screamed. "Do you know what you're doing?"

"Yes. I'm enforcing the law. Before you 'find' something you've missed. Get going," Hanson told Christian and Jerry, hooking his thumb over his shoulder.

Now nothing but dead silence and bright light filled the street, pierced only by huge tides of emotion. Christian nodded to Jerry. They opened the car doors and got in. Jerry slowly drove forward, trying to see through the shattered glass.

"Get to a phone!" Christian cried in a dry voice.

Shaking uncontrollably, Christian put a dime in the telephone and had Jerry dial the number, unable to focus on the symbols himself.

"Hello?" Allen's voice answered.

"Clean up. Quickly. Thoroughly. You may only have a few minutes," Christian's tense voice exploded.

Without answering, Allen hung up to gather stash.

Christian had Jerry dial the lab number next, the one that was never to be used unless there was an emergency. The phone rang and rang.

Come on, Christian prayed. *Be there.*

He refused to hang up, but he was getting spacey, had to concentrate, each ring a lifetime of thought. Finally, a timid, "Hello?"

"Doug, thank God. Albert's coming in. Meet him at the airport at ten. He's being tailed. Do not go home or to work. Understand?"

"Are you sure?"

"Very sure. Check into a hotel. Let Benjamin Miller know where you are. I'll call you tomorrow."

Christian put a third coin into the phone. "Lance, you working late?"

"Christian? You sound funny. Is everything all right? Your voice is shaking."

"Something's come up this evening. Can I come by?"

"Sure."

"Call Richard, will you? Have him come down. He'll want to hear this."

50

BREMER AND MYLES
BERKELEY, CALIFORNIA
LATE DECEMBER 1969

Tobacco smoke floated in waves in the dim light of the bar, the neon signs offering little light. A jukebox played soulful tunes. Bremer and his men chose the quiet booths in the back. They were trying to piece together what had gone wrong. Already they were calling it the Brooks fiasco. Several ideas kept getting rehashed and reshaped as the drinks were poured. Each of the men had a speculation. Each of them, except Bremer himself. He knew exactly what had gone wrong.

At first, Bremer thought that maybe the LSD had gotten Corbet stoned, maybe later in the evening he had begun to see visions and hallucinations. Maybe that was the reason he couldn't leave his house to meet the squad. Anything was possible with that stuff. No one knew how it worked.

But from the second Hanson had appeared, he'd known. Corbet had finally had his revenge, had played him along for weeks.

Corbet had set him up, had watched him fail in the one moment when it was absolutely necessary that he succeed. Corbet, who had counted the moments and waited the years to repay Bremer for the humiliation of his arrest. Corbet, who was smarter than all of them and who had gone out of his way to prove it this evening.

Corbet, who had probably set up the Henry Street house himself as an excuse not to appear.

Sitting in the booth, Bremer said nothing of this, but he downed the drinks the men bought for him, slowly, patiently. By ones and twos, the men excused themselves until Bremer sat at the table with only Phillips and Wilson.

"What do you think?" Phillips asked him. "Any hope of saving any of it?"

"Maybe," Bremer answered unhurriedly. "We're tailing that kid. Took a plane to L.A."

"You've been quiet tonight," Wilson said. "What's on your mind?"

"You saw Hanson show up?" Bremer asked.

"Yeah."

"Corbet sent him. Corbet masterminded the whole setup and the failure. Corbet," Bremer added leaning closer to the men over his glass, "warned Brooks and Putnam."

"You think so?" Wilson's eyes widened.

"I know so." Bremer leaned back in the chair. "And he's made sure I'll take the heat for the missing base." He threw back the last of his drink.

"Jesus," Phillips mumbled.

"I'm thinking of paying Corbet a little visit this evening. Would anyone care to join me?"

Wilson laughed loudly, shrugging his shoulders, loosening up, ready to move. "No kidding? Boy, would I!"

Myles sat on the edge of his bed, his eyes closed, his head dropped into his hands. Why had he gone overboard? If only he hadn't sent Hanson, he could have pleaded innocent. Bremer could only have suspected. True, he would still have had to continue working . . . no Brooks, no lab, no base. But now, what would Bremer's wrath be?

As if in answer, he heard a pounding on the front door.

Shit! he thought, the knot of fear tightening his stomach. *I won't answer.*

"Open up, Corbet," Bremer's voice was thick. "I know you're in there. If you don't open this goddamned door, I'll take it off its hinges!"

"Coming," he called. "Just a minute."

Running to the bathroom, he flushed a small stash of smoke down the toilet and then ran to the door. He opened it partially and noted that Bremer leaned heavily on the frame. Phillips and Wilson stood behind.

"It's late," he said to Bremer. "Couldn't this have waited until morning?"

"I don' thin' so," Bremer said, his words slurred together. He shoved the door open.

Myles felt a deep chill creep into what little confidence he had remaining. The smell of alcohol entered the room with the men. Bremer's face was hard, angry, ugly. He swaggered as he crossed the room. "So . . . " Bremer eyed him.

"What's going on?" Myles muttered, forcing himself not to look at the men who took positions behind him.

"You missed the rendezvous this evening. I was worried about you. Did you get dosed?" Bremer asked.

"I've been feeling kind of funny since it happened."

"You thin' so? You'd better have a damned good excuse for not showin' up."

"What happened?" Myles asked, now nervously glancing over his shoulder at Wilson.

"You don' know what happened?" Bremer asked, signaling.

Wilson grabbed Myles's arms, pinning them behind him.

"Wait!" Myles cried. "I can explain!"

"You don' have to, Corbet," Bremer answered coldly.

Phillips planted his fist deep into Myles's stomach. Myles exhaled hoarsely, his legs buckling beneath him.

"I can explain it for you. You set me up, you bastard." A nod and Phillips planted another fist into Myles's stomach, leaving him retching, gasping for air.

Myles tried to find air to speak. A warm trickle of urine ran down his leg.

"You've been settin' me up for weeks. Not just me, but our whole department. You warned Brooks and Putnam . . . "

This time, Phillips's fist hit Myles squarely on the jaw.

"Not his face," Bremer told them. "He has to testify tomorrow."

Another fist found Myles's ribs.

"You put Hanson on the scene. You set up that LSD bomb in the vacant house. What'd you think, Myles? Did you think I'd go in first?"

Wilson dropped him to the floor, and Phillips kicked him squarely in his kidney.

"You thought you'd win, eh? You thought you'd finally take ol' Dolph down. We're goin' to show you what winnin' feels like, punk."

Bremer nodded, and at once, Wilson and Phillips went to work furiously and effectively with their feet on Myles's body.

Stepping back, they looked down at him, a look of satisfaction on their faces.

"We'll see you in court tomorrow," Bremer told Myles. "Ten o'clock. If you don' show . . . I'll come back and kill you."

Myles heard the door slam but was so sunken into the pain of his body that there was no relief at their departure. He heard his voice groan, found his face lying in a puddle of his own vomit. He moved slowly, trying to get to his knees. His ribs . . . God, his ribs were broken. He started crying, crying because of the pain, crying because he had lost his bid for closure.

Bremer's words pierced his returning thoughts. *You thought you'd win . . . you set me up.*

Myles got to his knees, holding his ribs against the movement of his sobs, still gasping for air. He leaned forward to touch the floor with his forehead, tears falling in great drops to the wood. Then the sobs were broken by quiet laughter, wild and hysterical.

How stupid he'd been! Bremer was right! If he'd worked to set Bremer up as he'd always wished to do, he could not have chosen a better plan. Unconsciously, he'd fulfilled all his desires. Bremer was right. He'd won.

Heavy on the floor, lying shakily in vomit and tears, Myles was forced to ask why victory hurt so much.

Myles must have passed out; when he opened his eyes, Jerry and Christian were leaning over him.

"We came by to let you know we survived the night, and it looks like you almost didn't," Jerry said.

Myles tried to speak, "Bremer . . . ," but it hurt too much to breathe.

"We saw them leaving," Christian murmured, his eyes very dilated, his mind clear. "When we left Lance's office, we thought we should maybe come by to check on you. It's a good thing we did. Let's get you to the emergency room."

The next morning, Myles sat at the back of the courtroom with Jerry and Christian on either side of him. McKinley never called him to the witness stand. They could not be sure of what he'd say.

At lunch recess, Bremer walked up to them. "Beat it, punk," he told Christian. "Why don't you go destroy some more minds so we can cool your ass."

Christian looked toward Myles questioningly.

"Give me a minute," Myles told Bremer.

"Look," Myles said to Christian and Jerry, once they had moved a short distance away. "It's over. None of us can struggle against this and win. I have to follow the road I've made for myself. I'll catch you guys around sometime."

"You'll be alright?"

"In broad daylight? In the courthouse? He's sober now. Yeah, I'll be alright."

Christian held out a hand. "Take care of yourself . . . brother."

"Sure." Myles smiled weakly. "You too."

"Myles . . . ," Jerry began uncertainly.

"I hear you're following Benjamin to his next teaching position."

Jerry nodded. "Yeah. Grad school. Maybe we'll meet at some conference someday."

"Time to go." Christian nodded to Jerry, noting Bremer's impatience.

"I'll be in touch," Jerry whispered. He brushed Myles's hand, looked deeply into his eyes, and saw surprise, and something more . . . hope . . . the possibility of love rekindled. Then Jerry turned and hurriedly followed the hallway to the exit.

Desire rose in Myles so strong, he closed his eyes against it.

Jerry, his mind whispered.

Bremer grabbed him by the arm. "Let's step upstairs for a minute, Corbet."

Walking was hard. Myles's back and legs were covered in large yellow-blue bruises. The doctor had told him one rib was cracked. Every muscle in his body ached. Halfway up the stairs, Bremer released his arm. Myles wasn't going anywhere very fast.

"Sit down," Bremer told him in an amiable voice once they'd entered a dim office.

Laboriously, Myles lowered himself into a chair.

"You know, Myles," Bremer began, "I've been thinking. I've been thinking that we both won and we both lost. You know that?"

Myles said nothing.

"I'm sorry about last night," Bremer continued. "I mean it. I just got a little carried away."

"How's your hangover?"

"Come on. I didn't have that much to drink. You're my best agent. The best I have. So we lost one. With luck, we'll have scores more in the next years. That was our agreement, wasn't it? You'd continue working?"

Myles nodded.

Bremer grinned. "I got a call from Washington. They've got this guy on the line. They know he's bringing in bags of coke from Bolivia. They want to know the sources. Something about the fields, the laboratories, shipping routes through the jungle and out of the country. How and in what quantities it's being transported to the United States. They're looking for someone good. I mentioned you."

"You're asking me to take a position out of the country?"

Bremer held his hands open, palms up, shrugging his shoulders. "To Bolivia. As a government advisor attached to the Bureau in Washington. Might not be the hash crowd, but I think you can handle any drug lord you meet, being so smart and all. What better place to be a botanist than the jungles of South America? That'll be your cover."

Myles took a deep breath and looked down at the floor.

"You're going to need a few weeks," Bremer continued. "You look a little stiff. That should give you some time to get your affairs in order. Here." Bremer threw Myles his passport across the table. "Updated and with a visa. Good luck, Corbet."

"Yeah. Thanks." Myles stood gingerly, the pain shooting through his ribs. He picked up the passport.

"Phillips will give you a lift home after court today."

"No need." Myles stopped, one hand on the doorknob, and looked back toward Bremer. "By the way, best of luck to you, too. You may need it."

"Hey," Bremer grinned, raising his palms again. "We both won and we both lost, right?"

Instead of opening the door, Myles turned and gazed squarely into Bremer's eyes. "I'm going to say this only once." His voice was resolute. "If you ever threaten me again, I'll not only press charges, but I'll go to the *Barb* with my story. All of it. Do you hear? You've got enough legal problems. You don't need any more." He reached once again for the doorknob, ready to leave, then stopped, his back to Bremer. "This . . . this was all to protect my mother. But she's going to hear the whole story. Today. From me."

Myles walked into the hall.

51

R ichard sat at the defense table with Lance, his heart pounding wildly, uncontrollably, his hands shaking so much that he gripped the table in order to steady them. The members of the jury were still taking their places in the jury box, ready to pronounce the verdict.

Hope warred with logic. Would the jury take into account all Lance had revealed during the trial? Would they release him? Dear God, if they didn't, how much time would they give him? How much of his life would be taken from Marcie, John, and the new baby? Eighteen to sixty months, Lance had predicted, a year and a half to five years. Even one night away seemed like a lifetime, and when all those nights were strung together, it was like looking across a wide, pain-filled ocean with no shore in sight. He felt himself drowning in despair but knew he had to breathe, had to stand against the crushing waves of hopelessness; behind him, Marcie waited, her heart pounding as hard as his. Closing his eyes, he began a silent mantra, seeking courage.

"All rise."

"Good afternoon, ladies and gentlemen of the jury. Have you reached a verdict?"

The foreman stood. "We have, Your Honor. We, the jury, find the defendant, Richard Blake Harrison, guilty on all counts."

Everything else followed so quickly that for months afterward,

Richard could only try to replay it so that he might understand what
had been said and what it meant.

". . . therefore sentence you to five to fifteen years . . . "

After that, he'd heard no more. Marcie had gasped in horror at the
words, and he had turned from the judge to look into her eyes. Nothing else in the world existed, everything falling away, only the depths
of her love speaking to him.

Suddenly, an officer was on either side, taking him away, while he
vaguely heard Lance say that everything was not as bad as it seemed, an
indeterminate sentence, parole possible in two and a half years, something about an appeal, and other things he would later try to decipher.
For the moment, he was asking whether he could say good-bye to his
family, was devastated they would not allow it, a simple hug for his wife
and son, he asked, while they pulled him into the bowels of the jail.

The door to the courtroom slammed, and he was lost to them.

52

After the verdict, the judge called Lance Bormann and Dolph Bremer into his chambers.

"Mr. Bormann, I called you here because I didn't like your defense tactics in this case. Your constant contempt of court. Your flagrant disregard of my rulings. Your use of the media. I'm sure you're aware of the stories in this morning's paper of Mr. Bremer's alleged alcohol problems. Along with other insinuations that not only label him a liar but come very close to calling him a murderer. Do you have any evidence that proves he shot that Indian boy?"

"I did. But it disappeared with Joe O'Brian the night he was killed." Jennifer had just returned from the Hoopa reservation, white-faced and defeated, knowing she would never know what really happened to Joe on the night he died. "Now the boy who witnessed the shooting has disappeared again. You wouldn't know anything about that, would you, Bremer?" Lance asked angrily.

"That's quite enough, Mr. Bormann," Judge Burgess ordered.

"Why'd you give Harrison five to fifteen years, for God's sake? Bremer here would have done less time for murder."

Even if he did get paroled in two and a half years, that was a long time for a man with a young family. Lance was furious, and at the moment, he didn't care if he did go to jail for contempt. Not after what Christian and Jerry had told him the night before.

"The agent in the case didn't testify today," he continued tightly. "Do you know why? Do you know Bremer went over to his house last night in a drunken rage and beat the shit out of him with two of his goons?"

"Try and maintain some perspective, Mr. Bormann," the judge said, equally angry now. "Harrison was guilty. The evidence was all against him. And, quite frankly, you brought it on your own client. There were too many eyes on this case. I had to show the public that strong law enforcement is being carried out. Without the eyes, perhaps he could have done less time."

"You sentenced a man to fifteen years to spite me?" Lance turned away from the desk wild with frustration. "He's . . . he's a good kid."

"He's a piece of shit, Mr. Bormann. And probably a wealthy piece of shit or you wouldn't be here."

Lance turned back to the judge, defiant. "We're going to appeal your decision. You know that, don't you?"

"And you know it won't do any good. No judge will overturn my decision, even if you can get a hearing. Why did you become so emotionally involved?"

Lance stared at the bespectacled man, incredulous. "Are you kidding? Don't you see what's involved here? The slaying of innocent men by a gun-happy thug wearing a badge. A twenty-one-year-old man doesn't have to be shot in the back for selling marijuana!"

"Wait a minute." Bremer stepped forward forcefully.

"You wait, you son-of-a-bitch," Lance shouted, confronting him. "Go on. Tell the good judge about kicking your own agent senseless last night. Don't you get it? He's no longer a scared nineteen-year-old. He's a law officer. Tell the judge about how you operate your own private secret army. How you can do anything to increase your arrest record without worrying about whether it's legal or not. And you," Lance pointed a finger at Judge Burgess, "you condone his actions out of personal bigotry and your desire for reelection."

"Mr. Bormann, you will leave these chambers and never appear in my court again. Or I will have you arrested on sight."

"I know for a fact," Lance continued, ignoring the command, "that

Phillips lied in his report about me. I know for a fact that they planted the '*evidence*' themselves. What about me? What about my case? How many years will I get based on a lie?"

Judge Burgess stood. "You will know that, Mr. Bormann, when you stand trial. Like any other citizen."

"Like any other citizen? Like Bremer here? Around here, you don't stand trial if you have a badge. Around here, if you have a badge, you can use the law to your own ends."

"Do yourself a favor," the judge told Lance in a barely controlled voice, "get out before I have you removed."

"I'm taking my case to the American people," Lance spat at him. "Let's see what sort of society they want to live in. And I'm going to make sure you get indicted, Bremer," Lance continued to shout as he walked to the door. "I'm going to dig up everything you've ever done and notify the press and whoever will listen until the charges stick."

Lance slammed the door behind him.

When the sound of the door finished reverberating in the room, Judge Burgess looked toward Bremer. For a long moment, neither spoke.

"I'll tell you what I'm going to do, Dolph," the judge finally said. "I'm going to let you take a little vacation. Quietly, of course. There's a small hospital in Northern California that does alcoholic rehabilitation work. I want you in therapy for at least three months. You're going to stop drinking. After that, we will see if the position of field supervisor is still open."

"And if I don't?"

"You will," the judge said firmly, "or I might just take a closer look at Mr. Bormann's evidence. I might even get curious about what actually did happen to Joe O'Brian. I'll allow you to suggest someone to take over during your absence, if you'd like. I'll give that name to the police commissioner."

Dolph swallowed hard. "Wilson. Ed Wilson," he said with a dry mouth.

"Then, good day, Mr. Bremer."

53

MARCIE, KATHY, AND CHRISTIAN
BERKELEY, CALIFORNIA
LATE DECEMBER 1969

Kathy walked along the shoreline near the Berkeley Marina with Marcie and John, the women overwhelmed by the sentence Richard had received just a few hours before. Even though the late afternoon sun brought some warmth to the December day, the sea breeze had picked up, and she was cold to her bones.

For the first time since leaving him in India, Kathy had seen Christian. She'd gasped to see him sitting brazenly with Jerry Putnam and Myles Corbet in the courtroom, thinking he must have lost his mind to taunt Bremer that way.

At the recess, she'd looked for him, but he'd vanished. Marcie said he was leaving the country and would be gone for a long time. The thought brought her to the edge of despair. As she staggered across the sand, a slow, seeping guilt enveloped her for all the months she'd avoided him.

Surely, surely, I could have gone to Richard's gathering, she cried to herself. *I should have told him then about the baby. Explained. Marcie's right. He would have understood everything.*

John was having a great time, oblivious to the feelings of his mother and godmother. His short legs took the path over the rocks and through the sand, his eyes following the flight of seagulls. He lifted his arms, laughing. While he ran, the women walked slowly, arms linked together, each step labored.

"They took him," Marcie said suddenly, stopping, her eyes looking out toward the Golden Gate. "They wouldn't even let us say good-bye."

The judge's sentence had been devastating. What made it all the worse was that the outcome was unsettled. Richard could be gone anywhere from two and a half to fifteen years. If he served five years, John would be in second grade before he spent time with his father again. For the first time, Marcie was beginning to ask what happened to the children of the incarcerated. How did they manage without one of their parents? Her chest hurt so painfully that she wondered if her heart would fail.

"Marcie, I'm so sorry."

"He knew. You could see it in the faces of the jurors. The hostile actions of the judge. But there was simply no place to run."

From deep inside, the ache had begun, an ache that would only be soothed each time she went to the prison for a visit, each time she looked into his eyes, touched him. Losing Richard had cleaved her in two, and from that moment until he returned, she would always be incomplete. Sadness had already settled into her features.

Warily, she glanced at Kathy. "Did you see Christian?"

"Yes. He's a madman."

Marcie gave a weak smile at the pride in Kathy's voice. "You need to speak to him, you know. Before he leaves. You need to tell him about the baby."

"I . . . can't."

"Oh, Kathy, why not?"

"Because he wouldn't go if I told him. And you know what'll happen if he stays. They'll find a way to bust him—with or without goods."

At the sound of a car horn, Marcie turned to look back to the parking lot, shielding her eyes with her hand to better see against the glare on the water.

"I'll be right back," she said, picking up John.

Jerry stepped out of the car and raced up the beach. He took Marcie and John in his arms and held them for a long moment. Someone else had reached them, and Kathy watched helplessly as Marcie pointed a finger toward where she waited, poised on a rock of shore break.

Christian climbed toward her, and in a voice as soft as the waves lapping along the edge of the bay, he said simply, "Hello, Kathy." He looked up at her for some moments, his hands in his jacket pockets, his eyes searching her.

Heat and color rushed to her face, shamefully remembering the blood and scars of their last meeting. Finally, she answered, a tremor in her voice. "I was looking for you earlier today."

"Marcie told me."

"What are you doing here?" she asked.

"I came to see Marcie. And you." He shook his head grimly. "Richard's sentence was a blow. Walk with me for a few minutes."

He held up a hand to help her down, and she jumped to the sand, steadied by his arm.

"I've made arrangements to purchase a small tabbing machine," he told her as they took the shoreline toward a point that jutted into the bay. "Merlin's agreed to put it up at the farm. But Albert and Doug may need help transferring crystal from the lab. If they need you, can you go down there and get it up to Merlin?"

"Sure," she nodded, her brow knitted together, concerned. "You know I'll do anything to help. Is Albert's going to continue?"

"For as long as the ET holds out. I'll be looking for more on my travels."

"Are you sure you should still be doing this? Now that they know who you are?"

He picked up a small stone and skimmed it lightly over the water, watching it bounce once, twice, three, four times before falling beneath the sea. Finally, he answered, as if he'd been thinking about this very question. "It's the only thing I believe in. My dilemma in Bodh Gaya . . . how to put together all the spiritual paths that run through me . . . they only come together with acid."

Another stone skimmed across the water. "I went to see my father. Daya Nanda told me my healing wouldn't begin until I did."

Kathy nodded, aware of the times in the last year when she'd woken to his nightmares, the torturous scream, his body bathed in sweat. She knew, too, how he had feared a visit to his father. Watching him closely, listening to the troubled sound of his voice, she could appreciate what courage it had taken to make that journey.

"Are things better between you?"

"Better? Yes. I asked his forgiveness. But I still can't be the minister he wants me to be. That still hurts him. What we do have is time to keep talking."

"Are you tempted to become Daya Nanda's disciple?" *And live in the ashram with Kali*, Kathy wondered silently.

He shoved his hands back into his jacket pockets. "I was a fool to ignore all I'd heard about the Master of the ashram. Arrogant." He cast her a knowing look. "A tragic flaw in my character."

"I happen to like that arrogance. Sometimes."

He grinned slightly at the equal measures of approval and petulance in her voice. "But no. I'm not ready to live in an ashram. Or in a monastery in Nepal."

Kathy stopped walking and looked directly into his face, her voice serious. "Christian, have you stopped to think that you've been brought to this place in your life for very good reasons? Look at how many major events have put you here. Don't you see how involved you are with the world? Maybe you're doing exactly what you should be doing."

Without answering, he ambled forward again, and she followed. When they reached the point and could go no further, they stood silent. The unsheltered wind blew harder here, and Kathy wrapped her arms about herself.

"What are Alan and Linda going to do now that you've closed your house?" she asked.

"They're moving back East to work for a group called Amnesty International. The organization works for the release of prisoners of conscience. People who have been imprisoned because of their political opinion or religion."

"Maybe they can work on Richard's case."

"What about you? Are you still thinking of law school?"

"I've applied to begin at Boalt in the fall. But it's going to mean taking some extra units to graduate on time. I . . . I missed fall quarter."

"And Danny?"

Kathy smiled, proud of Danny. "Now that he's got his acceptance letter to Cal, we're going to continue our partnership. There's talk of a College of Natural Resources. And eventually, he's looking toward the new Goldman School of Public Policy. Maybe someday he and I will write new law together."

"Sounds like you've chosen your next journey."

"Yes," she nodded. "It's . . . exciting. It's the right thing for me."

With her arms still wrapped around her body, cold, she turned to walk back the way they had come, away from the full impact of the wind. "Have you talked to Jennifer?"

"Yesterday." He nodded. "She's . . . devastated. Busy trying to tie up loose ends. Joe's death has changed her whole life. But devastated or not, she's still Jennifer. She's decided to go into teaching. 'American history,' she told me, 'not American myth.' She wants a whole new generation of kids to hear of a government 'by the people.'"

They were halfway to the car when Christian suddenly stopped and turned to look meaningfully at her. "Kathy, I'm leaving today."

The sand seemed to shift under her feet, and she struggled to control her next words, desperately wanting him to stay, to explain, to share all the truths that would make them whole again. But instead of begging him to understand all her fears, she said instead, "Where did you have in mind to go?"

"Good question. I've burnt out a number of continents. I thought I might try South America."

"South America!" she exclaimed.

"Only until things settle down and we see what the movements of the universe bring. Jerry doesn't have to be back in school until September. We're going to Mexico and then on to Ecuador and into the Amazon rainforest."

"I . . . I thought you might try . . . well . . . Hawaii. Someplace closer."

His body turned away from her. "There's not much happening in Hawaii for me."

The unmistakable pain in his voice alerted Kathy to some news she had yet to learn. "What's going on in Hawaii?"

"I loaned Keith the money for his land payment. You know, I think he's getting it down. Looks like he's growing some outrageous herb in that red Maui dirt. Eventually, he'll pay me back."

"As soon as I have a break, I'll make it over to see Julie. I'm sure she can use a shoulder and some company."

His face was grim. "I don't know. Julie, Bliss, and the kids joined the Hare Krishna Temple. They took the last of Bob and Dharma's pesos and donated them to the ashram."

Stunned, Kathy could hardly find the words. "But . . . the land Bob wanted. Maybe . . . maybe she just fell apart with the news of Bob's sentence. Maybe she felt deserted. I should have gone to her. I was just so wrapped up in everything going on around here . . . in myself . . . "

"God, Kathy. Stop. What more can you do? You've been supporting everyone. Marcie. Selling Richard's stash so he can make his attorney's fees. Carrying your own business while Danny finishes his finals. And now, you've just said you'll move crystal to help me."

"And Carolyn? She was spending a lot of time praying and meditating the last I heard."

He shook his head. "She didn't enter the temple commune with Julie. Keith says she moved in with a friend of his. I know the dude. He's cool. They're going to try growing."

Kathy closed her eyes and said a quick, silent prayer for Carolyn's future. She could not imagine what it must have been like to come down from the high of a first acid trip, full of all the promises she'd made to be Larry's true partner, then to understand the reality of his death. That had to have been devastating. "I'm glad she's found someone," she said quietly. "But what's Bob going to say when he hears he's lost the land he wanted?"

Frustration clouded Christian's eyes. "I don't know."

"Have you heard any more about when they'll be released?"

"Yes," he answered with a heavy sigh. "The sentence was reduced to two years. Less with good behavior. Not seven. But, still, a long time. Another year."

She regarded him. "Are you still blaming yourself for what happened in Greece?"

"In large part, yes. If I'd only done the right thing. Paid attention to getting that load back."

Kathy pulled her coat more tightly around her body, felt herself shiver, whether from emotion or cold, she did not know. "There's a rumor going around that Lance scooped some of Bob's bucks. True?"

"True." Christian stiffened. "His . . . fee. But that was before his bust. He seems to finally be getting it."

"Then it's probably also true that you put up the money for Bob and Dharma's new attorney. You need contributions?"

Christian shook his head. "It's covered."

"You don't have to do penance, you know. We can all help."

"If it's a penance, it's mine to do. By the way . . . " He pulled the pack from his shoulder and opened it to produce a long brown envelope.

"What's that?"

"The three grand you said I owed you."

Suddenly, she was both furious and ashamed. Without warning, she began to cry, quietly, huge, hot tears of love and sorrow overflowing from her eyes. "You know I was only being cavalier at the time. Just stop this. I won't take it. Don't you know I'd do it all again in a second if it meant helping you?"

Taking a deep breath, looking into her eyes, he reached out to wipe a tear from her cheek. "Why were you looking for me this morning?"

His touch took her breath away, her entire body responding. "I was worried. Richard told us about that scene with Bremer last night. I needed to make sure you were alright."

"Still worrying about me?"

"Of course I was worried," she cried, angry again, trying to stop her tears and failing, praying she would not break down completely. "From the first moment I saw you, I loved you."

"Please don't cry," he said softly.

"Bremer didn't hurt you, did he?"

He shook his head and laughed. "Just a backhand across the face. I'm sure you'd like to give me a few backhands yourself."

"Maybe." She tried to smile with him, but her lips still quivered. Wiping her face, she forced her voice to become smooth with some tenor of the old teasing seduction. "Or maybe I'd like to give you something else."

He stood very still, looking into her eyes, then spoke softly. "Kali was a fantasy. If you had listened to me in Varanasi, you would have heard what I was trying to tell you. She and I both knew . . . even before the police came through the door . . . that it would never work. We'd already glimpsed our differences. We knew we didn't have the kind of affection . . . the shared goals . . . it takes to love and live in the day to day. That's the kind of love she holds for Nareesh. They're going to be married in the spring, you know. Then they're moving to Connecticut to begin a retreat center."

He found the courage to take her by the shoulders. "I made a huge mistake leaving you and traveling to India without a word that I was going. I compounded it by pushing Kali into an affair she didn't really want." Suddenly, his eyes filled with tears, and Kathy was almost undone. "I am so sorry for what you had to endure," he whispered, blinking, trying to control his voice. "And now Bob and Dharma are paying part of the price, too. So yes, I do have a penance."

"Christian . . . " she whispered.

But he shook his head. "I was so sure of myself. About how I thought the world should be. I blamed my father for mistakes he'd made, only to find that I was blaming him for being human." He had to finish what he'd come to say. "Now I find I'm trying to forgive myself for being human. I'm trying to understand that my mistakes are simply a part of learning to live. Choosing my karma." The sadness in his eyes was pleading. "Can you forgive me?"

"Forgive you?" she said wrapping her arms about him, laying her head on his chest. "I'm the one who should ask your forgiveness. I'd give anything to have the last months back again. I've been so stupid. How could I know we'd run out of time? There are so many things I want to tell you . . . "

"Shh . . . " he tried calming the rising distress in her voice. "We have the future. I'll be back, and we can spend the rest of our lives talking."

Wondering desperately if she should mention the child, she turned from him to look across the water, afraid he would read the secret in her eyes. Near the horizon, the sun was lowering, turning the water a wavering red-gold. A seagull swooped low, then another. Kathy followed the birds as they came to rest on the waves. In the background, San Francisco stood on its peninsula, glaring against a glowing sky.

The moment of temptation passed, and she swallowed the words that burned in her throat. He had to leave. He had to be safe.

"I'm remembering Haight Street," she said softly. "How we started in love and friendship. How passing out sacraments brought people together."

"They still do."

She looked up at him with a tremulous smile. His lashes were wet, but light filled his eyes, the blue of them gold-tinged, picking up the color of the sky. Each moment they had spent together crossed her mind in precious, palpable memories. "When you come home this summer, we can go up to Merlin's and take off our clothes."

"I love you, lady. I always will. You're my connection to my past experience. To our Tribe. The Brotherhood."

Pulling her into his arms, he covered her mouth with his own. In the softness of his lips, the familiar stirring of her body, the sound of her moan against his mouth, she knew all the months of waiting, the longing, and hesitated in her resolve.

"I don't want to leave you," she heard his whisper in her ear.

Forcing herself to control the rush of desire, not just for his body, but for the life with him she wanted to begin again, she stepped back and held him at arm's length, grateful for the thick winter coat that hid her body.

"If you don't go, then tomorrow, or the next day, or the next week, they'll bust you. You know their routine. Let some time pass. Then they'll be on to other things."

Christian looked toward Jerry, and Kathy saw Jerry touch his watch.

Turning back to her, wiping his eyes, serious again, wanting her to understand, he said, "Listen. Richard's long sentence is a warning. Things are changing. I'm told by people who know that it's going to get a lot worse before it gets better. Nixon's thinking about dramatically increasing the federal drug agency. He wants to create what he's calling a War on Drugs. That means the state boys may be taking a backseat to a new kind of federal repression. This new war's going to have stiffer penalties and sentencing. Be really careful when you go back to work."

"Christian, we've always known the possible consequences. And you're right. It is a war. One for hearts and minds. It's as if the entire history of the world has come down to this one moment. All our experiences, our journeys of higher consciousness, have shown us that we can create a new world that supports the rights of people and peace. One that defies the military and the big corporations who foster misery for profit. And yes, it will take risk."

He looked long and hard into her face, and she thought he looked as if he wanted to memorize everything he saw.

"I'll miss you so much," he whispered. "I love you. I'll be back. Wait for me."

With one arm around his waist, Kathy walked slowly with him toward Jerry, Marcie, and John.

"Sorry," Jerry said, looking miserable, "but we'll miss our plane if we don't go now." He reached for Kathy's hand, sought her eyes. "If not for you selling my mushrooms, I might not have been able to go back to school. Because of you, I've been accepted to a doctoral program with Ben at his new university."

"Safe journey, dear friend," Kathy murmured, hugging him, at that moment wishing more than anything she could join them in the green world of the rainforest.

Christian picked up John, clasped him against his chest, and then slowly passed him back to his mother.

He's always wanted children, Kathy knew.

A huge part of her once again cried to give him the news of his own child as a parting gift, a strength to hold to while he traveled, a dream to await his homecoming.

"Did you tell him?' Marcie whispered, watching Kathy wipe her eyes as the men walked back toward where they had parked.

The question broke the spell of her speculations.

"No," Kathy said softly, shaking her head. "You know why."

"Well," Marcie sighed, giving Kathy a rueful smile as they watched the car take the freeway entrance, "here we are again. Just as we once were. You and me. Standing on the side of the road and stepping into new adventure."

"Oh, Marcie," Kathy cried, her voice suddenly strong, her arms reaching out to draw Marcie and John close. "Christian will be back. And I have such hope for the future! For you and me. Our children! For the Tribes and what we're going to do. The changes we're making. We're going to get Richard out. And it won't take five years. I promise you."

In the west, the sun touched the horizon between the towers of the Golden Gate, perfectly round and bright red, a shining mandala. The two women stood looking out over the bay and the bridge and the ocean beyond, their faces radiant, bathed in soft, rose-colored light. In minutes, only the tiniest tip of the arc of the sun was visible above the horizon line, a glowing ember, slowly fading. In the blink of an eye, it was gone.

LIST OF CHARACTERS

Albert Wright
Chemist, child genius, student at California Institute of Technology, Doug's partner

Alex
Richard's grammar school friend and business partner, dealer, Honey's ex–old man

Annie
Keith's old lady on Maui

Benjamin Miller
Professor and botanist at the University of California, Berkeley

Bert Parker
Lance's law partner

Bliss
Dharma's old lady on Maui

Bob
Member of the Brotherhood of Eternal Love, surfer, dealer in Laguna Beach

Bremer, Supervisor Dolph
Northern California Bureau of Narcotic Enforcement

Carolyn
Larry's old lady in Tucson

Christian Brooks (Alden)
UC Berkeley history student, son of Christian missionaries in India, dealer in Berkeley

Danny
Kathy's friend and dealing partner in Berkeley

David
Dealer in Haight-Ashbury, likes women and coke

Daya Nanda
Master of the Ananda Shiva Ashram

Debbie
Kevin's old lady in the Haight-Ashbury, skilled in embroidery and clothing design

Dharma
Surfboard craftsman, motorcycle mechanic, dealer in Laguna Beach

Eduardo Garza
Larry's new Mexican connection, formerly Steve's associate, younger brother of Mario

Greta
Merlin's old lady in Humboldt

Hanson, Lieutenant Frank
Berkeley Police, Narcotics Department

Hyatollah Tokhis
Brother of Nazrula, Brotherhood of Eternal Love hash connection in Afghanistan

Janata, Colonel
Officer of the prison in Varanasi, India

Jennifer
Joe O'Brian's secretary, partner, and old lady

Jerry Putnam
Botany student at UC Berkeley; Myles's one-time best friend, partner, and academic colleague

Joe O'Brian
Private investigator working closely with Lance Bormann, former Free Speech Movement activist

Jose
Larry's friend from pacifist training, business partner, dealer in Tucson

Julie
Bob's old lady in Laguna Beach and on Maui

Kali
See Lisa

Kathy (Kathleen) Murray
Former student at Louisiana State University Baton Rouge, political activist, transports marijuana from Tucson to the San Francisco Bay area

Keith
Member of the Brotherhood in Maui, grower

Krishna
Manager of Ananda Shiva Ashram in Santa Monica; becomes student
and manager of ashram in India

Lama Loden Rinpoche
Christian's Buddhist teacher, Tibetan *tulku* and monk

Lance Bormann
One of the new "drug attorneys," former Free Speech Movement activist

Larry
Dealer in Tucson, Carolyn's old man; Kathy's love interest and contact

Lisa
Dropout philosophy major at the University of California, Berkeley; a
devotee at the Ananda Shiva Ashram, renamed Kali

Marcie (Marcelle) Arceneaux
Kathy's best friend, political activist, Richard's old lady

Mario Garza
Steve's Mexican connection, elder brother of Eduardo

Merlin
Richard and Alex's former runner, Greta's old man in Humboldt

Miguel
Member of the Tucson ranch commune, Rosie's old man

Myles Corbet
Botany student at the University of California, Berkeley; informant
and, later, American narcotics agent working with Interpol

Nareesh
Christian's boyhood friend and brother in spirit, becomes Padmananda the Disciple to Daya Nanda of Ananda Shiva Ashram

Nazrula Tokhis
Younger brother of Hyatollah, Brotherhood of Eternal Love hash connection in Afghanistan

Neil Bolton
Mountain redneck, burns hippies out

Padmananda
Disciple of the Master of the Ananda Shiva Ashram

Phillips, Agent Ted "Phil"
Northern California Bureau of Narcotic Enforcement

Ram Seva
Nareesh's father

Richard Harrison
Dealer in Haight-Ashbury, Marcie's old man

Rosie
Member of the Tucson ranch commune, Miguel's old lady

Steve
Carolyn's lover; dealer in Laguna Beach; sells his Mexican connections, Mario and Eduardo, to Larry

Wilson, Agent Ed
Northern California Bureau of Narcotic Enforcement, Bremer's protégé

GLOSSARY

A

Acid: n. Lysergic acid diethylamide, a psychedelic altering thinking processes, producing visuals and synesthesia and documented spiritual experiences; a key sacrament in the 1960s counterculture; used currently by medical researchers in understanding death and dying and anxiety disorders

B

Baksheesh: n. Charitable giving, a source of good karma

Base: n. Ergotamine tartrate, an alkaloid of the ergot fungus from which lysergic acid can be made, used medically as a vascular constrictor and migraine medicine

Brahmin (class): n. a member of the upper priestly class among the Hindus of India

Brotherhood of Eternal Love: n. A loose-knit confederation of men and women who believe that higher consciousness can be achieved through the psychedelic experience; originally begun in the Laguna Beach area of Southern California by John Griggs

Bukhara: n. A distinctive rug from Central Asia made from wool, framed with a rectangular border and with geometrical designs in the center

C

Chakra: n. Any one of the seven major energy centers in the body in Hindu and Buddhist religions

Charas: n. Hand-rolled hashish from the Himalayan foothills of India, dark in color

Chillum: n. A straight conical pipe

Cocaine (coke): n. A naturally derived central nervous system stimulant produced from a plant grown in the Andean region of South America

Cop: n. A police officer; v. to buy from someone

Currandero (m.)/Currandera (f.): n. A Latin American shaman who heals and divines through herbs and psychoactive substances

D

Drop: v. To take LSD; to release a batch of LSD into the market

E

Ergotamine tartrate: n. An alkaloid of the ergot fungus from which lysergic acid can be made, used medically as a vascular constrictor and migraine medicine

G

Geshe: n. A Tibetan monk or lama with a high degree in the study of Buddhism

Ghat: n. Most generally, steps leading down into the Ganges River in India

Grass: n. Marijuana, one of the various species of *Cannabis*: *Cannabis sativa*, *Cannabis indica*, or *Cannabis ruderalis*

H

Hashish (hash): n. A product composed of compressed *Cannabis* resin

Hippie: n. One of the flower children of the 1960s, believing in the principles of peace and love, especially those of the Haight-Ashbury district in San Francisco

J

Joint: n. A marijuana cigarette

K

Kachina: n. A masked dancer that embodies a spirit in Hopi religion; a small carved figure representing a masked dancer

Kali: n. The Hindu goddess of destruction, yet in destruction, the possibilities of rebirth

Karma: n. A complicated system of cause and effect that occurs on different levels of existence; in this world, the generally immediate results from personal choices, and in the next, the result of the accumulated actions that produce a destination of rebirth or afterlife.

L

Lid: n. An ounce of marijuana

Load: n. The product that is transported or bought

Lysergic acid: n. A crystalline alkaloid that is a major constituent of ergot and used in the manufacturing of LSD

M

Man, the: n. The authorities, police, narcotics agents

Mic: n. Short for microgram, usually relating to dosages of LSD

Mudra: n. A gesture or position of the hands, generally used in meditation or prayer

N

Namaste: n. A salutation among Hindus of South Asia; lit. "I bow to the divine within you"

O

Old lady: n. A female partner and lover in common law living or marriage

Old man: n. A male partner and lover in common law living or marriage

Om: n. Onomatopoeic sound used in meditation

Orange Sunshine: n. Very good LSD produced in 1969 by Tim Scully and Nick Sand

P

Puja: n. A Hindu ritual showing reverence or honor at home, in a temple, or in an ashram

R

Roach: n. The short remains of a marijuana cigarette, often relit to smoke and held in a roach clip

Roach clip: n. Any metal holder that can hold a roach so that the fingers are not burned

Rolling box: n. A shallow box that allows for marijuana leaves to be separated from seeds by tipping the box so that the seeds roll to one side

Runner: n. A lieutenant who works for a dealer

S

Sadhu: n. An ascetic Hindu holy man

Satsang: n. A religious meeting where practitioners listen to teachings on a religious, moral, or spiritual principle

Stash: n. A supply of drugs, usually hidden, for personal or business use

Summer of Love: n. The summer of 1967, when approximately 100,000 people converged on the Haight-Ashbury district of San Francisco as part of the hippie movement

T

Tab: n. A pharmaceutical tablet; v. to create tablets, usually by machine

Toke: v. To inhale while smoking, usually marijuana

Trip: n. An experience brought on by the use of psychedelic medicine; v. to use psychoactive medicine

V

Velada: n. The traditional and sacred mushroom ceremony of a shaman to heal or divine

W

Weed: n. Marijuana, any species of *Cannabis*

A PREVIEW *of*

IN VIOLATION
OF
HUMAN RIGHTS

1

Once again, she woke in the darkness, fully alert. Kathleen Murray rolled over to view the clock at her bedside, hoping it wasn't 4:00 a.m. But the digital numbers were disappointing: 4:10, the clock pronounced.

In the dim light cast from the display, she rose, deciding she could no longer take another night of tossing and turning, always waking at the same time in the morning's wee hours. In the past months, there had been too many sleepless nights. Images of the faces of clients; of reams of paper; of affidavits, briefs, and appeals; entire case files chased each other in the darkness, and to hide from them, if only for a few hours, she had to change her headspace.

In the kitchen, she pushed the spigot on the spring water dispenser, filled a glass, and drank. The blinking of the telephone answering machine resting on the counter caught her attention. Sighing at whatever new issue might be waiting, she turned on the light over the stove, leaned against the counter, and pushed the button to retrieve messages.

"Hey, Kathy. It's me. Danny . . . "

Kathy smiled at Danny's announcing himself. Like she wouldn't know his voice after a twenty-one year partnership.

"Um . . . something's come up. It's . . . something . . . " He hesitated. For several moments, there was just a long blank on the tape. Finally, she heard, "How about if I come in to see you tomorrow? I'd like to come to the office. More private. I'll call in the morning to see what your schedule looks like."

Kathy furrowed her brow. What was this? Perhaps a new case he didn't want to mention on the phone? They could never be sure that the phones weren't tapped, were careful to be circumspect and entirely legal and never discussed strategy for an important court case—even though the recent technological advances in eavesdropping forced her to question whether there *was* any place that was entirely safe to speak frankly.

"Kathy," Danny's voice again, concerned and unsure. "I've got to talk to you before John's birthday party this weekend."

For the first time, Kathy felt some trepidation. This sounded like more than a client's defense or the details of the huge environmental law case they were representing. Could it have something to do with family? Danny had never in his entire life had any difficulty telling her anything. In the dark, with only her thoughts, Kathy's imagination ran wild. Had something happened to Richard or Marcie? Merlin or Greta? One of the kids? Had her son, Aiden, found trouble he'd conveniently neglected to mention? Whatever it was Danny had to say, he was having a hard time saying it. She'd heard that hesitation in hundreds of voices while interrogating witnesses on the stand. At the end of the silence, there would be pain for someone.

Alright, she sighed heavily. *Tomorrow. If it were anything really urgent, he'd be here.*

Taking another drink of water, she placed the glass back on the counter and promised herself, one more time, that tomorrow, she would begin to meditate. This time, she told herself, she was serious. If not, she'd probably never sleep again.

* * *

Years ago, after graduating from Boalt Hall School of Law at UC Berkeley, Kathy had had no problem in deciding that she would be a criminal attorney. While she was in school, she had worked diligently as a paralegal for the well-known, popular, and controversial lawyer Lance Bormann, researching the law, learning its finer points, and—more important—finding every fragment of case law that would help to reduce Richard Harrison's sentence.

Richard was more than Lance's client. In 1967, Kathy and Marcelle Arceneaux, her best friend and college roommate, had hitched to California without money or direction after the last day of classes at LSU, arriving just at the beginning of the Summer of Love in the Haight-Ashbury. Richard had given them a place to stay off the cold, fog-shrouded San Francisco streets. Three years later, Richard and Marcie married, with a son John and a new baby on the way, Richard had been busted with crystal grams of LSD and a tabbing machine. After a dramatic trial, he had been sentenced to five to fifteen years in prison.

The year of Richard's trial, 1969, had been a hard year. The entire city of Berkeley had come under martial law during the People's Park demonstrations. Students and bystanders had been gassed, a man blinded by police buckshot and another killed, thousands wounded. Kevin, a close friend, had been shot and killed in a separate police raid, Richard busted and sentenced, Christian—Aiden's father and the source of Richard's acid—forced to flee the country or risk arrest on a manufacturing charge. Even though Woodstock had been a beacon of hope in that dismal year, the tribal leaders of the psychedelic movement were being systematically killed, imprisoned, or forced underground.

In good part because of Kathy's diligence, Lance had found just the appeal angle needed to reduce Richard's sentence and to have him released after two and a half years. Making a series of motions to the appellate court, Lance had questioned the role of the agent who had set Richard up—Myles Corbet. The motion Lance had submitted evidenced Corbet's secret intrusions into the homes of private citizens, evidence planting, and his questionable testimony. The appellate court had agreed, and Richard was freed. At the time, Kathy had grinned broadly, believing that times were changing, that people were beginning to understand that psychedelics were the key to higher consciousness.

The three-panel appellate court judges' decision was a by-product of changing social norms.

That was before the mandatory minimum laws enacted by states and Congress.

In New York in the early 1970s, Governor Nelson Rockefeller had decided to try to tackle the problem of drug addiction. Heroin use was skyrocketing, and junkies could be seen everywhere in New York City, in good part because of the war in Vietnam and the number of American servicemen returning addicted to the cheap heroin they'd found overseas. At the time, Rockefeller believed drugs to be a social problem, not a criminal one, and he established drug rehabilitation centers and looked at housing and job training. But sometime during 1972, he began to study Japan's treatment of drug offenders and, one day, turned to his aide and claimed that his program was a failure. What was needed for drug dealers was a life sentence without probation or parole. In that moment, the current approach to drug use and treatment had been established.

With backing from the vast majority of New Yorkers, he created the Rockefeller Laws, mandatory prison sentences of fifteen years to life for both dealers and addicts, anyone with anything over four ounces of marijuana, cocaine, or heroin. Other states followed. Michigan enacted the 650-Lifer Law: Anything over 650 grams of cocaine or heroin, about 1.45 pounds, required mandatory life imprisonment.

Then, in 1986, the US legislature established federal mandatory minimums in the Anti-Drug Abuse Act of 1986, setting guidelines for sentencing that judges had to follow, without exception. That same law also mandated five years for possession of five grams of crack cocaine, while allowing the same sentence, five years, for five hundred grams of powder cocaine. Cheaper and just as effective as powder, crack was the preferred coke-based drug for black Americans, whereas white America generally used powder cocaine. The harsh and unequal laws deeply affected the African American community and created a huge sentence disparity between blacks and whites.

After graduation from law school in 1973 and passage of the bar exam, one of the foremost decisions Kathy faced was the kind of office she wanted to establish. Lance Bormann had offered her a position as an associate attorney with an office in his building. Although Lance's old partner, Bert Parks, had split their partnership and moved independently to San Francisco in early 1970, Lance had quickly found two associates to replace him, expanding the office space when suites became available. Now he owned the entire ivy-covered building on Shattuck Avenue, and invited Kathy to join the firm. Lance had a reputation, a large clientele, and, in all honesty, could use the grunt work of a new and untried associate. Kathy, he had learned, was meticulous in her attention to detail, and once her teeth had sunk into a case, she never relented. She, on the other hand, could benefit from the experience and the cases that would be handpicked for her.

Kathy had pondered Lance's offer carefully, and then politely declined. She had instead chosen an old home on Walnut Street to convert into a law office. In the beginning, she had rented the building. Eventually, she had bought it. The house was off a main thoroughfare on a tree-lined street on the edge of commercial zoning. In its relaxed atmosphere, she hoped to offer a nonthreatening space in which clients might feel more at ease, more able to confide in her.

This modesty of unpretentiousness had been learned a long time ago from Joe O'Brian. Joe, dead now some twenty years, had been a private investigator closely connected to Lance Bormann and a man who believed his abilities should be used to serve those who most needed the law. Joe had pushed aside the hindrances of authority. No large desk separated him from his clients and no imposing books lined a wall. Kathy had decided to do the same, meeting with her clients around a coffee table with comfortable chairs, soft lighting, and a note pad on her lap. Like Joe, she believed she was there to serve.

In the first two years of her practice, she was a constant sight at Bormann's office, asking advice on the numerous ambiguities she found in the law, and getting pointers in courtroom procedure. As time passed, she stood more and more on her own feet.

For the past fifteen years, she had worked out of the Walnut Street office. Some remodeling had created a front room that she used as a reception area. Liz Burnside, secretary and good friend, dealt with the mechanics of the business—typing, scheduling appointments, taking calls, and holding her hand when necessary. Down a hallway lit with a skylight, and to the left, was a former back bedroom that had been converted into her office. A desk sat before large, wood-framed windows that cast natural light into the room. To one side was a sitting area with chairs and low tables.

From that window, she had watched the seasons change and the years pass, her gaze finding solace in the trees and gardens lining the street—the changing reds and yellows of fall, the bare tree limbs in winter allowing weak sunlight, the bright green buds of spreading leaves in March, the burst of azalea and climbing bougainvillea throughout spring and summer.

Had she turned right at the end of the hallway, a second former bedroom was now available. The partner with whom she'd been working, Mark Resnick, had decided to move to Washington, DC, to work with an emerging prison rights group.

Today, as on many other days, Kathy unlocked the front door of the building and moved into the reception room, balancing a heavy briefcase, a stack of books, and a purse over her shoulder. A few of Mark's boxes were near the front door, and she absently remembered that they were being picked up today by a moving company.

Once in her office, she hung up her jacket and thought again about Mark's offer. *Come with me*, he'd asked. And indeed, she was tempted. This new organization looked good. She had devoted her life to prison reform, her own ideas a complicated miasma about what constituted crime, justice, and the very meaning of incarceration. Even though the offer was still on the table, she'd told Mark she had too many clients who relied on her. In fact, she had only to look at the files of open cases on her desk to have a pretty good idea about why she was waking up at 4:00 a.m.

Still, she had seriously considered the offer. Was still considering.

Was even willing to admit that something more than political motivation was at play in her deliberation of Mark's suggestion—some new restlessness, a dissatisfaction she could not explain.

Standing in the office, removing papers from her briefcase and sorting them on the desk, she considered the full life of friends and family surrounding her. True, she had always lived on the edge—*was* living on the edge. Over the years, she'd gotten used to the excitement, anticipation, and anxiety of walking into court, of holding someone's fate in her hands. Those people she defended were often important, even vital, to some political idea—the environment, spiritual awareness. Others were people merely trapped in a system without someone to speak for them, someone to make them important. Taking risks had become commonplace. But Danny's cryptic and worrying phone call in the sleepless early morning hours had bought up something new. Was danger becoming tiresome?

Many years ago, she had picked up Danny hitchhiking on the freeway between Tucson and Phoenix, Arizona. He had been sixteen and running away from home. He'd charmed her for hours . . . until confessing that Kathy's van reeked of weed. Indeed, she'd been moving about two hundred kilos from Tucson to San Francisco. Inviting Danny to share her College Avenue apartment, he had eventually become a full business partner. Together, they'd moved literally tons of pot. Until 1969. In that year, everything had begun to change—dispensing sacraments had become more dangerous and unpredictable.

In time, Danny had graduated from Berkeley High School, attended UC Berkeley, and received his diploma with honors. Afterwards, he had gone on to complete graduate school at Berkeley in public policy. Upon graduation, he'd begun an environmental watchdog group, the Center for Environmental Action, dealing with both local and international issues.

If Danny felt something was really important, he wouldn't trust the phones. What was it that had caused those ponderous, gaping holes in the message tape? Was it about the toxic mine tailings close to a residential area they'd been asked to look into?

And what did all of this have to do with John's birthday celebration? *Before the weekend party*, he'd said.

The entire Tribe was gathering for the weekend on the land Richard and Marcie had purchased near Sebastopol in Sonoma County. John was their first son and Kathy's godson, and in a few days, he would be twenty-one years old. Every member of the original Haight-Ashbury commune would be there. Greta and Merlin were driving down from Humboldt. Debbie was flying in from Houston, where she'd established her clothing factory. Honey lived in Cotati, close to Richard and Marcie, and grew organic herbs for Mary Ann and Keith's chain of Green Grocer stores. Even Albert and Doug, alchemists during the sixties, had been tracked down. All the kids would be there, adults now, some with toddlers of their own. Lots of people Kathy hadn't seen in a long time. Everyone from the Ashbury Street house . . . well, almost everyone.

Richard and Marcie had been making arrangements for months, sending out invitations with a list of hotels in the area and preparing campsites for those who would set up tents. A caterer had been hired for the night. A series of colorful canopies arranged for shade. Tables and chairs brought in. A stage had been built on the edge of the vineyard and a band hired. Solar showers hung in the old oaks, and portable toilets stood in a row, just like at Woodstock. In truth, this weekend was more than John's party. This birthday ceremony was a way to bring people together on a scale that had not been done in many years—a gathering of the Tribes.

ABOUT THE AUTHOR

 PAMELA JOHNSON was born in New Orleans, Louisiana, and migrated to Berkeley, California, in 1966. A Phi Beta Kappa graduate of UC Berkeley in anthropology, she went on to earn master's degrees in education at Mills College and in English at Holy Names University, both schools in Oakland. A former teacher and university professor, she is actively involved in social and environmental issues and views her writing as an extension of her politics. She is married and currently divides her time between a ranch in the Sierra foothills of California and Ocho Rios, Jamaica. Look for her next book *In Violation of Human Rights*, to be released through Stone Harbour Press.